Castle, Crown & Conscience

Castle, Crown & Conscience

SUNA FLORES

CITIOFBOOKS, INC.
3736 Eubank NE Suite A1
Albuquerque, NM 87111-3579
www.citiofbooks.com
Hotline 1 (877) 389-2759
Fax: 1 (505) 930-7244

Ordering Information:
Quantity sales. Special discounts are available on quantity purchases by corporations, associations, and others. For details, contact the publisher at the address above.

Printed in the United States of America.

ISBN-13:   Softcover   979-8-89391-123-7
               eBook   979-8-89391-124-4

Library of Congress Control Number: 2024909799

Table Of Contents

Introduction

Envision a world where there is no understanding of right and wrong. Look around you. Maybe we are already here. Is there a way that the world can focus on honesty, kindness and being good to others or are we past that in society today?

Maybe so, but I think the answer is Consciences. The Consciences in this book become real for a reason. They discuss issues, have opinions, and are not always right. As with humans, they are imperfect, but I think that the idea of discussing important problems with a voice inside you is valuable enough to deserve focus.

This is a novel that might be called a fantasy unless you look closely. It takes place in the Middle Ages but the individuals and situations are so familiar that you may recognize them when you see them on TV. You might say that this ancient time frame was used to reveal the present. You *might* say that.

Consciences were intended to have a real impact on human behavior, particularly due to the existence of Auras. Auras, for lack of a better definition, are evil impulses that may cause a human to make decisions they would not otherwise make. Auras are not as famous as Consciences, but in the real world, we all know that they exist.

This novel was written to create an awareness of the politics we see around us and cause us to consider the importance of inner voices, both Auras and Consciences, and their impact on the choices being made today.

Suna Flores

Do Consciences have names? For clarity, I have given them the names of their host humans, with only a C in front of that name (example: George's Conscience is named Cgeorge.)

1

The Lay of the Land

Lord Doran Drum was a wealthy landowner in the era of kings and queens, barons and lords, commoners and peasants. He lived in River Kingdom, a thriving country community comprised of manors of the wealthy and villages of peasants. The Kingdom was spread along the edge of a huge river running from the mountains to the sea—The Great River.

Most of the inhabitants of the area were peasants and farmers who worked for wealthy lords and served the needs of that lord, known as their "masters." The lords controlled the lives of those who worked for them from morning to night and were extremely powerful, but all lords were pledged to the support of the local king, King Sol.

This was a harsh economic system where the common people labored to grow, harvest, and trade their produce in the local villages, but turned over their harvest and earnings to their lords. In exchange, they received only a few sheckles or a dole of the produce that they themselves had planted and harvested.

The lords of the manors, in turn, supported their local royalty or "The Castle" with taxes and a percentage of their produce, which was stored in Royal Storehouses for support of the Royal Guard of The Kingdom and The Castle itself.

River Kingdom (referred to as The Kingdom) was the oldest and largest kingdom in the area. It supported a huge castle (known as "The Castle") and was a relatively peaceful place. A neighboring kingdom, the Kingdom of Urhonordo (Urhonordo) erected its own slightly smaller castle on the opposite side of The Great River and ruled its own citizens on that side. The two kingdoms had become friendly, and a sturdy bridge downstream (The Bridge) united the kingdoms for the trade of goods and services.

The Great River (The River) was the source of water for both kingdoms and their farms that were their primary source of food. The River was also essential to the structure of local peace.

Many strict Water Rights Treaties existed between the kingdoms, thus acknowledging their mutual dependence on the water as well as knowledge of The River's natural potential for destruction if not controlled. Heavy rains had brought their farms too much water in the past, and droughts had provided too little. Respect for The River was essential.

The two kingdoms monitored The River regularly. To manage it, they had cleverly erected a series of levees on both sides with which they could raise and lower the amount of water they were using for their fields every year in response to changes in the climate. The treaties were adjusted at yearly meetings between the kingdoms. These meetings were considered mandatory due to The River's importance.

And where were Consciences in this medieval society? Consciences were at work with humans of both kingdoms, practicing their consultation skills as the humans interacted with each other and went about their lives.

Consciences were openly conversational in these early days. They offered their opinion out loud to their host humans and to each other. They did not hold back. But although their voices could be heard by their host human and other nearby Consciences, they were not heard by anyone else. (The practice of not being heard by other humans still exists with most Consciences today.)

Consciences and the evil temptations of Auras existed on both sides of The River. Auras had caused great wars between these kingdoms in the past but were almost inactive now. It was a peaceful time.

At the southern end of both The Kingdom and Urhonordo was a territory that was not part of either kingdom. It was an ungoverned arid land inhabited by gentle nomads and known as "The Lowlands." Their dry, sandy territory received the last trickling remnants of The Great River as it flowed between the two upper kingdoms on its way to the sea. The River was not wide here, but it was vital. Those who lived in The Lowlands were a peaceful people known as Lowlanders.

The Lowlands were warmer than the upper kingdoms and sometimes visited by wealthy lords and ladies as holiday destinations, but they had not been coveted for farm use due to their limited water. The Lowlands had no king or queen, but the proud Lowlanders themselves welcomed visitors and in turn were welcomed by the two kingdoms above them, frequently working in the kingdoms' fields for a share of their more plentiful produce.

Consciences and Auras existed in The Lowlands as well, but because there was no royalty in The Lowlands, there was none of the politics between barons and lords, much less kings and queens. Lowlanders liked it that way. They lived simpler lives. The Consciences of the upper kingdoms envied that simplicity. The Auras seemed to pay them little attention.

So, all was peaceful on the banks of The River, and the local citizens assumed that this would continue forever. But their Consciences were skeptical and determined to remain vigilant in case needs changed. The Auras would always exist, waiting for a chance to invade the lives of humans, and the Consciences knew it.

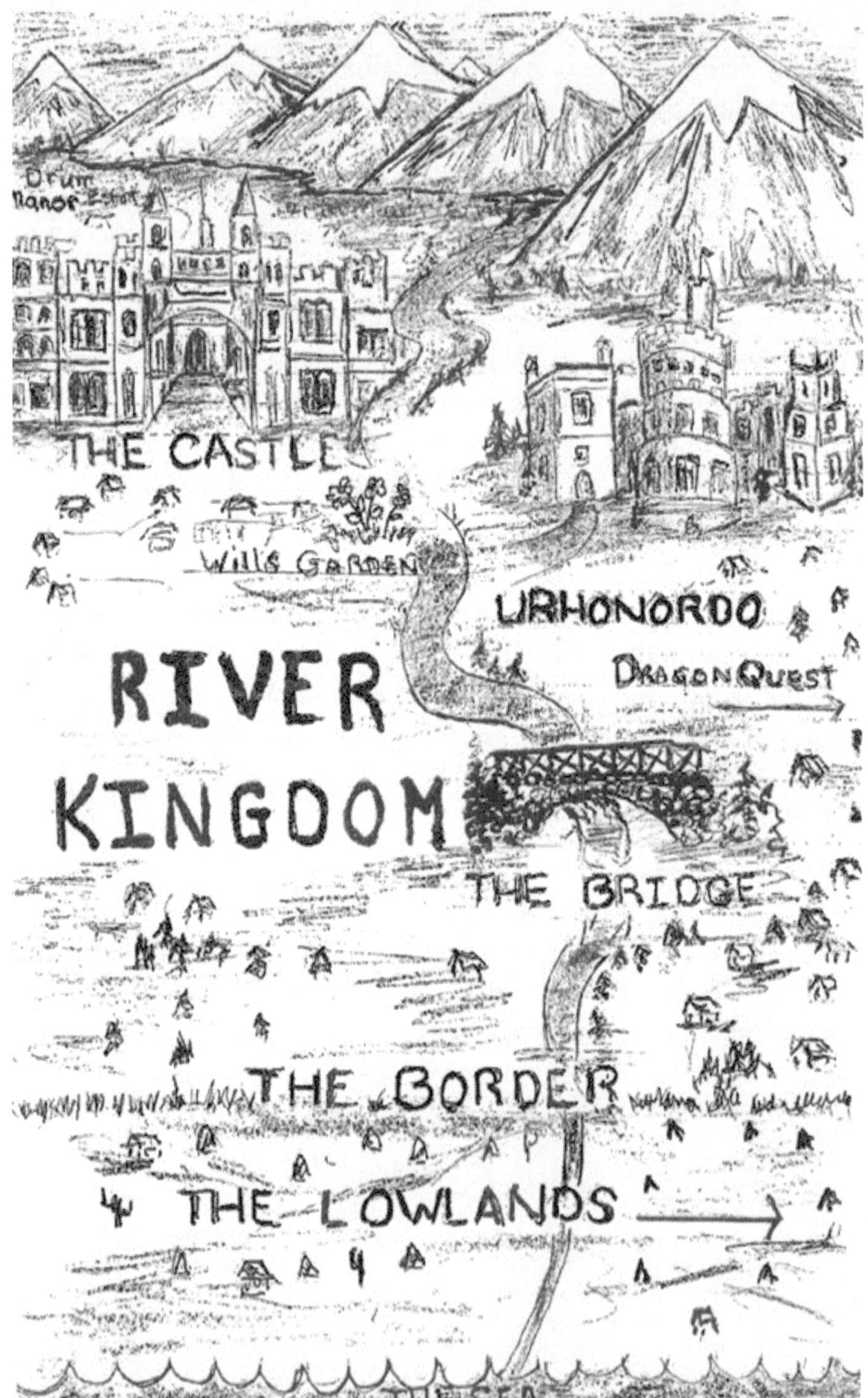

Drum Manor Estate
THE CASTLE
Will's Garden
URHONORDO
DragonQuest
RIVER
KINGDOM
THE BRIDGE
THE BORDER
THE LOWLANDS
THE SEA

2

Drum and Cdrum

Cdrum was the proud Conscience of Lord Doran Drum. He had a right to feel proud because although he had a difficult host human, he never backed off. His fellow Consciences took note of his dedication. His human host was definitely a challenge.

Lord Drum was a wealthy aristocrat whose landholdings covered the northern segments of River Kingdom along the upper west side of The River. Drum was prideful by nature. His lands and manor houses were the biggest and most well known in The Kingdom.

Lord Drum owned what could be called "a real estate empire" of its time, but his empire was not always problem-free. Sometimes his properties were not well managed. Sometimes his taxes weren't paid. His farmers occasionally missed their necessary food allotments. There were issues with the banks.

Drum enjoyed a relatively easy life as most of his wealth had been left to him by his ancestors. Hired help of questionable character supervised different aspects of his holdings, but he didn't really care if they were profitable.

His forefathers had been champions of the Auras in their day, engaging in numerous wars and corruption, but those obvious evil times were mostly hidden in history. More recent members of the Drum family line had been content to oversee their many peasants and their quiet production of crops in the valley of The River. They had parlayed their gains from more violent times into enormous landholdings that were known as Drum Manor Estates, and now, after many years, all their gains had trickled down to Drum.

Drum's ancestors were much more industrious than the current Drum ever intended to be. He enjoyed his inherited fortune and applied little additional effort of his own. He had tried his hand at more active participation in the past but had not been successful. As a matter of fact, he had already squandered some of his inheritance through poor investments, numerous wives, and a lack of appreciation for the costs of an overly grand lifestyle. Local lords were not impressed with his business acumen.

As his Conscience, Cdrum hadn't offered advice on many of Drum's business problems. Drum was only losing his own inheritance. He figured it was a family issue.

Cdrum was concerned with Drum's extravagant lifestyle, however. "You don't need another elegant carriage," Cdrum told him. "You don't need another manor house, and you certainly don't need another wife. Your desire to acquire more and more things is greedy, you know. Greed makes you susceptible to the Auras."

"The things I own increase my appearance of importance in The Kingdom," Drum countered.

"It's not that important to look important," was Cdrum's reply.

"Keep your opinions to yourself, Conscience," Drum snapped. "No one can see you so you don't care what you look like. Some of us have an image to project."

Drum invested most of his time in what he liked most—cultivating high society and or investors for his next deal. Wealthy important friends made Drum feel important, and he collected these personages like trophies to demonstrate his standing in the community.

Drum's Conscience knew that Drum's ever-present need to be noticed and feel important was a weakness, but it was not evil enough to keep the Auras interested as far as he could tell. Cdrum had decided not to put too much energy into trying to block it.

Cdrum was a member of an informal gathering called the "Conscience Forum" where Consciences met on a regular basis to exchange ideas and techniques for improving Conscience performance. Some older Consciences didn't agree with Cdrum's rather permissive approach to his work with Drum. "Such a need for self- importance and approval has a tendency to grow," they warned. "'In the past, we've seen this need for self-promotion spiral into a complete disregard for everyone else."

But Cdrum just shrugged when other Consciences talked to him about Drum. Cdrum felt that the other Consciences didn't understand Drum.

"Doran Drum is unique. His only real focus is himself," he agreed, "and he just wants to be a big cheese. There's no law against that. He likes to be the center of attention, and his wealth allows him to do that all he wants. That doesn't really hurt anyone."

Cdrum's fellow Consciences rolled their eyes. "Your man is famous, but he's only famous for being famous. Try encouraging his more productive instincts," they suggested.

"If I find some, I'll encourage them." Cdrum laughed.

Drum's skill at self-promotion had put him in contact with people in high places. The King knew him. All the King's Royal Advisors knew him. He was invited to the weddings of the wealthy. He made sure he was regarded as an important person in The Kingdom. Not too bad for a guy who didn't do anything to earn it.

Cdrum's biggest real worry was Drum's honesty. For some reason, Drum lied all the time for no reason at all. He would say that he did when he didn't. He would say that he would when he wouldn't. In general, he would say whatever was most convenient at the time, and everyone that knew him knew this was true. "Drum will lie when the truth sounds better," they would grumble.

Cdrum lectured Drum about lying, but Drum denied the problem. He even lied about lying. "I never lie," he stated convincingly. "If you have a problem with what I say, that's your problem. I say what I want to say.

If you don't like it, don't listen. You can't prove that I lie. That's fake news." But Cdrum was a dedicated Conscience. He was determined to stick with it. "Dishonesty is an Aura, Drum. You're playing fast and loose with the truth too often," he warned. "Someday, lying is going to get you into more trouble than you can handle."

Drum ignored him. "I'm smart. I'm charming and I'm popular. I am a a *very* good guy that's very rich. I don't see a problem."

Drum believed very strongly in work—as long as someone else was doing it. He was, however, able to put to work a few of his own natural talents. The first was a talent for cultivating popularity by complimenting and praising. "Everyone seems to love that," he told Cdrum, "and I am very good at it."

Women in particular were drawn in by this talent, so he enjoyed the company of many women, some of whom he married. He also had additional consorts who enjoyed his attention until he tired of them. Then they would conveniently disappear. It was just one of the blessings that came with being the lord of several manors that were a distance apart.

Drum also had a talent for being at the right place at the right time. He usually found someone to impress, something witty to say or a deal he could use to his benefit. He had made many "deals" this way, but many suspected they were a bit "off."

"You don't know what I know. No one knows as much as I do," he would respond when confronted. "I just do what I think is good to do, and it usually is. It's almost an art form. You might say that I'm a master of the art of the deal. My negotiating skills are phenomenal."

No one knew exactly how much wealth Drum had or didn't have either, and he went to great lengths to keep it that way. This brought up an additional talent—creating an impression of affluence and success with the right people rather than revealing an actual accounting of his worth or ability. This was another one of Drum's talents.

Cdrum was not impressed with these particular talents and thought they might put Drum's integrity in question. Was he a fake? Possibly. Cdrum questioned Drum regularly, but couldn't really prove a thing. And this didn't slow Drum down at all.

Instead, he began to lavish even more of his time and wealth on parties and public appearances, with the goal of impressing the influential persons that he met. This was the way to get ahead in The Kingdom. Drum was sure of it. On countless evenings, there were torches burning far into the night at Drum manor houses, all to satisfy Lord Drum's desire to keep himself in the light and assure all that he was . . . important. "You can never tell. Many times, what people think is more important than what is."

To enhance the impression of his abilities, Drum adopted a new slogan: "When you are as wealthy as I am, money is no object." This statement worked wonders on his reputation. Drum's fellow party-going lords assumed that the wealth they saw on display was a true indication of Drum's well- managed real estate and financial value. That wasn't really a lie, but it wasn't the truth either. Cdrum worried about this probably inaccurate impression, but he couldn't put his finger on what harm it would do.

3

William of Dale

What maintained Lord Drum's look of importance in The Kingdom was Drum Manor Estates. Dozens of farmers and other peasants worked hard in Drum's fields all through the year, planting and harvesting great amounts of produce. Their pay was not generous, however. It was only a very meager allotment of the beans or barley they had produced.

This allotment was doled out to his farmers and peasants in the fall by a growling stingy overseer, and it was supposed to feed them all winter. Another equally insufficient allotment was provided in the spring for use until the fall harvest. The protocol was established by medieval custom and law although the lack of generosity was not.

Medieval lords always had an overseer, especially chosen to be in charge of these doles and farm operations. Their hungry workers knew that these men were not selected for their openhandedness, and Drum's overseer was particularly harsh and hoarding by nature. But this was Drum's manner. He had even become more this way for years.

Winters were a lean time. There was work to be done on Drum Manor Estates every winter. It was cold, wet work and the food was sparse, but the work still had to be done. The overseer insisted on it and punished the slow and infirm with beatings and reduced rations.

This winter, however, Drum's overseer did not show up so a young peasant named William of Dale began working on the winter chores by himself.

Will, as his friends called him, didn't say much, but he saw what needed to be done and quietly did it. His fellow farmhands understood the process, so when he asked them, they followed his lead. The work got done as it was supposed to, but now it was early spring after a cold, wet winter. It was time for the spring dole.

The food that the farmers and their families had been parceling out from their fall dole was practically gone, and after their winter labor, they were more than ready for the spring allotment. But this spring, the dole for Drum's farmers was not just small. It was nonexistent.

There was no dole—nothing. The overseer was still not around. The farmers hung out at the food storage sheds for a while, but no one came. The sheds were locked tight. They would have broken in, but that was a hanging offense. They decided against it.

Drum's farmers grumbled loud and long. They had worked hard. They had earned their dole. Where was the usual stingy dole guy? Drum's overseer was nowhere around, and the spring dole that the farmers needed to feed their families was still locked up and rotting.

The farmers needed that food. Somebody should tell Drum, but Drum didn't speak with lowly farmers. He was a lord. Their stomachs were growling. They looked at each other.

"You tell him."

"Not me."

"Not me."

And where was Drum? Drum's focus was where it always was—elsewhere. He didn't know of his farmers' problem nor care. He had discovered a new form of amusement for himself and his wealthy friends. It was a game with a stick and a little white ball, and it currently had all his attention.

"You should stop playing and check on the welfare of the people that work for you," urged Cdrum. "I hear that your farmhands didn't get their spring dole yet. No one seems to be working at the shed. You need to at least see to it that your farmers get their food."

"Farming is boring," responded Drum, "and farmers are stupid. Otherwise, they wouldn't be farmers. Why else would they do all that hard work for nearly nothing?" He adjusted his latest hand-stitched robe.

"I, of course, am brilliant so I recognized the uselessness of the situation and fired my overseer last fall. Why did I need him? I figured that if the farmers got smart, they should be able to get food for themselves. If they didn't, they would starve. They grow the stuff every day, don't they? They should just get some of what they grow and eat it—and not bother me."

But the economic system of the Middle Ages didn't allow that. Drum had never paid attention to the rules of the economic system or the protocol of the dole. He had never cared how the farmers got their food. His food was served to him warm, on a plate, by a servant. Wasn't everyone's?

Drum's lack of interest in and knowledge of his workers worried Will, but he said nothing. He was a farmer, a humble man. It was not his place. But he was hungry too.

Will's friends were past hungry. They were starving. Suddenly, hunger gave them an idea. Will was the guy that had been getting chores done this winter. He didn't talk about doing things. He just did them. Maybe there was a chance that he could get something done like that with Drum and the food situation. It was worth a try.

Will was only a peasant himself, but his friends had seen that he took his work seriously. Possibly this was because he believed that their work was his only way to stay alive. But now that was again true. Things were coming to a head. If no one did anything, they would not stay alive now either.

They were angry. They were restless. No one was in charge. Commodities earned were theirs by right! They would have gone on strike, but strikes hadn't been invented yet. Hunger was rampant. This was a crisis. They went to Will.

"Take care of this for us, Will," they begged.

"We've got to get our food out of that shed or we'll starve."

"You know how to get stuff done. Go tell Drum to give us our dole."

Will was only a peasant. He was not about to go in and talk to Drum in person. That was not going to happen. Doing extra farmwork was one thing. Talking in person to a lord was another. He was not a beggar.

Cwill, Will's Conscience, went to work. "So I see that you are better at getting your friends to do winter work for Drum than you are at getting them paid for doing it," he scoffed. "I never knew that about you. I thought you would be better to your friends than that."

Lord Drum won't even talk to me, thought Will. *I'm just a peasant.* "True. And I see now that you're also a pitiful, petrified peasant who won't help his friends even though they helped you this winter. That's the way I see it," added Cwill.

Then Cwill had a brainstorm. "On the other hand, you *could* be doing Drum a big favor. Maybe Drum just doesn't know that the dole man is gone. He doesn't come out to the fields much. He's a businessman. Somebody needs to tell him about the dole and his missing overseer. He would probably want to know."

Cdrum didn't think Drum would care at all, but it was a decent approach from a proud Conscience.

That thought made sense to Will. He would be giving Drum information and helping his friends, not just begging for food. This new idea gave him courage, and again, there was no one else to do it. For several days, Will traveled on foot from one elegant manor house to another. Finally, he found Drum. He was lounging on the lawn of a grand house, trying out his new game with his friends. The object was to hit a small white ball with a stick. The other lords and barons were gathered around, laughing and joking and trying to hit the ball as well.

Will felt very out of place among the wealthy lords. Now they stopped joking and looked down at him and his dusty work clothes. He was obviously a peasant. They drew back in disgust. Will shuffled his feet.

Cwill knew he still had Conscience work to do. Will was too shy. Cwill's part of this job now would be pushing Will to say something, convincing him to do what needed to be done (just as he had quietly done on the farm this winter). Will was a good man, but being confrontational was not as easy for Will as farm work had been.

"Come on, Will. You're doing a good deed. You're helping your friends and your boss," coaxed Cwill. He hoped "doing for others" was an angle that would motivate Will.

It worked. Will began. "Please, sir . . . your usual dole guy isn't where he usually is in the spring."

"I know. I fired him," said Drum, swinging at the ball with his stick. "Get off my lawn."

"Oh," said Will. "In that case, since your farmers are hungry, maybe you will want me to open up the dole shed for you while you're busy with your friends, right?" Will shuffled his feet some more and looked at the grass.

"Wrong," said Drum.

Cdrum, Drum's Conscience, heard Will and Cwill and spoke up to Drum.

"Aren't you going to pay attention to your business at all, Drum? Come on, dude. These are *your* farmers that are hungry. They take care of *your* business."

"Farmers should be smart enough to get their own food," Drum barked, digging his game ball out of a hole. "I'm not about to pay someone to get food for them that they can get for themselves."

Cdrum spoke up again. "You need to use the dole system, Drum. It's the law of the land, and the farmers are used to it. Besides, this guy, Will, is smart enough to get his own food. That's why he's here asking you for it."

It's a stupid law, and it ought to be repealed, thought Drum. But he did find me and ask.

Workers' rights were not Drum's thing. Besides, he was busy. He was trying to hit another little white ball with his stick. It went into another hole. Drum seemed to be happy about that.

Cwill had heard Drum's Conscience lobby Drum. Cwill pushed Will one more time. He had a strategy. "You did great so far, Will. Drum actually heard what you said, and I think he's winning at his game. The secret here is to work cheap and ask quick while he's in a good mood."

"I don't need any pay, sir. I just need the key to the shed," Will said quietly. He plucked the game ball out of the hole and handed it to Drum.

Drum took the ball, smiled, took a key off his key ring, and handed it to Will. That was all there was to it. Drum hit the ball into the weeds with the next stroke, but Will had the key.

"Good job, Will." Cwill and Cdrum laughed.

Soon the farmers had their dole. Within a week, the word got out, and Drum's peasants all decided that Will was a guy they could depend on. Why? He was dependable. Cwill was rather proud.

Today might not sound like much, but because of this one act, Will's leadership with his fellow farmers became a regular part of his job. Without thinking about it, Will took on duties that seemed natural, and his friends accepted his role. But no good deed goes unpunished. Another problem soon surfaced at Drum Manor Estates.

Lord Drum had also forgotten to appoint anyone to organize what was needed for planting on the farms of his estates, and spring was coming on fast. Seeds had not been gathered, and Drum had said nothing about the water that would be needed for the massive estates. The fields were abnormally dry for spring, so water was going to be a problem.

There was still no overseer, so Will tried to respectfully inform Drum again. He was braver now. He figured that Drum would remember him from before.

But Will was wrong. Will tracked Drum down again on the lawn of one of his manors, but Drum didn't remember Will or want to remember him. Will tried to ask him about The River and the dry land and the seeds. Drum brushed Will's questions aside. Climate change and its effect on his property were not important to him at all.

"The fields will take care of themselves. They always have." And he was busy cultivating friendships on the social ladder, not cultivating produce on a farm. These farm-related matters were of no interest. He wasn't available for a discussion about them either and particularly not with a peasant farmer that he had never seen before.

"Farmers are only farmers because they can't do anything else," Drum shared with his wealthy friends. "But think about it. They have been farming for hundreds of years, so they must know how to do it no matter what the weather is. Dig, plant, harvest. Dig, plant, harvest. What else is there? Let them do their thing the way they have always done it. It will all work out okay. Trust me. I know about these things."

Gradually, Will decided that he was going to have to do something himself again if he were to keep himself and his friends from losing their livelihood while Drum didn't feel that his farm's operation was worth his time and attention. Will had no idea if he should do what he was going to do, and there was no one to ask but his Conscience.

"I'm nobody. Should I do this?" Will asked nervously.

Cwill had no trouble responding. "If somebody doesn't do it, there will be no more Drum Manor Estates, the way I see it. Then your friends will be completely out of luck. I don't think Drum wants to take care of The Estates anymore. It's boring to him. He's got his sights on something bigger. If you and your friends want to keep his real estate producing, *you're* going to have to do it. That's what I think, but that's just me."

So Will, little by little, took over the management of Drum Manor Estates. Cdrum talked to Drum, but his sense of responsibility was gone. "This Will guy is completely managing *all* the lands that are producing *all your income, Drum.* Did you know that? He has become pretty good at it. The least you should do is recognize him for all of his work or you might lose him."

"He's only a peasant," Drum smugly argued. "Peasants come and go. They are replaceable. I, however, am a genius, a very stable genius. I know more about managing farmlands than all the noblemen, not to mention all the peasant farmers. I could control everything in this valley from right here where I sit if I wanted to, so obviously, there is no value in any single peasant."

Cdrum persisted. "Maybe you *could* control everything, but you don't. Having a peasant like Will out actually doing what needs to be done is of real value, whether you know it or not."

"Does this dirt grubber own land? Does he have rank or position? I don't think so. Therefore, his value is limited. Life is a transaction, and peasants like this Will person are a shekel a wagon load as I see it, my friend."

"Oh, so now you call me 'friend'?" mocked Cdrum. "Well, listen to this, 'friend.' William of Dale and the other peasants tend *your* land. *Your* land produces the food that makes *you* important. *You* like to be important, right? That makes Will important to you. Have you ever thought of that?"

Drum rolled his eyes, but Cdrum stood his ground. This kind of guilt argument sometimes worked for a good Conscience.

Cdrum was right. Drum reluctantly knew this, but he responded in his own style. In a move of brilliance, he named Will "Drum Manor Estates Overseer." With such a title, Will would be the one to see to it that the plowing got done, the farmworkers got their dole, and the seeds for the farm's crops got planted. In other words, Will would do everything that Drum didn't want to do.

Will would get a title. That's all his Conscience had insisted on. If he didn't like the offer, Drum would get somebody else. He was only a peasant farmer. Drum now felt he had paid this useless peasant with some recognition, but that didn't mean he needed to spend time or money on a commoner like Will.

Cdrum knew that Drum had made things somewhat better for the peasants by officially giving Will a title to go with his responsibility, but this payless solution did not show much improvement in Drum's character. Drum's workers would no longer be starving, but Will was the only one who cared about them. Cdrum could tell that Drum really had no interest in anyone or anything other than his own self-interest—and his new game with the little white ball and the stick. As a Conscience, this lack of empathy for anyone bothered Cdrum, but he wasn't sure how to tackle it.

Not surprisingly, the first month of Will's management brought healthier, happier farmers on Drum Manor Estates. The farmers got extra dole for the extra work they had done over the winter, and it was clean and neat and mostly edible. It had been a long time since something like that had happened, so the Consciences of the farmers spoke up. "You really ought to thank someone for this welcome change," they said.

The farmers agreed with their Consciences and gathered at the front of one of Drum's lavish manor houses. "Thanks, Lord Drum, for the great dole," they all shouted out over one another.

"We like the new food allotment." "We'll work really hard to earn it." "It's the best ever!"

It was only after the shouts of appreciation finished that the farmers' Consciences discovered that they had forgotten to tell the farmers who to thank. Will, as usual, didn't say a thing.

Drum grandly stepped forward and accepted the farmers' gratitude. "I have been watching you all closely," he lied.

"Not true," shouted Cdrum in Drum's ear. "You haven't paid attention to the farmers for a minute. You're lying again."

"And I could see that you all deserved the generous dole that your families need to live on," Drum continued. "No one has ever valued your hard work more than I have, as you know. From now on, you will see that I alone have improved the local labor situation and made sure that every one of my workers has the best work conditions in River Kingdom."

"That Drum is a heck of a smart guy," said the farmers as they spread the word to their friends.

Will, Cwill, and Cdrum were part of the listening farmer group. They all shook their heads at Drum's boasts, but the rest of the peasants cheered. Drum loved the response. Popularity among even the common folk was a good thing. He had never thought of that before, but he definitely liked it. He would try to remember that.

Cwill went after Cdrum at the next Conscience Forum. "He was lying through his teeth, Cdrum," commented Cwill. "Are you going to keep letting him get away with that? You know that Will did all the work that Drum was getting credit for. You know that, for sure."

"I know, I know," agreed Cdrum. "Drum lies all the time, and he has always taken credit for other people's work. But most of his lies are harmless. If I jumped every time he lied, I would be on him all the time. Drum has a lot of issues. I know that. I'm just trying to deal with the ones that are most likely to attract major Auras. Thank goodness he isn't involved in anything important."

4

𝕱lawless

Lord Drum had enjoyed the company of many wives and other assorted young ladies in the past, spending his time between the several manor houses that he had built with his inheritance. He had also enjoyed traveling with his lady friends in elegant carriages from one home to another. Lately, however, his primary female companion was the firstborn of his daughters, Mistress Flawless Drum.

Flawless was his favorite and most trusted companion. When her mother disappeared, Flawless had stayed, maturing into a beautiful young woman, obediently traveling with her father from manor house to manor house and never questioning his decisions.

As an aristocratic young woman of her time, she left all decisions of consequence to her father. As a man who valued his own opinion above everyone else's, Drum told his friends that she was the perfect female. For this reason, Drum never deserted her as he had his other children, and he felt she could do no wrong.

Fortunately, she didn't do much wrong. Cflawless, her Conscience, had a pretty easy job. Mistress Flawless was amazingly gentle and generous considering the pampered lifestyle she enjoyed with her father. She honestly cared about others and sometimes even talked to her father about it.

"Look how beautiful our fields look today. The peasants have been working so hard. Maybe we should invite them to a party and tell them how wonderful they are."

"They're peasants, Flawless. What are you thinking?"

"My bad."

Flawless was beautiful, and due to her sweetness and her father's lavish lifestyle, she too was famous in The Kingdom. She had many friends both elegant and not so elegant and treated everyone she met with the same respect. Her father could not understand or appreciate this, but he allowed it because he ignored it.

Flawless charmed the servants and sometimes even helped them complete their tasks. She was courted by the rich and famous but was not as impressed by them as her father. And although she had had many suitors, Flawless remained single, accompanying Drum from one richly decorated manor to another and gracefully hostessing his many gatherings. Drum did realize that her open and friendly manner helped immensely with his elegant dinners and balls, but he expected it.

Drum was a great fan of loyalty, and Flawless was a loyal asset. Drum was fond of discussing many of life's ideas with her to get her opinion, but he never listened to it. This was her favorite part of their relationship even though he never took her advice. She was used to it. He didn't trust anyone's opinion but his own, feeling that he already knew the important things. Of course, he did. He was a man.

Since she loved her father, Flawless agreed with whatever he chose to do, but something odd was happening. She was beginning to ask questions. She was wondering if there was not more to life than this. At night, Flawless thought things over and formed her own opinions—a very unique process for a young lady of her time. Her father hadn't caught on to this yet.

Flawless's major failing according to her Conscience was the fact that she seldom openly questioned her father's decisions. She never seemed to catch him in his lies. She never pushed him to be more honest or to help others. Like most of the women of the age, she accepted whatever he did without question, even though she silently questioned many things.

Cflawless was a bit ahead of her time. She tried to nudge Flawless in this direction. In truth, some other female Consciences were also beginning to give their human hosts new ideas about having their own opinions. That, however, was scandalous behavior for a female of the Middle Ages, and Flawless wasn't there yet.

And there was one more thing. Although Flawless was lovely and charming to all of her father's friends, she had a few close friends of her own. She was frequently lonely for people her own age. Her father didn't see a problem, so there were seldom young people around. Flawless said she understood, but she was still lonely. Cflawless saw this clearly and vowed to push Flawless in the right direction if good prospects ever showed up.

5

King Sol

King Sol was the respected monarch of River Kingdom and was, for the most part, a good king. He was a bit overly conservative and cautious by nature, seldom entertaining at The Castle and always saving the wealth of his storehouses for what might be needed in the future. Although he was not particularly social, he was considered fair by his people and the neighboring kingdom of Urhonordo, and he was also admired by the Lowlanders whom he thought of as friends.

"Lowlanders are different," he observed. "They are hardworking freemen, and they like it that way. They don't bow down to any king, queen, or baron. They're all equal. I respect that. They live on rough, dry land and make do with a tiny bit of water, but they never start wars. That makes them pretty good neighbors, I think."

"That makes you a good judge of character," agreed Csol. "You know good people when you see them."

King Sol was fond of his neighbors to the east as well. This was the realm of the young queen of Urhonordo, Queen Luna. Some people had thought that Queen Luna and King Sol might someday merge their kingdoms, but King Sol was older and set in his ways and Luna was a much stronger, more self-directed female than he was used to. He respected her but would have a rough time taking her on as a partner.

Queen Luna, although the young ruler of a smaller kingdom, was tough in negotiations and never backed down. Cluna, her Conscience, liked that about her. King Sol had worked with Luna's father and now with Luna since her father had died. He found little difference in their determination and strength. Luna was no pushover.

Urhonordo and The Kingdom both saw strong levees as the guardians of their respective kingdoms and peace. King Sol and Queen Luna honored each other's concerns and met frequently to discuss the weather and refine their decisions.

Of course, the primary focus and concern of both kingdoms was the climate and the yearly changing flow of The River. To Urhonordo and River Kingdom, the appropriate height of the levees was essential to keeping each kingdom's farmlands producing and feeding their people. Some farmlands were low, and high levees were necessary to keep them from flooding as had happened in the past. Some farms were higher, and they would need lower levees during dry spells. The changing climate made every year different, and they had learned from their mistakes.

For this reason, the need for levee alterations on either side required yearly negotiation of Water Rights Treaties. These negotiations were given the greatest priority and had allowed the two kingdoms on either side of The Great River to live in peace for many years.

6

Threat from the East

Water was not the only thing that affected peace, however. Sometimes there were completely unanticipated challenges that could not be avoided. And this year, the peace of River Kingdom was about to be interrupted.

The harsh winter had begun to give way to a warm spring when a runner staggered in from the plains east of Urhonordo. Breathlessly, he demanded entrance to The Castle and collapsed in front of King Sol. He had obviously run a long way with a message of great urgency.

"Dragons are threatening to take over the far eastern regions! My kingdom is just past Urhonordo's flatlands and eastern prairies!" he gasped when he at last revived. "River Kingdom is our only hope. *You* are the largest kingdom in the area, King Sol. *You* have the strongest Royal Guard. The eastern regions are in danger of being overrun! You've got to help us!"

Csol had always been afraid of dragons (although he had never seen one), and he began lobbying King Sol to do something immediately. "You should probably pull together a strike force of your Royal Guard for a search-and-destroy mission, don't you think? I mean, if dragons are involved, there is no time to waste and they're not that far away. We have to get them before they get us, right? Sooner rather than later, right? That seems like a good idea, don't you think? I'm just sayin' . . ."

King Sol listened patiently but was definitely not as excited about a Dragon Quest as his Conscience. He was interested in stability and leadership in the kingdom, and at his age, he no longer pictured himself as a dragon slayer.

"We have important treaties in place with our neighbors, and that's a good thing," he told his Conscience. "These treaties keep the peace between kingdoms, so it is essential that we maintain that peace here and stay true to our word.

"I know that there are greedy individuals in River Kingdom who wouldn't think twice about breaking treaties. Some have been after me for years to let River Kingdom do things the way that they want to do them. The Queen of Urhonordo would not like their ideas, and neither would I."

King Sol began to pace. "A strong king in place is essential for the peace and security of The Kingdom. It is my duty to stay here and do my job. *I* should definitely not go on a Dragon Quest," he concluded.

"I hear you," said Csol. "I see that you are a man of conviction . . . *and truly boring,*" he added under his breath. "I know that a strong leader is really important here. But . . . does that mean that you are going to let the dragons eat the whole Eastern Region?" Csol had decided to offer up his idea of a persuasive question.

King Sol did think some more about the dragon problem.

The fearful Csol had another compelling piece of information to share. "Since dragon territory is only several days to the east, I should probably remind you that after the dragons finish off the Eastern Region, they may be eating their way through Urhonordo to us. I offer that as food for thought, Your Majesty."

Now there was no choice. Sol's duty became clear. His Conscience had helped him make the decision, and there was no doubt. The thought of being eaten by dragons was a strong deciding factor. King Sol made a kingly decision: "A Dragon Quest is the right thing to do."

But as the conservative king that he was, King Sol thought things through some more and concluded that if he was not going to be here to keep the peace, he would need to leave River Kingdom in the hands of a watchdog, someone that was equally (or almost equally) capable and strong. Someone who would keep things going as peacefully as he would until he returned. He needed to find a Royal Caretaker that he could trust.

King Sol reviewed his situation. The Royal Advisors of River Kingdom knew their role. He had a Royal Advisor for every important position— Defense, Finance, Agriculture, Community Relations. All systems had their experienced specialist. These men had served King Sol for years and were loyal to his way of governing. They would take care of the daily business of The Kingdom while he was gone. Sol knew he could trust them.

The position of Royal Caretaker would need to be a position of greater authority than any of the other advisors, however. This person would be an overseer of The Kingdom, and this position would, therefore, need to be held by a man of high integrity and judgment such as himself. He should be well known and admired, an individual who could maintain the trust of all the Royal Advisors and the peace between The Kingdom, Urhonordo, and The Lowlands while he was gone. This strength of character was essential to the prosperity and safety of River Kingdom.

And so King Sol's search for a Royal Caretaker began. The word went out by Royal Courier across The Kingdom. Nearly all the wealthy barons and lords flocked to The Castle, each insisting that they knew what the King wanted and was the best choice to fulfill his requirements.

Did Lord Daron Drum throw his hat in the ring? Of course! It was as though he had been grooming himself for a chance like this all his life.

After several days of interviewing most of the "aristocratic establishment" of River Kingdom, however, King Sol became completely discouraged.

Some of the candidates were too old. This position required vigor.

Some were too young. This position required *some* experience in the ways of the world.

Some possibilities were down on their luck and needed money. They could not be trusted.

Some individuals were known to be just plain greedy. They couldn't be trusted either.

On the last day and after reviewing his entire list of prospects, King Sol couldn't imagine anyone that he could confidently place in this important position. He paced the floor and gazed across his beloved kingdom from his balcony. He needed to find a not-too-young, not-too-old wealthy man who would care for The Castle *and* The Kingdom successfully and maintain its peace and prosperity as he would. Someone just like himself . . . of course.

Tonight, a bright light in the distance caught his eye. It was one of Lord Doran Drum's manor houses lit up for a large social gathering taking place there. King Sol was not a partier. He had never been to one of Drum's parties. But it looked like there were a lot of people there. "He must be very popular. I should go to one of his parties someday," he mused sleepily.

Then it occurred to him. *Why didn't I think of Lord Drum?* King Sol asked himself. *Doran Drum is obviously a popular landowner and a well-known member of The Kingdom. Why didn't I think of him?*

"You were looking for someone like yourself, and Drum is nothing like you," commented Csol.

"True," agreed King Sol, but suddenly Drum appeared a very interesting choice. He had wealth of his own, was middle-aged and healthy, and appeared to be admired by many members of The Kingdom. Upon further review, he might be a good fit.

King Sol didn't say a thing to anyone. He was only *thinking* about Drum, but somehow the word got out. To be honest, it was Csol's fault.

He had heard what Sol was thinking and shared it with a few of his Conscience friends. Csol had some questions. He didn't want King Sol to make a mistake.

Csol was anxious for King Sol to go on his mission, but he was not so sure about Lord Drum as a Royal Caretaker. He had heard some less- than-positive comments about Drum in the Conscience Forums. At casual discussions with his fellow Consciences, he had listened particularly to Cdrum and the challenges he had experienced with Drum. Cdrum was a hardworking Conscience. He would let Csol know if Drum had any serious Aura issues.

That very night, Csol called a Conscience Forum to discuss the Royal Caretaker selection. The King's choice would affect the well-being of all the good people of The Kingdom. As Sol's Conscience, it was his duty to give the King's choice careful thought and help him make the right decision.

"Guess what," Csol announced to the group. "King Sol is thinking seriously about appointing Doran Drum to the position of Royal Caretaker. What do you all think about that?"

Cdrum was lounging on a beam under The Castle floorboards, a frequent gathering place for Conscience Forums. Now he grinned and stood up. "What I think is that it will ever happen," he laughed. "Like I've told you before, my human is not that much into responsibility. Don't get me wrong. Drum's not really a bad guy. But I don't think he's 'Caretaker material' really. Being a Royal Caretaker would require a lot of honest work, and Drum, as we know, is not into either honesty or work."

"Yeah. I heard that he lies a lot. Why does he do that? What does he lie about?" asked Csol.

"I'm not sure why, actually. I guess he just likes to make himself look good," answered Cdrum. "Mostly he just brags . . . what he does is better, what he has is grander . . . what he knows is more—that sort of thing. And he likes to take credit for doing things that somebody else did. I'm working on that with him, but he loves to make himself look good. I don't approve, but his lies never seem to hurt anything."

"Hmm. Harmless lies, huh? That doesn't sound too bad, I guess," commented a Conscience for one of the Royal Advisors. "A lot of rich guys lie. And he would be watched by the Royal Advisors who have been doing the real work of The Castle forever. They should be able to keep a stand-in Caretaker honest."

"That's true. That would help a lot," agreed Csol, "but—"

"And fortunately, there are lots of Royal Advisors, so he wouldn't have to know much or work too hard," snickered a Conscience for another one of the Royal Advisors.

"I think this Royal Caretaker position might be just a figurehead position, anyway," contributed Conscience of Castle Cook. "The Royal Advisors for The Kingdom are smart. They will do the work while the Royal Caretaker just nods his head and orders good food from The Castle kitchen."

"Drum would probably like that," admitted Cdrum, "but there's one more thing: Drum is sort of a party animal, you know. He's a playboy, and he loves his women. He holds parties and hangs out with ladies on a regular basis. It makes him feel important."

"Yeah, I heard that too. But that's not a *real* bad thing. Drum has his own money, doesn't he? If he spends it on some parties while he's living a few months in The Castle, that could keep the Castle Staff amused while King Sol is away. A lot of people say that King Sol's boring, anyway."

Csol listened to the Consciences of the Royal Advisors and shrugged. "If you guys think Drum could do it, then I guess I'm okay with it, but I'm still not sure Drum's a good idea. Drum sounds pretty self-centered."

"Oh, that's true, for sure," agreed Cdrum. "I had to bang on him hard to get him to take care of his peasant farmers at all, let alone fairly. He hardly knows they're alive. In fact, he finally turned the whole thing over to a peasant named William of Dale so he wouldn't have to even think about them. Fortunately, that guy is honest so things are going okay with Will in charge of everything, but Drum does look out for number one. That's true."

Csol listened closely. "Is that true, Cwill?"

"Yeah. That's true, but my guy's doing a pretty good job."

"So do you all think Drum would make a good Caretaker or not?" asked Csol hesitantly.

Now a quiet voice was heard from the back of the room. It was Cben, the Conscience of Ben, a Lowlander friend of Will.

"Let me get this straight. If I heard you all right, you agreed that this guy Drum is a self-centered party animal that doesn't do much and lies all the time. That doesn't sound like a good Royal Caretaker to me."

The Consciences looked at each other. In truth, they were blowing off an important decision. Maybe the Consciences needed their own Consciences, and Cben had summed their shortcomings up pretty well. They were taking Drum's problem issues too lightly.

The discussion began again and much more seriously. The Consciences of Drum's wealthy "friends" now contributed even more unflattering stories about Drum.

"He isn't just selfish. He feels he *deserves everything.*" "He doesn't care about anyone but himself."

"He tells lies every time he opens his mouth . . . lots of them." "He's had several wives and has not treated them all well."

"He is completely self-centered and doesn't do *anything* he doesn't want to do."

"In other words, Drum will *not* be a good Royal Caretaker for The Kingdom, and Csol should tell the King the truth."

Depressed, Csol straggled sadly back to The Castle. He knew, as an honest Conscience, he had to advise against Drum. But the King couldn't leave to fight the terribly frightening dragons without a Royal Caretaker, and Csol was afraid of dragons. What should he tell King Sol? Should he tell him that he shouldn't go on the Dragon Quest at all? Definitely not! Csol had to think this through. Hopefully, he would figure it out tomorrow.

7

Auras' Influence

And where were the Auras? The Auras didn't know about the Conscience Forum or its negative conclusion, but they wouldn't have cared if they knew. They were Drum fans. Drum was a man who could ruin a good kingdom if the Auras could get him into the right position, and they began to think that this could be their moment.

The Auras maneuvered slowly into temptation position. Here was a wide-open opportunity for evil, and no one seemed to be around to run interference. Good.

Of course, Consciences knew about Auras. They had always known about them. The problem was, however, River Kingdom had been at peace for so many years that Consciences were not watching as closely for Auras' threats to take hold as they had in the past.

Even without knowing of the Conscience Forum, the Auras had decided that tonight might be a lucky night. The king had not interviewed Drum yet. They had been hovering around him for a long time, imagining him in a true leadership position. He lied a lot and was slightly dishonest. He was self-centered and an upward climber. What more could an evil force want? With this MO, he could ruin River Kingdom in a short period of time. He could be fun to watch.

He was their choice, but they had to be sly. They would not overplay their hand, but they *could* definitely take advantage of Drum's most frequently used talents—flattery and lying and being at the right place at the right time.

The Auras awakened Drum. He sat up with a start in the pitch dark of midnight. He could feel that his Conscience was not nearby. The Auras had planted dreams of his superior ability inside him for years. Now they surrounded him with visions of the potential power of the position of Royal Caretaker. He was made for this job. If he worked it right, he could get that position, they insisted.

"It's all about looking like a popular, healthy, unneedy aristocrat," the Auras instructed. "Show this King what he thinks he needs, and the job will be yours. And you know what he wants to see. He wants his Royal Caretaker to be supported by the people and able to keep his kingdom peaceful while he's gone. It is important that you show him that you are a person like that."

The King must believe that The Kingdom loves me, Drum calculated to himself. And of course, everyone does love me. They all just came to my party.

He needs to see that this is true, which, of course, it is. It's all about the King's perception. I need to create that image. But I can do this. I've been doing it all my life.

"Yes, you have," agreed the Auras. "It is the 'wonderful you' that everyone knows."

Drum could not contain his excitement, and Cdrum was saying nothing.

He wasn't there.

In the morning, Drum sent his own private messengers to the partygoers that had attended most of his parties. Cdrum, tired from the Conscience Forum the night before, slept through the whole thing.

By Royal Invitation: King Sol's Royal Caretaker Party!

Only the elite of The Kingdom are hereby invited to King Sol's Royal Caretaker Party, the first party ever held on the grounds of The Castle! This party will include only those select few who are in line to become a Royal Caretaker! Someone from this party will be chosen!

King Sol will be there! *The King will actually come to his balcony and make his selection from the elite present. Be there and be chosen!*

Sincerely,
Lord Doran
Drum

The invitations raised a bonfire of expectation among the well-connected and those who thought they should be considered "elite." It was a chance for another one of Drum's parties, which by itself was not that exciting, but the invite said "King Sol will be there" and one of the elite would be chosen to be the Royal Caretaker. This party was "the place to be." By evening, most of the lords and barons of The Kingdom had gathered from far and near and crowded in joyful expectation under The Castle balcony.

Drum strode back and forth in front of the partygoers like a cheerleader, laughing and clapping his hands.

"Who throws the best parties in The Kingdom?" "Drum, Drum, Drum!" the crowd shouted.

"If you want more food and drink at this party, who will provide it?" Drum yelled to the partygoers. Drum's servants circulated with plenty of drinks.

"Drum! Drum! Drum!" the happy crowd responded, holding out their glasses.

The wonderful treats and drinks kept coming, and the partygoers in the courtyard continued to grow, wait for the King, and ask Drum for more. Predictably, the noise became almost deafening as even more folks joined in for the fun.

The King in his chambers was exhausted and getting ready for bed. All day he had been worrying about his Caretaker selection as well as his upcoming Dragon Quest duties, and now, what was this? Noise and laughter outside in his own courtyard? People were yelling Drum's name. Why on earth was this happening?

Wrapping himself in hasty robes, his crown tilted slightly on his head, Sol poked his nose past the door to his balcony and peered down at the ground below. There were dozens of people gathered in his front courtyard, of all places. And they were all cheering and yelling things like, "You know what we want! You're the man!"

"Atta boy, Drum!" "Great job, Drum!"

Obviously, Drum's friends know him, thought King Sol. Must be they are here to support him for Caretaker. They look like they really like him. They must want me to choose him. How nice of everyone to let me know.

The grateful monarch stepped to the edge of his balcony and waved. He smiled down at the crowd below him and then withdrew to his chambers, content that he knew now who he should choose to protect his kingdom. It was time to prepare for Dragon Quest.

Drum's friends laughed and waved at King Sol. They were happy. The King had come to their party, just as Drum had said he would. They partied on. They felt superior and enjoyed themselves until the food and drinks that Drum had provided suddenly disappeared. Then they drifted off to their homes, content with dreams and hopes regarding who would be chosen.

The first "King's Caretaker Party" was a big success. Tomorrow they would learn of the King's selection. They all had high hopes.

Drum knew that his show was a success. The King had seen that his friends loved him, and it had only cost him a bit of party food and drinks to demonstrate it. He didn't care what his friends really thought right now. He was only concerned about what it looked like they thought. It was all about perception.

Cdrum had been up all night the night before at Conscience Forum. He had accompanied Drum to his party, but he had no idea about its origin. It was just another party as far as he could tell, and he hadn't paid much attention. He should have guessed that there was something fishy about the venue, but he didn't.

He was flabbergasted, therefore, when the Royal Couriers arrived at Drum's manor house the next afternoon with an invitation to meet with the King at The Castle.

"The King hasn't interviewed you yet, has he?" asked Cdrum cautiously. "No, not yet." Drum smiled. "But my friends at the party last night told him I would be perfect for the job, and he believed them."

"I was there," Cdrum snorted. "Your friends never said that."

"No, but the King thought they did." Drum smiled.

While Cdrum was trying to understand this answer, a rumor began to circulate in the village. Word had it that the King might have inexplicably decided that Drum was his man. He had sent for Drum. What else could that mean?

As more of the word got out, Drum's party-going friends were first stunned but then suspicious. Drum had thrown the party last night at The Castle. He had been in charge of the party. The King had seen that. Had that party inspired the King?

Suspicion soon became anger. They understood immediately. They had been duped.

The Auras were ecstatic. They had backed Drum for a job he wasn't qualified for, and now they had inspired jealousy in the gullible aristocracy. It was a "win-win."

The aristocratic hierarchy was furious. Drum was a showman. He was a huckster. How could the King allow a man like Drum to even set foot in The Castle, much less become the Royal Caretaker? How could they have let this happen?

Drum was nothing but a con man, they told each other. They knew that now for sure. A thick aura of Eforce anger began to circulate around their feet. Jealousy was one of the Auras' main ingredients, and the lords' aura was definitely green.

"We should have known that Drum would get this position without earning it," the lords told the barons.

"That's how he got everything he owns," the barons told the lords. "Drum has no royal blood."

"He has no experience in running a kingdom or anything else."

"And he's just plain lazy. My hound dog has more work ethic than he has."

"He threw a great party, and we fell for it." "We praised him. We called out his name."

"What does he know about being a Royal Caretaker?" "Nothing."

"Nothing!"

"The King should have picked me." "Or me."

"Or me."

The air was green, indeed.

Cdrum had not completely processed what the party at The Castle had caused until he and Drum were on their way to The Castle. Flawless was coming with them to meet with King Sol as well. This was serious. Cdrum suddenly realized that this outlandish, ridiculous, unimaginable "Royal Caretaker idea" might actually be taking place. Drum as the Royal Caretaker? Really?

Lord Doran Drum didn't know or want to know how to take care of a farm or a manor house, much less a kingdom. The Conscience Forum had been right. Cdrum had no idea how Drum had created the King's new interest in Drum, but he now determined that he needed to talk Drum out of this mistake.

"Drum, my man, you really need to give this some more thought," Cdrum began. "It's not too late. You're okay as a rich guy. Believe me. I'm on your side. But I'm not convinced you're right for this position, my friend. You're sort of a playboy, and this Royal Caretaker thing is a real job.

"You've had several wives and spent a lot of time giving parties. Although you're big in real estate, you don't even take care of your own properties. You put on a good show, but that's all. Your friends all know that. They say you might be an okay guy, but you don't have a clue about running a kingdom."

"My friends are just jealous," Drum countered as they entered The Castle.

"This is true, but that's not the issue," insisted Cdrum in Drum's ear. "Just think about it." Cdrum now became even more serious. "The King is going to depend on you to honestly do what the King would do if he were here. Honesty is not your thing. Doing anything you don't want to do is not your thing. This whole gig is not your thing!"

King Sol's Conscience had come to meet them and heard the last remark. "That was pretty harsh, Cdrum," said Csol. "Drum's friends at the party the other night seemed to think he's going to be a good Caretaker. I was going to tell the King what the Conscience Counsel said, but Sol was so impressed when Drum's friends were supportive, I thought we Consciences might have been wrong. The King thinks that Drum's friends want Drum to be the Royal Caretaker."

"That's what Drum wants him to think," groaned Cdrum. "He mainly just wants to look good and have a good time, but his honesty continues to be up for grabs. I'm not sure, but I think his party on The Castle lawn might have been a con job. The more I think about it, the more I wonder if the Auras put him up to it. Seriously, Csol. You might want to give King Sol a heads-up before he leaves The Kingdom."

Flawless was blissfully unaware of this discussion but Cflawless listened closely. Flawless was happily following her father into a position that she knew nothing about, but three important Consciences were now worried.

Sadly, Csol now realized that he had made a mistake by waiting to warn King Sol. He was a good Conscience, but this had been bad timing on his part, and he might have let his human make the wrong decision.

Csol rushed to King Sol and valiantly tried to pass on what he had just heard from Cdrum, but the King had already made up his mind. He had heard what he needed to hear from Drum's fans at the party.

The meeting with Drum and Flawless went well with no hint of potential problems. King Sol was even more pleased with his choice when he met Flawless. He could see that she was a young lady of quality that would enhance The Castle while she was here. The decision was made.

Csol was ashamed. He had wanted King Sol to fight the dragons. Why had he not paid more attention to the man that the king would leave behind?

He was the King's Conscience, and now he feared that he had not warned him as he should.

The preparations for Dragon Quest were massive. This was where King Sol's attention was now focused. Most of the Royal Guard would be going. The following days were spent in planning and loading battle gear and supplies. They would be traveling across the prairies and into the wild eastern territory with hope of conquering a frightening foe. The King's mind was on all this now. His Conscience was no longer relevant.

And then the day came. Lord Doran Drum bowed low and wished King Sol well. "Godspeed you in your endeavor and bring you home safely, Your Highness," he murmured respectfully.

The Dragon Quest Army gathered its forces and set off across The Bridge to the eastern fields on their dangerous mission. Lord Doran Drum was now the Royal Caretaker of River Kingdom.

8

Drum and The Castle

The position of Royal Caretaker was not the same as being a king, but it satisfied the desire Drum had always had to live like royalty. He felt he deserved it. Having no royal blood, this was as close as he would ever get to a royal position, and he was thrilled. Cdrum remained worried, however. How would his human behave now that real work might be demanded of him?

The first thing Drum did was to move into The Castle, of course. He was excited until he realized that many of the rooms in The Castle were not as elegantly appointed as those in his manor houses. King Sol was a frugal sort. The place was huge, however, and it definitely had historical significance so Drum could see its potential as a party palace.

"I know what you're thinking," warned Cdrum. "You're thinking of huge parties and prestige and power instead of responsibility. I know you. Don't think I don't."

"Nag, nag, nag," returned Drum. "I know how to do this job. All I have to do is keep the peace and . . . live like a king!" Drum was on top of the whole idea.

"You had better pay attention," Cdrum continued. "This position is more demanding than anything you have done before."

"I have run huge real estate holdings where hundreds have worked for me. I think I can handle this," Drum answered smugly.

Cdrum rolled his eyes.

Drum's first Royal Caretaker order was to demand that the interior of The Castle be brought up to his standards. For this, he raided the riches of the King's Royal Storehouses and moved in piles of tapestries, carpets, and rare items of decor.

Flawless moved into The Castle as well and set about interior decorating. She didn't inquire about the source or cost. She had never had to worry about such things before, so she didn't now. She knew her father's lavish style and arranged what he had delivered to her artfully, loving every minute of it.

"Can you believe it, Flawless?" chortled Drum as he admired her grand displays. "We are living in The Castle, surrounded by the King's riches and servants and lackeys. We are envied by even the most titled aristocracy. I know they have always thought that they were better than I, but I am the one that is truly living like a king. Everyone will now bow down to me, and they will have to do my bidding. No one will dare to tell me no. This is a dream come true."

"I am so happy for you, Daddy. I know you have always wanted something like this. You will *almost* be like a real king," agreed Flawless. A slow smile began in Sir Drum's eyes and wafted over his entire face. "Like a real king," he repeated quietly. The Eforces gathered around Drum, present and patient. They had Drum where they wanted him.

"And you can do wonderful things for people while you are here," Flawless continued happily. "Everyone will love you. You are in a position to really help people."

Cflawless was not as cheerful. She was wary. "This is a very different place, Flawless," she warned. "People will be watching everything your father does, and I'm not sure that 'helping people' is the main thing on his mind."

Cflawless had attended the Conscience Forum with Cdrum and Csol, and she hoped Flawless could help her father do a better job than some of the other Consciences had predicted. She was going to try to help Flawless, but Flawless was an innocent.

Flawless heard Cflawless, but she wasn't worried. Her father was happy, and she was feeling positive. Her father really could do good things, and she would help him.

Cdrum slid down Drum's sleeve and stared back up at him. He had decided to be hopeful as well, but cautious. Drum was prone to selfishness, but maybe this new position and encouragement from Flawless would change him for the better. Maybe the Conscience Forum had been worrying for nothing.

Cdrum was a proud Conscience. He would give it his best. He ran back up to Drum's shoulder with some test ideas. "Flawless is right,

Drum. Now that you're living in The Castle, you *can* improve things for others.

"Just think of it. *You* can keep the wages high for your peasants and encourage your wealthy friends to adopt better working conditions for their peasants. You can open more fair-trade routes with other kingdoms and eliminate poverty for the beggars in the streets. This is your chance to do some great things. That's what real kings do."

But the Aura was enjoying Drum's increased feelings of superiority as well. Seductively, the Aurs curled around Drum and settled on his other shoulder like a cat. Drum reacted immediately to its presence.

"Why don't you mind your own business, Conscience?" Drum replied. "Haven't you noticed? I am *really* important now. I don't care about peasants . . . never have, never will. And you don't know any more about being a king than I do so don't act like you do."

Drum looked inward darkly. Feeling his power, he made a formal announcement to Cdrum. *I know what I want now, Conscience, and you're not it.*

He strode grandly around the throne room, finishing his dismissal aloud. "I don't need anyone telling me what to do. I have the best brain in The Kingdom, and I intend to use it. You should leave and find somebody who needs you. In my position, I won't need you at all anymore."

Flawless blanched. Why was her father saying such hateful things to her? What had she done? "I'm sorry, Daddy. I didn't mean anything."

Drum stopped short and winced. "I'm sorry too, Flawless. I wasn't talking to you. Sometimes my Conscience gets on my nerves, and I have to tell him off."

Flawless grinned. "Oh, you actually *have* a Conscience, Daddy? I didn't know you had one." She laughed and gave her father a hug.

Drum melted a bit and laughed too. "Of course, I have a Conscience, daughter, but don't tell anybody. *And* I really do plan on doing wonderful things, just like you said. King Sol was boring. The Kingdom is not as much fun as it needs to be. There aren't enough parties. I can make

River Kingdom great the way I like it. With my strong leadership, it will be the greatest kingdom in the world."

Cdrum listened. "Greatest kingdom in the world" sounded hopeful. "Not enough parties," not so much. Cdrum backed off and waited for evidence of what Drum was truly thinking, but he could feel the Eforces and suspected that he and Drum had entered into a whole new level of challenges. Drum was not just standing in for King Sol. As of now, he was taking over, and what he did, right or wrong, would have real consequences. Cdrum had his work cut out for him. He watched the catlike Eforces slink into a corner.

The next morning, before any Auras appeared to be stirring, Cdrum tried a gentle warning to Drum about his power. This power was only temporary. Drum needed to remember that.

"Power can cloud a person's understanding of right and wrong, big guy. So you need to watch out," Cdrum said quietly, trying not to preach. "With power, good judgment can disappear just like that."

Drum did hear Cdrum and grinned from ear to ear. "I'll be careful, no problem," he said smugly. "But I have some important things I want to do to take advantage of my position, and there's no doubt that I'm going to do them. Stand back."

Drum strode onto his balcony and gazed out over the land. This was his kingdom now. He had arrived. Below him, people looked up and saluted. Behind him, he could hear the scurrying feet of servants and advisors who were there just to serve him.

And he had the keys to everything—the storehouses of the kingdom's harvests, gold and silver, everything. His awareness of this truth began growing stronger. He could actually do anything he wanted no matter the cost. Who had the power to say no? No one.

With a growing awareness, Drum pictured his friends when they heard of his new position. They had said they were happy for him, but he wondered if they really felt like that. He suspected that they were jealous. He had heard some mumbling. And what was the antidote for jealousy? Loyalty.

It was hard to know who to trust. Loyalty became a sudden issue for Drum. Loyalty, he decided, would be the cornerstone of his administration. His plans for success would need to be centered around loyalty, complete loyalty.

First to be evaluated for loyalty must be the Royal Advisors who had been chosen by King Sol. Would they be loyal to him? Who among them would deserve *his* trust? He would need to sort out the loyal advisors from the disloyal and eliminate those who might not be loyal enough. How to do this? How to do this?

"Aren't we getting a little bit paranoid, Drum?" whispered Cdrum. "These Royal Advisors have a lot of experience. They can be very helpful to a new guy. Why don't you just kick back for a month or two and get a feel for this place. It looks like it's running pretty well to me. Relax . . . enjoy."

Drum gazed out again from the balcony, but he was not finished with his thoughts about loyalty and his new position. He was where he supposed to be. Some people might not think so, but this was his destiny. He had earned the perks of his office, and he would keep those who recognized that and dismiss those who didn't. Who was who now needed to be evaluated. He would find out in his own way.

9

Will and Ben and the Garden

Back on Drum Manor Estates, Will was at work in the fields before sunup as usual. William of Dale knew the importance of the job that he had been given by Lord Drum, and he tended to it with even more care now that Drum was living at The Castle. Although he had hardly even thought about Drum in the past, he knew that his "boss" would be demanding a show of good production now from his fields. The Kingdom would be watching.

Will was a peasant farmer, born the son of a peasant farmer. He was nothing special, but his father had taught him about the sun and the rain, the rotation of the seasons, and the need for constant care of the crops. It was early spring, and Drum was, even now, less important to him than the fields and his fellow workers.

"Plants are sort of like people," Will's father had told him. "You take care of them, and they will give you what you need."

Will's mother had added to that message. "The wheat and beans will keep you alive, but flowers and people will give you joy. Don't forget the flowers and people." Will's mother had been wise.

"I like mornings like this," Will whispered to himself, grinning.

"Me too," agreed Ben from nearby. "It smells good out here." Ben was a Lowlander, a long time coworker, and friend. He and Will had worked together for years now, and they frequently felt like brothers. The sun was just rising, and the air was fresh with the perfume of dew on the freshly turned dirt. The Castle was barely visible in the morning mist.

"It's getting warm early," Ben observed. "Harvest should be good this year, but we'll need more water. Drum will be a happy guy if a good harvest rolls in on his watch at The Castle. We'll need to get permission from the Ag Advisor, though, if we're going to be lowering the levees."

"I'll talk to Arnold about it," agreed Will as he dug another row for his bean crop.

"Good idea." Ben grinned. "A good harvest will mean a lot of parties for Drum."

"Haven't you heard?" Will dug further into his row. "Lord Drum is living in The Castle now. He is the Royal Caretaker. That's big. He won't have time for parties anymore."

"Yeah, I heard that." Ben grinned. "And here's what I think'll happen. I think Drum's parties will be bigger than ever. The difference is that Drum won't pay for 'em. The King's storehouses will. That's what I think."

"That's just gossip," Will grumbled. "Drum is an important person in The Kingdom now. We should be proud that we work for him. And we should be working instead of gossiping." Will glanced up at The Castle with respect and then returned to his digging.

"Right," agreed Ben, following Will's lead. "But I still think I'm right." The Consciences of these two workers didn't say a thing. They didn't need to. They had attended the Conscience Forum the other night, and they

thought what Ben thought too.

"I guess that makes you a 'Caretaker for the Royal Caretaker,' right?" Ben laughed. "Drum's not even going to be anywhere around. He won't care at all about what happens out here in the fields, not that he ever did, of course. He'll be living the high life. That leaves all the real work up to you even more than usual."

Will had thought about that, and Ben was right. Now there was really no one but him to watch Drum's real estate, and the manor was definitely a big source of the food for the people of The Kingdom. The more Will thought about it, the more he realized that his responsibility had grown.

"You think you should give yourself a raise?" Ben laughed as he moved to dig the next row. The Eforces listened.

"Sure. I handle all of Drum's storehouses, right? I'll just give you and me a great big raise. That'll be great." Will slapped Ben on the back. "We can both get rich and go to live in one of Drum's manor houses."

"Now you're talkin'! And maybe that pretty daughter of his will want to marry one of us," Ben continued with a hoot. "Have you ever seen her?" "Nope, but I hear she's beautiful. At any rate, we shouldn't probably talk about her like this. Drum is our master, and she is way beyond our pay grade." The Auras were bored and moved on. Nothing to see here.

Ben's Conscience, Cben, shook his head. "There isn't anything wrong with gossip this far out here in the middle of a field," he told Ben defensively. "Will is a goody-goody stuffed shirt."

Ben laughed. "We're in the middle of a field, Will. My Conscience says we don't need to worry about gossiping out here. We can say Drum's daughter is a looker all we want."

But that was the kind of people Ben and Will were. Doing things right was important to both of them. No wonder that they bored the Eforces.

The Auras were bored by Will and Ben and also annoyed by the flower garden that Will had created in a small patch near The River. It honored his mother's love for flowers and Will's appreciation for them now that both his parents were gone.

To Will, flowers seemed like his defense against frustration and anger. No one had a real use for flowers in these early days, but to Will, they had meaning. They just made him feel good. Cwill liked this about Will, but sometimes he worried that his hardworking human spent more time with plants than he did with people.

Every night, after a long day in the fields, Will visited the garden that he had secretly planted near The Castle. He had been doing this for years, and he had gathered many species. It was peaceful, and the beauty of the place made this the happiest part of his day. On some warm nights, he fell asleep in the garden, awakening in the morning to wash in The River before going off to work.

Tonight, Will's mind wandered as he pulled at the few weeds that had dared to gather around the base of his rosebushes. When he was gardening, he had time to think of other things. He gazed up at The Castle. His secret garden was closer to The Castle than Drum's fields. The Castle lights were coming on. *That figures*, Will thought absently. *Drum's probably planning his first party, just like Ben said. He's got a perfect place for parties now.* "That's not your problem," commented Cwill. "You don't need to be worrying about Drum and his parties. You are going to have enough to do keeping his farmland in good shape." Cwill was very good at reading thoughts.

"You're right," mumbled Will and went back to his roses.

10

The Party Planners

Yes, indeed. The lights were on in The Castle, and as Will had predicted, Drum's first party was the one idea that had been churning inside him since he moved into The Castle only a few days earlier.

Was Drum intent on learning the ways of The Castle? No.

Had he asked if King Sol had left important instructions or requests? No. Had Drum introduced himself to any of the Royal Advisors or staff? No. Drum had been touring the grand, but sparsely decorated castle with disdain. "The Castle needs work. There is no elegance to it at all. I'll have to get Flawless on the job drumming up more decor right away if

I'm going to stay here."

Tonight, the Royal Castle Staff was respectfully following behind Drum as he had ordered, waiting for instruction.

"This Castle is a waste of space," Drum mourned. "There is no doubt that King Sol was a boring guy. There is nothing here that indicates a good time. What did he do for fun . . . anything?" No one answered.

Drum wandered from room to room. In each of them, he turned and glowered at the Royal Staff. "Light the lamps, for heaven's sake, people. We look like we are living in a tomb." The Royal Staff scrambled to do as they were told.

The Royal Finance Advisor was part of the contingent and began clucking his tongue. He lowered his head and tried to remain respectful, but all this lighting of lamps was wasteful. This was something that King Sol would not approve of.

This newcomer might not know this, he thought. With appropriate restraint, he spoke up quietly.

"Sir Drum, King Sol does not usually light rooms that are unoccupied," he murmured.

Drum was a tall, heavy, imposing figure. This was a quality from which he had benefited in the past, using his size to intimidate and impress. Now he turned and glared directly down at the slightly stooped older man who seemed to shrink before him. "Do you see King Sol anywhere around here?" he growled.

"No, sir, but . . ."

"Then what King Sol would or wouldn't do doesn't really matter, now, does it?"

"*I* see your point, but—"

"I want the lights on, and I am here saying so. Do you understand that?" With each deliberate word, the Royal Financial Advisor's understanding became clearer. This man was going to be a spendthrift for sure . . . way different from King Sol *and* intent on getting his own way. The rest of the entourage took note.

"Yes, sir," the old man said in a quivering voice. "Good."

"That was a pretty bossy start to working with a Royal Advisor, Drum," commented Cdrum. "You shamed him."

I suppose, thought Drum, *but these people need to find out who's boss in this place.* "When I tell you I want something done, I want it done," Drum growled aloud. Cdrum shook his head.

The entire group of Royal Staff backed up timidly and nodded. Drum looked around and enjoyed the reaction he had received. Now was a perfect time to introduce the real reason that he was surveying the rooms of The Castle. They were in the biggest room they had visited so far, the Grand Ballroom. With an air of authority, Drum stepped up on a large platform at the front of the room and addressed the gaggle of castle staff directly. "So, gentlemen, as you may have guessed, I am about to put together a huge inauguration dinner and ball to celebrate *me, myself,* in my new position. It will be the biggest party the kingdom has ever seen, so this room is entirely too small. We will have jugglers and musicians and dancers here to entertain all the wealthy lords and ladies of the aristocracy. Noblemen will swarm here from miles around. We will need to enlarge this room and decorate it accordingly.

"I am famous and popular, so all my friends will flock to me and the rich and famous of River Kingdom will be thrilled that they know me. This party must be excellent, which is why we must enlarge this hall. Who is with me on this?"

The collection of Royal Staff looked at one another. What should they say? What should they do? King Sol had never ever wanted to enlarge the already enormous castle.

One advisor rushed to the front of the group. "I am with you, sir. Of course, we will need a bigger hall," the man gushed enthusiastically. "We all know that. That is a 'given.' And we *must* build that hall immediately!" Drum was startled but then grinned widely. The rest of the Royal Staff and Advisors looked from side to side but chimed in. "We should build a larger hall!" they echoed. "Of course, we should build a larger hall."

Drum was thrilled. This was a perfect response. "Who wants to be in charge?" he called next over the din.

No one moved. Then from the ranks of the Royal Staff, the hand of the same enthusiastic advisor shot up high.

"Choose me, sir. Choose me!" The hand belonged to Metta Morf, a longtime member of the Royal Advisors. Actually, he had been the King's Royal Community Relations Advisor. He prided himself on being able to find creative solutions to any problem. He was even sure that he himself would have been good at the Royal Caretaker job.

Morf felt that his creative flexibility was an asset that would make him a good caretaker. He had actually pined for the position, but in the end, he hadn't even mentioned it to King Sol. The truth was that he was a follower more than a leader. That was disappointing, but his creative flexibility allowed him to change perspective easily.

Now, Morf decided he would become an excellent *follower*. The Auras took note. Being a follower could make him useful in the future. Followers frequently had value to the Eforces.

Morf was content to be a follower because he was a survivor. He knew he was smarter than this Drum guy. That was obvious . . . but Drum was now in charge. He couldn't change that. Morf's current goal was, at the very least, to stay relevant in The Castle until the King got back.

In this way, he was a little like Drum. Appearing important was important to Morf. He would study Drum's style. Being creative and able to roll with the punches had always been a strength. Morf had surveyed the current situation and had already begun to plan his next move.

Drum was new to The Castle, but Morf had heard through his sources that this man liked his parties. If Morf was to remain important in The Castle, he would have to become necessary to this fellow. He would have to get himself on Drum's good side quickly. He made up his mind. He was still the Royal Community Relations Advisor. Parties should be his thing, so whatever Drum wanted, Morf would provide.

"Your Majesty," Morf began, bowing low. "Oh dear! I am so sorry, Sir Drum. Did I say the wrong thing when I said 'Your Majesty'? You just seem so kingly in your manner that I misspoke." Morf looked up at Drum with an engaging smile.

Morf's Conscience closed his eyes and groaned. This type of behavior was pretty disgusting. "Are you going to keep fawning like this with this guy?" he whispered.

Drum grinned and spread his arms out wide, displaying a generous and forgiving pose. "Don't apologize, my friend. I am flattered that you call me 'Your Majesty.'"

"He was just flattering you. Don't get used to that," whispered Cdrum.

Drum ignored him. "So you raised your hand to take charge of building my splendid new Royal Party Hall. Of course, this new hall is meant to honor my inauguration to the position of Royal Caretaker. You certainly seem to have the right respect for my position and enthusiasm for the job. Does this mean that you would like to be my Inauguration Party Planner as well?"

"Indeed, Sir Drum. It would be my honor. My name is Meta Morf, 'Morf' for short. I was the King's Community Relations Advisor." Morf bowed again. This groveling was working. He could tell. He would keep it up.

"Fine then. You've got both jobs."

The Royal Advisors looked at one another. Drum didn't even know Morf. Morf had never enlarged a building. He had never planned a big party. Was this how the new man was going to give out Royal Assignments? They all took note.

"I will ask my daughter, Flawless, to give you the list of my friends so that the throngs can gather to appreciate my arrival to The Castle," smirked the confident Drum.

Morf had done it. He had been given two important jobs by the man who was now in power. This was insurance. He knew he could produce the best party that this guy had ever seen. This was a perfect first step to locking down his own importance. He took his place at Drum's side with pride.

Cmorf was mortified. "I can't believe you," he hissed. "You are the biggest suck-up I have ever seen. You didn't act like this before, and you don't know what you're doing. Why are you doing this?"

Position, Morf thought confidently. *You can't stay important if you're not in the right position.* Cmorf heard the rustle of Eforces. He was not surprised.

Suddenly, there was a commotion at the back of the group. No one was looking at Drum or Morf anymore. Morf was aggravated. He was having a moment of positive recognition with his new boss, and someone or something was interrupting it.

Then Morf caught a glimpse of the reason for the hubbub. Flawless had quietly entered the chamber and was working her way through the advisors toward her father. The gaggle of Royal Staff parted and instinctively bowed. So did Morf.

The young woman was beautiful. Arrayed in a long gown of rust-colored velvet, she reflected the glow of the surrounding lamps as though she were part of them. Everyone inhaled at once and waited for her to step up to her father's platform.

Flawless appeared unaware of the stir she had caused. She smiled broadly as everyone stared at her. "Hello to all of you. I hear my father is already planning one of his parties. How wonderful! The Castle will be a splendid place for a party. I can't wait."

Flawless was happy and ready for the next party. This was one of her favorite activities as well and ever so much more fun than carriage rides between manor houses. "Do you want me to help you, Father?"

The Castle Staff exhaled as one and began to chatter excitedly. There was going to be a party in The Castle. The thrifty King Sol had seldom held any festivities, and this beautiful girl would be part of this one. This was exciting.

Morf congratulated himself. He had definitely put himself in the right place at the right time. He sidled up to Drum and nodded to his daughter. She grinned and held out her hand. They were off to a good start.

Bowing low again, Morf murmured quietly, "It will be my great honor to be of use to both of you." Morf had already decided that fawning was going to be one of his new specialties.

Drum expected the flattery he had always coveted and said nothing, but Flawless smiled at the groveling Morf. "Your assistance will be greatly appreciated, Sir Morf," she answered sweetly.

Morf nearly fainted. Not only had she accepted his offer, but she had extended her hand and spoken to him by name. In a blissful state, Morf stood tall and proclaimed with unexpected eagerness, "I am at your service, Your Highness," and this time He didn't even think of apologizing for referring to her as royalty.

"Thank you, Sir Morf. What should we do first?"

11

The Morphing Morf

orf went to work immediately. He was going to love his work. Soon he discovered that Flawless was more than willing to be a wonderful partner in their task.

First, they gathered all the best craftsmen in the Kingdom, and Flawless explained the way she knew that her father wanted the new Royal Party Hall to look. It was to be longer than three huge rooms together and plated with gold, she said. Walls would need to be torn down and windows added. Gilt would need to be plated on richly carved archways and draperies from the Royal Storehouses should be draped on every wall. The floor was to be rose-colored marble with a red carpet down the center.

Morf's jaw dropped at the description of such extravagance.

"You look shocked, Morf. Do you think it's too much?" Flawless asked timidly. "It seems a bit gawdy to me too. Maybe we should ask Daddy to make it a little less showy."

"If you don't mind my saying so," offered Morf politely, "I think your father is intent on impressing his wealthy friends. This decor would certainly do that."

Flawless nodded. "Daddy does like to impress people," she mused. "Well, let me put it another way. If you think your father wants it, we

should probably do it," offered Morf. This production was crucial to Morf's plan for ongoing importance in The Castle. It had to be top-notch. He drew up the plans for the craftsmen to go to work, and they began the next day. Next, Flawless provided her father's list of the most talented jugglers and musicians that had performed for his parties in the past. Morf had no such list as parties were not King Sol's way of doing things, and he soon realized that he would need to work on recruitment immediately.

Morf dispatched Royal Couriers to all these performers. This part of the plan was going to be easy. With great excitement, he and Flawless drew up plans for a wonderful array of festivities.

Third came a much more sensitive part. "Who, exactly, should be on the exclusive invitation list and who should not?" Flawless brought the question to her father.

Drum considered the possibilities carefully. Many titled and aristocratic persons had taken advantage of his parties at one time or another in the past. Although he wasn't that close to all of these individuals, they were each important due to wealth or heritage and needed to be impressed. When they saw each other, they would impress each other, Drum felt. To make this the most influential party ever, *all* these people needed to be on the invitation list.

Drum could picture each of them being grateful to him for remembering them and inviting them to the grandest party ever held at The Castle. He leaned back and relished the glorious vision of their gratitude. He was really an important person now. He could feel it.

So could the Auras that were gathering in The Castle corners and balancing on the rafters. Drum's Conscience took note of the increasing number of Eforces, which now seemed intent on encouraging Drum's pride and self-indulgence. Cdrum climbed to Drum's ear with a warning.

"Watch yourself," Cdrum stated with scorn. "Now that you're in The Castle, you think that you are so cool that everyone will adore you. Get over it. You have responsibility for a whole kingdom, not just the rich. All you are thinking about is being the center of attention for the elite.

"And here is another thought: Have you forgotten that some of your regular partygoers may be mad that you tricked them into supporting you at that 'King's Royal Caretaker Party'? Do you think they are just going to forget that?"

"Get out of my face, Conscience," responded Drum. "I told you that I didn't need you anymore and I don't. I have tons of entitled friends who love me and will love me more now that I am a man of importance in The Castle. I certainly don't need a little voice in my ear trying to put me down." The Auras continued their support, wafting around Drum's feet. They would not allow him to tolerate the possibility of rejection.

"I'm not trying to put you down," Cdrum shot back. "I'm just trying to keep you real. All your party friends may not be actual friends like you think they are. Think a little bit before you risk your reputation and expect everyone to think you're 'all that.'"

Drum closed his mind to Cdrum's chatter. Taking a deep breath, he inhaled the cool scent of the Auras around him. All the rich and famous would be here and at his command. He knew it. They would all bow and ask for favors. The groveling would be awesome.

"Give that Morf fellow a list of every person who has ever attended my parties before," he told Flawless with authority. "They will flock to me now that I am the Royal Caretaker and more important than any of them." "You're completely full of yourself, and you're going to be sorry for that," warned Cdrum.

Flawless stared at her father's list. There were literally hundreds of names on it. Many were unfamiliar to her. Who were all these people?

Morf was stunned by the size of the list. "This is a gigantic number of people, Mistress Flawless. Are you sure that we should invite this many guests? We will need to hire more cooks than we currently have at The Castle and pull in great amounts of food from your father's storehouses and even the King's. This could be a very costly affair. Can your father afford such a lavish party?"

Again, Flawless went to her father. "Do we have to invite *all* these people, Father? Even the ones that are mad at you? Maybe some don't even want to come. This party might be too big and expensive, even for you."

"Cost is no object now that we are in The Castle, daughter, and we must *especially* invite the people who might be mad or jealous. The idea of a big party is to impress and cultivate as many people as we can while we're here in The Castle. These people and their influence will be golden to me when I leave here. A grand party is our chance to *own* their gratitude *now* for their support in the future. Never lose track of the next gig. Have you learned nothing?"

Drum dismissed the issue of expense as someone else's problem. The cost of the party would take care of itself. The cost would be worth whatever it was. He never liked to bother with the financial details, anyway.

Flawless mulled the situation over. She agreed with Morf that the party plans were really getting big, and she really didn't understand her father's motivation. Parties were for fun, and this one was sort of out of control. It would be hard to be a good hostess if she couldn't remember the names of half the people.

Morf had concerns for practical reasons. He knew the Royal Financial Advisor, and he knew that the Advisor would not like this extra expense. He knew this, but flexibility and loyalty to the new guy were now his way of life. He was determined to please Drum at all costs.

Morf shook off his old way of thinking. He had always been against deficit spending in the past, but Drum was the key to his future. He dispatched a huge mass of invitations as Drum wanted and quietly checked for extra supplies in the Royal Storehouses. He was going to need them. Hopefully this would be the end of the overspending.

But no.

It was only after Morf had delivered the first round of Inauguration Celebration fliers that Drum had another idea. Continuing to ignore costs, Drum ordered that Morf provide *engraved* hand-delivered invitations to those of the highest lineage and wealth.

"Engraved invitations will definitely show all those pompous blowhards that I know how to operate with class," Drum crowed. The Eforces silently cheered. Drum's need to impress was impressive.

Morf rolled his eyes. "Are you sure you want to send out such fancy invitations?" he murmured. This was a major breach of protocol as well as extravagance. "This type of invitation is usually used by kings and queens only."

"I know," responded Drum confidently. Eforce delusions of grandeur were on a roll.

"Only the super wealthy are personally invited," warned Cdrum. "Folk that gets an engraved invite will believe that you think you are better than they are."

"I do."

"Everyone else will say that you are acting like royalty." "I am."

"You don't get it, do you?" Cdrum groaned. "People will accuse you of trying to be a King rather than a Royal Caretaker."

Who cares? Let them think what they want. I have enough influential friends so that I don't need them all, anyway, Drum thought.

"Drum, get over yourself," Cdrum pleaded. "You are only going into a temporary position where you must consider what's best for the whole kingdom, not just for yourself. *I* am your Conscience. I am trying to help you do this right. Please . . . let *me* be your *influential* friend and stop trying to impress *influential humans.*"

Drum seemed to listen.

Morf couldn't hear Cdrum, and he was in "grovel mode." "The wealthy of rank will envy you, sir," he gushed with enthusiasm.

"That's what I'm talking about!" said Drum with a grin. "Morf gets it!"

Cdrum had lost this argument, but Morf was learning fast what he would need to say and do to stay in Drum's good graces. He had always prided himself in being able to adapt, and desperate times now were calling for desperate measures. He would need to be a toady. He would need to deliver an ego boost on cue, at a moment's notice. If he wanted to stay in position, he definitely needed to keep morphing.

Morf laughed at himself, but he squared his shoulders and ordered that the fancy invitations be engraved and hand-delivered as requested to all those that Drum considered worthy of receiving them.

Drum was now satisfied that the festivities were going to be splendid. Anyone who was anyone was getting a fancy invitation. Drum sat very still as a royal seamstress measured and labored over a new fur-lined cape. He needed to look the part.

Morf moved on to the next of the many important tasks necessary for the upcoming celebration. He suddenly realized he was just getting started. What about food? Mountains of food needed to be prepared for such an enormous party.

Morf discussed the matter with The Castle Cooks who stared at him in disbelief.

"Hundreds of wealthy aristocrats?" "You've got to be kidding."

"There is absolutely no way we can feed that many picky rich people." "King Sol has never asked for such a stupid thing."

Morf tried to smooth-talk The Castle Cooks. He had always gotten along with them in the past and had been able to get an extra plum pudding anytime he wanted one. But it wasn't working this time. The Castle Cooks were balking.

So Morf morphed again. He tried threats. "This new Royal Caretaker is no one to mess with," he warned the Cooks. "I must get the required huge amount of food prepared and prepared well or heads will roll."

The Auras began to be impressed with Morf. Maybe he had more potential than they thought.

Threat one: "You could be thrown in the dungeons." "Oh, Morf. We know you. You wouldn't do such a thing." Threat two: "You could be boiled in oil."

Laughter.

Then Morf came up with a really hateful threat. "I could go out and recruit every good cook in The Kingdom to replace you *after you are thrown in the dungeon.*"

Nice threat, thought the Eforces. *The man is getting the hang of his.*

"You wouldn't do such a mean thing, Morf . . . would you?" Cmorf pulled Morf's hair.

Rubbing his head, Morf softened and modified his threat. "I could, unless you professional Castle Cooks find your own assistant cooks to help you carry the load. All of you could be in charge of these lesser Cooks, of course. You Castle Cooks could tell your assistants what to do. You could be their *bosses.*"

The Castle Cooks quivered a little but liked the "boss" idea and scurried out of The Castle on a mission. It was going to be hard to find the necessary "assistants," but their professional survival depended on it.

"He never used to be like that," they whispered knowingly to each other.

Morf smiled proudly as he watched the Cooks depart on their task. Cmorf was not pleased. "You could have made the Cooks happy to do what you wanted them to do instead of threatening them."

"Like I said, my name is Morf. Sometimes I have to throw a changeup." Morf was feeling cocky. He was getting used to his new power.

When Morf reported on what the Cooks were doing at his suggestion, Drum gloated over the need for such recruitment for his huge party. But Cdrum continued to object.

"This party is over the top," he stated flatly in Drum's ear. "Can't you see it? Your new position is going to your head. You need to remember one fact. You're not a king. You're a rich property owner turned Caretaker. That's all you are."

Drum folded his arms and scowled. "I know, I know. But this is my time to shine. Relax, Conscience. When this party is over, I will settle down. In the meantime, let me have my fun."

Just as Morf was feeling smug about his success with The Castle Cooks, he discovered an even worse problem. One by one, a surprising number of musicians that had been on Drum's entertainment list "could not be found." Dancers and jugglers seemed to be experiencing a rash of "sprained ankles" and "broken toes" and could not perform. Something odd was going on.

Morf contacted all the individuals on Drum's list again, this time by Royal Courier, but everyone seemed to be universally unavailable. No one was going to perform at an important function at The Castle? This was humiliating for Morf. What was causing this catastrophe?

A failure of entertainment would spell doom for Morf's importance as a party planner, not to mention doom for the party itself. If there were no performers, there could be no fancy party. Rich people needed to be entertained. This was a fact. Morf was mortified.

But the next day, Morf again morphed—and became creative. He was determined to get to the root of this issue and solve it. Shedding all the distinguished garb of his Royal Advisor position, Morf dressed in the ragged clothes of a common drifter and scurried into the villages of River Kingdom in search of answers. He was now a spy.

None of the other Royal Advisors had ever dressed as a commoner before, and this step down was a bit frightening even for the adaptive Morf. He swallowed hard and assumed an unassuming demeanor.

One by one, he stopped at local taverns, fitting in quietly and focusing on learning just what was happening to the reluctant performers of The Kingdom. Taverns were the best places to collect such information, he guessed. Taverns also had good beer.

As he entered the fourth tavern of the day, Morf was beginning to weave slightly but finally spotted a group of patrons who might have answers. There at a table in the corner sat several jugglers engrossed in discussion, and Drum's name rose above the din of the pub. Morf called for a mug of ale as had been his custom all day and tottered to a nearby table to pick up on their conversation.

"You gonna perform for the Drum party at The Castle, or will you blow it off like me?" asked a dandy-looking patron in a fancy hat. Morf judged that this fellow was a good juggler since his hat displayed tassels and embroidery, a sign that his skills had earned him some finer engagements. "I'm givin' it a pass for sure, Reggie," replied another spritely juggler with a snicker. "Drum is still Drum whether he's livin' in The Castle or not. That guy don't pay his bills. It took me 'most a year to get one coin out of 'im last time."

"I hear you. He's got time for partyin' but no time for payin'. That's my take on it." The men laughed and slapped each other on the back in solidarity.

Morf's mug landed on the table with a thump. That was it. Drum had a reputation for not paying his bills. No wonder performers weren't answering his call. Morf placed this in his slightly tipsy memory bank.

Now he knew the problem, but he could still see a fancy celebration ahead that would have no performers. The jugglers and even a few musicians who wandered in later were full of stories about Drum and his inability to be trusted to pay. None of them were willing to work for him again. None of them offered a solution to the problem either.

On the way back to The Castle, Morf wobbled along as he contemplated his options. Providing no entertainment would reduce Morf in Drum's eyes, but he didn't really blame the entertainers for not wanting to do their act for nothing. Drum was a stingy, selfish guy in their eyes. Morf believed them. He was starting to get to know his new boss.

"Watch out for this Drum character," Cmorf mumbled, also affected by the ale. "If the performers don't trust him, you shouldn't either."

"He's the only game in town," Morf slurred. "If I don't please him, I'm out of The Castle."

"I'm just sayin' . . ."

As Morf wandered on toward The Castle, thoughts began to jumble themselves in his ale-sloshed head. He knew he had to do something creative, another change of pace, to save himself. In truth, however, he had downed a bit too much ale. Tonight, he was not ready to be creative.

At last, he reached The Castle and staggered in. Thankfully, no one was around, but his room was at the other end of a long hall. He could hear snoring from the sleeping areas of the other Royal Advisors. His room was too far away. Without another thought, Morf found a dark corner of the corridor and went to sleep.

In the morning, after finding himself shivering in the hall for a reason he couldn't quite remember, Morf splashed water on his face from the hall fountain and came up with an idea.

"Be careful," warned Cmorf. "We're completely hung over. We might not be making good decisions right now."

"Speak for yourself. I have to do what I have to do," Morf replied, splashing more water on his aching head.

Though definitely not at his best, Morf rounded up ten Royal Scribes from the catacombs where they usually spent day and night carefully copying religious doctrine and the tales of famous and imaginary battles. To them, he dictated a note to be sent to the performers. The scribes questioned their task but wrote dutifully on Royal Stationary with an elegant script.

Their note was primarily a royal promise to pay. In addition, in very large letters, was another short but meaningful sentence. "Show up or die," after which Morf added a strangely unreadable scrawl at the bottom.

"Is that supposed to be Drum's signature?" Cmorf questioned.

"Sort of," Morf replied, holding the notes up to dry one at a time. "I think it will pass."

"That's an actual threat."

"I know. I am finding threats helpful these days."

"You never used to do such things before. You're changing, and not for the best."

"I'm morphing," Morf said flatly.

"This approach isn't honest, you know," scolded Cmorf.

"What's wrong with it? It's Drum's party. He would sign these things if he had the time."

"He's not that busy, and you know now that he can't be trusted."

"I'm just making it convenient for the Finance Advisor," Morf offered smugly, handing the invitations to the Royal Couriers, "and I'm making sure that at least some performers will be here and get paid."

"It's good that you want to pay the performers," admitted Cmorf. "That's a good thing."

"I thought so," answered Morf confidently.

"But I have to let you know that lying and threatening isn't good at all.

Those are bad things." "Not that bad."

"Ha. Says you," scoffed Cmorf. "A threat is a threat, and a lie is a lie." "Bending the rules gets the job done and keeps me in my job. Be quiet." Morf stomped off, but Cmorf was uncomfortable. Morf had lied and threatened for a man that couldn't be trusted. He was taking on Drum's style.

Within a day of their delivery, however, the responses from the Royal Promissory Notes began to come in. Enough performers responded so there would be a respectable show for Drum's Inaugural Celebration. Morf breathed a sigh of relief. Success!

12

The Inaugural

The day of the grand Inaugural Celebration dawned clear and dry. Drum and Flawless dressed in new finery and took their places on elegant chairs at one end of the beautifully remodeled ballroom, now to be known as the Royal Party Hall. At Morf's direction, the already large room had been tripled to accommodate the hundreds expected. Huge tables stretched along the walls, laden with fruits and wine and separated by elegant red carpets. All was in readiness to receive the best people in The Kingdom.

Morf had supervised the entire remodeling project, spending day and night as a type of foreman for the expansion—another change of identity which he had assumed unexpectedly. No one else that Drum knew seemed willing to do it. Morf was exhausted.

He stood proudly at Drum's side. He had checked the performers gathered at the rear of The Castle, tensely waiting for their entrances. None of the jugglers had recognized him, dressed in his own fine party attire. Morf loved that. It proved to him that he could adapt to whatever was needed. This was becoming a very handy skill for someone who wanted to stay in favor during Drum's time at The Castle.

Cmorf settled into the collar of Morf's new outfit and asked a practical question, "How do you keep track of who you really are? Are you good, or are you bad? If you change who you are too many times, who are you, really?"

"It's not a matter of good or bad. It's more about getting it done or not getting it done. I'm just a flexible person who's going to stay in

Drum's good graces, that's all," Morf answered under his breath. "And this is how you do it. You morph."

The Royal Castle Staff was ready. Morf had checked the platoons of housewife-cooks (supervised by Castle Cooks) who were roasting record amounts of mutton, beef, and pork along with mounds of vegetables. The Castle ovens had been baking loaves of bread for days. Additional servants were gathered at the rear of the Royal Party Room, waiting with serving trays. Morf felt that this was his celebration as much as it was Drum's.

He, Flawless, and Drum proudly surveyed the gawdy gold-encrusted walls and tapestries with satisfaction. Drum hadn't said anything, but Morf knew he was pleased.

At last, Drum gave the signal to the Royal Guard at the door. The waiting crowd would be allowed to enter as the huge gilded doors swung open wide.

Morf held his breath. Drum and Flawless assumed the regal positions that Drum had thought would be expected. The first two guests entered and proceeded a bit hesitantly toward Drum and his daughter.

"Hello, Sir Drum," said the gentleman with a slight head nod. "I hear there's going to be a big celebration here tonight, right?" He laughed in an attempt to sound jolly as his voice echoed through the still empty hall. "This place is a bit bigger and fancier than the manor house I visited a while back with my first wife, right? Well, let me introduce you to my lovely *current* wife. She and I are thinking about building a new manor house for ourselves in a unique spot. Maybe you could help us get the land for it, now that you are the big Royal Caretaker. What do you think, big guy?"

Not very respectful, thought Morf. *Oh well. He must be a very close friend.*

Drum looked perplexed. He had seen this man before, but he couldn't remember his name. Flawless came to his aid with a welcoming smile.

"It is so good to see you again, Lord Dipswitch and your new Lady Dipswitch. We are pleased to see you, sir, after so long. And I am glad that you were first to arrive." She rose from her chair and offered her hand to them both. Drum smiled and followed her lead.

Seeing no one else around, the couple stepped up closer. "Indeed. We wanted to be first, but . . . are we early? Since there are only a few people outside, we were afraid that we were too early or perhaps we had the wrong date." Sir Dipswitch nudged Drum in a slightly conspiratorial manner. "However, since we are still alone, maybe we can discuss a little business. You've landed in a great position, haven't you, Drum? Maybe we can help each other out, eh?"

Drum was still smiling, but he wasn't listening to the undisguised offer of a deal. He was focused instead on the fact that Lord Dipswitch had referred to "only a few people outside."

"A few people, you say? There are only a few people outside? Just a few? How many would you say?" Morf, Flawless, and Drum leaned in to hear the answer.

"Yes. Only twenty or so. I did see Baron Hornswoggle. He brought his lovely daughters with him. I believe he wants to talk to you about positions for them in The Castle."

"Positions in The Castle?" asked Flawless innocently.

Sir Dipswitch winked at Drum. "He will discuss the type of positions he would like with your father later, if you know what I mean," he said. "His girls are both eligible young ladies, you know." He laughed and winked again. "I, however, wanted to discuss something more practical. Lady Dipswitch and I have our eyes on a piece of land at the south end of The Great River for our new manor house. We were thinking that we would construct a beauty overlooking The River and just above The Border with The Lowlands. It is a lovely, warm area where fruit trees might grow. Is that land available for . . . a sum?"

Morf stopped listening to the conversation altogether. Where were the rest of the guests? Quietly, he slipped down the richly draped wall toward the rear entrance of the Royal Party Hall. Another couple was entering there but with studied indifference to Drum and Flawless. They were gawking instead at the elegant decor and not smiling at all. Their mood was definitely not partylike. *What strange friends Drum seems to have,* thought Morf.

He scurried outside. The first guests had been right. There were only a few people here and there. There was no rush to come inside. Instead, those present were engaged in animated discussions with each other and gesturing angrily rather than having a good time. They did not look friendly, and they were *not* early. Why were they still outside? What was wrong with these people?

Morf smoothed his new cape and brushed down the velvet collar where Cmorf was still riding and staring in wonder at the grumpy partygoers. There was something odd going on here. He was determined to get to the bottom of it.

With appropriate dignity, Morf approached a slightly nervous-looking gentleman whose feathered head gear was tipped askew. This fellow looked out of place and began to tremble self-consciously, mopping his brow.

"Hello, fine sir. How are you this afternoon?" said Morf, extending his hand. The little man blew a drooping hat feather from his face but did not smile. Quickly, he extended his hand to Morf and began to pump it up and down, saying, "Hello to you. Hello . . . hello. How do you do? I don't know anyone here. I am not one of these elite people. This hat is driving me crazy. Are you Lord Doran Drum?"

"No. I am Sir Metta Morf III of the House of Morf. Who might you be, sir?"

"Milton Fandango of the house of . . . I do certainly have a house of . . . Oh. You're not Drum, then? Well, I don't need to talk to you, I guess. Point me at the new Royal Caretaker so I can make my pitch before anybody else does."

Morf blinked and withdrew his hand. How crude.

"This man is obviously a hustler of some kind," contributed Cmorf.

Obviously, Morf thought, motioning the man toward the entrance to the hall. The strange fellow secured his feathered hat and scurried away.

Hmm, thought Morf. *I wonder if this is a clue to the rest of the guests that might be attending the party today. Both this man and the couple inside want something.*

Morf gazed out over the lawn. Not only were there a very few people near The Castle, but there was nearly no one on their way. Trying to look casual, he meandered slowly toward a lone, obviously aristocratic arrival. Without hesitation, the adaptable Morf decided to pose as a guest himself, hoping he could collect more clues about this uncelebrational scene.

"It looks as though people have decided to come 'fashionably late' to Drum's Inaugural Celebration, wouldn't you say?" he began with a smile. The man looked down at Morf in a superior manner. "I would say they are not coming at all," he replied tersely. "That is what I would have preferred. I, for one, do not want to watch this 'royalty wannabe' show off.

How he tweaked the situation to get himself into this position, I'll never know, but I've heard stories."

Morf decided on a different approach. "You predict that we'll have a lot of no-shows to this celebration, then. Am I right?" he offered with a comrade-like nudge.

"You've got that right," the man growled. "If you could just direct me to where Drum is holding forth, I will tell him what I want quickly and leave. This party is not my idea of a celebration. It's just one of Drum's bigger 'transactions.'"

Morf was now sure that his first clue had been a good one. Many of the people who were attending Drum's inaugural today were not celebrating with him. They were here to do business. They looked wealthy and important, but they were all after something. Morf could identify the type. With a sudden self-awareness, he acknowledged that he was one of them.

"Glad you recognize the truth," commented Cmorf.

But this party was *Morf's* baby, and no one was here. He needed to know more. Hiding his panic, Morf led his new acquaintance toward the Royal Party Hall doorway. "My name is Metta Morf III," he offered. "I am actually one of *King Sol's* Royal Advisors. Drum is new. I don't know him that well. You say this party is just a transaction for Lord Drum? Why so?" "A Royal Advisor, you say? So you were on the inside of The Castle before, eh, Sir Morf? Glad to know you. My name is Thorndike. Everyone in Drum's circle knows who I am. I am here to stake my claim to a possible future deal with Drum more than to participate in an overhyped party.

There are a few others here who may have similar motives, if I don't miss my guess."

"I see," agreed Morf, nodding sagely. "But you do understand that Drum is only a Royal Caretaker, right? He'll never be king, so why do you call him a 'royalty wannabe'? Surely, he will be satisfied with his new position."

The gentleman obviously knew Drum. He answered Morf freely. "Of course, he will not be satisfied. When you know this man, you will definitely *understand* what I mean. And I certainly know him. We all do. This man has no skill and no readiness for this job. He owns a lot of property, throws a lot of parties, and he's a hustler. Nothing more. He just likes to impress people and act like a big man. That's what's going on here, *but* if he can maneuver his way to the throne itself, he will do it, and I wouldn't put it past him.

"Now, Sir Morf, before the rest of the Kingdom catches on, I intend to check out Drum's possible interest in my ideas for some of what he will have access to while stodgy King Sol isn't here—like worthy positions of power in the administration of The Castle, for example. Together, we might be able to benefit each other . . . if he's not too afraid of me to give me a worthwhile opportunity. Lead me to him."

Morf shuddered. It wasn't hard to tell that this anti-Drum aristocrat would be a pro-Drum aristocrat in a second if he could swing the right deal. Morf quickly decided that he hoped that wouldn't happen. This man had an evil way about him, and he was, above all, "pro-Thorndike." *Oh well,* Morf concluded. *I'm "pro-Morf." I get it.*

"I am sure Drum will be glad to speak with you, Sir Thorndike, but I still don't understand the 'royalty wannabe' reference. He has no royal blood. He can't get to the throne, at least not yet." Morf grinned, now understanding a part of what was happening.

LORD DIPSWITCH
LORD THORNDIKE

MILTON FANDANGO

"I'm simply repeating what all the local establishment is saying about him. Only kings can afford to send engraved invitations like Drum sent out. Only kings can throw massive parties like this. Drum is undoubtedly in The Castle to take advantage of his good luck and act like a king. That's the way he is, but I want in on it. If ol' Drum wants to act like a king, let him start with me."

The man gave Morf a cold smile. Morf nodded in understanding and led him forward. Did all of Drum's friends believe what this man said? "It'll be good to be one of Drum's friends, right?" he asked as they made their way to the front entrance.

"Drum doesn't have many friends. We just like his parties. He's entertaining in a way. But now, he'll have even fewer 'friends' since he moved into The Castle. He obviously thinks that he is better than the rest of us now. That engraved invite must have cost a fortune and this huge party in The Castle as well. Moving into The Castle has gone to his head."

As Morf followed the grousing gentleman into the beautiful hall, Morf noticed that a few more persons of wealth were arriving. *How many of Drum's friends are not really the friends he thinks they are?* he wondered. *Are they all just jealous and ready to make use of his new position?*

Morf now realized that he had jumped to get on Drum's good side, but he really didn't know him. What was this Drum really like?

"You really don't know him, do you?" whispered Cmorf. "That's what you get for trying to wangle an important position before anybody else."

I hate to admit it, but you're probably right, thought Morf as he hustled back to Drum's side. *But a card laid is a card played, and if these rich guys are ready to take advantage, I am too.*

"I read you, and I don't approve," commented Cmorf.

At the far end of the hall, some of the jugglers Morf had persuaded were already juggling, and the musicians were tuning up. The red carpets running down the length of the room glowed as they stretched from one end to the other. All was in readiness, but the number of guests was still pitifully small and looking lonely as they clustered around Flawless and Drum at the front of the hall. The rest of the yawning Royal Party Hall was empty and quiet.

Morf returned to his position beside the Drums.

"Where is everyone?" Drum was whispering to Flawless.

"I don't know. Where is everyone?" whispered Flawless to Morf. The small gaggle of guests nearby was beginning to look from side to side and raise their eyebrows. This absence of the expected throng was not a good sign. Whether it was jealousy or just lack of real friendship, the rich and famous were not showing up as Drum had expected.

Morf knew a personal disaster when he saw one. In spite of what the gentleman guest had told him about the reason for the no-shows and their disregard for Drum, Morf could not help but feel that Drum would blame him for the poor turnout. That would not be good for his future in Drum Castle.

It was time for Morf to get creative again. He could not let Drum—or himself—look like a failure. Morf concentrated. The problem at hand was "no people." The answer had to be "people."

Create a crowd! Drum has got to believe that a crowd came to his party, Morf hastily decided in desperation.

"You have got to be kidding me," snorted Cmorf. "I give up. All this morphing yourself from one problem solver to another has finally made you balmy. There is no crowd here, and you can't just decide to make one. Settle down and confess to Drum that because his friends have caught on to him, you can't *make* a crowd at a crowdless party that nobody but scammers wants to come to."

But Morf was already working on a solution. He had another idea. In a flash, he excused himself, rushed from the Royal Party Hall, and began scrambling through the back rooms of The Castle. From the kitchens to the laundry, to the storage, to the livery, Morf ran, waving his arms and gathering up the servants.

Within minutes, he had rustled the Royal Castle Staff together at the rear of the Royal Party Hall, telling them in threatening tones to stand there or else. "Spread out and try to fill in the empty space here at the back of the hall. Mill about and talk to each other. This is a crisis.

"Drum is too far away at the other end to be able to see who you are. Take off your aprons. He must think that he is seeing 'guests.' You all must act like guests if you want to be working here tomorrow."

The huge staff assembled nervously and did as they were told. At the far end of the hall, safely out of Drum's clear vision, they became "a crowd of guests."

"And I know it sounds odd," Morf added when they were all assembled, "but now you must make some unhappy noises. Mill around. Groan. Mingle. Cough. Gag. Sputter. Look sick. Sir Drum is a very strange guy. Sometimes he likes other people's misery. He will fire you all if he doesn't hear lots of very sick people."

"And you will lose your job," added Cmorf in Morf's ear. "I swear, Morf. You are just getting weirder and weirder. You make my Conscience job interesting . . . But figuring out what is right or wrong in what you do is almost impossible."

"Quiet," Morf hissed. "We're in an emergency here."

Trying to do their best, the servants began to mill about and make halfhearted coughing and gagging noises.

Next, Morf assembled all the entertainers with slightly different but equally threatening instructions. "Stay back here in the practice area and perform."

"This is ridiculous," they were saying as Morf herded them into performance positions, also nearly out of Drum's sight in the back of the hall.

"Why are we performing now, and why are we back here?" "There's nobody here yet."

"The guests at the front of the Party Room can't even see us."

"That's the whole idea," admitted Morf.

"What is happening?"

"Where is everyone?"

"This is just your rehearsal," growled Morf. "You didn't expect to perform without a dress rehearsal, did you? Your real performance is tomorrow. You want to get paid, don't you? Tomorrow is when you'll really perform, and that's when you'll get paid—or you can go to the dungeons now. Take your pick."

"I think I get what you're doing, but you're lying and threatening again," grumbled Cmorf. "Lying is getting too easy for you. You used to be pretty honest . . . and nice, even."

"A man's gotta do what a man's gotta do," answered Morf.

A few jugglers slammed their equipment into the ground and left, but the rest needed their payment and valued their freedom too much to say no. They settled down to their respective "rehearsals" in the back of the room, a good distance from Drum and his few guests at the front.

Morf's mind was still racing. Was this going to work? A plausible justification for what was happening formed on his lips as he ran back up the red carpet toward Drum.

"Good grief," croaked Morf to Flawless and Drum as he rushed up to them. "Sir Drum, Sir Drum! I just discovered why there are so few people here," he gasped.

Morf fell to his knees for yet another creative performance. "Our Inaugural Celebration is going to have to be postponed," he announced with a show of great misery and hand wringing. "I know you had thousands of friends on your friends' list, sir, but a great plague of stomach flu appears to have struck The Kingdom today, and most of them couldn't come."

"More lies," snorted Cmorf. "More and more lies. The rich people are just no-shows and you know it."

"There seems to be a large number of people gathered at the back of the hall, Daddy," Flawless offered hopefully.

Drum squinted down the hall. "I see that many of my fans have arrived at the far end of the hall. I have thousands of friends, of course. Perhaps I should go down there and talk to them since they are here. They all love me, you know."

"Oh, of course they do, sir. Of course, they do, but the guests gathered at the other end of the hall have also just become . . . very sick," squeaked Morf. "Very, very sick. You can hear them groaning, can't you? You mustn't go near them."

"What?"

"That's right. All those people down there were watching the entertainment . . . that you see . . . when they became deathly sick. It swept through them suddenly. It was very strange. I know you can't see that from here, but they all just came down with the flu as well. They struggled to be here. They didn't want to disappoint you so they tried to stay here, but I am going to send them all home now so they don't spread the contagion." "They *all* have the flu?" cried Flawless. "How terrible! But how loyal and true-blue of them to try to come here in spite of it. Thank them all for coming and for being such good friends. But *do* tell them they should go home right away and get well."

The guests who were near Drum and Flawless began to grumble. Both Morf and Drum could see and hear this.

Morf gulped and ran down the red carpet again to the milling, confused gathering of servants and disgruntled performers. Panting hard from the two sprints he had just endured, he sent the servants back to their stations, telling them he would explain everything to them soon.

Then he turned to the performers and informed them that Drum was not feeling well but would probably feel better tomorrow and would definitely need them to come back and perform—which they must do if they wished to be paid.

Slowly, the unhappy performers dispersed, grousing under their breath about Drum and saying, "We should have known."

Morf struggled back to Drum and Flawless. Without hesitation, he spread himself on the ground in front of Drum. "Forgive me, sir. I have failed you," he stammered.

Drum scowled down at Morf. "Of course, you have failed me," he agreed, "and I thought you were going to be good at this. I was obviously wrong. I should have chosen someone who could deliver a healthy crowd on cue."

Morf lay still. He could tell he was about to get walked out of The Castle by the Royal Guard in spite of all his work. He was too tired to object.

Drum looked around at the few attendees that were still close. For an instant, he understood the indifference that the empty hall suggested. But he couldn't allow that to be the reason. He had always been popular. His parties had always been successful before, but his wealthy friends were not swarming to him now. Were they all sick?

Eforces swarmed Drum's chair. They were about to lose him to reality.

They couldn't let that happen.

Suddenly, with a fierce jolt of self-assurance, Drum stood up straight and tall and adjusted his thinking—a plausible reconstruction had arrived. *Of course, they were all sick,* he decided. He now believed Morf's answer. *There must be thousands throughout The Kingdom who are at home on their sick beds. Otherwise, all my friends would certainly be here,* he concluded with confidence.

Morf had constructed an explanation that worked for him, and Drum had accepted it. The Eforces began to relax.

Drum glowered down at the drooping Morf. "I appreciate the loyalty of those that showed up today, but I can't risk talking to my sick friends in person. I am very important to The Kingdom now. It would not do at all for me to get the flu too. Those who did not arrive stayed away to protect me from their deadly illness. I see that they had to do that because they love me. Things like that happen."

He bought it, thought Morf to himself. *He actually believed my story!*

"They were very, very ill, sir," repeated Morf aloud as he scrambled from the floor, "or they would have been here for sure."

"True, true. I can understand that. Well, at least I do see several loyal people here with me now." Drum had changed gears.

"You go tend to my sick friends, Morf, while I speak to these loyal folks who are up close. They all seem healthy and ready to talk to me in my new and influential position." He turned back to the waiting group with a stunning smile of magnanimous importance. "What can I do for you, fine people?" he proudly asked them all.

Morf knew that his ingenuity had saved him, at least for a while, but he also knew that today had showed him a brand-new game that he needed to get good at. The new game was a self-esteem preservation game where Drum was an obvious champion. By the look of things, Drum had probably played this game for a long time. He was very good at it.

13

The New Game

As the last of the guests filed out of the empty, echoing hall, Drum became silent. He wasn't stupid. The small number of people he had talked to were jealous and greedy. He could feel it, and he understood it. His new position was not as full of glory as he had thought it would be. Quietly, he slumped in the grand chair he had had made for the occasion. Flawless gently tried to comfort him.

"This wasn't your fault, Daddy. You and Morf and I prepared a wonderful party. It's a shame that people got sick. It just happened so suddenly." Flawless hugged her father and patted him gently. She wanted to believe the best.

"You don't have any real friends among these rich guys, do you, Drum?" Cdrum observed frankly in Drum's ear. "All the rich guys are jealous, or they want something or both."

"Shut up. You don't know everything."

"What?" answered the kindhearted Flawless.

"Sorry, Flawless dear. I was just arguing with my Conscience again."

Morf watched the pair from a distance, standing on one foot and then the other. He had no idea what he was going to do now.

"I am forgiving you for telling a big bunch of lies just now because it helped soften the blow for Drum and Flawless," commented Cmorf in his ear. "And actually, your lies were pretty inventive. But you and I both know they were told to save your own skin as well. You'll have to pay some dues for those lies."

In this Royal Advisor business, you can't be too picky, thought Morf absently. You just do what you've got to do. Look at Drum. Drum is lying to himself about being popular, but he knows the truth and he's miserable. And look at Flawless. She feels sorry for her dad so she's sad too. I really need to get creative one more time.

"It would be pretty nice if you could make them both feel better and do something good at the same time," offered Cmorf. "You think you're creative. Can't you think of something nice to do?"

Morf paced a bit, glancing occasionally back at Drum and his daughter. They had actually been dumped by people they thought were their friends. There was no doubt about it. Morf felt bad for them both, even if Drum was arrogant and pushy and wanted to be important too much and had spent more than he should have on the Royal Party Room and the tons of food that no one was eating.

What a waste. All that food is still just stacked in the many castle kitchens, Morf thought sadly. Suddenly, Morf's creativity kicked into action again. Very quietly, he spoke so that no one but Drum could hear.

"Sir Drum, I have an interesting thought. I know that you are a wealthy person and have not spent too much time among the peasants, but it occurs to me that we have made food for thousands and none of it was eaten by those with . . . stomach flu.

"If you were so generous as to *donate* all that food to the peasants of The Kingdom, they would be very grateful. They are frequently hungry. They would bless your picture."

Drum listened.

"They would sing your praises."

Drum listened some more. So did Cdrum and Cmorf.

"All the commoners of The Kingdom would think that you were more wonderful than King Sol if you simply gave all the leftover food to the peasants. King Sol has never done anything like that for the common people before."

"That was a pretty creative idea." Cmorf smiled. "That was a terrific idea!" exclaimed Cdrum.

Drum processed the thought some more. "Even more wonderful than King Sol," he heard. "King Sol has never done anything directly for the common people before," Morf had said.

But then Drum's selfish nature assumed its usual position. Old familiar Auras began to flow through him as they had for years. "I don't care about the common people," he growled. "They can't do anything for me."

But surprisingly, new more creative Eforces countered. "Don't be a fool, Drum," they whispered. "If your rich friends don't support you, you need *someone* in your corner, particularly after King Sol gets back. People who like you are people. Remember how they cheered for you back at your manor house? *And* there are more common people in the Kingdom than rich people. If the common people love you in your position, you don't need the aristocrats. You can tell the establishment to pound sand. If enough common people love you, the rich people won't have enough power to resist you."

"I have an idea," shouted Drum. He brightened and jumped to *his* feet, almost knocking Flawless to the ground. "Listen to me, daughter! We have leftover food that will go to waste if someone doesn't eat it. Let's give it to the peasants of the Kingdom tomorrow and let them enjoy it."

"Oh, Daddy, that is such a wonderful idea! I can't believe you thought of it. The people will be so excited." Flawless's generous nature was overjoyed. "It just came to me," Drum chortled. "We must send Royal Couriers throughout The Kingdom tonight and tell them that I, their beloved new Royal Caretaker, will make River Kingdom great by giving them lots of free food. Tell them that if they want to Make River Kingdom Great for themselves, they should join me here tomorrow. 'Make River Kingdom

Great.' That will be my new motto."

Cdrum and Cmorf gave each other a high-five, but Cdrum had heard the Eforces. He wasn't sold on Drum's sudden generosity, and he was right. "Also, Morf, or whatever your name is, have the Royal Seamstresses make some hats for me—thousands of them. Tell all the common people of The Kingdom that since they are here to 'Make the Kingdom Great,' and since they are all working peasants, they will each get a beautiful hat to remember me by . . . if they show up. Tell the whole kingdom that.

Everybody likes hats."

Morf's head bobbed up and down. He couldn't believe that Drum had decided to agree with him so quickly. He was gone before Drum finished his sentence. It didn't matter whose idea it was. It was his second chance.

Drum's Conscience was stunned. "Wow!" he gasped in Drum's ear. "Giving food to the common folk is a good idea, but do you know how much those hats will cost? You don't have enough stored away in your storehouses for all those hats."

Don't worry about the finances, Drum justified silently to himself. I'm the Royal Caretaker now. If I am going to be successful, I will need loyalty. The hats, if people wear them, will show that loyalty. I won't have to guess how people feel. I'm going to Make the Kingdom Great. So The Kingdom will pay for loyalty hats."

Cdrum heard Drum's rationale and worried. *He really had been wounded by the no-shows, Cdrum observed to himself. None of the elite were loyal. He was completely crushed. These hats would show loyalty if people wore them. He would need this.*

Morf was important to Drum again, and he was glad. Staying important was the goal. Quick and unusual adjustments in thinking were now becoming a regular part of the technique he would need if he were to stay in The Castle. For better or worse, Morf was getting used to it. He went to work.

The next morning dawned fair and warm. Morf had pushed and pulled the expanded number of Castle Cooks into all-night duty, arranging food throughout the streets of the villages. The town criers had called out a new Inaugural Celebration invitation, this time to the common people.

The paths and roadways became crowded and happy—and Drum's hats were everywhere. They weren't much, but they were dipped in a bright red dye and people wore the simple headgear like a badge. The new man in The Castle had given them hats, and they were thrilled.

Again, the jugglers arrived and juggled, musicians played, and dancers danced. Flags were flying, and piles of food were being given out on every corner. The crowds continued pouring in from neighboring villages.

"This is the way a celebration for me was always supposed to be," Drum chortled as he strutted and grinned from his balcony. "The crowds are growing. They are all wearing hats. Now they are all my fans. These peasants love me. All these hats show that!"

"Yes, sir," said Morf with a yawn. He had been up all night with the seamstresses, coaching, coaxing, sometimes even stitching and cutting cloth himself, trying to get hundreds of hats made in a night.

"Have the women make some more hats like these, all bright red. We may run out today, and I want all the commoners in River Kingdom to have one. We are Making the Kingdom Great! Do you like my new motto? The hats will remind everyone that I fed them and gave them something. And who are all these people? They are now my loyal fans. I can feel it. They believe in me."

"Yes, sir," Morf mumbled.

Cflawless and Flawless were also on the balcony. "Morf is about ready to fall asleep on his feet. Somebody should tell him thank you for putting all this together," whispered Cflawless.

"Morf worked hard for days on this party, Daddy," Flawless spoke up quickly. "You should appreciate him. Tell him thank you."

"Sure, daughter. Thanks, Morf. You redeemed yourself. Great job."
"It was my pleasure," responded Morf, again employing his now consistent deep bow.

"And this party is so much nicer than yesterday's party with only those few rich people," Flawless continued.

Drum snapped around with an obvious grimace that was so sudden and such a change that Flawless and Morf stepped back in fright.

"What do you mean 'only a few rich people'?" Drum snarled. "There were hundreds of rich people here yesterday! Maybe even thousands! That was the biggest Inauguration Celebration ever held at any castle. King Sol never had a party that big at The Castle. That was the biggest party ever!"

Cdrum choked. "What?"

Morf and Flawless stared at Drum and then at each other. Was he serious, or was he joking?

"Really, Daddy?" ventured Flawless. "The biggest party ever?"

Drum stood strong and walked up to his daughter so that his nose was nearly touching hers. "It was the biggest party that there ever was anywhere, right?" he challenged. "You were there. You saw it. All the important people of The Kingdom were streaming in at the back of the hall when they suddenly came down with the flu. That couldn't be helped.

"But they were all there! King Sol would have been shocked to see how many of his fancy aristocrats turned out to greet *me* and congratulate *me* for my wonderful new position. King Sol would have been jealous."

Cdrum had to say something. "You know that isn't completely true, don't you? People may or may not have gotten the flu, but there weren't that many there at all. That's why we have leftover food."

"We have leftover food because all my important friends got the flu," Drum insisted with authority. "But thousands tried to be there. I saw them at the back of the hall. Thousands!" *I think he actually believes that now,* thought Cdrum incredulously.

Morf shuddered at his remembrance of the frantic trick he had put in place the day before. Flawless blinked but said, "Yes, but the party today is even more wonderful. Don't you just love it?"

Drum smiled and turned to the crowd below him again. "Yes, indeed. I do love it. Today's party is even bigger. These peasants are now my people. I must have more parties like this. We will call them rallies—where the common people can gather together just to show their loyalty to me as they are doing today. They love me . . . and they love hats. Morf, be sure to have more hats made."

"Yes, Sir Drum," answered Morf sleepily. *This is the new game,* he thought. *Loyal support and creative reconstruction of facts.*

Loyalty hats were not a bad idea, mused Cmorf.

14

The Partygoers

William of Dale and Ben wandered along the courtyard below The Castle, marveling at the number of people milling about. "I have never seen this many farmers in town at the same time. Plowing for planting must have come to a stop all over the kingdom," mumbled Will through a large bite of mutton.

"I wasn't going to take time off today, but the town criers came by and practically insisted," Ben agreed. "And it's a party for Drum himself, I guess. We work for him, right? There's free food and entertainment, right? Why not? If we take a few hours off from his fields, he won't care. It's his party."

Will finished his mutton and grabbed a biscuit. "The couriers said there were hats. I could use a new hat. Did you see where to get one?"

Ben shuffled along at Will's side, his attention focused on a piece of pie. "Forget about hats. Look at this pie I got. Get one. It's delicious. I can't believe Drum is just giving away all this great food. Generosity isn't usually his thing."

Will laughed at Ben. Eating was his favorite pastime. Then suddenly, Will stopped. "Forget about hats and food," he gulped. He was staring up above the crowded courtyard at The Castle balcony. A ray of light had the perfect angle, and captured in its rays, there was a goddess. She had to be a goddess. She was too perfect to be a normal human.

Ben, his face now buried in his piece of pie, did not look up and so stumbled headfirst into his friend, knocking his precious morsel to the ground.

"Look what you did, Will, you apple head. You stopped in the middle of traffic and made me drop the best thing I ever ate. What did you think you were doing?"

"I was looking at a goddess," whispered Will. "Look at her."

Ben picked up his dripping hunk of pie and began picking off pieces of hay. He was not going to give it up just because of a little dirt. He glanced up impatiently and followed Will's gaze.

Ben blinked hard in appreciation. He whistled. "That is one lovely wench," he admired respectfully. "That's the one I was telling you about, Will. That's Drum's daughter. I guess she moved into The Castle when Drum did. Well, at least there is someone good-looking in The Castle for a change."

Will appeared to be at a loss for words. He stared. Ben nudged him with a sticky finger. "Wake up, Will. Listen to me before I have to whack you with my pie. This amazing woman who is standing by that chunky dude on the balcony is Flawless Drum, our boss's daughter, and her father. She's out of reach for the likes of you and me."

"I can't believe he's her father," Will finally recovered enough to say. "I might be wrong because I've never looked at him much, but I can't believe that Drum is the father of that beautiful goddess."

"I see your point. That girl just dropped down out of heaven. They couldn't be related. No way! No sir."

Will pulled Ben out of the party traffic and leaned against a stall. "I know Drum threw this party to celebrate that he's the Royal Caretaker now. And I have always known he had a daughter too. But this party is always going to be special to me for another reason. I really never even guessed that his daughter looked like this, but now I know."

"Okay. Whoopie do. Now you know." Ben went back to his prize.

"I have to meet her," Will stated earnestly.

"And I have to finish this pie and get another piece before it's gone."

The crowd passed the two friends who were both intent on something they had not expected but could not ignore.

Oblivious to the adoration below her, Flawless gazed happily over the crowd. "This is so much fun," she exclaimed from her perch on the balcony. "I have never seen most of these people before, but they certainly seem friendly. They are all smiling and eating and having a good time. And they really do love their hats. I would like to meet them all."

Almost on cue, someone in the throng waved and began to yell. "Hats and food! This is the best day in River Kingdom ever! Long live Drum!" The crowd gathered below the balcony and began to wave their new hats with one hand while gathering up bunches of grapes and loaves of bread with the other. Some of these locals did not eat regularly, and they were grateful. "Drum! Drum! Drum! Do this again! Stay on in The Castle forever!"

Drum waved back and began clapping his hands. What were they doing? They were calling his name! The people adored him. They wanted him to "stay in The Castle forever." His wealthy friends had never said such a thing. These people were appreciative.

"They think you're wonderful, Daddy," bubbled Flawless. "They are so much more enthusiastic than your rich friends. These people seem to love you."

Drum surveyed the crowd of people, common for sure and without rank definitely, but great in number. But they did seem to love him. His need for loyalty and appreciation was being satisfied more today than he ever would have expected. These people seemed to understand him.

"Don't sound so surprised, daughter. I see now that these peasants may be the best friends of The Castle from now on. It took me a while to understand it, but in my current position, the loyalty of the many common people may be much more valuable than that of a few of the so-called establishment elite.

"Wealthy people have issues. Greed is one. Jealousy is another. The noblemen have always thought that they were better than me. That's a fact. These common people like me and they also like me here, where they think I will be good to them. All I have to do is keep these people loyal to me, and I can keep this position for as long as I wish. It's like I've always said. Loyalty is the key."

Drum smiled down at the crowd below and waved his own red hat. The crowd cheered. Drum had learned something important. "These hats were a brilliant idea," he smirked. "Loyalty can be created with hats."

"Glad you liked 'em," Morf managed to reply as he staggered slightly, nearly asleep at Drum's side. Somewhere, a hundred seamstresses that Morf had supervised were slumbering, but Morf heard and understood, even in his haze, what Drum had just discovered. Morf had scored some points with the hats, and loyalty was going to keep Drum in The Castle—and Morf as well.

Drum's Conscience drifted away from his happy human and looked around. He had never really talked personally to Morf's Conscience before, and he didn't see him now. These two Consciences were probably going to see a lot of each other in the near future. He went on a search.

Cmorf was sprawled out and resting in a corner of the deserted Royal Party Hall when Cdrum found him. Cdrum sat down beside him. "Rough night, huh, Cmorf?" he snickered. "I guess you never knew that being a Conscience for a Royal Advisor included supervising all-night seamstresses and cutting out hats. I don't suppose that was in the job description."

Cmorf sat up and shook his head. "Morf is obsessed with pleasing Drum," he groaned. "Morf was King Sol's Royal Community Relations Advisor, but he didn't have much to do. A dinner here and there was about it. Now he has decided that the best way to keep his job in The Castle is to get in tight with Drum. He is determined to become Drum's most loyal supporter."

"Loyalty's not too bad an idea with Drum," Cdrum admitted, munching on a dropped crumb of party food. "A lot of Drum's wealthy friends seem to have snubbed him. I don't think they were ever too loyal, anyway. But he earned himself some new friends with the food and the hat ideas. If Drum keeps on being popular with the common people, he might have found a new group of admirers to solve the loyalty and popularity needs that he's always had."

"Yeah," Cmorf agreed. "A lot of rich people are just stuck-up and jealous, even with other rich people, I've noticed. Hats and food made Drum popular with all the peasants and their families. They are not used to getting gifts, and they loved it. The food was Morf's idea. I was pretty proud of him for that."

"Don't let Morf take credit for it, though," warned Cdrum. "Drum wants the credit for anything that happens that's good."

"Thanks for the heads-up," said Cmorf. "But I hope he doesn't do something like big parties and hats too often. This Inauguration

Celebration cost a boat load from King Sol's operating budget. The Royal Finance Advisor is going to pitch a fit."

"Right. I'll try to warn Drum to keep the spending down . . . but that's kind of the way Drum operates. He loves to entertain and make decisions off the cuff," Cdrum acknowledged, taking another bite of his found goodie. "I still can't help wondering about everybody who didn't show up yesterday, though. That was weird. It couldn't have just been the flu. Those wealthy partiers have always showed up in droves to his parties before."

"Jealousy is a big thing, you know, Cdrum. Get used to dealing with it here at The Castle more than you ever did before. But don't worry. The so- called 'important people' will still come around when they want something. They always do."

"True, true. Well, I've got to get back to work. Drum is still active. I shouldn't leave him alone for too long. He needs constant supervision. See you around."

"Yeah. Looks like you *will* be seeing a lot of me if I can keep up with Morf's pace," groaned Cmorf, rolling up in a ball and starting to snore. Cmorf knew Morf would soon be sleeping too after his long night. He knew Morf probably wouldn't need his Conscience anytime soon.

Cdrum caught up with Doran Drum as he finally strode away from the rejoicing farmers below his balcony. Their apparent adoration was new and completely unexpected. He loved it. He had trusted that his real estate holdings and party regulars would ensure his popularity at The Castle, but he now had a new perspective.

Today felt more like *real* popularity and *real* loyalty. The rich might be useful again from time to time, but the common folk were his new fan club. These peasants recognized his greatness and his right to be in The Castle. Yes, this Castle was *his right*. The Eforces agreed.

Cdrum scrambled back into position near Drum's ear. He didn't expect to be needed on this happy day, but he could feel that something had changed. Drum was *truly* appreciated by a new group of people. This was different, and appreciation for perceived good deeds was a new thing. This could mean a positive change for Drum. Cdrum kicked back and rode along, concealed in Drum's collar. Sometimes Conscience life was easy. Sometimes it was much more challenging. Cdrum would enjoy today as long as he could.

Flawless joined her father now as they headed slowly into The Castle. "That was so amazing, Daddy. The people all seemed to love you. I wish we could have a party like this one more often." Flawless was already a grown woman, but sometimes she was still his little girl. They had become dependent on each other for approval since her mother had moved on.

"You liked that party, didn't you, Flawless? Well then, we should have lots more of them. Would you like that?"

"Of course, I'd like that, Daddy, but I know we can't do it. Parties like that cost too much for us to do it too often. King Sol wouldn't like it."

"Hogwash." Drum chuckled. "King Sol isn't here. I can do whatever I want. I'm in charge now, and my people love me. Besides, I didn't use the King's money for this party. I used my own money, so don't worry about it."

"What did you just say?" whispered Cdrum. "You said 'my own money,' did you not? You used the King's money. You know you did. You just told your daughter a lie."

"But if any of the King's money was used, I didn't do it," Drum amended quickly—more plausible deniability. "If Morf used the King's money, it's not my problem."

"Really?" whispered Cdrum. "You're blaming Morf? That's the way you're playing this? Really?"

Drum was not answering any more questions. Flawless shrugged her shoulders. She didn't know much about finance, and that sounded right to her.

Cdrum was not through. "You just lied to your daughter, and you are not changing it. She trusts you. You don't want to lose that. You should tell her the truth," he warned.

"I deserved this party," Drum concluded. Flawless smiled and nodded, again assuming that her father was talking to her. Cdrum took note of some difficult times ahead. The Eforces just smiled.

"I deserved this party," Drum concluded. Flawless smiled and nodded, again assuming that her father was talking to her. Cdrum took note of some difficult times ahead. The Eforces just smiled.

15

The Royal Advisors

The next day, Drum was full of energy and ready to take control of his new position. He called Morf to the throne room early. The throne room? Of course. Drum didn't see any reason that he shouldn't use that room—*and* the Royal BedChamber next to it. He was in charge.

Morf bowed low again. He had decided that this was what Drum liked best. "At your service, Sir Drum," he announced.

"Of course, you are," Drum responded. "And don't forget it. And the King's other Royal Advisors are at my service as well. I demand respect and loyalty. By the way, where are my other advisors?"

"They are all working at their respective positions, Sir Drum. Would you like to see someone?"

"Indeed. I have decided to see them all immediately."

"All of them?"

"Indeed. All of them. They used to work for King Sol. Now they work for me. I'm checking for loyalty."

"Why?"

"The King is not here and I am. Whether or not they are useful to me as their new boss is something that only I can decide." Drum smiled proudly. "I learned yesterday that I need loyal friends to run this operation, so I am only going to work with friends. Let's see how many of these advisors will be friendly. Go get them." He donned one of the new red hats that he and everyone had worn the day before and smiled triumphantly.

Morf scurried from the throne room. A man on the king's throne in a funny hat was not very dignified, but Morf had taken Cdrum's loyalty warning to heart and did not want to question it. One by one, wearing his own hat, he hurried from advisor to advisor, delivering his message. "Sir Drum will see you immediately in the throne room."

The Royal Advisors' work spaces were rooms chiseled into the rock walls that lined the lower corridors of The Castle. Although they were much like caves, they were very elegant rooms. They contained finely made furnishings—polished wooden tables, sleeping platforms with down mattresses, and an ample supply of coverlets. These accommodations were not as fine as those of the throne room or any of the rooms in the King's suite, but were greatly above the living conditions of the farmers in the valley. Morf had his own well-appointed space on this same corridor.

There were, of course, candles and lanterns for light, pens for writing, and the "tools of the trade" in the quarters of each advisor. These were possessions of honor that indicated each advisor's position.

For the Defense Advisor, there were such important items as swords, shields, and armor lining the walls as well as an extra table covered with leather maps so that strategy could be plotted in times of conflict.

For the Agriculture Advisor, there were bags of seed, baskets of harvest, and finely crafted tools with polished handles.

The Finance Advisor lined his room with the commodities that River Kingdom had to offer other kingdoms in trade. There were woven tapestries, golden goblets, and of course, the finest wines and ales. Most notable, however, was a table stacked high with ledgers on which the advisor's daily and seasonal tallies were meticulously inscribed.

The Royal Advisors were men of stature. Each was appreciated for their particular knowledge and expertise, and they had always been held in great esteem by King Sol.

Morf hustled from one room to another, informing his colleagues that they had been summoned by the Royal Caretaker. And he added another suggestion to his first request, hoping to smooth the relationship between these good men that he had worked with for years and what he had already learned about the new guy. "Try to wear one of the hats from yesterday," he suggested. "Lord Drum would like that."

"I'm not going to kiss this guy's ring," scoffed Marvin, the Finance Advisor. "He's only a Caretaker, not a king. I didn't wear a stupid hat yesterday. I didn't even go to his silly celebration. I was too busy paying the bills for a party, which was, I might add, overly expensive and completely unnecessary."

The Finance Advisor was almost buried in a pile of receipts and notices that covered his writing table and littered the floor.

"I understand, Marvin. I really do," Morf responded quickly to his old colleague. Sir Marvin was an aging, cranky gentleman, but he was very good with numbers. He knew how much was on hand, down to the last piece of silver. He was well respected by King Sol who had often joked that Marvin would chase the last penny through a crack in the floor before he would let it go missing.

Sir Marvin threw his pen to the floor with disgust. "This Drum character piled up more bills yesterday than I have seen accumulated in a year under King Sol, and he did so in only a day. Now he wants to chitchat? Is that what you are telling me, Morf?"

"Actually, those bills came from more than just yesterday, and *actually*, it was *me* that pushed most of them through at Drum's request. *Actually*, you should be mad at me, not Drum," confessed Morf.

"I *am* mad at you, you numskull! Why did you do it? You never used to spend like this. You are the Royal Community Something-or-other Advisor, not the Queen of Sheba. You spent too much. And I should have been consulted beforehand. What was the matter with you?"

"This man is calling you out, Morf. And what he is saying is dead on," snickered Cmorf.

Morf chose not to listen. He was a Royal Advisor and was not used to being criticized by anyone, much less a man of equal rank. "I ordered these things because Lord Drum wanted them," he answered defensively, "and he is the Royal Caretaker. Now he wants you. Be sure to wear a hat." With that, Morf turned abruptly and left the paper-strewn Finance Advisor sputtering angrily behind him.

Morf loyally marched from advisor to advisor along the long lamp-lit hall. No one was happy to see him even though they were associates and had been for years. They sensed that he had aligned himself with Drum somehow, and they were all too busy with their regular tasks to drop everything for a social visit. By the end of the day, however, a line of muttering Royal Advisors had formed outside the draperies that constituted the grand entrance to the throne room.

The Royal Advisors waited. They grumbled. They waited some more. At last, a maid servant poked her head through the curtains and told the advisors that Lord Drum was resting and would see them all tomorrow.

What?

Dismissed, disgruntled and disrespected, the Royal Advisors returned to their individual domains but were now determined to inform this new guy that he didn't understand his position. He was ignorant of castle protocol and respect. This was not the way King Sol had done things, and they didn't like it.

The Royal Advisors gathered again outside the throne room the next morning looking more like an angry mob than dignified advisors. Morf slid in the side entrance of the throne room. True to his new pledge of loyalty, he thought a warning to Drum as to the mood of the advisors might help.

Drum was aware that the advisors were waiting, but was unconcerned. He was watching a group of dancers perform an elaborate routine while the man with the feathered hat that Morf had met on inauguration day looked on. Sir Fandango, was it? Morf was shocked. What about the advisors?

Drum waved Morf aside until the dancers finished. Morf was dumbfounded. He could hear the advisors grumbling in the hall. "The Royal Advisors are waiting to see you, sir," he mumbled, bowing as usual.

"Let them wait," Drum said with authority. "I've decided that I will start my day with a bit of entertainment, not to mention the local news. These girls are not only talented, but they are also informative. They connect with a lot of people on a regular basis, and people tend to tell them everything it appears. I like to know what The Kingdom thinks before I deal with boring people like advisors. These popular girls always bring me the news in a very enjoyable way. It's amazing how informative pretty girls can be."

Morf tried to maintain a respectful countenance. "I think you won't find these advisors to be boring," he said quietly. "They're feeling pretty aggravated."

Drum spun around. "Why? What do they know? What have you heard?

Are they against me?"

Morf had not expected the sudden paranoia, so he blurted out his response without thinking. "The Royal Advisors are just mad because they got summoned when they were busy and then you told them to wait like flunkies and now—"

Drum put up a flat hand as though he was directing traffic. "Stop!" he said deliberately.

Morf froze and started to shake, sure that he had said too much and sure that he was about to be demoted and replaced.

Instead, Drum looked at him closely. "I hear what you say, Morf. This information is valuable to me. You have been around this Castle for years. I can use what you know. What do you think these advisors need right now?" Again, Morf was broadsided. What should he say? In answer to Drum's reasonable question, he returned to his new understanding of Drum's loyalty fetish. He bowed low while his mind churned.

"The Royal Advisors need to learn . . . who is boss now," he said loudly, facing the floor.

"Wimp," whispered Cmorf.

"Brilliant!" shouted Drum, patting Morf on the head. "Show them in, but only one at a time. I'll need to check them each out one by one. I will check for intelligence. I will check for respect. But most of all, I will check for loyalty. Go get me the Royal Defense Advisor first. I love a strong military."

And thus it began. Every morning, Morf waited for the dancers to perform for Drum and tell him the gossip that was circulating in The Kingdom. Then when the gossip providers left, Morf entered with his contributions—information he had gathered, possible threats from unknown areas that he had uncovered, missives from other kingdoms or territories, or appointments that Drum had requested. He was now careful, however, to present every offering in a way that was as favorable and flattering to Drum as he could muster. Drum listened to what interested him and dismissed what did not. Thinned-down matters of interest became the ritual.

Drum seemed to enjoy most of this routine, but after several days, he decided not to read the boring missives from the other Royal Advisors. He dismissed requests from other kingdoms as well. He even ignored heroic accounts from Dragon Quest. Finally, he came to rely solely on the news of the day from the pretty dancing girls and Morf's loyal laundering of information.

As far as Morf could see, Drum was not taking his position seriously, but Morf trusted that King Sol's Royal Advisors knew what they were doing so he was fairly satisfied that everything was under control. He wasn't worried.

Morf settled into a routine of his own. His first duty was to bow and scrape before Drum on a daily basis. He delivered information, also daily, couched to fit Drum's mood. He never read messages from King Sol or Dragon Quest. They only reminded Drum that his position was temporary. Finally, mail of any kind was tossed into an empty corner for the maid servants to carry away.

Morf's Conscience was not pleased with Morf's behavior. "Half the time what you say is a bald-faced lie just to make Drum happy. You know that, don't you?" offered his Cmorf.

"I don't tell real lies. I only stretch the truth a bit," Morf countered.

"A lie is a lie," drawled Cmorf. But Morf continued his practice, and for this reason, Drum seldom heard bad news and Morf felt secure in his position.

Drum was particularly interested in Morf's version of economic news, and Morf was becoming an expert reporter.

Debris gathering in the streets became "the overflow of the blossoming trade environment."

Battles between competing manor houses were dismissed as "healthy competition between producers."

Beggars in the streets were obviously an "available workforce."

Morf became very adept at selective news programming as well, so he did not inform Drum that the farmers were worried about early spring heat threatening their planting season. There were reasons for this omission.

First, Morf determined that peasants were only peasants, and for that reason, Drum would feel that they were unimportant. Second, weather was not something that anyone could do anything about. The whole world knew that. Third, planting was a yearly agricultural function, not an issue of importance to The Castle. Fourth, and probably most important, it was not a happy story. Drum wouldn't like it.

Morf decided not to mention this issue to Drum at all because it was a complaint, but he did refer the matter to the Royal Agriculture Advisor, Arnold.

Morf's decision was a good one, but not good enough. Arnold evaluated the situation and informed Morf that the problem was much more significant than it looked.

Early heat meant that the fields were too dry for planting. If the crops needed more water, the levees might need to be lowered. If the levees needed to be lowered, Drum and Arnold would need to meet with the Queen of Urhonordo to discuss Water Rights Treaties immediately.

This was a big issue, but not big a problem. Issues like this frequently happened in the spring as changes in the levees affected both sides of The River. Water Rights Treaties could be altered easily if done properly. Both kingdoms had equal rights to The River that ran between them, so both needed to be involved in any decisions made.

Levees were a major issue every year because The River was essential and not to be tampered with carelessly. If one side took too much water, the other side might not get enough water downstream. Some years the balance was delicate. This might be one of those years. The River was high, but the ground inland was very dry. Changes would need to be made carefully. The River needed to be treated with respect.

As Morf suspected, weather and levees were not the least bit interesting to Drum even though he owned large tracts of land next to The River. Today, however, several of the prominent manors had contacted Drum directly with written letters. They needed more water for their crops, and they needed it quickly.

Morf carefully mentioned the letters, but Drum was busy with a new dancing girl that morning. He looked at Morf with disgust, asking, "Haven't you learned yet? Farm problems are Arnold's problems. 'The Castle' is not interested in such trivialities."

So the new letters were referred to Arnold. Arnold, noting the urgency of the letters, asked to see Drum in person and immediately to set up negotiations with Urhonordo.

But it was a warm day, and Drum grinned and asked one of the dancing girls to draw him a nice bath. As far as he could see, there was no immediate water problem.

Morf tried respectfully to justify the delay to Arnold who was his peer and a man he respected. "Unfortunately, Sir Arnold, The Castle is extremely busy right now. When Lord Drum is no longer busy, I will arrange a meeting for you."

"I know that guy isn't busy, Morf. The King was never too busy to talk to me about water rights. Go tell 'The Castle' that I have been doing this job for years, and I know what I am doing. Changes in the levee structure need to be done early and by treaty. We have dammed up too much water for a hot year, and the need is urgent. Get on it!"

Morf didn't want to let Arnold down (or show weakness). He shuttled back to Drum, but Drum was now blowing bubbles at the dancing girls from his tub.

"Goodbye, Morf." Drum laughed. "Can't you see that dammed water is not my issue of concern right now?" Morf was worried. Arnold had said that the need was urgent.

"Tell Drum the truth, Morf," counseled Cmorf.

"I hear that this levee issue is really urgent for the whole Kingdom right now. We've dammed up too much water for a dry year."

Drum blew more bubbles. "Not my problem." He grinned.

An aggravated Morf now returned to Arnold and got serious. "Here's the truth, Arnold," he confessed. "Drum doesn't really care about this today. To be blunt, he feels that the dammed water is your dammed problem."

Arnold threw up his hands. "This is something that King Sol would never have done. This cannot be ignored. Even Drum's own man, William of Dale, sent me a personal request for more water. Here, show Drum this message from his own overseer. Maybe he will 'care' about that." Sir Arnold shook his head in disgust.

Morf scurried back to Drum who was still lounging in his bath while the dancer who had been chasing bubbles earlier fanned him with a feathered fan.

Cmorf jumped into action again. "Don't let him blow you off this time," he hissed to Morf.

Morf bowed low. "Sir Arnold says that *your own* fields need more water right away, sir. He says that *your* foreman has asked for permission to lower the levees on *your* farm as soon as possible."

Drum switched his focus from the dancer and thought a minute. "That's right," he said. "That Will fellow who takes care of my farms is a farmer, right? And *he* is saying that *he and his fellow farmers* need more water, right?"

Morf had broken through. Drum was actually paying attention. "Yes," Morf said triumphantly. "That's what the Ag Advisor told me." "Why wasn't I told about this before?" Drum shouted. "Why doesn't

anybody tell me anything? The farmers are my fans. They are my loyal supporters. Remember how they flocked to me at my Inauguration Celebration? Were the rich and famous there? No! Were barons and lords there? No. The *peasants* and farmers are my people now."

Drum waved the dancer away with a flick of his fingers. Morf looked at Drum's eyes and realized that he had the same look that he had had when he spoke about the hats. The levees weren't his concern at all. It was all about loyalty. Peasant loyalty was now another key.

"My foreman and all those farmer peasants are probably the same people who were enjoying my inaugural in front of my balcony the other day, right?"

"That's right, sir."

"Those were good people. Those were wonderful people. Those were the people who liked my hats . . . and me. So this is what we will do. We will call them all back together, and I will announce to them that I have ordered the lowering of all the levees just for them. The water will flow to wherever *they* need it. I can see it all now. They will love that . . . and me." "That sounds good," replied Morf. He was happy, and he thought that

Sir Arnold would be happy too. "Thank you, sir. I will tell Sir Arnold to send out the word."

"No, you won't," Drum cut in quickly. "Instead, you will get me the Royal Couriers so that I can announce a grand rally to be held tomorrow night. Then at the rally, *I* will tell them. It was *my* idea, not Sir Arnold's."

"But Sir Arnold—" Morf began.

"Sir Arnold is an old man with old ideas left over from the previous administration. He doesn't need to be out there in front of my people. Tell him that I will take care of this and then send me the Royal Couriers . . . and tell them to wear their hats."

The Auras began to bubble. This was the kind of thing they had been waiting for. Drum was full of his own importance. His use of the power that he loved was growing. This behavior had potential.

But Cdrum was on the case. "Whoa!" he shouted. "What are you doing, Drum? The Ag Advisor isn't a bad guy. He tried to tell you about the levees before, but you didn't listen. This is *his* area. He knows about the levees and how much water to take from where. Stand back and let him do it."

"But he doesn't know *my* fans, the peasants, like I do. This is something that the peasant farmers and I can do together. We will bond over this. Lowering the levees will make our relationship even stronger than it already is. The Ag guy will be okay with it. I'll send him a hat or something," said Drum with a confident grin.

Oh brother, thought Cdrum. *He's sending a hat in place of respect.* "This is a bad move, Drum." But Drum's invite was delivered by the Royal Couriers to the farmers that afternoon.

The next night, Drum stepped out on The Castle balcony again with his red hat and a big smile on full display. Below him stretched a sea of red hats on the heads of hundreds of farmers. At the first sighting of Drum, the crowd erupted into a cheerful chant. "Drum, Drum, Drum!"

Drum stood back a bit and basked in the sound. This was a sign. The crowd was with him. They liked him. He could do no wrong. Morf stood to the side, out of the way. He was stunned at the response of the crowd. What would happen next?

Drum stepped forward again and leaned over the crowd. "Thank you all . . . and thank you for remembering your hats. As you can see, I have mine. You all have yours. That means that we are friends, right?"

A huge new roar arose from the crowd. "Friends, friends, friends!" they shouted.

"That's what I thought," Drum returned the shout. "This is the reason that I have come to you all today. I have just issued a Royal Decree. Tomorrow is hereby decreed to be 'Take Down the Levees Day'! Are you for it?"

The joyful crowd took up the chant. "Take 'em down! Take 'em down!" Drum clapped along with their chant and then continued. "The old Agricultural Advisor didn't want to do this right away without asking Urhonordo, but I said if you don't give my farmers their water right now, we'll lock you up."

The chant changed. "Lock him up! Lock him up!" The chant went on for over a minute as Drum strolled back and forth and listened, his pleasure and confidence growing. Flawless heard the noise and stepped out onto the balcony.

"Daddy! What is this all about? What is happening?" She stood behind her father and peeked over his shoulder.

"I'm meeting with my fans, daughter," Drum answered, waving his arms over the cheering crowd. They continued to chant.

Drum smiled benevolently. "No, no. There's no need to lock Arnold up, of course. Instead, we will just 'put him out to pasture.'" Drum laughed at his own joke, and the crowd laughed with him, resuming their first chant, "Drum, Drum, Drum!"

Flawless stepped cautiously forward and surveyed the huge gathering. "Wow, Daddy! This is wonderful. This looks like a party. What's the occasion? What are they cheering about?"

Morf pulled himself together and stepped forward. "This is more like a rally than a party, Flawless," he explained over the crowd. "Your father has just told the crowd that he is going to lower the levees that are holding too much of The River water back from their dry fields. These are farmers. They are pretty happy about it."

"Levees? What's a levee? Where are they?" asked Flawless.

"Those are good questions, Flawless," responded Drum. "I'm not really sure."

"Shall I go ask the Agriculture Advisor, Daddy? He would know," asked Flawless.

"No," answered Drum. "I have a better idea." He leaned out over the crowd again to speak. "My friends, since Sir Arnold is old and out of touch with you people, I think I need someone younger for a new position—the position of 'Royal Levee Advisor.' That way, I can deliver orders straight to *him* when I am ready to give them instead of involving Arnold. Who should I choose to do that?"

Drum grinned and pointed.

The crowd below turned in one direction. Drum was pointing at one of them. It was Will.

The rally cheered, and Will looked slightly embarrassed, raising his hand in a shy salute. Drum had only seen Will a few times, but he knew this was the right choice. This man worked for him already. Drum could tell him what to do. *His* lands would get the first infusion of the needed water. It was perfect.

The rally continued with happiness and cheers all around. The farmers were content that their crops would get more water, and the rally ended with everyone feeling good and munching on snacks that had been prepared for them by The Castle Cooks.

"Everyone wonders what will happen next," offered Cdrum. "How much are the levees going to be lowered, and when does that start? Do you have a plan?"

"These are only farmers," Drum responded nonchalantly. "They don't need a plan. I issued a Royal Decree. William What's-His-Name will take care of it. He's the new Royal Levee Advisor."

"Do you realize that you just chose your own man to be a Royal Advisor?" Cdrum asked. "You should have talked to Arnold first. The lords of other manors are going to know that you showed favoritism toward your own property by hiring your own man. They will smell a rat for sure." "I'm not worried about the lords of the other manors. Their farmers love me." Drum grinned. "The peasants will get all the water they want. Don't worry about their lords."

Drum didn't bother to tell the Royal Agricultural Advisor what he had done. But Morf knew his colleague needed to be informed. When Morf told Arnold, the old man sank onto his chair and wiped his brow. "Drum shouldn't have done that," he said slowly. "You have to be careful with levees. Levees are pretty fussy. You can't just knock down any levee at any time. There are treaties with Urhonordo involved. I'll have to go out and warn Will."

"You might want to do that right away," said Morf. "The farmers and Will already met with Drum to thank him after the rally. He signed his big Royal Decree right then and there in front of them. It was a wonderful meeting and everyone wore their hats and celebrated."

"I see. But the levee situation is complicated, and there is a lot that the farmers don't understand." Arnold sighed. "I know William of Dale. He is a good man, and I don't want to pour water on his happy promotion, but I don't think Will knows about Water Rights Treaties.

"I am the Royal Agriculture Advisor," he announced with pride. "I alone have been appointed by the King to negotiate for the King with Queen Luna about levees and the Water Rights Treaties. That is something between kingdoms that the King and I have always done. We can't change how much water is siphoned out of The River or where it comes out until we meet with Urhonordo and come to mutual agreement. Water is tricky. You don't want too little, but you also don't want too much. Water is a very sensitive issue." Arnold was correct. Will was a farmer, not a water man, but he had heard about the importance of Water Rights Treaties. At least he knew there was such a thing. He wanted to help his fellow farmers fast, but he wanted to do it right.

"I'm going to need to go to The Castle and talk to Arnold before we do anything. And he will need to come out here and take a look," Will continued, "but that will take time."

"If we don't get water to these fields right away, we won't need to plant at all," Ben grumbled. "And if we are going to get the levees lowered quick enough to do any good, the farmers are going to need more labor to help do it."

Ben and Will were sitting on the edge of the dusty field where rows had already been dug but nothing was planted. Everyone was waiting. This Levee Advisor position was flattering, but it was new to Will and time was wasting.

Ben was a good problem solver and had been in the fields as long as Will. They would work on this situation together as was their habit. The two friends thought about it hard while dry puffs of soil wafted in the breeze.

"I have an idea," offered Ben. "My people in The Lowlands are having the same trouble with the dry weather that we are up here in River Kingdom, only worse from what I hear. They're already conserving water, and they fear they will be reduced to eating cactus all winter. Why don't I go get some of them up here to help lower levees while you talk to Arnold? Arnold will tell us what we can do, and my people will already be up here to do it. My Lowlanders can get paid in The Kingdom's produce when it comes in, in the fall. No more cactus! That would help everybody."

"Great idea!" exclaimed Will. "Why didn't I think of that?"

Ben grinned. "Because you are already thinking like a big cheese," teased Ben. "I'll take off right now."

"Absolutely. And I'll tell Arnold and Lord Drum what we are doing and get a promise for the fall food."

Ben hurried down the dusty road, full of purpose and sure that his family and friends would be ready and willing for the challenge ahead. It would be a win-win.

Will was now alone with his thoughts. He needed to talk to Arnold and tell Drum what he was doing, but Will had more than two old men on his mind—Drum's daughter, the beautiful girl he had seen during the Inaugural Celebration and the rally. Flawless was her name.

He had been thinking about her ever since he had first seen her face. He was sure that she had not noticed him. She didn't even know he existed. Will determined that he needed to fix that, and he was headed for The Castle. This might be a chance to see her.

Opportunity was knocking, but would Will be able to take advantage of it? "That's what I've been telling you," Cwill groused. "You're too shy. You spend too much time with plants."

If Ben was here with him, Will knew what he would say. "If you think you like the girl, go talk to her."

And Ben would be right. Will was determined to follow Ben's way of thinking. He brushed back his hair and washed his face. He was quitting a little early, and Ben was off on his mission. Will needed to go to The Castle, anyway, he figured.

But first, he headed for his flower garden. Maybe this beautiful girl would like a flower.

"You're chicken. This is another stall tactic," snickered Cwill.

Maybe so, but the flower garden was thriving. This was not a surprise to Will who had been watering it nearly every evening. A large bucket from the edge of the nearby river was sufficient if you did it often enough. Tonight, he had decided to pick one "gift flower." He wandered through the blooms, trying to decide on just the right one. Suddenly he spotted something else, a movement through the leaves and blooms. He ducked behind a tree.

The movement gracefully revealed itself to be a woman, walking among the flowers, stooping to touch, to smell, to smile. Will was unable to move. It was Flawless herself.

Will panicked. He was not brave with the ladies so he ducked behind a patch of hollyhocks, hoping she wouldn't notice him. No, that wasn't true. Will's Conscience knew right away that Will was really just lying to himself. He *wanted* her to notice him. Will coughed a shy cough and stepped into the clearing.

Flawless jumped a bit and then smiled. "Are you the man that cares for these beautiful flowers?"

Will coughed again and almost choked before he managed a humble yes. "They are really wonderful," Flawless offered. "I've seen flowers growing by the side of the road sometimes, but I have never seen a whole group of many different kinds planted in rows like this. You must work on it a lot."

"I just like flowers," Will said lamely. Why was he so stupid? A beautiful woman was smiling and talking to him, and all he could think of was "I just like flowers"?

Flawless smiled and approached Will in a shy fashion. "I think I have seen you before, haven't I? Don't you manage my father's property?"

Will was shocked. The goddess had actually noticed him. He tried to answer. His mind raced, looking for the necessary words to say something smart. Nothing.

"I-I . . ."

Flawless laughed. To Will, her laughter was light and musical like the sound from The River nearby. "I'm sorry that I surprised you. My name is Flawless. I am Lord Drum's daughter. What is your name?"

This was a question Will thought he could answer. "I'm Will. I mean, William of Dale, Mistress Flawless. And you're right. I do work for your father." He said it all in one breath and then looked at his feet.

Flawless took a step closer and held out her hand in greeting, a bold but delightful move for a lady of rank. Will took a step forward as well and took her hand in his. For the first time, they looked at each other closely. Neither was disappointed. Several seconds passed. Then they smiled. That was all that was needed.

"I am so pleased to meet you," Flawless murmured shyly. She turned and walked away, but looked back. "I hope I will see you and your beautiful flowers again soon." She smiled and drifted off in the direction of The Castle.

Will stood rooted among his flowers. The most wonderful and unexpected thing had just happened. He looked around. All he could see was a small but vibrant patch of flowers. Now he suddenly knew what flowers were for. They were for someone as wonderful as Flawless to appreciate.

Will reached into the satchel that was hanging around his neck. Fishing down to its bottom, he felt for something he had just gathered "by the side of the road" as Flawless had put it. They were seeds for a new flower that Will had been planning to try. With the joy of the day's surprising and unimaginable event in his heart, he dug into the rich river-dampened soil and carefully planted the seeds of several sunflowers one by one.

16

The Lowlanders

At the southern end of River Kingdom, another moment of joy soon took place. After several hours' travel, Ben arrived at his birthplace in The Lowlands, and his relatives happily swarmed him with hugs and handshakes and offers of food. It had been months since he had been back to his homeland.

After his welcome and a hearty meal, Ben got down to the news that he had brought them.

"You won't believe what I have to tell you all," he announced grandly to those nearby. Ben knew that his friends and relations led a very spare life with much poverty in their dry homeland. There was always a need for the kind news he was bringing. They all leaned in with excitement.

"The Royal Caretaker of The Castle himself has given permission to lower all the levees in The Kingdom, and the Royal Levee Advisor has requested help from us Lowlanders to get the job done. Our payment will be food for the winter. What do you think about that?" A cheer went up from the friends and family members nearby.

Ben jumped onto a nearby table and continued so that everybody around him could hear. "Lord Drum has given his approval for a massive irrigation project to help the fields of River Kingdom during the current dry spell. The best part of that project is that he wants it done immediately for planting season so he needs more workers than the manors have. More workers! Did you hear me? He wants all of us

Lowlanders to come up and help their existing farmhands to lower the levees on the manors."

Now the cheers of the gathered crowd vibrated across the dunes of The Lowlands. River Kingdom was huge. The number of levees in River Kingdom must be huge too. The work needed to reduce these levees for all the farmers would also be . . . huge! If good crops were grown with enough water, the Lowlanders and River Kingdom could both eat well this winter.

The rest of the day, there was dancing among the tents and cabins that made up the Lowlanders' village. Then there were the preparations for travel. This work would be a blessing for the families of The Lowlands. The men laughed and joked while their women packed a few changes of clothing and wagons of digging tools. Soon it would be a time to work, but now was a time to celebrate.

Among the happy Lowlanders, there was one person who remained solemn and thoughtful. It was Ben's grandfather, Ben Sr. He was quite elderly now, but he had experience and memories that some of the younger folk didn't have. He also had something to say.

"A dry spring in River Kingdom means an even dryer summer for us in The Lowlands. I remember a summer before there were levees along The Great River. The water leaked into the low farms of Urhonordo and water was in such short supply in The Lowlands that some of our people died of thirst. If the levees are lowered too much this year for The Kingdom and Urhonordo, that could take too much water away from us down here."

The workers stopped their celebrating and packing for a minute. Ben Sr. knew what Ag Advisor Arnold knew. Water was important and "tricky." So they talked it over, but only for a short while. The Lowlanders needed work now to earn food for the winter. They had already been storing their river water in jugs as was their common practice, but they would need food. Their men were now reminded to be as careful as they could be of the precious water up north because of the needs of their homeland.

They would deal with the water issue when it happened, they decided. If their men worked this summer, food earned from The Kingdom would sustain all of them in the fall. The preparations continued.

Ben's grandfather watched, but he worried. "Respect The Great River," he warned.

In the morning, Ben, his family, and most of the Lowlander men began the trek northward. They were traveling along the bank of The River as this was always the most direct route. It was also the most pleasant. The farther north they went, the wider and more beautiful The River flowed. The Lowlanders, accustomed to only the trickling remnants of The River through their dry flatlands, grew happier with every step.

Soon, alongside The River, there were sections of rich farmland already furrowed and ready for planting. The sight was magnificent, but a little dry. The Lowlanders knew they were going to do the work that would keep all this wonderful land watered and healthy. The springtime rush of The River on the other side of the massive levees assured them that there would be plenty of water to go around.

As they approached a shady, unplowed field near The Castle, Ben suggested that the travelers camp and rest overnight. They could bathe in The River, eat a bite, and get ready to be assigned to the appropriate manors in the morning. After hours on the trail with all their belongings, the idea was met with immediate approval.

Ben left the happy Lowlanders singing and resting and munching on their minimal provisions. With a splash of water to his face, he continued on to find Will. He was proud to have brought dozens of great workers with him. Will and the other farmers would be happy.

As it was getting close to evening, Ben headed toward the flower garden. He knew that was where Will would be. Suddenly he stopped short. He heard voices. Who was at the flower garden other than Will? Almost no one knew about it but Will and Ben. Did whoever it was mean Will harm?

Ben snuck up quietly, flattening his body as best as he could behind an ancient Willow.

"I see you, Ben," called Will. "You are good at a lot of things, but hiding isn't one of them." A giggle followed.

Ben peered into the blossom-filled clearing. The other person at the flower garden was a woman. And not just any woman. It was Flawless Drum. Ben slicked his hair back out of his eyes and straightened his tunic.

She was even more beautiful up close than she had been at a distance, but what was she doing here? Ben shuffled from one foot to another. He looked around for something intelligent to say, but the only thing he could come up with was, "Hi, Will. I see you have company."

"This is Mistress Flawless Drum, Ben," Will began. "Mistress Flawless, this is Ben, the guy I told you about."

"How do you do, Mistress Drum," Ben managed to gurgle out. He turned to Will. "Since when did you know Flawless Drum?" he asked Will accusingly. "When were you going to tell me about this?"

"I just met her yesterday." explained Will. "Oh . . . really?"

"Yes, really," offered Flawless. "I came to the garden alone, and here was Will. I didn't know how they got here, but I saw all these flowers. They were so pretty that I have come back again and again to see them and find out how they got here."

Ben melted. The woman was not only beautiful, but nice—and a flower lover. That made her perfect. "I water the flowers sometimes too. I'm glad you found us," stammered Ben.

"Us?" Will snickered at Ben who was obviously approving of Flawless and making a bid for her to like him too.

"Sure, 'us.' We're all here in the garden together now, right?" defended Ben. "All three of us."

Flawless giggled. Ben was going to be a good friend.

"So Mistress Flawless has just been warning me about a problem we might have with lowering the levees. I'm glad you're here to hear it too."

"We don't have no stinkin' problem," quipped Ben with macho bravado. "Soon there will be no such thing as a levee problem. Wait 'til you see who I brought you. I have dozens of the hardest-working Lowlanders that you ever met, and they are, as we speak, just a way down the road. They're bedding down for the night now. Tomorrow they will spread out and tackle any levee problem you might *think* you have." Ben's chest puffed up with pride. 'Maybe not," sighed Will. "Tell Ben what you just told me, Mistress Flawless."

"Will you please just call me Flawless? 'Mistress Flawless' makes me feel like one of my father's wives."

Ben was enchanted. "Look, Will. Flawless is just like a real person."

Will blushed and said, "Okay. Please tell Ben what you were telling me, . . . Flawless."

Flawless grinned. "Alright. Here is the problem. The Agriculture Advisor for The Kingdom has just toured the levees as Will asked him to do. He sent word to Dad that he shouldn't allow too much to be dug from the levees, so he will need to monitor it daily. He feels that too much lowering of them will take too much water out of The River and make it difficult for The Kingdom of Urhonordo to water their fields downstream. Also, it might cause The Lowlands to go completely dry."

Will just smiled. "We will talk to the Agriculture Advisor right away, Flawless. Ben and I and our Lowlander crew understand that already. We know better than to lower any levee too much. That was never our plan."

Ben nodded. "Will's right, Flawless. My grandfather warned me about that. We know about sharing The River's water. Don't worry. Tell your father that we will take care to lower the levees just enough to help but not too much to hurt."

"Well, that's just it." Flawless sighed. "My father doesn't agree with that 'sharing the water' idea of the Ag Advisor. He says he told all the farmers that he was going to give them *all the water they wanted* and now the farmers expect that. He wants *all* the levees taken completely down. He says that he will not go back on any of his promises to the farmers. They are his fans."

"Excuse me, but your father doesn't get it. Taking down the levees too much will drown the crops," said Ben in disbelief. "That would give River Kingdom more than its share and leave Urhonordo and The Lowlands high and dry. That's not even smart. It would hurt everybody."

"Flawless knows," explained Will as Flawless nodded, "but Drum says he doesn't care about Urhonordo or The Lowlands. They can take care of themselves. It's River Kingdom First, *so that's* our problem."

"Oh." Ben thought for a minute. Then he smiled. "I know what we can do," he announced smugly. "We can go to your father and explain the situation. Since he is *your* father and *you* are smart, I am sure he is smart and will change his mind once we explain it to him."

"You don't know my father." Flawless sighed.

"Stand up for what's right, Will," counseled Cwill loudly in his ear. "Be a man." Will listened.

"We should definitely try talking to him, though," Will said at last, looking determined. "He can't change his mind if he doesn't understand the possible problems. It's up to us to make sure he understands. It's the right thing to do. When can we meet with your father?"

"I hear you," said Flawless. "You two want to do the right thing. I love my father and he loves me, so hopefully I can get him to talk to you right away." Flawless smiled but looked a bit skeptical as she walked away. "I will talk to him right now. If you stay here in the garden, I can find you when I have an answer."

"We'll be here," answered Will and Ben together.

Will returned to tending his garden. Ben, tired from his day's travel and not too thrilled about taking care of flowers anyway, stretched out under a lilac bush and went to sleep. Less than an hour had passed when a breathless Flawless popped through the bushes. "He will see you now," she said, beaming.

Ben was up, and Will was brushed off and ready in a second. The daylight was fading fast so they hurried. They need not have worried about the darkness, however, as the lamps were all being lit in The Castle. They passed through the many glowing rooms that were set for guests, but no one was there.

"The Castle is using up a lot of lamp oil that no one will ever see," Ben grumbled. "My mother told me that was a waste."

"I know," said Flawless as she led the way. "And the Finance Advisor is not happy about it either. He complains to my father every day, but Dad says he wants The Castle to glow and reflect that *he* is now in charge, so that's the way it is."

Flawless stopped and turned back to Will. "That was what I was warning you about," she said simply. "My father has always done just what he wanted to do because he could do that at his own houses. He believes he can be the same way here. He feels that he can do what he wants to do in The Castle as well, and no one can tell him not to."

"He acts like he thinks he's king." Ben laughed.

Flawless became very serious for a moment and looked down, but did not say a thing. She was beginning to get the same feeling. She moved forward now, and the boys followed.

At last they reached the throne room. Through the curtains at the entry, the first thing that caught Will's eye was the form of the Ag Advisor lying flat on the floor. Standing over him were two members of the Royal Guard. Doran Drum sat above them on the elaborate throne of the king, obviously in charge of the situation. "Come in, all of you," he said calmly without looking up.

The three pulled aside the heavy curtains and entered slowly. Something was happening here that did not look happy.

"Rise, Arnold," Drum ordered.

The Ag Advisor laboriously pulled himself up and stood crookedly, his head bowed.

"So now we agree, am I right, Arnold?" Drum stood up, looking even more imposing as he stared down at the trembling older man.

"Yes, sir," quavered Arnold.

"Good. I thought we would. Fine. You are dismissed."

The two guards half escorted, half carried Arnold from the throne room. The tone changed immediately. Drum beamed at his daughter. "And who have you brought with you to visit me, Flawless my love? Two new farmer friends? That's wonderful. What are your names?"

Will raised an eyebrow quizzically. "You know me, don't you, Sir Drum? My name is William of Dale. I work for you, remember? And this is my partner, Ben of The Lowlands."

Drum blinked and refocused. "Oh yes, of course, I know you, Will. I just didn't get a good look at you. And this fellow with you is a Lowlander, am I right?"

"Yes, sir," chimed Will and Ben proudly in one voice. Flawless stood back and watched.

"Well, that's alright. I'm not prejudiced."

"What?" gasped Will, Ben and Flawless in one breath.

"Yes. Of course. It is a pleasure to see you and your little Lowland friend here in The Castle, William. Have you ever been in The Castle before? Pretty fancy, eh?"

"Yes, sir," mumbled Ben and Will.

"When Flawless said that you wanted to see me, I said, 'What for? Did they read my mind?'" Drum chuckled at an inner joke. Ben, Flawless, and Will looked confused.

"As you could probably see, the poor old Ag Advisor is getting a little 'long in the tooth,' as they say. He was just telling me that he wants to retire, at which point I said to myself, 'I know just the man to fill the now-vacant Royal Ag Advisor position. Levee Advisor isn't a real position. My man, William of Dale, should be Royal Ag Advisor! That's just the man for that job! What do you think?" Drum smiled at Will and offered his hand.

Will shook his hand, but then stepped back. "You mean you want *me* to be the Royal Agriculture Advisor, sir?"

"Indeed, I do," chortled Drum. "You already work for me. Sometimes the Royal Ag Advisor has worked *against* me. Now you will work *for* me . . . and the whole kingdom too, of course. You are the perfect man for the job. And your little friend here can be your 'Lowlander Assistant' as I hear that there are many of them here to lower *all* the levees. It is an excellent situation, don't you think? It was all my idea."

Flawless now jumped into the discussion with joy. "Oh, Daddy! That's such a wonderful idea! You didn't tell me about Will. I am so excited."

Will was overcome. This was not why he was here, and he had never thought about such a lofty position as Royal Agriculture Advisor. He blushed. Flawless was glowing and shaking his hand.

Ben was frowning. He was not Will's "little friend," but he decided that this was not the right time to say so. Instead he said, "What do you say, Will my man? Are you up for it? Are you ready to be promoted to Ag Advisor? I know you'll be good at it."

Will smiled. "Royal Agriculture Advisor," he repeated slowly. He was proud. He wished that his mother and father were here to see this. This was a wonderful opportunity. "Thank you, sir," he answered.

Will shook Drum's hand again as Ben stood back and watched. It was a happy scene, so happy that Will had almost forgotten why he had come to see Drum in the first place.

"Are you going to let a fancy title and position keep you from telling Drum why you're really here?" Cwill taunted. "I thought you were a better man than that."

Will stopped for a minute and thought. He might ruin his chances to be a Royal Advisor if he said something Drum didn't like, but the treaties were important. He had almost forgotten. He squared his shoulders.

"Sir Drum," he began. "I am honored that you have offered Ben and I these wonderful positions, but I need to speak to you about the levees before we accept the jobs."

Ben bit his lip and looked away. He really wanted Will and himself to have their new positions, but what Will was going to say might lose them those jobs before they even started.

"A man of principle, eh? I like that," said Drum. He folded his arms and squinted at Will. "Flawless says you have a problem with completely lowering all the levees. What do you need to say to me about the levees, William of Dale?"

Will gulped and proceeded. "Well, I have heard that you want to lower all the levees all the way," he said quickly. "I can't agree with that. If we lower the levees too much, it will bring too much water into

River Kingdom crops . . . more than we need. Urhonordo may not have enough water. It would not be fair to them. I have heard that we have Water Rights Treaties with them that we should honor."

"Oh, is that all you are worried about, my young friend? Don't worry about any Water Rights Treaty. I will be repealing that treaty. You can count on that. Sounds like a stupid treaty that could cost River Kingdom farmers their desired farming practices. I do not intend to abide by such a thing.

"That treaty was something that the previous administration thought was good politics. I do not. We need to consider River Kingdom first and let Urhonordo take care of itself. We need more water. We're bigger."

Will and Ben sagged. This wasn't right. It wasn't good farming practice or good politics either. You couldn't just rip up a treaty that two sides had agreed to, could you? This change in Water Rights policy could be dangerous. It could ruin their neighbors and River Kingdom itself.

Drum noticed the reaction. *These two might be a problem for me and my beloved farmers*, he thought, *but not one I can't fix.* He took a deep breath and smiled beguilingly.

"Of course, we will honor all the agreements previously made until I have time to review them and update them," he crooned. "Please see if you can find a copy of this so-called treaty among Arnold's things when you go down there. He'll be moving out tomorrow. Meanwhile, there is no reason that the Levee Lowering Project cannot get started tomorrow."

That sounded a bit better. Once he reviewed the treaty, maybe Drum would understand why it had been put in place.

"The Castle will, of course, be your home as a Royal Advisor if you want it, Will," Drum continued. "All of *my* advisors live in The Castle. In the meantime, you must start working on the levees tomorrow so that we can make the dry fields of River Kingdom as great as they should be."

Will and Ben were relieved. They had accomplished their mission for now. Drum was new at this. He would soon understand the entire issue. Will and Ben stayed with Drum for a few more minutes so that they could proudly explain just how many of Ben's countrymen would be ready to work on the levees tomorrow.

The lit lanterns of The Castle shone bright on the happy scene. Soon after, the young men said good night to Flawless and thanked her for her help. Almost everyone was content with the solution. That is, everyone except Cdrum.

When everyone was gone, Drum's Conscience yanked on Drum's ear. He was not content at all. "What did you just say? What did you just do? Are you drunk with power? You know that Arnold doesn't know that he's 'retiring,' don't you? You're firing him for saying what that kid, Will, just said, and poor Arnold doesn't even know yet that he has lost his job. Don't you understand how two-faced all that was? And the farmers will all expect the levees to come down completely. That is not what Will wants to happen. This is a setup for disaster."

Drum leaned back comfortably on the throne. He heard his Conscience, but he didn't care. "Let that Lowlander work crew deal with it. The farmers will tell them what to do, and they'll do it. The Lowlanders do what they're told because they need the work, and they want to be paid. Everybody will be happy."

"Let me list the evil of what you just did so it's clear in your head," growled Cdrum. "First, you humiliated that old man, Arnold, and made him grovel for his job."

"I did, didn't I?" Drum smirked.

"Yes. And then you took away his job without telling him he was fired.

He still thinks he is the Ag Advisor."

"I'll have someone tell him in the morning."

"Then you gave his job to a young guy that already works for you in your fields. He doesn't know the particulars of any treaties with Urhonordo, and he presumes that you are going to work them out . .

. which you won't. Promoting Will was wrong as well as a conflict of interest."

"It's not a conflict of my interest, and besides, Flawless likes him so I can't go wrong."

"That's not all," fumed Cdrum. "You gave that Will kid the impression that you will let him honor the agreements with the Urhonordo Kingdom. Are you really going to do that?"

"Of course not, but the kid doesn't know that. The farmers will do what I say. The Lowlanders will do what the farmers say, and I will Make River Kingdom Great. Count on it."

"Why are you doing all these underhanded things?" screamed Cdrum. "I am your Conscience! Don't you intend to listen to your Conscience anymore? I realize that I've been pretty easy on you up until now. Maybe I should have been tougher all along. But you seem to be more underhanded now that you are Royal Caretaker than you were before. Why?"

"Why not?" Drum smiled. "The rules are different for people in power and much more lenient than they are for everyone else. Everybody knows that."

"You don't have that much power," Cdrum snorted. "You are only a Royal Caretaker. You aren't a king."

"Not yet," Drum responded as he toddled off to bed.

17

The New Ag Advisor

The next morning, Will was full of energy. By noon, he was able to check out his new living space in The Castle. It was sort of a mess as it looked like Arnold had left in a hurry. Will carefully searched through what was left, trying to find the now-famous Water Rights Treaty, but it was nowhere to be found. Apparently, Arnold had taken it with him.

Ben was already rounding up the Lowlanders and doling them out to the manors of The Kingdom that needed the work done on their levees first. They would start with the southern farms where the need was greatest. Eventually, they would work on nearly all the farms as the water from the levees would need to be directed inland as far as it could go. It would be a big job.

The tools of the men were shovels and heavy picks, pitchforks, and hoes. According to Will, the Lowlanders, together with the local peasants, would dig carefully into each levee, just far enough to let the right amount of water through. Then they would dig ditches to the dusty back rows so that the water could reach them. The Lowlanders had done this many times in the past with their own land, making use of the tiny bit of water that still existed when The River reached them at home. It was a smart plan, but very hot, dirty work.

"The local manors will feed us daily, but you will be given your actual pay from the Royal Caretaker as soon as you have finished the job," explained Will to the Lowlanders. "When the crops are harvested, fresh produce will be added to wheat, barley, and beans. Everyone should do well this winter. We expect a bumper crop."

Drum had promised this, and the Lowlanders were completely agreeable. There were still two remaining questions, however: how much water should be released from the newly dug levees, and what should be done with the leftover rubble?

Will huddled with the farmers. They were all his friends and either worked Drum's lands with Will or worked for other manors nearby. Carefully, Will explained about limits on water and treaties as Arnold would have done. He told them he couldn't find the treaty with Urhonordo, but maybe if they used their heads, they could be fair about the water until Drum found one and got back to him.

Reluctantly, the farmers all agreed to take only the water they needed. After all, they had friends on the other side of The River. And they also had memories of Will's fairness. Will had pried their pay out of Drum in the past. They loved Drum's enthusiastic promise of "all the water they wanted," but practically, they decided to quietly trust Will, at least for now. That took care of one problem. The next problem was the rubble; the extra dirt and rock being removed from the levees had to be put someplace. Will had never thought of the rubble issue before, but as the first day ended, he discovered it was going to be a big problem for . . . the new Royal Ag Advisor. Growing piles of the stuff were beginning to sprawl everywhere. It was mostly clay and large rocks. The village people could not get their carts past the debris. Will knew he had to find a better place for the huge mess to go.

"Here's a thought, Will. We Lowlanders build walls out of that stuff," offered Ben. "That stuff is good to build with. Maybe someone can make use of it."

Good idea, thought Will as he picked a bouquet from his garden. He headed for his new housing space in The Castle. He was going to the throne room as well to discuss rubble, but on his way, he stopped in front of the room that the servants knew belonged to Flawless. The housemaids that had guided him there stood back giggling as Will softly called her name.

Flawless pulled back the curtain in surprise. "Will? Is that you?" Noticing the spray of hollyhocks in Will's arms, she smiled warmly.

He handed them to her carefully. "You will need a potful of water for them," he explained. "They need water just like our fields do. They should stay fresh for several days, though, if you keep their stems in water."

Flawless was charmed. She had never had a bouquet of flowers before. "Thank you so much, Will," she said shyly. "You are so kind."

"I'm happy that you like them," said Will, also shy. There was a moment where the two just looked at each other as though there was no one else in the world. Then the servants giggled, the spell was broken, and Will continued down the hall on his mission to see Flawless's father.

Drum was eating in the throne room, musicians were playing soft music, and a dancing girl was resting at his feet. Will cleared his throat.

Drum whirled around with a start. So did the musicians and the dancing girl. Will suddenly knew that he shouldn't be there. It was at that moment that Morf swooped forward from a spot beside the door, which he had begun to occupy in his role as all-around problem solver. Morf shoved Will out of the doorway and down the hall. "Who are you, and what are you doing here?" he hissed sharply.

"I'm William of Dale. I'm the new Royal Agriculture Advisor."

"The new what? Where is Arnold? I know nothing about a new Ag Advisor."

"I'm very sorry," Will stammered. "It just happened last night. I didn't know what I should do. It's about the levees. I have to speak to Lord Drum about them right away."

Morf loosened his grip on the young man. He seemed sincere, but what was he saying about Arnold? Morf had spoken to Arnold just yesterday. Arnold was worried about lowering the levees too much. He had told Morf he was going to talk to Drum about it.

Now Morf's friend, the longtime Ag Advisor was gone. This fact sent shivers down Morf's back. *Drum does not like to be contradicted,* Morf reminded himself. *Arnold must have argued with Drum somehow. Think loyalty, loyalty, loyalty.*

"So you're the new Ag guy, huh? Congratulations." Morf was changing gears. "Tell me what you want to say to Lord Drum about the levees. As you can see, he is very . . . busy right now."

Will gathered himself together. He was going to have to learn the ways of The Castle. This man was obviously some sort of gatekeeper or watchdog or assistant for Drum.

"It's a simple problem, really," said Will, trying to sound official, but unassuming. "I just felt I should ask for Lord Drum's advice as to the solution."

"Oh," said Morf, nodding sagely. "You seek advice? That's okay. Lord Drum doesn't like complaints, but he's great on advice. Come on in."

Morf reentered the doorway to the throne room with dignity and bowed his usual bow. "This young man is here to seek your wise advice on a matter that is important to him. He would like to know if you could spare some time for such a purpose."

Drum put down his food, and the dancer sat up straight. "He wants my advice? How wise of him," said Drum, leaning forward. "Oh, I see that it's you, William of Dale, my new Ag Advisor. Come in, my son. Of course, you need my excellent advice. You are new to your job, and I am wiser than anyone, this I can guarantee you. What would you like to know, William?"

Will exhaled notably and did his best to state the question. "It's about the rubble that we're hauling away from the levees," he stated. "There's a lot of it, and it's beginning to block the roads and pathways. We need to know where you want us to put it."

Drum leaned back and laughed out loud. "You want advice about rubble? That's funny. I have never thought about giving 'wise advice' about rubble." He sat back, chuckling. "But I will give it a shot. Let me see . . . This levee rubble is mostly dirt and large rocks. Am I right?"

"Yessir, . . . and clay. It's good building material, but right now, it is just in the way."

Drum thought again for a moment. He didn't really care where the rubble went. "Just leave it where it is," he answered. "Who cares if it's in the way?"

"You made the decision about the levees. Now you have to do something about that rubble," reminded Cdrum. "Don't forget. You said you wanted to help the common people, and the rubble is in *their* way."

I didn't say I wanted to help them, thought Drum. I just said that I wanted them to be loyal to me.

"You have to earn loyalty," responded Cdrum, reading his thoughts. "I don't see it. Loyalty is loyalty. I should just get it because I deserve it. They should just take care of their rubble because it's their rubble. There are plenty of workers now. There are even a bunch of Lowlanders . . . Lowlanders . . . hmm."

Then it occurred to him. Will had said that the rubble could be "building materials." There was a possible solution here that could make his peasants happy and make Drum a bit of extra income on the side. He knew somebody who might want this rubble and be willing to pay him for it. Excellent.

"You aren't supposed to make a profit when you are a Royal Caretaker," reminded Cdrum, reading Drum's idea.

You should mind your own business. If I make a bit of profit off this, it won't hurt anybody, thought Drum.

Drum and Cdrum were both suddenly remembering the very first guest who had appeared—and stayed—at his Inaugural Celebration. The man wanted to build a manor house down by the Lowlander Border, and this man, unlike other wealthy no-shows, was loyal enough to come early when invited. Of course, he had wanted something, but Drum expected that. Now Drum could *sell* him something. That was what this guy's kind of loyalty deserved—building materials for a price.

"Okay," Drum announced to the patient Will. "Here's my idea, and it is brilliant as are most of my ideas. Why don't you have the Lowlanders take all the rubble down south to The Border where River Kingdom joins The Lowlands? A friend of mine wants to build a manor house with a view down there. He can use that rock and clay to build his house and retaining wall, and it will be out of the way of my farmers up here. That will solve both problems."

Will considered the answer for a minute. He had never really visited The Border, but it sounded like a good solution. "Thank you, sir. That sounds good. I'll tell the workers that this is your wish."

"You do that, son. Thanks for checking with me." Drum turned back and took a big bite of his dinner. "Morf, I have a small errand for you to perform. Please find Lord Dipswitch for me and tell him he is about to be offered a deal that he can't refuse."

The lowering of the levees proceeded apace. It was a serious, hard business. The Lowlanders and the peasants were used to it, but it was slow and tedious. Things were going well, but the barons and lords of the manors were not a patient group. They had heard that their farmers had received permission to get their levees lowered as much as they wanted, and the aristocrats wanted that work done *now*.

Will was worried. He was being careful, but the Water Rights Treaty had still not surfaced. Will was working day and night. Not only did he need to prepare the fields of Drum Manor Estates, but he had to journey to every other manor along The River. It was his job as Agriculture Advisor to explain what was and was not happening and why.

"Your farmers and the Lowlanders are working as hard as they can on what they have permission to do now," he told the grumbling nobleman of each manor. "The levees are being lowered in order, south to north so that those that need the most water get it first. Each levee will only be lowered to the degree that is needed for that manor's plantings in order to conserve and share water with Urhonordo, but we are still waiting for the actual treaties." "That's not what the Royal Caretaker told our workers," the lords and barons now growled. "He said that our levees could be lowered as much as we wanted, and we want them lowered a lot and fast. Maybe we want to plow up more land. Maybe we want to expand. Whatever we want we should be get. Drum told the peasants they could get us what we want."

"There are treaties with Urhonordo that we must abide by before we go too far," Will tried to explain. "What we can do now is limited, and it takes time."

This idea did not go over well. Will needed the treaties that Drum had promised. And then there was the problem that the rubble was still causing. Lowlanders were using their valuable time taking the rubble down to The Border. He needed to talk to Drum again.

Carefully, Will approached Morf in The Castle hall. He had learned his lesson. He would not go to Drum directly.

Morf was sitting at the doorway of the throne room, his red hat firmly squared on his head. He looked official. Actually, however, he felt very nervous. He had just allowed the Finance Advisor into the throne room, and from the sounds escaping from within, things were not going well.

Will took off his own red hat and wiped his brow with it. He didn't like to wear the hat, especially when it was so hot, but he knew Drum liked it. Everybody did. Everyone was still wearing them.

"You're here to see Lord Drum, right? Well, find another chair," announced Morf. "Marvin, the Royal Finance Advisor is in there, complaining again about the nighttime lighting in The Castle. Marvin is a conservative dude. He earned a lot of respect with King Sol, but Drum doesn't care. He doesn't like to do what anyone else says he should do, especially King Sol. If you have anything to say that he doesn't like, you should probably not bother saying it right now. We'll have to see how this Marvin thing works out, but you might want to come back tomorrow."

No sooner had Morf delivered his advice than the Royal Finance Advisor marched out the door. He stopped when he saw Morf.

"He's crazy!" Marvin spit out. "The man thinks The Kingdom is made of unlimited riches. We have a budget. He won't read it. He thinks he can do anything he wants." He stomped off down the hall, ledgers tucked protectively under his arm and robes flying out behind him.

"Like I said, maybe you should come back another day," Morf suggested to Will, shaking his head knowingly. "Looks like Drum's in a bad mood."

"Morf!"

Drum was bellowing from the throne room. Morf straightened his hat and hurried in. What should Will do in a circumstance like this?

"Are you going to tuck your tail between your legs and run off like a scared puppy? asked Cwill.

"You talk pretty big when nobody can see you," Will answered aloud.

"I'm just sayin'," Cwill continued. "You were excited about having the Royal Advisor job, and now, when the issues get tough, you're scared to talk to your boss about them."

"Did you just see the Finance Advisor storm out of a meeting with Drum?"

"I did. Now it's your turn. Get in there."

Will pulled back the massive draperies to the throne room and stepped in. Flawless was pouring her father a cool drink, and a lovely dancing girl was fanning fiercely. Morf stood twitching in front of Drum.

"Hello there, Will. I didn't know you were here," said Drum as he took a sip of his drink.

"Hi, Will," said Flawless brightly. "Look, Morf. Will is here. What a wonderful surprise. I haven't seen you in days, Will."

Morf looked a little embarrassed. He thought he had scared Will away. "So," concluded Drum. "We will continue to light the evening torches as I have requested, Morf. Are we all clear on that?"

Morf nodded vigorously. "But Marvin has already told the lighters—"

"I'm telling you what *I* want, Morf. I am not bound by anything that the previous administration did. I hope we are clear on that too."

"Indeed, we are, sir. I will take care of it right away, sir." Morf backed out the doorway and disappeared.

Drum smiled confidently. "Now, how can I help you, William of Dale?" Will tried to look confident and official. "I am here to discuss the concerns of your local manor owners regarding the lowering of the levees," he began boldly. "Have the Water Rights Treaties been found?"

"I really don't care about the manor owners who didn't bother to come to my inauguration. Forget them. And as for the leftover treaties from Sol's foreign entanglements with Urhonordo, forget them as well," Drum stated with authority. "*I* am in charge now, and the blasted treaties have been taken care of. Now, have you anything else to say?"

"I just wasn't sure what to tell the farmers about—" Will began to add.

"*My farmers?*" Drum interrupted, his face lighting up. "Tell me about the farmers. What about my farmers?"

"*Your farmers* are frustrated with the levees because their lords are demanding that the levees come down faster than they can to do it. The days are getting warmer, and the planting is not yet completed in many areas. No matter how the *farmers* and Lowlanders sweat, the lords demand more levees to be lowered deeper and quicker." Will was catching on. It was all about "the farmers."

"The farmers and Lowlanders are suffering?" asked the kindhearted Flawless.

"Not really. The lords are just impatient."

"Why are they impatient? Are the Lowlanders working too slow?" asked Drum.

"Everyone is working hard, sir. Very hard. But the Lowlanders do have a problem. It's the rubble again. They are spending so much of their time hauling away the rubble to the south that they can't work full-time on the levees. That slows things down. We need your input on the subject."

Drum stood on his royal platform. He looked at the throne beside him, the rich tapestries on the walls, his daughter, and his new young advisor waiting for him to speak. They needed his "input." He could almost feel his growing importance.

The lighting in The Castle was one thing, but Will was asking him to make a real decision—a decision that only he could make. He felt that his popularity with the farmers was at stake. Suddenly, Drum knew what he was going to do.

"I hear what you have to say, Will, and I thank you for bringing your problems to me as you should have. I have made my decision on what we should do to quiet the aristocrats and, what is more important, make my farmers happy. I will announce my solutions tonight at a rally for my fans, the farmers. *They* are the ones that I listen to. They are the ones that are working. They need to see that I understand their problem."

Drum laughed and slapped Will on the back. "And thanks, Will, for keeping me informed. Now, about the treaty. I have a brand-new

Water Rights Treaty right here in my superior brain, so not worry about a thing. I will see you and the farmers tonight. But right now, tell your little Lowland assistant to come see me. I am going to make a very helpful change in their routine."

Will was unsure of what had been decided, but he was relieved. There was finally a new Water Rights Treaty. Drum was in a good mood, and he would announce a solution to problems of the manor owners tonight. And Flawless was walking out of the throne room with him.

"Wow." Will grinned. "That was positive."

"I know. This is going to be interesting. Usually he tells me what he's thinking, but this time, I have no idea what he's going to do. Will I see you at the rally tonight, Will?"

"Absolutely." Will smiled. "I have missed you, but I have been working on the levees day and night. I have to get back to work now, but would you meet me in the garden?"

"Yes."

A long, hot day followed the morning meeting. It was still hot and the sun was still shining, but already hundreds of torchlights were lit around The Castle. Flawless laughed as she noted that her father was in a defiant mood.

She and Will met in the garden as planned. Flawless had picked out a splendid lavender gown that now matched the fragrant lilac branch Will had given her when they met. They were secretly holding hands as they walked to the rally among Will's friends and fellow farmers.

Will didn't look like a rRoyal Advisor, but he was wearing some fine new shoes that Arnold had left behind in his quarters. And he was cleaner than his friends tonight. He had bathed in The River. He thought it was the least he could do for Flawless since he had been working and digging in the dirt all day. His friends snickered, but they could understand. Flawless was a prize.

One thing surprised everyone as they waited for Drum to make his entrance on the balcony. Ben and the rest of the Lowlanders were nowhere in sight. Drum had required an announcement to be made by the Royal Couriers at each manor that day, but the Lowlanders were not here. Surely, they had heard it.

The greatest concentration of Castle light was on the balcony above the crowd where dozens of torches blazed impressively. Drum stepped out on the glowing platform, looking magnificent. He had spared no expense in draping himself in regal finery. In a very dignified fashion, he turned from side to side, waving and clapping with the crowd as they cheered his arrival. Someone started to chant, "Drum, Drum, Drum." Drum acknowledged the chant and beamed, raising his hands in approval.

"Look how much the people love him," Flawless marveled.

"He made a lot of friends with the food at that party and then lowering the levees," acknowledged Will. "He has become very popular with us farmers. I hope the rest of my friends will still love him when he explains that the levee repair might need to be slower than the barons want. And I wonder what the new Water Rights Treaty says."

"I'm sure everyone will understand," said Flawless, squeezing his hand. The cheering and chanting continued for several minutes while Drum strolled back and forth, soaking it in. Finally, he motioned that he wanted to speak, and the crowd settled down to hear what he had to say. They expected something good. Will was only hopeful.

"Gentleman of River Kingdom, thank you for that rousing welcome, especially after you have all been working on those darn levees so hard all day." He grinned at them sympathetically. The crowd roared. They could tell that Drum understood them.

"I see that many of you still wear the sweat and dirt from the work of the day. *You* are the real men of River Kingdom. That is why I have ordered something for you that I know you all want and need.

"First, the Lowlanders will no longer take time away from lowering the levees to remove the rubble. I am ordering members of my *Royal Guard* to deliver the rubble down to The Border on a regular basis. I am doing this for you who do the hard work of this Kingdom. You deserve to Make River Kingdom Great, and I am here to be sure that the Lowlanders are here to help you do it!" The crowd cheered. But Drum was not through.

"And now I have another surprise for you. Second, I have ordered a doubling of the work done by the Lowlanders who *will now finish their work on the levees twice as fast.*"

The crowd cheered again.

Will groaned. Twice as fast? How was he going to do that?

"Their work will now begin at dawn and conclude at midnight, taking advantage of additional nighttime hours. That is why you don't see them here tonight. They are already working on the new schedule."

The crowd yelled its approval. "Drum! Drum! Drum!"

"What?" groaned Will. "What did he say? He can't mean that."

The crowd was jumping up and down with excitement. The levees were going to be lowered twice as fast. The manor owners would finally be happy. Amazing!

"And you owe this new plan to my new Royal Agriculture Advisor," Drum continued. "William of Dale told me this afternoon what he wanted, and I ordered it immediately!" Again, the crowd stomped and waved their arms as they now began to chant Will's name. "Will, Will, Will."

"Is that what you asked Daddy to do?" asked Flawless.

"No." Will sighed. "The Lowlanders can't work around the clock. The work is too hard. What is your father thinking?"

"Maybe he misunderstood you?" she asked hopefully although remembering what she herself had heard Will say.

The crowd erupted into wild merriment. Only royalty could afford such a grand gesture to help the common people, and now it looked like The Castle was on their side for the first time. Their excitement could not be contained. Drum was not only solving their problems, but he was also making them feel entitled like people of importance. The chant of "Drum, Drum, Drum" grew until it filled the air.

"Long live Drum! Long live Drum! He's better than King Sol! He should be the king! Long live King Drum!" There it was. It had been said.

"King Drum?" Drum responded in an appropriately humble fashion. The crowd began to chant, "King Drum! King Drum!"

Will and Flawless crept to the edge of the crowd and watched in amazement. Drum was striding back and forth on the balcony, clapping his hands in time with the chants. The call he was hearing seemed to go on forever, and he was not in the mood to stop it. "King Drum! King Drum!" Finally, the crowd finished their cheering with one mighty roar and dispersed to the snacks that had been laid out for them. Tomorrow, the Royal Guard would take over removing the levee rubble, and the round-the-clock Lowlander work schedule was already underway. The levees would be lowered twice as fast. Maybe even faster. Their lords and barons would be thrilled. It had been a wonderful night.

What had just happened?

Will had one word for it—slavery. And he had been named for turning his Lowlander friends into nothing more than slaves. And the farmers were calling for Drum to be king? And the Royal Guard was being used to deliver rubble? Surely none of these things could be serious ideas. As a peasant, Will had always respected the decisions of royalty, but tonight had left him completely bewildered.

"I don't know what to tell you," whispered Flawless as the pair arrived at her bedroom curtains.

"I don't understand anything that your father said tonight," offered Will. "I hope I can do something about it . . . or at least understand it in the morning."

Flawless slipped through the curtains and into her room, but Will continued down the hall and out the back door. Some things couldn't wait until morning.

The night seemed to Will to be even hotter than the day had been and in more ways than one. He had to find Ben.

It wasn't hard to find him. He and his family and friends were still at work at midnight. Will climbed over a pile of rubble and approached a group of Lowlanders. They looked up, glared at Will, and went back to work, turning their backs in disgust.

All but one. Ben came forward, his clod-crusted pick hanging from his hand like a sword recently used in battle. "What do *you* want?" asked Ben without smiling. "I would put down my pick, but I can't afford the time it takes to do that."

"I came to tell you that I didn't ask for this," Will said simply.

"Then who did?" Ben shot back. "Aren't *you* the big Royal Ag Advisor now?"

"Drum just decided to do this himself without telling me," answered Will. "I don't know where he got the idea, but he didn't get it from me."

Ben just stared.

"Come on, Ben. You've known me for a long time. Does this sound like something I would do . . . especially to you and your family?"

"That was before you became a big cheese," spat Ben. "I see that you're all cleaned up and even wearing fancy shoes now."

Ben felt betrayed, and Will's simple explanation did nothing for the rage that he and his fellow Lowlanders now felt. Ben had convinced his countrymen to come here. Their winter food supply was riding on the trust he had placed in Will. Will was no longer the man he thought he was. Ben turned his pick over and over, glaring at the dusty ground in the moonlight. Ben's Conscience jumped into the discussion. "Don't be so hardheaded,

Ben. Will has always been your friend. You need to give him a break and listen to him at least."

Never. Never again, thought Ben. Never.

But Will stood his ground. He didn't shuffle or look from side to side. When Ben glanced up at last, he saw his old friend, miserable and sincere.

"See what I mean?" whispered Cben.

A small grimy smile crept to the corners of Ben's mouth. Then a big one. He held out his arms, and the two workers hugged as they had many times before. "What happened, Will?" Ben finally managed to say.

"I don't really know." Will sighed. "I just had to come tell you quick that whatever the Royal Couriers told you and your people this afternoon, it wasn't me that told them to say it. I told Drum that you and the farmers were hot and the lords of the manors were trying to rush you. I told him you had to spend too much time taking the rubble down south. I have no idea where the rest of the crazy ideas came from."

More of Ben's countrymen gathered around slowly, accusing looks on their faces. "This guy is your friend, right?" spit out one younger-looking worker. "If this is *not* his idea, what's he going to do about it?"

"Good question." Cwill popped up on Will's collar. "What *are* you going to do about it? Drum's decided what he wants done, and he's your boss."

Will had been trained by his father to do what bosses told him to do.

It was a matter of honor.

"On the other hand, you can't work your friends to death," Cwill continued. "As a Conscience, I would have to say that this is what we call in the trade a 'Conscience Conflict.' Let me work on it."

But Will thought for only a minute.

"Drum had no idea what he was talking about or the effect of what he ordered," offered Will to the men. "I think he just wanted to make the farmers at the rally happy with him. Obviously, you guys can't work all day *and* all night. That'll kill you."

"True."

"I think I'm dead already."

"We have all been working since early this morning."

"Then take the rest of the night off," said Will firmly. "I will go to the other work sites and tell all the Lowlanders to stop for tonight. If anybody asks you, tell them I said so." Will spoke with an air of authority that he had not known he had in him.

"Good move," whispered Cwill.

Gratefully, Ben and his friends laid down their tools and moved to nearby grassy spots where they could rest in spite of the heat.

Will spent the remainder of the night going to the Lowlanders at every manor, explaining that there had been a mix-up in the message that they had received and that they should stop work and rest until tomorrow.

As he journeyed through until dawn, many of the farmers near them began to admit to Will that they had wondered how the Lowlanders would manage to work all night and all day. Their fellow workers admitted that they couldn't do it. They had been caught up in the excitement of the rally. That part of the solution didn't make sense, but they were at least grateful that the rubble was being taken away by somebody other than the much- needed Lowlanders.

As the warm morning began building into a hot day, many of the farmers went to work on their levees, grateful for their Lowlander workforce when they struggled in a bit late and tired. They appreciated them. The work was too much for just the farmers alone. Everyone seemed to have learned something.

18

Drum and the Crown

And Drum? Drum had left the raucous crowd and returned to his bedchamber alone, the shouts of the farmers ringing in his ears. He was elated. "King, King, King!" they had shouted.

There on a special pedestal rested the magnificent crown of King Sol. It was just waiting for him. Drum picked it up and placed it on his head. Tonight had proved to him what he had always known should be true. He had the crown. He was more than ready. He was now King Drum.

"You are not a king," hissed Cdrum. "You are a Royal Caretaker, nothing more. Get over yourself."

But Drum wasn't listening. He had received a mandate from the farmers, had he not? The call for his leadership still echoed in The Castle courtyard. When his very own trusted fans called for him to wear the crown, who was he to say no?

Reverently, he removed the crown from his head and stared at it. It was beautiful. It fit him perfectly. It was meant to be his.

He donned the crown once more. Indeed, it felt right. The glow of the crown eclipsed the voice of Cdrum entirely, blending in with a supportive hum that only Cdrum could recognize. It was the gathering of Eforces.

Drum strode from the Royal Bed Chamber and into the throne room. For the first time, he felt that he truly belonged there. Back in the Royal Bed Chamber, the bedcovers were turned down as they were every night, but tonight they seemed to be turned down in a way that befitted a king. With the glow of the evening still wafting about him, he climbed into bed and fell asleep.

Unaware of anything going on in the countryside, Drum slept, thrilled and content, but the Auras were not asleep. They filled his dreams with the glory that had been his at the rally. The shouts of "King Drum " resounded through his dreams. Royalty was his . . . and theirs.

With this success, the Eforces multiplied themselves now with new and expanded plans for the future in River Kingdom. Quickly, they spread the word throughout The Castle. "The farmers have called for Drum to become king. He has been seen wearing the crown," they whispered. "What will Drum do now? Is he really going to act as king? If he's king, he can do what he wants, right? No one can stop him."

But still, in the late morning, the Royal Bed Chamber was very quiet. Drum was sleeping in late after his evening of celebration, even though the rest of The Castle was buzzing.

Cdrum as well was wide awake but in a terrible state. He had not slept all night. Drum had turned the Royal Guard into delivery boys, made slaves out of perfectly nice Lowlanders, and then decided on his own to make himself king. *King!*

And Drum had been serious about all of it. He had actually put the crown on his head. Cdrum had tried to intervene, tried to stop him from even contemplating such a ridiculous move, but he had failed. He couldn't believe it.

While Drum was asleep, Cdrum decided he must try to pull together a Conscience Forum as soon as he could get away. What Drum had said and done last night had all the markings of an unprecedented crisis for Consciences. If the Eforces hadn't started working to support this yet, they soon would. On second thought, they had probably inspired it.

Drum's bedroom door creaked open and Morf tiptoed in. This was the third time he had checked on Drum this morning and it was nearly noon. The rest of The Castle was already buzzing. Gossip was flying up and down the halls.

"Was it legal?"

"What would King Sol say if he knew?"

"What else would Drum do now if he had made himself king?" "Anything he wants," they concluded. "He has The Royal Guard on his side."

Cdrum hailed Cmorf from the doorway. "Cmorf! Cmorf! Wait. I need to talk to you."

Cmorf scooted down Morf's sleeve as Morf continued on toward the Royal BedChamber without him.

"What's up?" Cmorf answered, grinning from ear to ear. "How do you feel on this monumental morning? How does it feel to be the Conscience of a king?"

Cdrum stopped short. Actually, he hadn't realized that he had been given a raise in status at the same time that Drum had given one to himself.

"Wow . . . I guess you could say that's what I am, huh?"

"Of course, you can say that, Your Majesty," snickered Cmorf. "That's who you are now. Wait until you arrive at the next Conscience Forum. Everybody will be bowing and scraping and calling you 'sir.' You are now the most important Conscience around."

Cdrum shook his head. This was crazy. He wasn't really a Conscience to a real king. He was the Conscience of a guy who had lied and promised things that he couldn't and shouldn't deliver and named himself king. That wasn't the same thing . . . was it? It couldn't be.

"What do you think I should do?" Cdrum asked.

Cmorf didn't seem concerned. "Drum is just taking advantage of the current situation," he responded easily. "He's not really doing any harm. Besides, I have enough on my hands with Morf. If he grovels any lower, he'll be eating dirt. Let Drum do his thing for a while. What harm can it do?"

Cdrum listened and was slightly relieved, but . . .

Drum was now awake, yawning and stretching and accepting endless congratulations from Morf who had gone to his knees with respect for the "new royal status" of his boss.

Drum, still in his nightshirt, carefully decked himself in the crown that was lying in the bed beside him. Had he been sleeping with it?

"Your Highness," Morf offered as he rose from the floor.

Drum was bursting with pride and excitement. "I am actually king now, aren't I?" he said, sounding strangely like a little boy. "The crowd demanded it and I accepted. Am I right?"

"Indeed, you are," Morf bubbled. "You really are the king now. You were wonderful last night. The farmers loved you."

"Yes. The peasants love me, and I love them. I will keep it that way, always. The common people made me king, not the rich establishment that I used to think of as important. They are not more important than a king, are they, Morf?" Drum broke into a deep satisfied laugh.

"No, sir!" said Morf, laughing as well although he wasn't sure why. "They will have to bow to *you*, sir, and I will make sure that they do. It will be my honor." He bowed deep.

"Morf, you are such a shameful groveler," snarled Cmorf. "That was completely disgusting."

This is what is called for even more now, Morf thought silently. Get *used to it.*

Drum scratched his nose and smiled at Morf. "Thanks for letting me sleep in, Morf. Last night was a triumph. I never thought this would happen, but I have always known I deserved it."

Cdrum groaned. *I should have stopped it. What kind of Conscience am I to let him go this far? he thought. I have to do something to correct it, and soon.*

"You are not really a king. You do understand that, right?" began Cdrum sternly. "You don't have the rights of a king. There are rules for becoming a king, and you don't qualify. You think that being a king is just wearing the crown and doing what you please and getting the respect, but you're wrong. Wrong, wrong, wrong."

"Who's here to say so besides you?" Drum responded. "And what is on my schedule for today, Morf? I am ready to do the work of the king." He posed in front of a mirror, tilting the crown this way and that.

Morf straightened from his bow to almost a salute. "It's good that you're ready, Your Majesty, because you have someone here already waiting to see you. I believe he is one of those wealthy people who attended your inauguration. You asked me to summon him."

"Everyone who was anyone attended my inauguration, but the most loyal individuals came early and stayed late," bragged Drum.

"Yes, Your Highness. That is true, and this man was one of them," Morf agreed.

"Horse feathers," scoffed Cmorf. "You worked your tail off to make it look like there were a lot of people there. Stop lying."

"Indeed," continued Morf. "It was quite a celebration. I remember this fellow, though. He wanted to build a manor house down south along The Great River, as I recall. But isn't that where the rubble is going?"

Drum stopped short. Manor house? Rubble? Drum tried to remember, but reality was lost. He was still in an unstable haze from last night. He had summoned this wealthy man for a reason, but he couldn't remember why. Cdrum began to chuckle. "Boxed yourself into a corner, didn't you,

Drum? You decided to summon somebody like a king and now you're stuck. Serves you right."

Drum stared at his image again in front of the mirror. He was still in his nightshirt and crown, but his mind raced. He had come this far on his wits. All he had to do was use them now. Suddenly he remembered his idea. Ah yes! Genius returned. "Thank goodness I am a very stable genius,"

Drum announced to the cosmos.

He had the answer. It was a deal, something he had thought of yesterday that would solve his farmers' problem with rubble and make him richer at the same time. Drum shifted the king's crown on his head, almost as though he thought it had magical powers. This was a crown of power, and that power would help him seal the upcoming deal.

Cdrum was aware of Drum's thought. "I don't believe you and that crown," he hissed. "You know you're in over your head."

"Believe this," Drum said triumphantly to Cdrum and Morf. "Stand by and watch 'The Power of the Crown.' Send in the gentleman who is waiting to enter my throne room. If he is as rich and eager as I think he is, he will take the rubble off our hands and pay through the nose to do it."

Morf hustled out into the hall and escorted Lord Dipswitch into the empty throne room.

Drum kept him waiting for an additional hour. Drum figured that this is what kings could do. By the time he arrived, Dipswitch was furious, gathering up his cape and making ready to depart.

He didn't expect to see what he saw entering, however. Drum, complete with royal robes *and crown*, made his way in a slow, but regal fashion toward the King's magnificent throne. He was followed by servants laden with elegant-looking trays of food and drink.

"Ah, Lord Dipswitch. I remember you as one of the first to arrive at my inauguration," said Drum without emotion. "It is so pleasant to see you again." Drum lowered himself onto the throne.

Dipswitch was dumbfounded. This wasn't Drum, the party thrower and unimpressive Royal Caretaker. This was a king. Dipswitch stumbled forward and bowed low. "Your Majesty," he managed to mumble in respectful tones.

Drum was thrilled. "Rise, Lord Dipswitch. No need for such formalities among old friends," he said magnanimously.

"I had no idea that you had become King, Your Majesty," the man blurted nervously. "When did this happen? Did King Sol die?"

It was a reasonable question, but Drum had not expected to have to answer it so soon—or at all, for that matter. He hadn't even thought about it. Drum's brow wrinkled. It was time to think quickly. "Please, sit down and let my servants give you something to drink," he said in a manner that was calmer than he felt.

The guest did as he was told while the servants hustled to provide him the appropriate cups and plates as they had for King Sol.

Drum's eyes became big. *Where was King Sol?* he asked himself in shock. For the first time, he had no idea what to say. The sweat of panic dribbled instantly from under the crown. Morf saw at once that a disaster was at hand.

"Hurry. Help him before he faints dead away," hissed Cmorf.

Morf guided the helpless block of matter that was now the trapped "King Drum" and slid him carefully onto the throne. So far, so good.

"Well, you see, it was all very sudden," Morf concocted quickly. "Day before yesterday, we received news by way of special courier that King Sol had been gravely wounded in a fight against the dragons. The courier declared that King Sol could not return to River Kingdom soon . . . perhaps ever. He sent a request that Lord Drum take over as king until such time as he could return, if he ever can."

"What?" screamed Cmorf. "Are you out of your mind? That was two complete lies, and you know it. Anybody with half a brain will see through them."

"Flexibility is now required," whispered Morf sternly but quietly. "Yes, indeed," murmured Drum gratefully. "I hear you, Morf."

Sir Dipswitch sank into his chair with amazement and ate a crumpet without noticing Drum's momentary panic. He had thought that Drum was a ridiculous choice for Royal Caretaker, but king? That whole idea was impossible to comprehend.

Drum recovered and re established his royal demeanor as he quickly perceived the doubting response. His inner bluffer was ready. It always had been in the past, and practice had made it perfect.

"My dear Dipswitch, I know this is a shock to you. Believe me, it was a shock to me as well. I had no idea that this honor was going to come to me." Drum smiled and looked down at his guest in what he hoped was a kingly gaze. "That is why I am so glad to see you today, sir. You are just the kind of person I need among my friends to work with me in my new administration and 'Make River Kingdom Great.'"

"I was a friend of King Sol," offered Dipswitch. "I can't believe that he may never return to River Kingdom. He was a good king."

"Indeed, you were his friend, and he was a good king," Drum agreed in a mournful tone. "This is why I, *the current King,* stand at the ready now to grant you the land you and your lovely wife desire. That property on the magnificent western shore of The Great River overlooks The River and the Kingdom of Urhonordo to the east. It is, of course, a coveted spot. I am sure that King Sol would have wanted you to have it.

"And because you are a man of wealth and understanding, I know that you were ready to offer a generous amount for that land. In light of this most recent sad development, however, I want you to do me a favor, though. I am also requesting an *additional* sum, which I will send straight to Dragon Quest so that every comfort can be provided for our wounded King."

Lord Dipswitch was caught off guard. "An additional sum?"

"Yes. As a friend of King Sol . . . and myself, I was sure that you would insist on such a contribution."

Sir Dipswitch hesitated. "Well, I . . ."

"And for an additional small fee, I have made special arrangements for my Royal Guard to deliver many large loads of rock and clay suitable for the construction of your manor house and retaining wall. I knew you would be pleased."

"A small fee . . . ?"

"Yes. Not much for a person such as yourself at your grand . . . new . . . sunny location near The Border. Your wife liked the view, and you were thinking of planting fruit trees, as I remember."

Lord Dipswitch was not in Drum's negotiating league. "Well, yes. My wife does think—"

"Exactly. This climate will please your lovely wife and you will have an eager workforce in the nearby Lowlanders to assist with the planting of your trees. It should be a spectacular residence for a man in your position." Sensing some hesitation, Drum needed to top off his kingly negotiation. "*And* speaking of position, in *this* location, you would definitely need to become a member of my Royal Advisors . . . The Royal Advisor of Border Relations." "The Royal Advisor of Border Relations?" Sir Dipswitch swallowed hard. "But I don't know anything about The Border. I have never visited

Urhonordo, and I have never even talked to a Lowlander."

"That is why I am appointing you." Drum smiled. "You will be looking at The Border with Urhonordo and those little Lowland people with new eyes, ready to solve any problems there with a fresh perspective. What do you say? A new manor house and a new title all at the same time."

Drum smiled broadly at Lord Dipswitch. Lord Dipswitch smiled back. Dipswitch now fell to one knee. "I would be honored," he said solemnly. "Of course, I would like to collect the contribution to The King's Recovery Fund, etc., right away due to the immediate need, but this will not be a problem for a man of substance such as yourself, I'm sure." Bingo. This summed it up. This was the art of the deal.

"That sounds like a wonderful concept," crooned Sir Dipswitch. "I would be honored to take the lead at The Border and be of any assistance possible to poor King Sol. I will have the money forwarded to you, Your Highness, immediately."

"I knew I could count on you," responded Drum. The deal was set. Drum breathed a sigh of relief as the happy gentleman was guided toward the doorway by Morf.

The Auras were ecstatic. It hadn't taken Drum long, and this was what they had been waiting for. Small lies and promises were one thing, but this was big. Drum had made himself into a king. Then he had parlayed his self- anointed kingship into a great financial win, and one of his major doubters had bought the whole thing. *The whole thing!* If Drum had succeeded with this first negotiation, there was no limit to what more he could do. The Auras knew now that they were on fertile ground.

Morf was also impressed . . . with himself. Drum had survived a near catastrophe and "stuck" a winning landing. And Morf had been part of it. *I am becoming essential,* he thought.

"Don't get too impressed," counseled Cmorf. "I heard the lie you told to rescue Drum, and by my count, Drum lied at least three more times after that. These lies are not something to be proud of."

But Morf continued to be impressed. *This guy can make people do anything he wants them to do, he thought. He is smooth, but dangerous. It is far better to be for him than against him.*

"You were over the top, today," scolded Cdrum when they were alone. "I couldn't even get a word in. What was going on with all this lying and grabbing off money for stuff that isn't yours? Are you going to keep on pretending to be king? You used to tell harmless lies, but now you've advanced to a bigger league."

"I'm good at it, that's all. I've always been good at negotiating, and now I'm even better. Probably the best there ever was," Drum answered with a shrug. "And I *am* the King now, if you haven't noticed. I can do whatever I want."

"You're not the King. That's not the way it's supposed to work," said Cdrum.

"That's the way it works now." Drum smirked. "What's *your* excuse?" Cmorf asked Morf.

19

Kingly Decisions

The overly warm spring evolved into a boiling summer in River Kingdom. The Lowlanders' hard work on the levees continued as scheduled and was almost completed. With the abundant water, additional furrows were dug for the expansion of several manors. Crops were growing lush. Harvest of some early vegetables was even beginning already. Drum continued to act as king, enjoying the perks of royalty, the "news-sharing" dancing girls, and frequent rallies with his beloved farmers.

Flawless and Will continued to meet in the garden, in the hall, and by The River. They saw each other nearly every day, and there was no doubt that their love was blooming as much as Will's flower garden.

Flawless was aware that her father had only declared himself king, but she was not too worried about it. "It's only temporary," she told Will as they walked together in the garden. "He is just having a good time. He will give the crown back to King Sol when he returns. Right now, King Sol doesn't even know about it so it's not a problem. It's just a game."

Flawless's Conscience wasn't so sure. "What you are saying is what King Sol doesn't know won't hurt him, right?"

It was just then that Will asked, "Are you saying that what King Sol doesn't know won't hurt him?"

Flawless laughed out loud. "That's what my Conscience just asked me." She giggled.

"Well, it's a good question. Your father isn't legally a king, you know. I don't think he expects to do anything really bad, but I've noticed that he makes up his mind to say things or do things on the spur of the moment all the time, and *sometimes* things don't work the way he thinks it will. He doesn't think things through."

Flawless was a loyal daughter. She looked sideways at Will. "Like what?" she asked.

"Like saying that it was okay for the farmers to dig the levees all the way down and make the Lowlanders work on the levees 24/7. I had to go out that night and correct what he said."

"Is that what you did?" Flawless asked. "Yep."

"Good. That's why Daddy made you the Ag Advisor. He had fun saying what he said, and you took care of the details. See? It all worked out." Flawless smiled engagingly at Will. It was hard to argue with her beautiful logic.

But Will was still more than a little concerned. Drum had promised to pay the Lowlanders when the levee work was completed, and the time would soon be upon them. Will remembered the problems he had had getting his farm hands paid for work on Drum Manor Estates. He hoped there would be no problems with "King Drum" for the Lowlanders who were definitely counting on their payment to get them through the winter. But the weather was still warm, and the Lowlanders continued to work hard. They were now finishing large manor expansions. The lords and barons and other assorted aristocrats were taking advantage of the increased water now available from The River's more generous levees.

King Drum was a happy monarch. If Drum heard of any problems, he would just shake his head and explain that this problem had been caused by the previous administration and he was now going to fix it immediately. No one would do anything and soon the problem would be forgotten, but no one seemed to care. And the peasants loved Drum, so what could go wrong? Marvin, the Royal Finance Advisor, did not love Drum. He was continuously sounding the alarm about

Drum's increased spending. His rallies were numerous and costly. He had ordered the Lowlanders' work schedule to be prolonged due to the manor expansions. The Lowlanders had now worked long enough to be earning actual coin in addition to their

winter food supply although they had not been paid anything yet.

The Royal Guard was spending longer and more costly periods of time down south at the building site of the new Dipswitch Manor and the oil in The Castle lanterns seemed to always be burning. The Royal Storehouses were literally being emptied, and Marvin didn't accept Drum as King either though he had held his tongue.

At last Marvin was fed up. He needed to speak with King Drum, and he needed to do so immediately. At least that is what he explained to Morf. Morf, as was his custom, greeted Marvin who had aimed himself toward the throne room curtains, armed with ledgers and paperwork. This new King, or whatever he called himself, was a financial disaster, and Marvin needed to get him back in line before it was too late.

Morf stood in front of Marvin, barring the entryway, but he smiled in his most engaging fashion. He was aware that his colleague was upset, but the King was enjoying a morning of watching some particularly entertaining dancing girls and listening to some very flattering news they had gathered from the farmers. He would not appreciate an irate Finance Advisor at this time.

Morf had settled into his role as primary supporter/protector of "King Drum" with comfort. He made it his habit to seldom disagree with Drum, even though Drum frequently told outrageous lies and was almost never consistent. The Kingdom seemed to be humming along just fine so Morf had little trouble being somewhat of a lapdog.

Cmorf was fairly disgusted with Morf's submissive behavior, but had reduced his nagging due to the fact that it didn't seem to do any good. In addition, fawning wasn't exactly illegal. It was just embarrassing.

Morf had become particularly good at calming the ruffled feathers of disgruntled visitors before they got to Drum. Flareups with other members of what was now "The Drum Administration" usually came and went as Morf patiently explained that complaining wasn't going to change anything unless what they wanted was what King Drum also wanted—and positive changes were billed as Drum's idea.

Today, it was only the Financial Advisor again. Morf had dealt with him numerous times. Morf put an arm around the tense shoulder of the determined Advisor. "You have yourself all fired up, Marvin," he said gently. "Why don't you give me your paperwork and let me present it to King Drum. He appreciates all your hard work, and he knows that you two need to talk. When he has reviewed everything, I will call you, and you can work out some of the solutions you seek."

Marvin noticed that Morf spent a lot of time with Drum. Morf was like Drum's shadow. He had been a good man in the past. What role was he playing now? Marvin looked at Morf suspiciously. "That's what you said last week. You seem to spend more time with Drum and understand him better than the rest of us," Marvin commented. "How do you do it?"

"I just try to stay creative and flexible." Morf shrugged.

"And you suck up all the time. That's what you really do," added Cmorf. "Now that Drum acts like a king, you're selling out to a fraud." Morf ignored him.

"Alright," Marvin grumbled. "Leaving the paperwork might be a good way to do this, but I am concerned about this 'King Drum.' What does he know about finance? Does he realize that he has promised more than the contents of one whole storehouse of food for the costs of the levees being lowered? Meanwhile, he has spent enormous amounts on pleasure—like dancers. Dancers? I can't find a logical justification for that. And then there's that new game with the little white ball and a stick. Lately, he has taken to playing with that on The Castle lawn instead of doing the work of The Kingdom at all. Resources are getting dangerously low, and he doesn't seem to be paying attention. He has no right to bankrupt The Kingdom completely. Does he really think he is the King?"

"Yes," said Morf calmly.

"Pish tosh!" fussed Marvin. "Did you know that there is a manor house being built with rock and clay that's being transported by the Royal Guard at the expense of The Kingdom? Did you know that? We were paying the Royal Guard to take the building materials down to The Border and now they are still down there working. Who bought that service? And where is the payment for that clay and rock? Where are those payments going? I need to see the paperwork."

Morf gulped. What? Did Drum know that Marvin knew all this? This was what Drum had agreed to with Lord Dipswitch. Morf had to think quickly.

"The Royal Border Advisor is doing The Kingdom a service by supervising The Border with The Lowlands and Urhonordo. You don't expect him to sleep on the bare ground and have no troops to protect him while he does that, do you?"

Marvin raised his eyebrows. "I didn't expect a 'Border Advisor' in the first place," he said. "Tell the King that I will be back to discuss his need to cut back *and* keep me informed about any payments paid *and* received *tomorrow*. The budget cannot stand for any more of his reckless financial decisions."

The Royal Finance Advisor dropped his ledgers and papers at Morf's feet, turned on his heel with a threatening glare, and marched down the hall in a huff.

Morf hauled the heavy ledgers through the draperies at the throne room door and placed them carefully to one side. The area in front of King Drum was occupied by the dancing girls and their reports of "news of the day." They were covered or nearly covered by an assortment of feathers and silk. It was a glorious sight and it happened on a regular basis, but Morf never tired of it.

DRUM 4: THE DANCING GIRLS

It was only after thoroughly enjoying the sight of the girls that Morf focused on who else was in the room. It was Milton Fandango, the nervous little man with the feathered hat that Morf had met on inauguration day months ago. What in the world was he doing here in the throne room?

Then it came to him: feathers on a hat . . . dancing girls in feathers. The "feather man" was merely a vendor who furnished the girls that Drum was listening to and happily watching almost daily. He was not even an aristocrat.

King Drum was in a very good mood. Morf guessed he had been too enthralled with the girls to take notice of Fandango. He would ask him to leave and come back later.

Morf's Conscience was on duty today and snapped Morf to attention. "Speak up, Morf. Don't worry about the weird little man." Cmorf nudged. "It's your duty to let Drum know about the serious problems with the budget. Quit watching the girls and tend to business."

Morf sidled carefully up to the side of the throne. "Your Majesty, I am sorry to interrupt, but I need to make you aware of some information that may be important." He stepped back and waited.

"Can't you see that I'm busy?" asked Drum without taking his eyes off the girls.

"Yes, indeed, but I feel that I should let you know about anything that may eventually cause you trouble." Morf stood on one foot and then the other.

Amazingly, Milton Fandango spoke up. "Your King has told you he is busy," he said in a whiney, nasal voice. "What your King wants to do, he should be allowed to do. My girls are here. This is what he wants to do. You should respect that."

Morf almost flew at the man with his fists. How dare this man with the feathers and the nervous mannerisms speak to a Royal Advisor that way? He had no standing. He was just entertainment.

But the feather man's comments did not seem to raise any problem with Drum. As a matter of fact, Drum smiled at him with approval.

"Did you hear that, Morf? That is the voice of a man who knows how to treat a king. He's got respect. I like that in a man."

Morf glared at the feather man in disgust, but said nothing. Milton Fandango smiled a strangely knowing smile and ignored Morf. "Would you like the girls to begin another dance, Your Majesty? They have a dance with more feathers or less, whichever you prefer."

Drum laughed out loud. "You are too good at what you do, Milton. Your girls are my favorite part of the day. But Morf here has something to discuss that he feels is very important, so I guess we should listen to him." Sir Fandango lowered his eyes respectfully, but glanced sideways at Morf with a sneer.

"Don't say a thing," Cmorf counseled him. "For some reason, the King likes him."

Morf cleared his throat. "Thank you, Your Majesty. I do need to speak of something important. I will wait until Sir Fandango and his ladies leave as it is a very private matter." He crossed his arms and stared at the feather man, but the feather man was not budging.

"Oh, you don't need to wait," said Drum in a relaxed manner. "Milton is here nearly every day. He and his girls hear everything that is worth hearing in the entire Kingdom and report it straight to me. I'm sure that he can hear anything *you* need to say, Morf."

Morf's jaw dropped. He clenched his fists. Milton Fandango was only a back-channel gossiper. He had no right to know the King's business. "But, King Drum, I…"

"Come on, Morf. Tell me what you think is so important. If it's that important, tell me what it is."

Morf took a deep breath and stared again at Fandango, but began. "Your Royal Finance Advisor was just here, sir," Morf began. "He was not happy. He feels that The Kingdom is spending too much of its storehouse reserves . . . on things like *dancing girls*." Morf stopped for emphasis, hoping that Drum would tell the little man to leave now that he knew the discussion was about finances.

But Morf was wrong. Drum simply scratched his chin and looked at Morf from under his eyebrows. "How many storehouses do we have, would you say, Morf?"

Morf looked at Fandango again and said quietly to Drum, "That's kind of a secret, wouldn't you say, sir?"

"I told you, I'm not worried about Milton. He's a good man. Now, how many storehouses do we have?"

"I'm not sure," Morf stammered. "I never counted them. But there are many . . . perhaps as many as five—"

"I thought there were a lot, and we've emptied one." Drum grinned. "So what's the problem?"

Morf was ready to make his point. "The Royal Financial Advisor says that you have already promised one storehouse for the anticipated cost of levees that will soon be completed. He also worries about the cost of the Royal Guard transporting rubble down to the manor house being built at The Border. He says that you are spending too much too fast," Morf blurted. That speech got Drum's attention. "What did you say?" Drum growled. "Who are you to tell the King when he is spending too much? Who do you think you are?"

Morf was immediately terrified. He had said too much. What should he do? The stupid feather man was chuckling in the corner, his feather-dressed dancing girls clustered behind him.

"It wasn't me that said such a thing," Morf squeaked. "It was the Finance Advisor. He's the one that said those things."

King Drum did not like to be criticized. He had never liked it. He had never actually experienced much of it, at least to his face. But he did know that as king, he shouldn't have to stand for any of it. "We have five storehouses or more, right? Why should I worry about using up one of them, then? The harvest will soon fill it up again. You say that the Finance Advisor thinks I should change my ways?"

"Yes, sir." Morf was trembling. "He left his paperwork here for you to see and said he would be back tomorrow. He was very angry. That's why I suggested that he come back tomorrow."

"He was angry with me, you say?" mumbled Drum.

"Yessir. He said he wouldn't stand for this kind of spending."

"Fine," concluded Drum. "I can see to it that he won't have to stand for anything like that anymore. I am the King, and I can spend what I want. Wouldn't you say, Milton?"

"Absolutely. That is exactly what I would say, Your Majesty," Milton answered smugly.

Morf clenched his teeth.

"Say something," whispered Cmorf. "Marvin is a friend of yours. He shouldn't be bad-mouthed over just telling the truth."

"The Royal Finance Advisor has been here at The Castle for a very long time, sir. Maybe if you just talked to him—"

"Are you trying to tell me what to do, Morf?" "No, sir."

"Good. In that case, I will tell you. Run down to the Royal Finance Advisor's quarters and tell him to pack his things. I have a new Finance Advisor that will be moving in tomorrow, someone who knows what I like."

King Drum smiled. He didn't need to have advisors who were trying to tell him how to do things.

Slowly, Drum turned to Sir Fandango. *Here is a man who knows exactly what I like. He is on my side and will help me do things my way,* Drum thought. "Sir Fandango, how would you like to be my new Royal Finance Advisor?"

The deed was done. Marvin was out. Milton was in.

Will was shocked when the Finance Advisor was replaced by Milton Fandango. The new man had a rather seedy reputation and didn't seem to know much about finance. Until now, he had spent most of his time shuffling some beautiful girls in and out of The Castle. Now there would be no more shuffling of girls *out* of The Castle as the elevated "Sir" Fandango and his girls had found lodging in The Castle in Marvin's richly furnished rooms and just down the hall from Flawless.

The girls made friends with Flawless who was happy to see more females nearby. The new developments didn't seem right to Will, and Cwill rolled his eyes frequently. But Will was busy with the farmers, the Lowlanders, and the levees, and he felt that Sir Fandango and the dancing girls weren't his business.

20

The Queen's Call

The work on the levees was long and exhausting. Ben had grown into his role of levee supervisor for the Lowlanders and was usually very happy with it. There were times, however, when he had to advise his workers and the farmers that they could not lower too much of a levee. He watched carefully. He knew there was only a certain amount of water in The River, and some of it belonged to the Urhonordos on the other side—and the Lowlanders. Will and Ben both knew that was what the new Water Rights Treaty would say although they had yet to see a copy.

It was a shock to all, however, when the Urhonordos crossed The River and proceeded toward The Castle late one afternoon. It was a large but friendly-looking contingent, impressively represented by flags and a well- dressed Royal Guard, their weapons shouldered peacefully on their backs. The Queen of the Urhonordos rode elegantly in a carriage of glistening mahogany emblazoned with her kingdom's royal crest.

Morf rushed into the throne room, breathlessly intent on informing King Drum that his expected company was arriving, but soon he became frantic. "Queen Luna is arriving! She is almost here! We had advance notice of this. Where is the welcoming party that I ordered?"

King Drum yawned and waved his hand lazily in the air. "I know. You told me she was coming several weeks ago, but I cancelled your order for a welcoming party. Don't worry about it. She's just the Queen of a small kingdom, and one that is much less important than ours. She's nothing special. Don't worry about it."

Morf was beside himself. "King Drum, you don't understand. Visits between kingdoms are extremely important. We have treaties and agreements for mutual protection and assistance. There is a definite protocol. These visits cannot be taken lightly."

"They are not important to the big dog in the area," Drum stated with a look of disdain. "River Kingdom is 'the big dog,' but I will provide her a brief audience with me in the throne room. Whatever Queen Luna has to say, I will listen politely, but I don't expect to arrange anything elaborate, and I will not buckle to anything if she has a complaint."

Cdrum gurgled anxiously. "You are only an acting King, you know. You might want to rethink your attitude, Drum," he said. "King Sol would never have behaved this way or said such a thing. He would have been much more respectful of the neighboring kingdom and its monarch. Such alliances are seen as essential to the peace of River Kingdom."

"King Sol was always a wimp, as far as I can see." Drum smirked. "Queen Luna is just a woman with a bunch of land on the other side of my river. She will do as I say and like it. Trust me. Just show the Queen into the waiting room, and I will meet her in my throne room when I am ready to do so." Drum retired to his bedchamber.

Morf was incredulous. He couldn't believe what he had heard from Drum. In the past, as Royal Community Relations Advisor, Morf had made elaborate preparations for visits from other heads of state. These visits were important occasions. Kingdoms needed to display their best royal behaviors and respect the protocols that had been refined for generations. Queen Luna would be offended.

Quickly, Morf pulled on his newest robe and hustled back to The Castle courtyard. Queen Luna was as beautiful and impressive as he remembered her. In soft rose-colored robes, she descended from her carriage and proceeded toward The Castle on the arm of a lady in waiting. If she was surprised that King Drum was not there to greet her as King Sol would have been in the past, she did not show it. She smiled warmly at Morf and even indicated that she remembered him from past visits. Morf was charmed.

Cmorf was in place and at the ready. He felt responsible for helping Morf make a good impression on Queen Luna, particularly since Drum didn't seem inclined to do so. "Send for Flawless," he hissed firmly. "Flawless has a way of making everybody feel welcomed and happy. Drum is not on that page today. Tell Flawless that she is needed to say nice things to the Queen and help her father."

Morf did not waste a minute before doing exactly what Cmorf had suggested, and soon Flawless was there with the lovely Queen, both engaged in friendly chit chat and enjoying each other. Cmorf and Morf congratulated themselves on this excellent outcome from Cmorf's suggestion.

Flawless and Queen Luna were on their second cup of tea when King Drum finally arrived in the throne room. As Queen Luna was escorted in with Flawless, he was cordial, but businesslike. "Welcome, Queen Luna. It is so nice to see you here in The Castle. I see that you've met my daughter. You have been here before, I presume."

"Indeed, I have," answered the Queen with a respectful nod of the head. "But at that time, I visited King Sol, an excellent monarch and neighbor. I see that you now wear the crown of King Sol. May I inquire as to his whereabouts and possible time of return?"

"Unfortunately, we don't expect him to return, Queen Luna. We believe he was overcome by dragons," announced Drum.

Cdrum choked.

Queen Luna stared at Drum in disbelief. Tears rose in her eyes and spilled down her cheeks. Her ladies in waiting rushed to comfort her. Flawless reached out and took her hand. Obviously, Queen Luna had had deep feelings for King Sol. The Queen bowed her head and sat motionless. "I can't believe you said that to her!" hissed Cdrum. "You don't lie to a Queen!"

"He may have even been eaten by dragons, according to the most recent reports we have received from Dragon Quest," Drum continued, relishing his new details and pretended sadness. "At least I hear that he will not be able to return to River Kingdom at all . . . or at least in one piece," announced Drum deliberately.

The Queen gasped.

"I can't believe you just said *that* either," cried Cdrum.

"And *you* are letting him get away with it," blasted Cmorf in Morf's ear.

Queen Luna sobbed. "Eaten by dragons? Are you sure? I can't believe that I never heard this. Why was I not informed as you were?"

"Perhaps *your* messenger didn't make it through," Drum suggested, wiping at a tear but hiding a smile. "We could scarcely go on when we heard. But . . . life here at River Kingdom does go on. The locals insisted that I take over as King since I had been chosen by King Sol to rule while he was gone. I felt obligated to do so."

"Horse pucky!" Cdrum slid down Drum's sleeve and off the throne. He had to leave. As a Conscience, he could only take so much.

Queen Luna was obviously shaken by the image that Drum had presented. Flawless could feel the pain that Luna now showed clearly on her face. And Flawless had not heard this news of the King's final demise either. Now her father really was King. Tragic for King Sol! And how did she feel about her father's position as the real king?

How do I feel about Daddy actually being a king? I don't know. That is not even the most important question right now. How would I feel if I heard something like dragons happened to Will? she wondered. She squeezed Luna's hand with sympathy. She knew she would feel the same, if not worse. Drum was satisfied with the Queen's response. He suspected that the young woman might faint dead away and need to be taken back to her castle to recover, but this was not to be so. Queen Luna dabbed at her eyes again but squared her shoulders and solemnly made ready to address the reason for her visit.

"King Drum then, is it?"

"Indeed. At your service."

"I am pleased to hear you say that, King Drum. As you read in my note to your kingdom, we of Urhonordo have become increasingly concerned by the continued lowering of the levees on your side of The Great River. As you must know, the Water Rights Treaty of The Great River is considered to cover the property of both your kingdom and ours. This, of course, is part of a long-standing series of treaties signed by King Sol and myself." Again, she wiped her eyes.

Drum thought for a moment. He had never read the Water Rights Treaty nor had he read Queen Luna's note. Reading was not a useful pastime for Drum. He preferred to figure out answers to problems as they came to him or were told to him by his "news girls."

Increasingly, he felt that treaties and couriers' messages and budgets were more likely to get in the way of his thinking and much less useful than his own superior ideas. As a genius, his judgment was more appropriate to his desires today than any preexisting treaty could possibly be.

"Of course, I have read it thoroughly, but here is the problem," Drum fabricated believably. "You see, madam, this treaty of which you speak was signed by you and King Sol, not by me. As you can undoubtedly understand, I cannot and will not be held to a promise that someone else made for *my* kingdom. *My* farmers wanted more water for their crops. The crops of River Kingdom must be my first concern." He gazed over her head in a kingly way and appeared resolute.

Queen Luna's face stiffened, and her lips drew into a straight line. She was shocked by this dismissive speech from Drum, but she was a lady. She would act with dignity.

"I understand that you only recently became king, and I congratulate you on your new position, King Drum, but surely you must understand that treaties are made between kingdoms, not individuals. This agreement was established so that the flow of The Great River would be shared equally between both of our great kingdoms. It clearly states that neither side can change its levees without consulting with the other.

"Some of the levees on your side are taking too much of the water and reducing the flow to some of our farms. The situation is not severe as yet, but this is the reason for my visit. By treaty, this would be an ideal time for your Royal Agriculture Advisor and mine to get together and work out a plan that is fair to both kingdoms."

"This treaty was made by King Sol . . . someone who isn't here anymore," replied Drum with cruel clarity. "What King Sol thought was beneficial to River Kingdom is no longer something that River Kingdom needs to live by."

Queen Luna stood and smoothed her skirts in calm fury. This man had no respect for The River, much less Royal Protocol and Treaties. He was obviously ignorant and oblivious as well as unconcerned with any harm that his actions might cause her kingdom. He was a newly installed, uncivilized creature that was going to endanger a relationship that had existed peacefully for years.

The Queen nodded to her traveling party. She would leave now and discuss this with *her* Royal Advisors, soon to determine a response that would take this idiot's behavior into account.

This treaty is rubbish, thought King Drum to himself. *I refuse to be governed by an emotional young woman and an old agreement that doesn't fit my current needs. My farmers like me. They want more water. If they want more water, they shall have it.*

Drum watched as the Queen prepared to exit with controlled anger. Morf was not saying anything, but Drum could see fear and worry on his face. This was probably not a good thing. Morf had been around for a while and knew some things about other kingdoms and their ways. If he was frightened, there might be a safer way to go right now. *Stall and dance, concluded Drum. Tell the Queen what she wants to hear and then . . . do what you want to do. That's the smartest plan for today.*

"I hear what you say, Queen Luna," said Drum, adopting a more agreeable tone. "And of course, I respect your position and that of your wonderful kingdom. For this reason, I will send my Ag Advisor to your side of The River immediately for talks on this issue. When would you like to begin?"

Queen Luna turned and squinted at Drum. This was an abrupt change of approach. Was the man serious? Could someone who changed his attitude and demeanor this quickly be trusted?

Morf was also watching and breathed a sigh of relief at Drum's words. Drum didn't realize that other kingdoms took treaties so seriously. Wars had been started over water rights.

Morf scooted forward. Again, he employed his signature bow, but now to both monarchs. With a sweeping gesture, he offered a peaceful piece of protocol. "If I may be of service, I would be most happy to bring *our* people to *your* people at your earliest convenience, Your Majesty."

Drum took his cue from Morf. "Indeed, Queen Luna. We here at River Kingdom are ready to meet you at any location of your choosing so that we may all be satisfied with the future use of The Great River."

Queen Luna listened and appeared to relax as did her entourage. This sounded better. This sounded more like the reception she was accustomed to. "I would be pleased to arrange a meeting with your Royal Agricultural Advisor as soon as possible," she stated. "I am sure that your advisor understands the reasoning behind the treaty as does mine. They have worked together in the past. Please ask your gentleman to contact mine so that they can arrange their meeting. Thank you for your time, King Drum."

With that, she nodded and swept from the throne room. This king was odd, she was in mourning, and she didn't see any reason to delay.

Flawless joined Queen Luna at the door of the throne room and escorted her gracefully to her carriage. She too had been listening to her father's conversation. She would need to make sure that Will heard what Drum had proposed. Will had been obligated to a visit with a queen for a very important discussion. He would want to prepare.

That night, Flawless and Will met in Will's garden. This had become a nightly ritual for the young couple. The roses were now at the height of their beauty, and their fragrance wafted through the garden. The pair seated themselves on a crude bench that Will had constructed for them.

"I need to give you a heads-up," Flawless began. "Queen Luna visited The Castle today."

"I heard about that," said Will. "What was the reason for the visit? Did she just want to meet the 'new' King?"

"The poor woman didn't even know there was a new king," Flawless responded. "She primarily came to talk about water rights and levees. It seems there's a Water Rights Treaty between us and Urhonordo."

"Yeah. I knew there was a treaty, but I've never seen it. I think it just means that both kingdoms share the water from The River. That doesn't sound too complicated."

"I think you are mostly right," agreed Flawless, "but apparently, the levees have been maintained at one height for years and the treaty says that they can't be changed without consultation and agreement between both sides . . . *before* any change is made."

"Oh, . . . *before* it's done? That's not good. We're already doing it."

"I know. So the Queen said that our Ag Advisor should meet with theirs right away and Morf will probably be looking for you tomorrow to set up a time for you to meet."

"I'm not really sure how to do that. I've never met with a Queen before, and I never even found the papers that contained the old treaty and I've never seen the new treaty. I feel pretty ignorant."

"The old treaty may not work anyway." Flawless sighed. "My father likes to make up his own rules about everything. I'm afraid he was never told no much as a child or an adult. He has never had to follow anybody else's rules about anything. Maybe you and Queen Luna can make up a new Water Rights Treaty. I spent time with her today. You'll like her. She's very nice."

"Well, it sounds like your father has already agreed to this meeting," mused Will. "When do you think he wants me to go?"

"If I know my father, maybe never." Flawless sighed. "What do you mean 'never'?"

"I mean, he doesn't really care if you go or not. He doesn't think it's important. He's determined to keep the levees the way that his farmers want, regardless of any treaty. He is much more concerned about the happiness of his loyal peasants and farmers than he is about the Queen of Urhonordo. He would rather hold a rally than worry about a treaty."

Will laughed and agreed, but this presented a big question for him. He was beginning to have a better understanding of this man that had employed him for so many years, but he had no idea how to proceed now. This man would not agree to anything that wasn't his idea. Cwill was also in a quandary.

"This is weird," commented Cwill. "Your boss has committed you to a meeting that *he* doesn't really care about. Does he care what you *say*, then? What are you going to do? How do you negotiate a Water Rights Treaty between a kingdom that thinks it's important and one that doesn't? Do you think it's important?"

Flawless was embarrassed. It was clear that her father had put Will in an odd position. "What do you think, Will? Do you think you should meet with the Queen?"

"I don't have any choice, as far as I can see it." Will shrugged. "Your father has said it will happen." Will's voice became strong. He, as a farmer of The Kingdom, knew this was a meeting of importance, even if Drum didn't. The use of The River was a major farming issue for both kingdoms. "This meeting should have happened long ago," he stated.

Will had respect for River Kingdom and the Urhonordos. River Kingdom had broken a treaty. They didn't mean to do anything wrong, but they did. And he was the person who was in charge of what they had done wrong. Will truly had no choice.

"I will talk to Morf tomorrow when he gets the meeting set up," Will said. "Hopefully he can help me work out a solution that the Queen and your dad will both accept. An apology from me to start will be the first order of business."

Flawless nodded. "As long as you don't expect one from my dad," she added. "He's never been good at apologies. He never believes he has done anything wrong." She laughed. Flawless was recognizing some traits in her father that she had not really noticed before.

Will sat quietly, mulling over the idea of broken treaties and the flow of The River itself. The spell of his meeting with Flawless was gone for the night. It happened so quickly that Flawless was sad. She wished she had waited to tell him her news until later. Slowly, Flawless gave Will a small kiss on the cheek and was already heading back to The Castle when a loud, crashing noise was heard on the other side of the garden.

Will and Flawless turned just in time to see Ben crashing through the bushes, landing on a pile of tools. "Why don't you pick up your tools, Will? Or do you leave them in a pile so that thieves will fall on them? Is that your strategy?"

Ben laughed and untangled himself from a pick and shovel. "I was trying to sneak up on you two and catch you kissing, but I fell over your booby-trap."

"If you killed yourself by trying to sneak up on us, you would deserve it." Will snickered.

"Hi, Ben," said Flawless. "I'm afraid there isn't going to be much kissing tonight."

"Oh, that's too bad. I had something serious that I wanted to tell Will, but I was hoping to have some fun first."

"What do you need to say, Ben? I've got a lot on my mind right now, so I don't really want to talk about stuff."

"I just needed to tell you that since you are the Ag Advisor now, some of your plans for lowering the levees may have run into a snag down at The Border."

"I already know that I have some trouble with the levees. It's all about water rights. The Queen of Urhonordo just paid King Drum a visit and told him that we have broken a treaty with them. Now I have to go to her and figure out what to do to make it up to her and fix the treaty."

"A broken treaty with a queen, huh? I guess that's a pretty important problem up here. But that's not your only water problem, I'm afraid. You know that rubble that we're clearing away from the levees? Well, it's being dumped down at The Border."

"I know. That's where the King said he wanted it. Some guy is building a house with it, I hear."

"Yeah? Well, I guess it seemed like a good idea to King Drum, but he didn't even think about what that house might do to us."

"Who?"

"Us Lowlanders . . . and Urhonordo too. The rubble is being used to build a huge manor house, alright, but they have planted the house and the retaining wall right where it blocks the water to The Lowlands. We already didn't have much water down there. Now there is going to be less. By fall, there won't be any."

"Oh my god. That's terrible," groaned Will. "Really? Where is the water going to go if it's blocked? You can't totally block a river."

"Right. The River's already starting to ooze toward the levees of Urhonordo."

Will shook his head. "That's bad. The Royal Guard should have been told to keep the rubble out of the riverbed. What were they thinking?"

"That sounds like my father's friend wasn't thinking about anything but himself . . . and maybe his wife," agreed Flawless. "Someone should tell him to fix this right away."

"Let me see," whispered Cwill to Will smugly. "The River is under the jurisdiction of the Ag Advisor, right? First, there are unpermitted levees up and down The River. Then there is a new manor house being built at The Border that's blocking lowland water. If I've got this right, I think the new Royal Ag Advisor just blew it again. How does it feel to be a big cheese now?"

Will bowed his head. *Not so good,* he thought.

"This is my fault too," said Will. "I knew that the rubble was going down there, but I was just glad to get rid of it. I should have made sure that it wasn't going to cause a worse problem down south than it was causing up here. Queen Luna must not even know about The Border yet or she would have said something to King Drum about that too. This adds another issue to our Water Rights Treaty meeting, for sure."

"Oh, Will, . . . Ben. I'm so sorry. I know my father didn't intend for this to happen," contributed Flawless. "How could Lord Dipswitch and the Royal Guard have been so thoughtless?"

"I just assumed that your father warned the guard and the rich guy not to block the water of The River," moaned Will. "It didn't even occur to me that they would do that."

Flawless sighed sadly. "Remember what you said about Daddy not thinking about consequences? He was so excited about his business deal that he probably never thought about The River."

Will smiled a little but closed his eyes and sat down hard again on the bench. Flawless sat down again as well. Ben just stood in front of them and felt bad. Both were his friends now, and he had brought them news that meant trouble. Ben thought that he had drawn the short straw that ruined what might have been a romantic night. He didn't know that he had just added a problem to problems that the couple was already facing.

21

Water Rights

The next morning, Will was at the throne room early, insisting to see King Drum. Morf was there too, refusing to let him in. "Come on, Morf. This is important. It's about the Water Rights Treaty."

"I know, I know. But you don't need to see *King Drum,*" Morf whispered. "You just need to see me. I am the one that spoke to Queen Luna about arranging a meeting with you so I am the one that will do that . . . very quietly. King Drum is not in favor of it. Just go down the hall where we can talk privately. By the way, you haven't seen a copy of the old Water Rights Treaty with Urhonordo, have you?"

"No, I haven't. I think Arnold took it with him. He wasn't too happy when he got replaced. I thought you and the King might have a copy."

"I haven't found one, and the King doesn't read anything so his files are a mess. Incoming messages, budgets, treaties—they're all just piled up. He isn't interested in that stuff. But I think you and I can work this out with Queen Luna. She has always seemed pretty reasonable, and I'm sure she has a copy of the treaty. We'll just look at her copy and go from there."

"No, we will not 'go from there.'"

Drum's head popped through the heavy curtains of the throne room, nightcap and all. "We are not going to look for a copy of the treaty, and we are not going to meet with any Urhonordos to talk about it."

Drum turned and marched back into the throne room. Will and Morf shrugged and followed obediently.

Drum removed his nightcap and put on his crown. He was an odd sight in his bedclothes and crown ensemble, but this was not a time to laugh.

Maybe he isn't entirely awake, thought Morf.

Maybe he is sleepwalking, thought Will.

But Drum was entirely awake. In fact, he had been awake most of the night. "That no-count little woman from the other side of The River is not going to tell King Doran Drum what to do," he barked. "Who does she think she is? She has nothing to say about what we do. River Kingdom is the biggest, richest kingdom there is, and there is not one thing that that foolish female has to say about what we do with *our* water."

Will stopped in his tracks. "Don't buckle, Will," whispered Cwill. "You know this is important."

Morf's jaw dropped. Cmorf jumped into Morf's ear. "This is Queen Luna that Drum is talking about!" Cmorf hissed to Morf. "He can't just ignore her. She is a *queen.* You *know* she has fighting troops. You don't just blow off a treaty that was signed with a woman like that."

"Wipe that stupid look off your face, Morf," growled Drum. "You're looking at *your* King, here. I make the rules in River Kingdom. No one else. Especially not a flimsy female from a forgotten little kingdom. This is just another unimportant business deal. They want it. We don't. Urhonordo would be nothing if River Kingdom was not here to protect it. It is about time that they figured that out."

Will stood quietly against a wall. He didn't like the sound of this, but he also didn't want to disrespect King Drum. He would wait for his moment. Morf had finally recovered enough to plead. "But, sir. I heard you promise that you would have our Ag Advisor meet with their Ag Advisor.

If we don't do what you say we are going to do, other kingdoms will lose faith in us."

"I never said such a thing," said Drum calmly. "Where did you get such an idea? I know better than to promise something that I would never do. That's fake news."

Cmorf spoke up. "Don't let him deny what he said. He's lying. You were there. I was there. We know what we heard."

Morf had to say something. "Maybe you didn't mean it the way it sounded, but you really *did* say that you would have our Royal Agriculture Advisor speak to theirs, and I said that I would arrange it."

"Look," said Drum. "I don't know what you said. I can't be responsible for that, but I never said that I would meet with anyone regarding the levees. Wherever you heard that, it was a hoax."

Morf stood back and dropped his head. "I am sure that you are correct, Your Highness." Cmorf was silent. There was nothing more he could think of to say.

It was at that very moment that a commotion was heard in the hall outside the throne room. The guards were holding someone at bay, but whoever it was, he was not giving up quietly.

"I am the Royal Border Advisor! Do you hear me? I don't care what you say. I am a Royal Advisor to King Drum, and I will not be treated this way! Ask King Drum if you don't believe me!"

Much scrambling and shuffling and shouting followed. Morf ran gratefully from the throne room. He could handle the banishment of unwanted intruders more easily than he could deal with Drum right now.

"What's going on out here?" Morf shouted above the melee. Then he saw at once what was going on. It was Sir Dipswitch, sprawled facedown on the floor in front of two Royal Guardsmen but still full of righteous indignation.

"Unhand me, you lawless ruffians! Wait until King Drum hears about this. You will all be thrown in the dungeon. I am a very important person!" This last pronouncement drew Drum out of the throne room immediately.

Since his poorly attended inauguration, anyone who thought they were "a very important person" was no longer important in Drum's eyes. He had just dismissed a queen. All the aristocrats and royalty that he had tried to impress before needed to try to impress *him* now or get out of his way. He was king.

But peeking out into the hallway, Drum suddenly realized that this man was in fact important. *This* was personal. *This* man meant business . . . his business. There was money involved. *Drum's* money. It was Lord Dipswitch. "Oh, I am so sorry, Lord Dipswitch," Drum said quickly. "My men didn't recognize you, sir. Here, let me help you up from the floor." He reached down a hand to pull the humiliated Dipswitch to his feet. Hat, cape, satchel, and shawl were quickly reassembled by the Guardsmen from the various parts of the hall floor onto which they had been flung.

Lord Dipswitch brushed away Drum's hand and rose, still in a red haze of the fury that he had not yet spent. He was ready to unload.

"What kind of Castle is this godforsaken place? Is there no discipline? Is there no understanding of proper treatment of important persons . . . no decorum, no training? Has the whole Castle gone to hell?"

Drum looked at the man and smiled. "Blame it on the previous administration," he stated. "The staff was like this when I got here. I can't change everything in just a month or two."

Sir Dipswitch regained a bit of his composure. "Sorry, Drum . . . not your fault . . . bad training . . . right," he mumbled.

"*King* Drum, if you please," Drum reminded Dipswitch.

"Yes. To be sure, *King* Drum," Dipswitch echoed contritely.

DIPSWITCH MANOR

Drum turned and walked into the throne room as Lord Dipswitch followed determinedly behind.

Will and Morf now retreated to an inconspicuous corner of the throne room. Will didn't know who this man was, but Will was here on a mission and he wasn't going to leave.

Morf recognized the man, and although he didn't particularly like him, he knew he shouldn't leave either. Drum was still in his nightclothes. Things were already not going well today. He had no idea what to expect.

Drum climbed onto his throne, and his bedclothes were soon covered by a more regal robe that a servant had quickly found for him. He assumed a pose of authority and looked at Lord Dipswitch. "Well?" he said.

Dipswitch was a man of means. He had not acquired these means by being unclear or indirect. And he was angry. He came straight to the point. "The progress on my manor house is being slowed by some scruffy, no-count Lowlanders, and you need to do something about it," he growled. "Lowlanders? What have Lowlanders got to do with your manor house?" inquired Drum with businesslike concern.

"That's what I asked them," agreed Dipswitch. "There I was, standing on my own King-approved land, building my own King-approved home with the rock and clay that you sold me and what happens? A handful of Lowlanders, mostly women and children, mind you, descend upon my workers in tears, sobbing that I am stealing their water. Can you believe it? My workers and I did not lay a hand on their water. All the water we were working with was on my side of my manor house wall, and it is currently forming a lovely pool. My wife is thrilled. Almost none of our water was on their side of my house."

Cwill heard and was immediately in action. "Did you hear that? That's what Ben was talking about. This dummy is damming up The River so that it can't get to The Lowlands. He's cutting The Lowlands off, the whole country."

Will was already rushing to the middle of the throne room. "King Drum, did I hear this gentleman correctly? Is he cutting off all the Lowlanders' water?"

"Of course, he's not doing such a thing!" declared Drum indignantly. "Who is spreading such a ridiculous accusation? That is another hoax."

"That's what I said," agreed Sir Dipswitch with indignation. "Those Lowlander women had absolutely no right to claim that they owned The Great River."

Will stood still in the middle of the room that seemed to be descending into a ridiculous argument. "Simmer down," advised his Conscience. "Just relax until you can find out the truth or something close to it at least."

"Just what, exactly, is happening to the water, sir?" asked Will quietly.

He was shocked at his own calm voice.

But Drum was not in the mood to be calm. "That's none of your business, young man. I allowed a house to be built by my friend, Lord Dipswitch, here. That's what you're doing, right, Dipswitch? Of course, you are because I, the King, told you that you could. We have a deal. You have the Royal Guard down there delivering rubble and helping out if I remember that correctly. If a gaggle of little Lowlanders bothers you, tell the Royal Guard to get them out of the way. Tell them that the King said so."

Sir Dipswitch nodded in triumph. "That's exactly what I thought you would say, Your Highness. It will be done."

"But the women and children of The Lowlands, Your Highness? They need their water," began Will.

"Who are you again? And what do you have to do with this?" Drum bellowed at Will.

"I am William of Dale, sir, your Royal Agriculture Advisor."

"Oh yes. Now I remember. Flawless likes you. Why are you here again?" "I am here because of a Water Rights meeting that is needed with Queen Luna, sir, but I also know about the Lowlanders. Their men are up here, serving you well. They are helping dig your levees. You mustn't allow the water to be cut off from their lands. They have almost finished the work with your farmers and will be returning to those very Lowlands. The women and children that this man speaks of are the families of your workers."

Lord Dipswitch approached Drum confidently. "These people are lowborn nomads, Your Majesty," he whispered. "I know you have hired some of them to do extra work in your fields, but you should see how they live. They have no king. They have no country. To be exact, they have no real value. If they disappear, no one will miss them.

"Meanwhile, I am prepared to sweeten our financial agreement for the completion of my wife's pool. It is developing nicely." He smiled a revealing smile.

Drum nodded. They appeared to negotiate a bit more, and in the end, both were smiling the same smile.

Will couldn't hear what was being said, but he suspected that it wasn't good for the Lowlanders.

Lord Dipswitch seemed to have recovered completely from his embarrassing incident in the hall. He sneered slightly at the seedy-looking commoner in front of him. This rube would obviously have no influence on what had been decided between him and the King. Whoever he was, he was not the decision maker here.

"I will be visiting with local friends of quality up north here for a few days," he announced to Drum. "When I return to the south, I will expect to move into my manor and enjoy my pool. I know my rights, and I intend to see that my demands are met and what I have purchased is accomplished." Dipswitch gathered up his belongings and glanced at Will.

"My pool will be huge. But if the ragtag Lowlanders want water, they may have whatever I don't need for my pool when I am finished," he snickered. "That should be good enough for the likes of them. Thank you for your assistance with this matter, Your Highness."

With a quick bow, he exited. This King Drum was strange, but he would be facilitating what Dipswitch wanted done. He was a useful king for a deserving person such as himself. That was all that counted.

Will straightened his red hat and tried to gather his thoughts. He would need to talk to Ben and fix the water problems at The Border, but first he had to find out about the Urhonordo Water Rights Treaty. It was his responsibility as Agriculture Advisor to do both, but one thing at a time.

Drum appeared to be strangely deep in thought, but Will stepped forward. "I was talking to Flawless about the meeting that occurred yesterday with the Queen of the Urhonordos," he started. "She told me that you might not be in favor of negotiating with the Queen about the Water Rights Treaty. Is that so?"

King Drum sat up abruptly on his throne. His mind was elsewhere. He seemed to still be focusing on Dipswitch for some reason, and Will was very sure he wasn't thinking about water rights.

"My daughter is very wise," Drum said in a matter-of-fact voice. "What she told you was correct. River Kingdom is great and getting greater. It is even spreading south as you just heard. Urhonordo is small and insignificant. They have never done anything for us. Why should we do anything for them?"

Will recognized that this was a dismissal, but tried again. "River Kingdom had a treaty with Urhonordo that we broke. I was a big part of that and—"

"That treaty was just the piece of paper that an uninformed king negotiated in years past. *No old* treaty should obligate River Kingdom or its current leadership to a tiny kingdom that doesn't understand business reality. "I am 'Making River Kingdom Great,' not Urhonordo. Tying us to something that would not be profitable to our kingdom would be pretty foolish, don't you think? Our kingdom is obviously the only thing that is important. Therefore, I am canceling the Water Rights Treaty." Drum smiled but then looked directly at Will.

Will didn't know what to say. "Canceling the treaty?" Will looked at Morf.

Morf shrugged and rolled his eyes.

"Yes," said Drum. "Now, let's talk about things that are *good* for River Kingdom. How are my levees doing? Are my farmers happy?" Drum's focus became sharper.

"They seem to be, sir," Will managed to answer. "The levees have almost all been lowered as far as they need to be and the crops are doing well, so, it's about time for the Lowlanders to return to their homeland. They are ready to go home."

"Such as it is," sneered Drum. "It's a worthless piece of sand from what I hear."

"It's pretty dry, but they like it," defended Will.

"I'm sure that some of them do," agreed Drum. "But they sure do hurry to get up here for work whenever they have a chance."

"Our kingdom frequently needs them, and they need the work, sir. The pay for this summer's work will help them a lot." Will was getting angry. Where was this going? "They did a good job for us when we asked them," he added firmly. "That's why we need to make sure that they get their pay soon so they can go back south."

Drum suddenly smiled broadly. He seemed to have solved his problem. "Oh, I agree completely," he said. "You are so right. Why didn't I think of this sooner? I *am* a verifiable genius."

Drum hopped down off his throne and began grinning happily. "I do have just one favor that I want your beloved Lowlanders to do before they get paid, though. But it takes place right near to their 'homeland' so I am sure they won't mind doing it. *Then* they can get paid. They will be happy. What do you think of that, William of Dale?"

This quick switch was not like Drum. There was something else on in his mind. What was the "favor" that he was he thinking about?

"I have another wonderful idea," Drum boasted. "I think I will be holding a Celebrational Rally tonight for my loyal peasants in honor of the completion of their levees, and I will have a new announcement to make at that time. Be sure to come. You will love it, William. Morf! Are you still around?"

Morf ran back to the throne and bowed.

"Of course, you are. Send out the Royal Couriers at once to announce a 'Levee Celebration Rally' for tonight. And tell everybody to wear their hats. I will have a surprise for everyone!" With that, Drum almost danced into his bedroom.

Morf rose from his bowing position and checked with Will. Will was just standing in one spot in the middle of the room.

"What just happened?" asked Morf.

"I don't have any idea. I think Drum is crazy," whispered Will. "We didn't discuss the water rights. We didn't discuss the Lowlanders' water. He just got all warm and fuzzy with some guy that wants to build a pool, and he's going to hold a celebration rally, for heaven's sake. Nothing that he said just now made any sense to me."

"He's the King. He doesn't have to make sense," Morf responded. "You don't believe that! You're just rolling over to keep your spot next to the throne!" yelled Cmorf. "You can't continue to do that. I am still your Conscience. You have to listen to me."

"I have to hear you, but I don't have to listen," said Morf as he walked out of the room. "I'm going to get the Royal Couriers."

Will could feel a strange current flowing through the room, but he had no idea what it was. Drum had made some sort of deal with a man named Dipswitch, canceled a long-standing treaty with another kingdom and scheduled a rally, all in just a few minutes. Will was confused about Urhonordo, afraid for his friends, and completely bewildered. Is this the way it always was with politics?

Will didn't need his Conscience to tell him that the deal Sir Dipswitch had discussed with Drum was not good news for the Lowlanders. Drum was smugly happy, and for some reason, he had just decided to have a rally. This was not a good sign, but he had no idea that it was Eforces at work.

And, what the Auras had just seen was several steps forward in the world of thoughtlessness that they loved. Theirs was an easy, labor-free job today. They were more than ready for a rally tonight.

22

Pool Promise

As evening fell, the farmers and farm hands began streaming to the rally, most of them wearing their precious red hats. They were happy Drum fans now. Their levees had been lowered, and their fields were responding with what looked to be a record harvest. Sir Drum was now King Drum, and their king had invited them to a celebration rally with treats to follow. They felt honored. They felt important. King Drum was on their side, and they loved it.

Will and Ben were among the farmers at the rally. Will decided not to stop in the garden to meet with Flawless tonight. Her father had not been speaking rationally this morning in the throne room, and Will was afraid of what Drum might commit him to tonight. Rallies like this seemed to have a habit of announcing Drum brainstorms that he had not thought through. And they always seemed to involve Will. It was unnerving for a nonpolitical soul like himself.

Will had already determined that he might actually love Flawless, but he knew that she was fiercely loyal to her father. He would need to work that out in the future somehow, but he was not ready to do that tonight.

Unfortunately, he didn't have a choice. She snuck up behind him. "You boys thought you could come here without me, didn't you?" She

laughed. "I'm glad I found you. My father was very secretive about this rally tonight, but he's in a good mood. I had to be here. He hinted that he might have a surprise for the farmers, and you're a farmer, Will." She laughed and grabbed his arm.

Will looked guilty. "I'm sorry, Flawless. I didn't mean to ditch you. The fact is, I don't know what your father is going to say tonight. I was sort of worried, and I didn't want to have it cause a problem between us."

Ben kept his mouth shut and moved to the side. Will had told him some of what Dipswitch and Drum had talked about this morning. He was worried too. "Hi, Flawless," was all he could say.

Flawless grinned at Will with confidence. "Daddy won't come between us," she said softly. "He knows that I like you." Will smiled briefly in response but said nothing. They waited in silence as the crowd of farmers and peasants jostled around them.

They didn't have to wait long. King Drum emerged onto the blazingly lit balcony, splendid in his beautiful crown. Majestically, he strode back and forth while the crowd below him chanted, "Drum, Drum, Drum."

Then without warning, Drum removed his crown and gave it to Morf who had entered onto the balcony behind him. Caught completely off guard, Morf bowed and received the crown. What was Drum doing now?

From under his robe, Drum produced a hidden red hat like the ones the commoners wore and fastened it securely to his head. Now he was one of them.

The farmers erupted into a roar of approval. Now their chant changed. "Long live King Drum!" they shouted in unison. Drum himself beamed in satisfaction. The crowd was with him. This was what it was all about—loyalty.

Drum put up his hands, and slowly, the crowd quieted. They were tense with anticipation. What was he going to say? The couriers had told them of a surprise announcement. What could it be?

"My friends, I am so glad to be with you at tonight's celebration. I hear that the lowering of the levees has almost been completed.

Urhonordo didn't want us to do it, of course, but I insisted. We are Making the Kingdom Great in spite of them, right?"

Will groaned, but the crowd cheered, "Make River Kingdom Great!" in unison.

Ben nudged Will. "That means that my friends and family will get paid pretty soon, right? They're anxious to get home."

"That's what that means, my friend," said Will. "I told Drum that you guys were more than ready to get back down to home. He said that he has a favor he wants to ask you guys to do first, but I know that the payment has been set aside already. Don't worry about it. I'll get the payment for you."

"Good man," Ben responded with a smile.

The cheering of the rally was still intense. "Make River Kingdom Great!" Drum was cheering too. He loved their enthusiasm. But at last, Drum put up his hands again, and the cheering drifted away. In its place was anticipation. It was time for the big announcement.

"Thank you, my loyal citizens of River Kingdom. I am one of you, as you can see. And I have been paying attention to all your hard work. I know that you have been working all day, every day in the hot, dry fields. Do the lords of your manors appreciate you like I do?"

"No!"

"Do they want to make you happy like I do?"

"No!"

"When do they let you cool off after a day's work?"

"Never!"

"Why can't you just jump in The River?"

A lot of laughter. "We'd drown . . . the current would take us down . . . we'd be goners."

"Wouldn't it be nice if you had your own pool like your masters have?"

"Yeah!" The crowd laughed and roared in agreement.

"That is why I brought you here tonight. As you know, I requested that the Royal Guard transport the rubble from your levees down south to The Border with The Lowlands. That rubble was originally being used to build a grand manor house for a rich guy."

The crowd hissed.

"But as a benefit to all of you, I have arranged for most of that rubble to be used to build . . . a pool!"

This was so unheard of that the crowd said nothing. They just looked at each other. A pool? Why was he building a pool? Who was that for?

Drum quickly regrouped. "Why did I build a pool, you ask? Why, for all of you, of course! For your own personal enjoyment."

The crowd was still confused. They didn't understand what he was doing for them. Drum continued quickly. "*You* all dug the levees. *You* all pulled the rock out of the ground. It is only right that the rock *you* dug up should be used to make a pool . . . but it's a pool just for *you to enjoy! It will be your pool!*"

Now the crowd got it. A pool had been built just for them out of the rocks they had dug! That was cool! That was thrilling! They began to cheer. They couldn't believe it. A pool was being built just for them! "Pool! Pool! Pool!" they chanted.

"And when is that pool going to be started? As a matter of fact, my Royal Border Advisor tells me that your pool has *already* been started. What do you think of that?" Drum asked with a flourish. The crowd cheered again on cue.

Will and Ben looked at each other. A pool? That didn't make sense. This was even crazier than Will and Ben had imagined this morning. The

King was telling everyone about a useless pool that no one wanted or needed, but suddenly, they all thought it was a wonderful idea. Why? And worse yet, where?

The peasants of River Kingdom would never use a pool. Their noblemen always had them working. "Family vacations" didn't exist. But they were being told that the Dipswitch pool was for *them* . . . and they loved the whole notion. And it would be built with their rocks, using the King's money. Brilliant!

Visions of a perk that rich people had, one that the King had arranged to be built just for them, sailed through the peasants. Drum really cared about them.

Ben stared in shock at Will. This would mean the end of Lowland water. Ben knew it. There would be no water flowing in the beloved small river that had always been The Lowland allotment of The Great River. The Lowlanders could not survive on their land as a people without The River. This would be the end of them.

Flawless looked at her friends with concern. She could see that something was terribly wrong, but she was bewildered. What was the problem? This sounded like something the farmers would love. After harvest, they and their families could go play in the water, couldn't they?

Did Flawless picture the pool being miles away? Not really. She had never been to The Lowlands.

Did she picture the pool blocking anyone's water? Of course not. A pool was just a wonderful thing for people to relax in.

Did Flawless see anything but good news in her father's gift to the farmers? Not one thing, and neither did the farmers. They were all thrilled.

But Drum was not finished with his announcement.

"And," he shouted over the crowd, "that's not all. Since you farmers have been working so hard on the levees, I have decided to speed up the finishing of your pool. It will be ready for use by the end of harvest!"

The crowd was thrilled again. No one had ever built a pool just for commoners before, and now it was going to be built fast. "Build that pool! Build that pool!" The chant became huge. The farmers were dancing with joy.

"How is that going to be done?" yelled someone from the crowd. "Who is going to finish our pool that fast?"

Drum was ready for this. "Am I not your King?" he asked. "Yes! Yes!" the crowd cheered.

"Do I not have the power to get this done for you fast?" "Yes!" Yes!" the crowd roared.

"Then you had better believe it," Drum shouted. "I have assigned this task to one of your own . . . William of Dale!" The crowd cheered and turned, looking for Will.

"Will, Will, Will," they chanted. One of their own was going to get a pool ready for them by the end of harvest! That was perfect. They were excited.

Will couldn't speak, but Flawless was hugging him with pride.

"Oh, Will. I had no idea you were going to do this for the farmers. I'm so proud of you. Why didn't you tell me?"

Will stared at her. What could he say? The crowd was surrounding them and slapping Will on the back. Ben was looking at him with horror. What was his friend doing to him now?

Will's Conscience knew Will needed help. Although Cwill himself was confused, he had to do his job. "Don't say anything. Will. This was not your doing. You didn't know. You are innocent of this craziness. Wait and go to The Castle tonight. You must get to the King and change this before it goes any further."

Will heard and listened in spite of what was going on around him. He took a deep breath. "I need to talk to your father again as soon as I can," he whispered to Flawless in a very serious tone.

Hearing the tone, she stepped back. She saw at once that Will was upset about something. Although she didn't understand what the problem was, she was here for Will. She had not told herself yet, but she had come to love him. "Come to the throne room as soon as the rally is over. I will meet you there," she answered, matching her serious tone to his. She was gone in an instant.

Ben was not going anywhere. He stared at Will's face, trying to read what he saw there.

"I didn't know anything about this," Will said sadly to his friend. "I had no idea he was going to say something this crazy. He was not making sense this morning, and he still isn't. Flawless is on her way to the throne room. I will definitely find out what this is all about. Do you want to come with me?"

"No way."

"Do you trust me?"

Ben gave Will a nudge. They had been friends for a long time. "I always do."

Cben spoke up. "Not always," he reminded him.

Ben looked up at Will and chuckled. "Well, almost always," he admitted with a half smile. "See what you can find out and let me know as soon as you can. Get back to me right away, okay?"

"Definitely," Will answered and the two went their separate ways. The joyous cheering at the rally continued, frequently erupting into "Build that pool. Build that pool."

Morf was twisting his red hat in his hands as he followed Drum from the balcony into the throne room. He had just attended an amazingly successful rally, but ridiculous promises had been made and he was sure they were going to cause trouble. Drum seemed to be out of control. Cmorf was quiet for once, so Morf was on his own with his own thoughts. He had hooked his future in The Castle to a man that made no sense, and this man was now the King.

Morf followed Drum into the throne room and was surprised to see Will waiting with Flawless. Morf was not surprised to see Will, however. He had expected him. As far as Morf knew, Will had not been in on Drum's "pool announcement" or his new orders. Obviously, he would have questions since this bizarre decision had been made without him. But Flawless was here too. Why? Morf slid into the shadows to watch.

Drum seated himself on his throne, replaced his red hat with his crown, and waited while Will bowed as was necessary.

"I take it that you were a bit surprised by my announcement tonight, eh?" Drum asked casually.

"Yessir," Will answered without emotion. Cwill was on duty and firmly anchored in Will's hair.

"I thought you would be," said Drum confidently. "I knew you would be here, but did you need to bring my daughter?"

"I came by myself first, Daddy," Flawless explained. "I wanted to know more about what you said tonight. How are you going to get that pool built so fast?"

"You doubt me, daughter?" Drum asked with a smile.

"Of course not, Daddy. I'm just curious." Flawless smiled engagingly and sat down confidently next to her father.

Drum laughed and patted her hand. "Now that I think about it, you would be interested in what I said that this Will guy of yours was going to do." He laughed some more. "I think he wants to know that too, right, William?"

"Right," answered Will.

Drum leaned forward as though he was explaining a secret deal. "Here's the plan, Will. I know you are friends with the Lowlanders, so this should not be a problem for you. I am taking the Lowlanders from the levees, which are almost done anyway, and assigning them to the finishing of the Dipswitch pool with you. What do you think of that idea?"

"I don't think it will work, sir," announced Will honestly.

Flawless and Drum sat back with a start. They both stared at Will. They had not expected a contrary answer from Will. He could do anything . . . according to Flawless.

"What is your problem, William? You said these Lowlanders are good workers. I'm just giving them a little more work. They'll love it."

Will closed his eyes and inhaled. Then he said slowly, "You should have said something to them or to me first, sir. This plan will not work at all. I am not sure that you have been to The Lowlands, sir, but if you had been there, you would have seen that the farmers don't need a pool there. The Lowlands just need water.

"They need to keep the small amount of The River's water that flows through their lands instead of blocking it for a pool. They will be glad to work for you on something else, but they need to be paid for what they have already done. A pool built with water that *they* need to live on is just not a good idea."

Drum scowled as though he had just heard war declared against him. "I see. Now that you know that my daughter likes you, you think you can say anything you want," he growled.

"Steady, Will. Steady," warned Cwill.

"I absolutely do not think that," Will answered as calmly as he could. "I'm just telling you the truth. The Lowlanders have finished the work they were hired for, sir. They are ready to be paid and go home . . . sir. *And I* need to make sure that the water they need is there when they get there."

"Don't believe what those little Lowlanders tell you about the pool. That's all a hoax. Those people lie all the time," sneered Drum. "Besides, they are poor people so they're used to being poor. They can make do without pay for a while.

"I am here to Make River Kingdom Great, not The Lowlands. The Lowlanders' water is not my problem. They have no rights to River Kingdom water. They are not even River Kingdom citizens."

"What?" Will could not believe what he had just heard.

"Daddy, that's not fair. The Lowlanders are good people. They need their pay and their water. You can't expect them to be our friends and work hard for us all summer if they don't get paid. And you can't expect Will to make them do it either. That's not right. Did you really mean that?"

Flawless stared at her father in amazement. For the first time since she was a little girl, she felt she couldn't stick up for him at all.

"You heard him exactly right, Flawless. You know you did," said Cflawless.

Drum stopped and studied Flawless. He was used to Flawless being on his side completely. He thought for a minute. Then he had the answer.

"Flawless dear, where is your faith in me? Of course, I will pay the Lowlanders," he murmured. "How could you doubt me? You run along to your room and don't worry about it. Will and I will work out the details."

Flawless smiled in relief. "Oh, Daddy, I'm so sorry I misjudged you. I'll leave you two men now to talk. I'm sorry I interfered." She blessed both of them with a winning smile and left. Will knew that the problem wouldn't be solved easily, but he smiled as well.

The room grew quiet. Drum sat on his throne and readjusted his crown with authority.

"So here I am with my new Ag Advisor trying to tell me how to run my kingdom. You have a lot of nerve, I must say," Drum said flatly. "I can see why my daughter likes you. You have grit. But you are young, and you have some things to learn. The first thing is, I am your King, your ruler, *and* your master, and you *will* do as I say. Do you understand that?"

"Yessir." Will felt trapped. Drum was right. He was the Royal Agriculture Advisor. He should do his job at the order of the King. That was a well-known rule. But the wonderful Flawless *and* his best friend trusted him to stand up for a *fair* resolution of this unfair situation. He was, indeed, trapped.

"Now, let me tell you how this is going to go," announced Drum confidently. "*You* are going to get my pool made as I have told the whole Kingdom *you* would. You will use the Lowlanders to do it. And *then* the Lowlanders will get paid . . . *if* you and they do as I say. If you don't, they won't."

"But the Lowlanders' water, sir—"

"Let them drink out of the pool if they get thirsty."

"That's cruel," barked Cdrum.

"That's practical. It's the best solution."

"That's not right," squeaked Cwill. "They finished the job you hired them for, Will. They need to get paid now . . . and to have their water . . . *their water.*"

Drum straightened his back and stood tall. "I need my pool, and the Lowlanders are the only ones that have the manpower to do what needs to be done quick. You are my Royal Agricultural Advisor, Will. You are the one I selected to take care of these hard jobs. You are in charge of what goes on with that pool, Will, so you must make the call. I have made up my mind."

"Yessir, but—"

"*And* if you want the Lowlanders to get paid at all, you will do as I say and begin tomorrow at the latest."

Drum rose from his throne and disappeared behind his bed curtains, leaving Will in complete confusion.

Suddenly, Morf stepped out of the shadows where he had been standing quietly out of sight. "Well, that leaves you in an interesting position, doesn't it?" Morf asked as he took a seat in an empty chair. "What are you going to do?"

Will just stood in one spot. The truth was, he didn't know what he was going to do.

"I've been in situations like this with Drum before," continued Morf. "I understand what you are going through. I call times like this your basic 'lose-lose' situation. There's really no way you can win. Everything is going wrong. You're doomed. Sound familiar?"

"That sounds about right," mumbled Will.

"I remember back when I started working on Drum's inaugural. There I was. There was no way I could win. There were no performers for the celebration. So I went drinking in the village."

"Did that help much?"

"The drinking didn't, but when I got sober, I got creative." "And that solved your problem with Drum's inaugural?"

"It solved one of them. The next problem I had was Inaugural Day itself. Absolutely everything was going wrong, so I just gave up and threw myself on the floor."

"Don't tell me that that solved your problem."

"No, . . . but I *did* get creative there on the floor and that helped a lot. I knew I would be doomed by Drum, so I got creative and told everybody to pretend they were sick."

"Don't tell me that getting sick was helpful." "Of course not. You're missing my point." "I think I am."

"Let me spell it out for you. *Get creative.* That's really all you can do when you're doomed. Just throw caution to the wind and get on with what needs to be done. If you stand still, you'll never figure it out. If you get creative, you'll probably fix your problem."

"I'm confused," groused Cwill. "Every option here is right for one reason and wrong on ten others."

"Tell me about it," Cmorf chimed in. "That's the way Drum works all the time."

Cwill nodded in sympathy.

"Of course, you *could* give up and quit, I suppose," offered Morf. "Yeah, just like you quit, I suppose," snarked Cmorf. "You and Will

both know Drum's wrong. The Lowlanders deserve their pay, and there should be no pool."

"But quitting isn't an option," responded Cwill.

"If I quit, my friends won't get paid at all and they will starve this winter, and if I get a pool built, they will eat but die of thirst," Will concluded.

"Let me say it again," Morf insisted. "If you work for Drum, you have to stay flexible and be creative. Someday, my creativity might fail me, but I'm not ready for that yet. I don't know what you're going to do, but I thought I ought to pass this trick on to you since I think you are in a rough position." Morf leaned back in his chair and glanced up at Will with sympathy.

"You are a complete sell-out," announced Cmorf in Morf's ear, "but I like what you're doing here. You should try being helpful more often."

Will had wondered how Morf felt about Drum, and now he knew. Mixed emotions, to say the least, but there was no one else to ask for advice. Somehow, what Morf said, though it was odd, made some sense. "I hear what you say, Morf. I don't know if I can be as creative as you, but I do know I have to make sure that the Lowlanders get their water, at least. I'll give it a shot."

The two parted. They understood each other, but both their Consciences were troubled. They weren't sure they were helping their humans the way they wanted to, but neither one had given up entirely.

Before the sun was up, Will tracked Ben down and told him what Drum had said. To his surprise, Ben was not surprised. "When I heard Drum promise that you were going to be responsible for building the pool fast, I knew we were the only workforce that could do it.

"The farmers and farm hands are busy in their fields. They are not going to stop to build a pool. A pool is such a crazy idea anyway. Why does Drum think they want a pool?"

"He thinks the farmers love him, and he wants to keep it that way. Since he promised the pool now, he thinks he has to deliver even though no one really wanted it until he suggested it. And there's one more reason. There's money involved, I'm pretty sure."

"That's not a shock," commented Ben. "Tell him the worst part," ordered Cwill.

"And, Ben, . . . Drum's not going to pay you or the rest of the Lowlanders until that pool is finished."

"No."

"Yes."

"After all our sweat and hard work on the levees, he's not going to pay us until we cut off our own water? You let him get away with that?"

"I'm sorry, Ben. I know it's not right. I tried to talk him out of it, but it didn't work."

"You were a wimp. You didn't try hard enough," commented Cwill. "The way Drum does things, we may not get paid at all," said Ben

angrily. "My family and friends will not be happy. The people at home are depending on our pay in food to live on. You know that. We had almost no crops this year due to almost no water. Now we will be completely without water and food."

"I hear you. I feel guilty for not getting you your money today. I do have one good thing, however. Morf gave it to me." He reached into his tunic and pulled out a piece of parchment. It was a promissory note, written in beautiful script and signed with a kingly scrawl at the bottom.

23

Dipswitch Manor

The sun was not yet up. As soon as Ben could gather them all together, Will and Ben and the Lowlanders headed south toward Dipswitch Manor. They were determined to do something with the foolish pool project so that they could get paid although Will had no idea what that was going to be. They had resigned themselves to Drum's unfair treatment, accepting it as just one more hurdle in their lives ruled by King Drum. They were only halfway to The Lowlands, however, when they spied an elderly Lowlander struggling toward them. It was Ben's grandfather.

"I am so glad you're coming in this direction," he gasped to his grandson. "There is an evil man down home who has built an enormous manor house on the mouth of The Great River. It's trapping most of what little water was coming to The Lowlands. Now he is building a wall that will close off Lowland water altogether. But that's not the worst thing." The old man began to crumple into the dirt.

Ben lifted him into the shade and dripped some of the contents of his water pouch into the man's parched mouth. Will and the other Lowlanders gathered around with comforting words and sympathy. Gradually, the old man recovered enough to tell them more.

"The Guardsmen took our women and children. They put them in cages . . . in cages, mind you! I was coming to find you. Many of our children and their mothers are already caged.

"It started right after you men left for the north," continued Ben Sr. "This terrible fellow showed up with his crew and began to pile up the earth, right where The River flows into our country. We tried to explain that if he could move his big ugly house just a little toward the west, we could still get our water. He just laughed and said he was building his house where his wife wanted it, and if we bothered him, he would have the Royal Guard put us in cages. Cages! And the Royal Guard was there all the time, bringing down rubble. At his command, they actually did it."

Will's heart sank as the facts of Dipswitch Manor became clearer and more terrible. Drum wanted a pool for his farmers and his money deal. He didn't care if he ruined the lives of the Lowlanders to get it. Dipswitch was already caging the families.

And what was also clear was that *Will* was the one that the King expected to make things even worse. He was supposed to ask Lowland men to create the very structure that would seal their waterless fate— while their women and children were held hostage. And the Royal Guard was already there to enforce his demands. It was a setup.

Will walked away from all the Lowlanders. He couldn't look them in the eyes. They had trusted him, and now his orders were to make them suffer even more because of him.

"You didn't know it would come to this," counseled Cwill. "I should have known." Will sighed aloud.

"But you didn't know," echoed Ben as he sat down on a stump near where Will was hunched, scratching in the earth.

His drawing was not very creative. First there was The River. River Kingdom was on the west side of The River. Urhonordo was on the east. The Lowlands covered the land below both kingdoms with what was left of The River down the middle. Now Will drew Dipswitch Manor. If it was the dam that Ben Sr. had described, it would soon stop all the water. Ben shook his head sadly.

Suddenly, Will stood up. His uncreative picture had actually created a solution to his problem. It was right there in front of his eyes. It was The River. The River made the pool impossible.

"Why didn't I see this before?" he said with excitement. "Building a pool that is part of a flowing river is impossible," he crowed with excitement. "Once a pool fills up, it will have to empty out someplace. It will cause a flood.

"If I had thought for only a minute yesterday, I could have showed Drum that a river just keeps flowing. It doesn't just make a pool and stop. Even if the flow is small, if it is dammed, eventually it will overflow. Even a king can't dam up a natural river. I should have just said that."

Ben's eyes opened wide. He looked at Will's picture. "I never thought about it that way," he said with wonder, "but I think you're right. But . . . you're just a farmer turned Ag Advisor and The River is small at The Border." Ben shrugged. "Will anybody believe you?"

Will grinned. "Eventually, they'll have to," he said. "If The River is already partially dammed, it will already have started to overflow. The facts will become obvious."

"Nothing is obvious to selfish people," Ben said sadly.

Slowly, Will walked back to where all the others were still gathered under a tree. "I am not sure what we are going to do when we get to Dipswitch Manor," he told the group firmly, "but we're not going to build a pool. First, we'll get your people out of their cages. Then we'll see what else we need to do."

The Lowlanders nodded in solemn agreement and took turns carrying Ben Sr. as they hurried southward. What greeted them as they rounded the final bend of their trek proved Will's drawing more correct than he could have imagined. The tiny stream of The River that was the lifeblood of The Lowlands had continued to flow, as was its nature. Blocked by already dumped piles of rubble, however, it had begun escaping, finding a new route of its own . . . into Urhonordo.

Over the years, Urhonordo had built large levees here that had protected its low-lying farms and manors along The River's banks. This had allowed The River to proceed to The Lowlands. Those levees were now gone.

The blocked Lowland water had grown into a lake and spread east. It had not taken long. Redirected by the dumped clay and rock, the coveted water was drowning the fertile farmlands of Urhonordo and had already turned them into leagues of muddy, useless swamp. This was a disaster. And not only was there a flood, but there were also no Lowlanders in sight. Will groaned. Fury fear gripped the Lowlander men. After all their hard work and sacrifice up north, they were returning to this. Where were their families? Where were their children? Where was their way of life?

Suddenly, hidden women scrambled out from behind clumps of grass and ran to meet them, but there was no rejoicing. "Somewhere, out there behind the big house, our children are caged like animals," a sobbing mother cried.

The Lowlanders who were left behind when the workers had gone to River Kingdom had been overcome. They were mostly women and children and old folk. They had been helpless, and the rights they had always had to their land and water were now devastated. "No one knows exactly where our families are or how to find them, and all our water is now a muddy lake," they cried.

"The King of River Kingdom has turned against us."

"He sent his Royal Guard to wall off our water and take our children."

"He wants us all to die."

THE POOL

Ben, of course, was a Lowlander, but Will was not. The miserable crowd surrounded Will, shaking their fists. Why was he here? Had the King sent him to torture them further? Knowing that he was not one of them, the Lowlanders glared at him suspiciously.

Will didn't blame them. *He* was the real cause of all their problems. But one thing was clear. "We have to find your children before anything else," Will said simply.

"He is my friend," added Ben. The rest of the men who had worked on the levees nodded.

Suspicion eased, but they needed to talk. Will and all the Lowlanders quickly gathered behind a nearby knoll. The Lowlanders felt the need to stay safely out of sight of the Royal Guard who were patrolling the manor house . . . and probably the cages.

The discussion was quick. Strategies came and went.

Charge the manor house?

No. The children might be harmed.

A sneak attack?

That wouldn't work. The Royal Guard appeared to be guarding the area closely.

Are the children near the manor house?

We think so.

Will could not wait anymore. Cwill tried to talk him out of the guilt he was feeling, but it didn't work. *He* had taken the men away from The Lowlands for pay that they didn't have. If they had not been up north with him, the Lowlander women and children would have been protected, and the water would not have been cut off. He had to find a solution to all this because he had caused it.

At last, Will knew what he had to do. He had to go to Dipswitch Manor alone, confront the Royal Guard, and try to get the children himself peacefully. It was his duty. And as a man that was not a Lowlander, he was probably the best choice. The Guardsmen did not appear to respect Lowlanders.

The Lowlander men were pretty sure that Will would be caged like the mothers had been when they tried to retrieve their children, so they formed a troop behind the manor house for backup. They would get their children one way or the other.

Will tried to reassure them—and himself—and set out bravely on his rescue mission. It was worth a try, and Cwill agreed that he needed to do it no matter what.

There was no bathwater in the parched Lowlands so Will was dressed in his dusty travel clothes and definitely did not present himself as an impressive negotiator, but suddenly, Morf's advice popped into his mind.

"Get creative." *Act impressive even if you have to fake it,* he said to himself.

With a dignified stride, he made his way toward the massive doors of the manor house, but he was surprised by the rude assault of two Royal Guards who immediately shoved him aside and barred his way.

"Be off, beggar! This is the home of a gentleman," they growled, shaking him by the scruff of his neck. Before he knew it, he was on the ground.

"I'm not a beggar," Will answered calmly, regaining his dignity as he picked himself up. "I've come for the children."

The guards stopped short and squinted at Will. "You don't look like a Lowlander. What do you want with Lowlander kids?"

"I want the children because they are *children* . . . and should not be in cages. Their mothers want them back. And their husbands want their mothers and wives back too," announced Will. "I understand that you have ladies in cages as well."

"Who is going to make us do such a thing?" scoffed one of the guards, making ready to shove Will to the ground again.

"I am," said Will, looking the Guardsman in the eye and taking a stronger position.

Behind him now, the Lowlander men stepped out from behind a corner of the manor house toward the front porch. There were dozens of them, and only two guards were here at the front door. Now, this was a different story. The guards stepped back and raised their weapons. Although they were surprised, they were trained fighters by nature and always ready to do battle.

But Will put out a hand open for shaking and stood firm. "I am William of Dale," he announced clearly. "I am the Royal Ag Advisor for King Drum. These men are the men that dug up the levees and created the rubble that you have been using to build the wall for this manor house. If you don't want me to have them take this manor house apart, then stand down and fetch me the owner of this home."

The guards were caught off guard. "He ain't home," one shot back, clearly not prepared for this professional-sounding announcement. They were also not prepared for the show of force. A few more Guardsmen peered out from the windows of the manor house.

Ben stepped forward and stood by Will. "That's okay," he said. "We don't need to see the owner. We just want our women and children."

The negotiation did not last too much longer. It was surprising how differently the few guards reacted to a clear request, much less a large group of angry-looking men. Somehow these factors made the right decision much easier to find than it had been when the poor mothers had come looking for their children.

Slowly, the Lowlanders were led to the back of the house where the caged children and mothers had been sleeping with assorted animals.

"We're Lowlanders, but we are humans like you and need to live on our land . . . with water and children," one of the mothers told a Guardsman indignantly, shaking her finger in his face as she was turned loose. "King Sol never would have let this happen."

Strangely, the Royal Guardsmen agreed. Their Consciences had already been reminding them that they had wives and children at home themselves. Gradually, the rest of the Royal Guardsman contingent joined the first two, and common sense began to settle about the strange combination of military men, Lowlander men, and their families. It appeared that none of the Guardsmen had been particularly happy with their assignments at Dipswitch Manor. Who knew?

Will watched the gentle transformation with surprise and gratitude. This was the beginning of forgiveness and understanding growing among very different people who were starting to see each other as very similar people. Consciences who had never met each other before were seeing each other for the first time. Figuring out what to do about the pool, however, was going to be much harder.

24

Invasion

Back up at The Castle, there was no hint of the drama that was currently taking place in The Lowlands. Flawless awoke to a beautiful day with no idea that Will was already gone. The levees had been completed, the local farmers were happy, and as far as Flawless knew, Will and Ben and his countrymen would soon be going to work on the farmers' pool. She was happy.

Flawless dressed in one of her prettiest gowns, hoping she would get a chance to talk to Will before he left for The Lowlands. She had even thought of going with him. She respected the farm women, all of whom she had recently noticed were hard workers. Maybe it was time for her to learn how to work too. She had never worked on anything before. Maybe she should go with Will and Ben and help them build the pool.

I must finally become useful, she thought as she walked slowly down the hall of The Castle. *Most people who live on the farms work every day. The women work with their husbands. If Will and I were to marry, he would still be a farmer. Would he want me to work with him? I think so,* she answered herself with a smile. She could hardly wait to see him.

As she reached the throne room, however, she could hear her father shouting angrily. What was going wrong this time? This should be a happy day. Cautiously, she peeked through the curtains of the throne room. Morf was trying hard to explain something to Drum that Drum didn't want to hear.

"What I am trying to say is that she is almost here," Morf said as calmly as he could. "She has a cadre of fighting men with her, and they are completely armed. It looks like she and her men are ready for war."

"This is crazy! You are undoubtedly wrong," shouted Drum. "Why would that stupid Queen be storming our kingdom with armed troops? Where did you get this fake news? I will not tolerate ridiculous rumors like this. You should be fired immediately."

"It's not fake news. The Royal Advisor for Defense told me," whined Morf.

Drum continued to shout. "If this was true, the Royal Advisor for Defense would have told me *himself!* I don't believe a word you say."

"Your Advisor is currently up in the tower, trying to get a better look at what appears to be an invasion force, Your Majesty," Morf hurried to explain. "He will be down here as soon as he figures out how many there are."

The possible truth was beginning to sink into Drum's thinking no matter how he tried to escape the thought. In place of denial, the cold chill of an unanticipated reality began to sink into his bones. River Kingdom was being invaded.

Flawless stepped into the room. Her father stopped fuming, but did not say anything to his daughter. He was now frozen with fear. Morf had told him that enemy troops were in River Kingdom. He had never thought of such a thing. This could not be so. Drum was not prepared. River Kingdom was a peaceful place. No one had ever discussed the use of force before. He was not ready.

"Daddy, what are you yelling about? Did I hear that someone is invading us?"

"Morf says that Queen Luna is marching on River Kingdom," sneered a quivering Drum as though he was repeating an obvious lie. "He hasn't seen a thing. He is only repeating hearsay. You can't depend on hearsay. He is undoubtedly wrong. The idea is a hoax."

"It's Queen Luna, Flawless," confirmed Morf. "Queen Luna has come over The Bridge, and she has brought troops with her. They have halted in formation on The River Kingdom side of The Bridge."

Flawless had never contemplated such a thing either. "Queen Luna is a good woman. She is very peaceful and sweet. I can't believe that she would do something like that without reason. I have talked with her," said Flawless matter-of-factly. "There must be some mistake."

"She's a woman!" Drum suddenly shouted. "*That's* the problem. A woman should never have been put in charge of a kingdom. They have no idea what they're doing. But if she is really trying to invade us, I will squash her and her troops like June bugs and take over her useless little kingdom! She will never know what hit her!" stormed Drum, his hand raised high in defiance, a slightly manic gleam in his eye.

Flawless blanched and then glared at her father. "You shouldn't say such things about Luna. She is a good woman. You don't like her just because she stands up to you." Flawless turned and found Morf cowering in a corner.

"You agree with me, don't you, Morf? You and Queen Luna worked out the treaty issues just as she requested, didn't you?"

Morf was caught. Of course, he had not done such a thing. He hadn't been allowed by Drum to even start.

"Of course, he did," interjected Drum. "The problems are all worked out. There never were any problems in the first place. That was all a hoax too. The levees are completed. No harm was done. What could that woman possibly want?"

Morf cringed. The King was lying again.

"Tell her," hissed Morf's Conscience. "Tell her that the King is lying. If Queen Luna is angry, she might have a right to be."

Morf just smiled a fake smile. He hoped Flawless would take that smile as a yes without his having to lie to her again.

"You are such a phony," said Cmorf. "I hope you know what a phony you are."

Flawless believed her father's lie and Morf's smile, but she was not leaving the throne room. "If Queen Luna is angry about something, Daddy, something else besides the levees must have happened. Let me talk to her. If there is a problem, I am sure it is only a misunderstanding. She and I can work it out."

"No!" said Morf suddenly. "No, you can't just work it out. It would be too dangerous. Queen Luna is coming here with an armed fighting force. A farmer down by The Bridge just reported it too. She and her men are ready for war!"

Now the curtains of the throne room parted abruptly, and a harried, breathless Defense Advisor clanked in. It was General Horace, complete with armor and a sword that appeared too heavy for his frail, aging body. "Well," the General began in a grave tone, "we are definitely being invaded. The Royal Guard of Urhonordo has halted just over The Bridge.

There are a lot of them, armed and ready to strike, sire. What do you suggest we do about it?"

"What do you mean, what do I suggest?" growled Drum, his fear-inspired rage growing. "*You* are the Defense Advisor. Take our superior fighting force down to The Bridge and drive that silly woman and her little insignificant batch of troops back over The Bridge. River Kingdom does not intend to be the slightest bit threatened by the likes of her."

The older gentleman drew himself up to the dignity that his age and experience had earned him. He had seen many battles and had the scars and medals to prove it. He was elderly, but entirely in command of what he knew. "That sounds quite appropriate, sire, and I would be glad to follow your orders, but I am afraid I can't."

"What do you mean by that, General? I am your king and therefore your commander in chief. By law, you must do exactly what I command you to do. How dare you even suggest that you can't?"

"I say this because I know this," responded General Horace, looking Drum straight in the eye. "Queen Luna has brought a large fighting force with her, and we, unfortunately, do not have enough men to do anything about it. I could not move her one inch, let alone back across The Bridge." Drum had begun striding back and forth across the throne room aggressively with a renewed air of confidence and determination. The Defense Advisor's comments brought him to an abrupt halt. He whirled around and stood glaring at the old General with menace, "What did you say?" he croaked in disbelief.

"Our numbers of Royal Guard here on site is painfully small, sir. I'm afraid we are currently not in a position to defend ourselves. If Queen Luna is on the warpath, someone better talk her out of it or we are doomed."

Drum backed away from the old General and stared in horrified disbelief. "What in the world are you talking about? River Kingdom has an enormous Royal Guard."

"Yes, indeed we do, but none of them are here where we can use them, Your Majesty. Most of the guard left with King Sol when he went on Dragon Quest. The rest of them have been sent to The Border of The Lowlands with the rubble from the levees. They have been going back and forth down there for months, and they are currently setting up rubble for the pool down by The Border."

Drum was furious. "What you are saying can't possibly be true. What kind of idiot would ask fighting men to move rubble? That is not what fighting men are for."

"It was on *your orders*, sire." General Horace shrugged. "Deny it! Deny it!" hissed the Eforces in the room.

Drum was beside himself. "Liar!" he shouted. "I'll have you thrown in the dungeon for such a lie. Get out of this room. I would never order such a thing. That would be stupid!"

The old General nodded but held his ground. "You did order it, sire. I tried to warn you that we would have no guard here at The Castle if they went on 'Rubble Duty at The Border' but Morf said that you didn't want to hear from me."

Drum bore down on Morf. "Did you do such a thing, Morf?" "Deny it. Deny it," repeated the Eforces near Morf.

Morf shriveled. "I don't recall, sir," he replied meekly.

"You don't recall? Hog wash," spat Cmorf. "Don't think that I don't hear the Eforces. I am beginning to wonder if you have any spine left at all." "He's acting like Drum," whispered Cdrum to Cmorf from his post nearby on Drum's shoulder. "The Auras are feeling bullish. Both our guys are less and less fond of the truth these days. I think we need a Conscience Forum. What you and I are doing as Consciences just isn't working enough."

Of course, Morf knew what Drum had ordered and what he denied, so he was not surprised by General Horace's unfortunate truth. Drum had paid very little attention to the actual duties of The Castle for a while now— too many rallies and mornings watching dancing girls and not enough actual attention to such things as borders and treaties. But Morf hadn't said anything. As long as there were no major problems, everything was going along well. Now, however, they seemed to be in a crisis.

Drum cringed on his throne. He could think of nothing to say. He might be in danger of losing his beautiful big kingdom to an upstart woman. This aging, old out-of-date General could not put together enough fighting force to go to war with a fly. Obviously, the General was not up to the job, but what was he going to do?

Drum reverted to form. This crisis must be somebody's fault, but whose? Someone had done something wrong or not done something right. Who was that person? Who was to blame for this?

"Your idea of your own wonderfulness won't allow you to admit that you have blown this, will it?" Cdrum asked quietly.

"Nobody asked you for your opinion," countered Drum under his breath.

In desperation, he thought of consulting Flawless. She was always on his side. She also had good ideas, or at least she had in the past. Drum turned in her direction. She had been standing in one spot during the whole discussion, but now, suddenly, she was gone. He was alone . . . and scared. General Horace stood at attention. Morf scurried around busily, straightening the doorway curtains and fluffing the pillows on the chairs, trying to look like there was nothing wrong although he could see clearly that Drum was increasingly frightened by this apparent threat that he had never thought of as possible.

It was then that Drum's fear became too much. "Get out!" he screamed at General Horace. "You are completely incompetent. No Defense Advisor should ever leave his King without protection. Why are you a Defense Advisor if you cannot provide defense? Get out, I say, and do not come back. You're fired!"

General Horace looked shocked . . . and then relieved. He drew himself up to attention and exited in a dignified fashion. His career was no longer in the hands of this fool although he pined for the Royal Guard he had led in the past and longed to do the job today that he knew needed to be done.

Morf groaned. Now what?

"Morf, you are the one person around here who seems to know what he is doing. My problem is that I appear to be surrounded by fools from a previous administration. What I need is someone who knows something . . . someone who thinks like I do. Someone I can work with in a crisis."

Drum paced frantically for a minute, and then an answer came to him. "Go get Lord Thorndike, Morf. Bring him here to me immediately! We're being invaded, you know."

Morf hustled to do Drum's bidding, but Thorndike? An unfriendly, power-hungry aristocrat who scoffed at Drum and his Inaugural Celebration? This was the man Drum wanted to see now?

Drum was frightened, but Flawless had very different ideas. She was on her way to The Bridge. Her morning decision to become useful had taken root. She refused to admit that Queen Luna was not a woman of reason, and yet the General had confirmed that Queen Luna and her troops were at The Bridge. Flawless was determined to speak with Luna, woman to woman, and find out exactly what the problem was.

The Bridge was a way from The Castle, but the path was smooth. She would actually pass Will's flower garden on the way. Maybe he would be there, and she and Will could talk to Queen Luna together.

The garden was bursting with colorful flowers of all kinds and lilies nodded gracefully before The River beyond, but Will was nowhere to be found. Without knowing exactly why, Flawless stooped to the lovely lily blooms and pinched off some of the long stems at their base. Folding them in the crook of her arm, she continued toward The Bridge. *These flowers look friendly,* thought Flawless. *Friendliness is my mission. Maybe these will help.*

The Bridge now loomed ahead. It was an imposing structure that had been carefully constructed out of huge logs by the Royal Guards of both kingdoms generations ago. It was a frequently used passage, but even more, it was a symbol of the alliance between the citizens of both kingdoms.

Flawless had never seen The Bridge look the way it looked today, however. Positioned on The River Kingdom side of The Bridge was an array of armor and weapons and members of the Urhonordo Royal Guard. The entrance to The Bridge was completely blocked, and in the center of the blockade stood Queen Luna, splendid in her own battle gear and demonstrating a commanding strength and determination that Flawless had never witnessed in a woman before.

Flawless was impressed. There was a doubt as to the correct protocol for such a formal and militaristic encounter. Flawless curtsied low, facing the ground and determined to hold her position until she was told to rise.

She had never been at the mercy of a war party or anyone else for that matter. Was she to be taken captive? Was she to be struck to the ground? She cringed and the flowers in her arms quivered uncontrollably.

She was completely surprised therefore when she felt a hand on her shoulder and heard a soft voice saying, "Rise, Flawless. You are my friend." Flawless stood slowly and was shocked to see the fierce Urhonordo

Queen standing close and smiling down at her like a schoolgirl.

"Queen Luna," she began hesitantly. Then she thrust her flowers forward and hung her head.

"Flowers?" questioned Luna.

"Friendship," Flawless answered quietly.

"They are beautiful," responded Luna.

Taking the lilies into her own arms, she said simply, "Thank you. You and I *are* friends, Flawless, at least for now. I am not here to wage war on River Kingdom. That is not my mission. I am here to formally respond to an invasion of Urhonordo territory by the forces of River Kingdom.

Why this has happened, I don't know, but such an invasion cannot be ignored." "An invasion of Urhonordo by River *Kingdom*? Really? That can't be true. Who told you such a thing? We are all at peace," Flawless stammered, looking at Luna incredulously. "There must be some mistake, Queen Luna.

No one in River Kingdom would ever even think of invading you. What makes you think this has happened?"

"I couldn't believe it myself." Luna sighed. "When my farmers and noblemen told me about it, I must say that I doubted them. I did have to admit that after no one from River Kingdom had made any moves to negotiate with us, I was angry. I was surprised and even insulted. But I certainly never expected an invasion."

"No one arranged to negotiate with you yet?" interrupted Flawless. "Really? I asked my father just today and he said . . ." The look on Luna's face stopped her.

"Your father has trouble . . . telling . . . the truth sometimes." Luna sighed. She was well aware that she was almost insulting Flawless's father.

"You mean he lies," said Flawless bluntly. "

Well said," commented Cflawless.

"I don't like to say such things about your father, but he was obligated to honor Urhonordo water rights, and he hasn't done so. He also promised to arrange a meeting with my people to discuss the Water Rights Treaty. He has not done so. I might have overlooked these things a while longer, but his most recent disregard of not only our rights, but also the land and homes of my people is no longer something I can ignore."

The Queen drew herself up tall to indicate both her power and her determination. "River Kingdom troops have invaded Urhonordo territory and laid waste to the farms and manors upon it. This cannot be tolerated!" Flawless stepped back. The friendly Queen no longer looked friendly.

The change was so sudden that Flawless immediately wanted to run. There was a stirring among the Urhonordo troops. They had felt Luna's hardening resolve as well.

But running was not an option. Flawless immediately knew that this crisis was the reason she had chosen to meet with Luna. She was being asked to step up and match strength with strength.

"I know of no such invasion, Queen Luna," she stated. "I am quite sure that I would have heard of such a thing if it were purposefully planned. Where is this reported 'invasion' supposed to have taken place?"

"The invasion occurred in our southern region, not far from The Lowland Border, and it is still underway. The rest of my troops are awaiting my orders to institute countermeasures there." There was no hesitation in her voice.

Flawless immediately assessed the sincerity of Queen Luna's answer. Whether there was actually an invasion or not, she could see that this woman believed her accusations.

"You say that the invasion is taking place in the south. I find this difficult to understand." *River Kingdom doesn't even have enough troops to commit them to an invasion of any kind even if we wanted to,* Flawless thought, remembering what General Horace had said.

Quickly, Flawless assessed the situation as carefully as she could. Queen Luna said there was an invasion on her land down by The Lowland Border. What did Flawless know right now about that area? Not much. Only that Will was going down there to build a pool. That was also where the Royal Guard had been taking the rubble from the levees.

Troops! The Royal Guardsmen were definitely "troops." Could this be what the Queen thought of as an invasion?

Flawless stepped forward with what she hoped looked like confidence. "Luna, my friend. I believe I may have some insight into the 'invasion' that you feel has occurred. If you would, could you please tell me at least some of what you have heard?"

Queen Luna was surprised at Flawless and her almost professional question. Flawless had seemed to be a sweet but gentle young woman. The strength she was exhibiting now was new. Luna knew she should honor this sincere question with an equally sincere response.

"I have had numerous reports from my southern farmers that the Royal Guard of your kingdom is erecting a fort between River Kingdom and Urhonordo land, Flawless. It is manned by the Royal Guard of River Kingdom.

"Day after day, the Guard has arrived with rock and clay. With it, they have built an enormous fort that extends right to our border. In addition, they are creating a huge rock wall to protect the fort. That wall is actually touching Urhonordo land, forcing The River to flood our land. Not only is there no regard for our sovereignty, but there is no respect for the people of our kingdom.

"Daily, the Guard patrols our side of The River as though it was theirs and offloads more boulders for fortification. Our farmers are afraid to come near their own fields and manors. There is no other way to view it. This occupation of our land is an invasion."

Flawless suspected that her information was at least partly correct. Rubble was being transported to The Border by the Royal Guard. Lord Dipswitch was building a manor house at The Border. That could all look menacing from the Urhonordo side of The River. Soon, Will would be going down there to build a pool as well, but it was all very innocent.

This is what Will had warned her about. Her father wasn't really a bad man. He just did things or ordered things on his own without consulting his Conscience or anyone else about possible unintended consequences.

The way it was viewed by Luna's people was a particularly bad consequence, however. Flawless could see that. What was she going to do about it?

"Use your head, Flawless," whispered CFlawless. "Your father has allowed Dipswitch to possibly take advantage of territory that wasn't his there. The situation can't be fixed fast, but . . . maybe it can be slowed down enough so that everyone can figure out what went wrong and restore peace."

*v*Flawless thought. "Try honesty," counseled Cflawless

Flawless took a deep breath and began. "My father made a business deal with an old friend of his," she began.

The two women talked for an hour. The Urhonordo Royal Guard sweat under their armor. More time passed, but in the end, a temporary truce was reached.

"Someone really needs to get your father under control, Flawless. I know you think he means well, but he is so focused on what he wants that he isn't paying attention to your kingdom . . . or to Urhonordo . . . or to anybody else. As King, he can't go on like this, or the next time something like this happens, we may not be able to settle it between you and I. Please tell your father that."

Flawless nodded. "I understand, Queen Luna. I will tell him."

"You must also tell him that a fort with a huge rock wall reaching onto our territory cannot continue to exist as the threat that it obviously is. We can't have troops on our land daily, scaring our farmers and occupying our land. Please tell him that he needs to remedy this situation or Urhonordo will."

Queen Luna did not wait for a response. She turned, motioned to her troops, and retreated over The Bridge to her side of The Great River.

Flawless stood for a moment and watched as the Queen and her entourage marched across The Bridge and disappeared into the lush foliage beyond The River's edge.

The sun beat down on the same beautiful day that she had seen when she awakened, but somehow the day didn't look nice anymore. The rocks along the pathway stood out sharply against the dirt. The blue of the sky seemed harsh and lower than usual. The gentle softness of the morning had disappeared into the reality of real life.

Flawless had averted a battle. She should feel proud, but she didn't. She had learned some things that she didn't want to know. Perhaps this was part of her growing up, her newfound determination to be useful as a woman.

She knew now that her father lied, not just about trivial things, but very important things as well. She had learned that her father had bargained away territory that wasn't his to give. She had learned that someone who should be a friend was demanding that these things "be fixed or Urhonordo will." That was a threat. It was a lot to swallow at one time.

Flawless was on her way back to The Castle when she again found herself near Will's garden. She stopped. In the excitement of her meeting with Luna, she had forgotten a most important thing. Will was now going to the very place where Luna had declared an invasion to be taking place. She needed to warn him. He was supposed to build a pool there?

Flawless knew that she needed to prepare Will for the dangers that were waiting, but he wasn't in the garden. She rushed on, intent on telling him what she had heard and then confronting her father.

25

Creative Solutions

Will, of course, was already more than aware of the problems at The Border. He was sitting in the middle of them. The caged children and their mothers had been released back to their families; Will was pretty proud of the way that had worked out, but the water flow from The River was still almost completely blocked from The Lowlands, and The Great River continued to ooze deeper onto Urhonordo territory. The flood was growing.

Will assessed the remaining situation. *I can't possibly make this mess into a pool as I was ordered,* he thought. *As I discovered on the way down here, a pool made from a blocked river is impossible . . . but a flood isn't. This flood of Urhonordo land for a pool is even illegal as well. That is another reason that I cannot do what King Drum has ordered. There will be no pool. So why do I feel guilty?*

"Because your father told you to follow your boss's orders," reminded Cwill. "But these orders are bad, so you're off the hook."

Many of the Royal Guard gathered with Will on the porch of the nearly completed manor house. They told him that they had blocked the water to The Lowlands even though they knew it was a bad idea because Dipswitch, as "Royal Border Advisor," had given them orders.

"They followed orders because they were Guardsmen, right?" asked Cwill.

"Yeah, I guess," mumbled Will.

The Guardsmen had also been pressed into construction of the manor house and wall by Dipswitch. The Royal Guard had thought,

"This shouldn't be our job," but they had followed orders and had done it.

Even worse, the Royal Guard had been told by Dipswitch that they must put Lowlanders into cages. Their Consciences had told them not to do it, but they had followed orders and done it.

"As a Conscience myself, I'm beginning to get the hang of this. Guardsmen are good soldiers. They did what they were told to do because a Royal Advisor had the authority to order them to do it, and they always followed orders, right?" added Cwill.

"Uh-huh," said Will, "but they were bad orders. They really didn't want to do those things." Will was still not getting the point.

"Think about it," whispered Cwill. "Dipswitch is a *Royal Advisor,* and he ordered them to do bad things and they did them even when they didn't want to. You're a Royal Advisor too, Will," hinted Cwill.

"So?"

"Being conflicted about not following Drum's bad orders is one thing, but not seeing the solution to the most important problem down here is another, Will. Were you listening when Morf talked to you? Use your creativity like Morf said. As a Royal Advisor, you can figure out what needs to be done about this mess, and this time, you can give the Guardsmen good orders to help you do it."

The resourceful Lowlanders still did not have access to their water. That was obvious. Since they were no longer afraid of the Guard, they were carrying buckets of water from the flooded banks of Urhonordo to a spot some distance behind Dipswitch Manor. It was where their homes had always been located and where the currently dry riverbed still existed.

"I never said a solution would be easy," said Cwill stubbornly, "but the Lowlanders are already taking the water of The River where it wants to go."

Will continued to watch the steady parade of Lowlanders carrying water from Urhonordo to their homes. They had been doing that all day. They had actually worn a path from the water to their land.

Will suddenly remembered what Drum had said to him when he ordered him down here. "You are in charge of what goes on at that pool. It will be your call." That was what Drum had said. Maybe that was what Cwill was trying to say.

He had the same kind of authority that Dipswitch had. He was the Royal Ag Advisor. If Dipswitch could order the Royal Guard to block water and fill up a pool, Will could order them to unblock the water and let The River flow back where it belonged. The King had even said so.

"Finally, you get creative." Cwill sighed.

With a sigh of understanding at last, Will jumped from his spot overlooking the offensive flood and began to shout. "Come here, everyone! I've got it! I've got our solution, and what's more, it's even legal."

Everyone gathered hesitantly around Will. There were Lowlander men, women, and children and the Royal Guard. They had all been through a challenging time, and they had been treated badly by nearly everyone in authority. Will could tell that they were not completely sure that they could trust any new idea.

"He sounds too happy. Maybe he has lost his mind," suggested Ben's grandfather.

"We should listen and find out." Ben grinned. Ben's grandfather decided to listen.

"Here's my idea," Will announced. "Over my shoulder is a handy path that you Lowlanders have made by dragging water to your land all day." The Lowlanders looked guilty but defiant.

"We have to do this, Will," defended Ben. "I thought you understood that."

"Oh, I do," answered Will. "I really do. The Royal Guard blocked the flow of The River so now you have to carry it all and store it in jugs."

"We had to do that," defended the Royal Guard. "You know that, Will.

We were under orders from the Royal Border Advisor."

"I understand that too," responded Will quickly. "But guess what. I am a Royal Advisor too, and I have some *different* orders.

"My orders are that we all get together and dig a ditch right where you Lowlanders already wore a path, only we will make your path deeper—a lot deeper. The ditch we dig will follow your path, directly past the manor house, and back to the riverbed on *your land where it belongs.*

"The Great River *wants* to flow in that direction, so all we need to do is make it easier for The River and its floodwaters to get there. The River won't be flowing the way it used to flow before the big manor house was built. It will be flowing in a new but an equally good way, *around* the house by way of a beautiful channel, on its way back to its own natural riverbed on your land!"

The crowd looked at each other and then looked at the path they had made all day.

"You mean we should take the water that belongs to the rich man? Won't he make the Royal Guard come after us?"

"The River water doesn't belong to the rich man," said Will. "I heard him say that the water on *his side* of his manor house is *his*. That's just fine to say, but The Great River is not his. When the water gets around his house and down to your land, *that* water will belong to you. All we have to do is give it a way to get there."

The assembled Lowlanders thought that over. They talked to each other and looked closely at Will, the Royal Guard, and the path.

The men of the Royal Guard were already smiling. "Finally, we get orders we like. We can do this," they mumbled in a funny sort of bashful way. "You're a Royal Advisor, right? We like your orders better than the ones we had from Dipswitch."

Ben was already excited. He and Will began to grin as one by one, the Lowlanders accepted the idea. They had trouble believing it. They had been through too much. It was almost too simple, but it was wonderful.

Quickly, the digging tools that had just come home from the levees up north were gladly picked up again, and the work on the ditch began.

26

Thorndike

It was still morning. Flawless had looked for Will but found him nowhere. Where had he gone? Quickly, she hurried to the throne room. Maybe he would check in with her father before he left for The Border. She also needed to tell her father about her meeting with Queen Luna. She was sure that he would be pleased with the peaceful solution that she had accomplished, but she needed to confront him about his need to repair his damaged relationship with this neighbor.

Flawless found her father in the throne room as expected, but he was not alone or with Will. The gentleman with him looked familiar, but Flawless was not sure where she had seen him before. Hopefully he was just passing through. She had averted a crisis, but she knew it was only temporary. She needed to talk to her father alone. Didn't he remember that they were dealing with a possible invasion? He didn't even know yet about her successful peace talks.

Flawless soon picked up an odd combination of vibrations. A strange, cold aura clung to the floor of the throne room, cancelling the optimism that had followed her from her talk with Luna. Cflawless knew right away that it was the Eforces in the room. She had a feeling about such things. She shivered.

Drum seemed to be happy and excited, however. He was waving his arms and making some kind of major point that Flawless didn't quite understand.

"I knew you were the man for the job," Drum finished, gloating. "You said that you wanted some authority from the beginning. Now you will have all the authority you want. It's perfect timing."

The other man was not nearly as animated. He stood calmly, looking at Drum with an unmistakable look of superiority. He said nothing.

That man is the source of the Eforce in this room, Cflawless thought. Flawless had burst in without warning, but she had no intention of waiting for whatever was going on with this unresponsive person. She had important things to discuss with her father. This man, whoever he was, could wait.

"Father! I need to speak with you immediately . . . and alone," she announced forcefully.

Drum looked up with a start. He hadn't seen her come in. "Oh hello, daughter," he said dismissively. "Sit down, dear. Lord Thorndike and I are having a serious discussion. I'll talk to you later."

Flawless did not sit down. Now, she flashed on her memory of this man. He had been one of the few guests that had actually spoken to her father at his Inaugural Celebration. Her memories rested on the face of someone who had been arrogant and rude at that time. He didn't appear to have changed. "Hello, Sir Thorndike," said Flawless as politely as she could. "Nice to see you again, but I need to talk to my father now. It's urgent. Could you please excuse us?"

Drum stepped back in surprise, but only slightly. "This is not a discussion for a young lady, Flawless. You can listen if you wish, but you must let the men here do the talking."

Flawless sat down to wait as she was told. She had fallen for a dismissal last night, but she had changed since this morning. She would not go away or wait long.

"What are you doing, Flawless?" whispered Cflawless. "You are being dismissed like a child. You have something important to say. Your father needs to hear it. What you need to tell him is important to the Kingdom, more important than this evil man, whoever he is."

I know, I know, thought Flawless. And look at this guy. I don't like him. I don't like the way he looks. I don't trust him. I am just going to wait a minute until he leaves and then tell Father what went on with Luna . . . and ask him what's going on with this guy.

"I think you're just wimping out," muttered Cflawless.

Maybe . . . Flawless leaned forward. Why was this unpleasant man here in the throne room in the middle of what her father should think was still a crisis? For all her father knew, Luna was still down at The Bridge. Flawless could feel a heartless aura surrounding the man with her father and so could Cflawless. This was not a good man.

King Drum regained control of his situation. He ignored the silence of his guest and began by explaining what sounded like the threat from Urhonordo. There was no longer a threat, but her father didn't know that.

Next, he moved on to coaxing. Flawless recognized the behavior. She had seen it before. Her father was making a deal.

"That stupid Queen is at The Bridge as we speak," he explained insultingly. "So far, she has not made a move toward The Castle. If you announce yourself as Royal Defense Advisor and General of The Royal Guard, I am sure that she will retreat. She is only a woman."

Flawless bristled but said nothing. This man was the Royal Defense Advisor now? Cflawless jumped up and down with impatience.

Sir Thorndike responded. "I am not worried about Queen Luna," he said calmly. "I *am* concerned about what comes afterward, however. With few troops remaining here at The Castle, how would you expect me to win an engagement against threats from any adversary, even Queen Luna?"

Drum smiled a strange but knowing smile. "You will have troops, Thorndike. You will have all the troops you want."

Flawless sat back on her chair. What troops was he talking about?

Thorndike stepped back in surprise as well. "Just where will you find these troops?" he sneered, showing the lack of respect and arrogance that Flawless had previously sensed in him.

"This man is the most *offensive Defense* Advisor ever. He's dangerous," hissed Cflawless.

"I know," Flawless said quietly. She could stay quiet no longer. "Father, if you are discussing the problem with Queen Luna, I would like to be a part of the discussion. I have something important to tell you about that." She stood up and calmly walked forward.

Sir Thorndike did not hide his disgust at the interruption. "I have a great deal of admiration for the beauty of your daughter, Sir Drum, but I feel that she is out of place in this discussion. It would be much more appropriate if she were dismissed and asked to come back at another time."

She was being dismissed like a yapping dog. "Thank you for your admiration, Sir Thorndike, but frankly, I feel that *your* comment is 'out of place,'" said Flawless. "I am a grown woman and the daughter of a king. I also happen to have knowledge of the situation with Queen Luna. I will *not* be dismissed."

Drum was flabbergasted. Flawless had never spoken up strongly before, especially in front of others. He was about to respond harshly when a small voice spoke in his ear.

"Don't dismiss Flawless," whispered Cdrum. "She has helped you before . . . and she's smart."

Drum hesitated. He felt frantic. There was an invasion on his border. He had not forgotten. He was in the middle of a deal that could, in his opinion, mean the survival of his reign or lack of it. Drum knew that Thorndike was strong enough to do what he wanted him to do, but Thorndike was also strong enough to take over River Kingdom himself if Drum wasn't careful. Drum knew instinctively that his best course was to work *with* Thorndike. Carefully he turned to Flawless and caught her eye.

"Thank you for caring and being here to help," Drum murmured. "You always help. But I ask you now, daughter. Listen and learn. Sir Thorndike and I need to iron out a very important matter, which I will share with you later." He was almost begging. Flawless sensed her father's desperation. He needed her to do as he asked without question. She sat. Cflawless said nothing.

"Be careful of this guy," coached Cdrum. Drum ignored him. "Thank you for your concern, Sir Thorndike, but I appreciate my daughter's presence so I will continue with her here. Now, let me first respond to the matter, which you just questioned. You wondered where I would get troops for any battle if we do not have enough troops here at The Castle. Am I right?"

"Indeed," Sir Thorndike agreed. "From what I can see, your understanding of troop availability is as flawed as your belief in your so- called Royalty. As you know, I have royalty in my blood. I interviewed for your position but was turned down on a technicality . . . something about a less-than-favorable financial situation, I believe. I was undergoing a momentary setback.

"I am eminently more qualified for your current position than you, but I am willing to concede King Sol's error in judgment in choosing you over me if you have a proposition, which I feel would be favorable to me. So far, I see nothing here of value. You're unprepared and under siege. There is nothing in this situation for me."

Flawless rose up out of her chair in instant rage. "You can't talk to my father like that, you pompous piece of leftover royalty!"

"Atta girl," chimed Cflawless.

Drum smiled slightly even though he was deep into the current situation.

Sir Thorndike recoiled in surprise.

Drum inhaled and carefully picked up the thread of his key proposal. He could take an insult from this also-ran because he knew he held the answer to Thorndike's wounded pride.

"Sir Thorndike, you are arrogant and, in addition, completely uninformed. I may not have royal blood, but I do have a kingdom full of farmers, peasants, and other assorted commoners. They all love me. They adore me. We have been developing a close relationship since the day after my inaugural.

"But of course, you wouldn't know anything about that. You have been off sulking somewhere, waiting for me to either fall apart or give you something. Well, now I have something that I know you want."

"And what would that be?" Thorndike sneered.

"Power," said Lord Doran Drum quietly, "and a kingdom of your own." Flawless sat back down in her chair with a thump.

"How do you figure?" Thorndike was suddenly very attentive. Flawless was stunned.

King Drum now began to strut. He had everyone's attention, and he had the solution he knew Thorndike wanted. Proudly he described his plan. "The commoners of River Kingdom are my commoners. There are hundreds of them and they are *my fans*," he bragged. "They will do anything for me. They are the ones that called for me to be King. Most recently, I promised them a beautiful pool down by The Border, not because they needed it, but because I could give them something that they had never thought they would have. I billed it as *their reward* for the work completed on their levees.

"They now anticipate that pool with pleasure. They are grateful. They feel that they deserve it, and they are thrilled with me. I know, if I ask them to, they will be willing to go to war for me because they believe in me."

Flawless couldn't move. She couldn't believe what she was hearing. Sir Thorndike, however, was alert and fascinated. Command of a brand-new strapping farmer fighting force? This sounded interesting, to say the least. But what had Drum said about ruling his own kingdom? What was that all about?

"I see," commented Sir Thorndike calmly, trying to give the impression that he was above everything. "And what about the 'other kingdom' you mentioned? Where, exactly, would that kingdom be, and how would I become its ruler?"

King Drum climbed back onto his throne where he knew he would look most impressive and achieve the best impact on his viewer. He adjusted his crown. "The pool that I have promised is between River Kingdom and Urhonordo, just above The Lowlands. The pool is already being built there.

I have my Ag Advisor and his Lowlander crew working to finish it as we speak. The crazy Queen that rules the Urhonordos will hate that pool. It will go against her stupid Water Rights Treaty. I am sure.

"All that the *right* man with the *right* force will have to do is go down there, claim the pool, and when Queen Luna and her puny Royal Guard object, claim her kingdom as well. There should be little or no opposition from the likes of her."

"That's out of bounds, Drum!" yelled Cdrum. "You can't do that."

"Father! You can't say that!" Flawless leapt from her chair and ran to the throne.

"I can *say* that and *do* that," Drum replied to both. "I am the King."

"He can do that, and I am ready to assist him," announced Thorndike.

"It is an excellent plan. I am amazed at you, Drum. I never perceived you to have this kind of foresight, planning, and nerve. I underestimated you. I believe we can work together, and I am looking forward to it."

"Daddy, you can't really be thinking of doing this!" Flawless cried. "I must restate my concern about your daughter, however," Thorndike continued. "I will be here tomorrow to draw up the plans for our operation. I am leaving for The Bridge now to inform the little Queen that we 'understand her concerns' and will be meeting with her shortly."

The man snickered slightly. "Meanwhile, I would appreciate you asking your beautiful daughter to *stay in her place and not interfere.*" With that and a slight bow in the direction of Drum, he strode from the room.

King Drum smiled at his daughter with a sigh of relief. "Well, what do you think?" he asked proudly. "We should be safe soon, wouldn't you say?" Cdrum threw up his hands. "I think you might as well not have a Conscience, Drum. You never listen! What good am I if you don't listen?"

"I think that man is a dangerous jackass," answered Flawless.

Drum stopped smiling. Could Thorndike be right? Was his daughter not able to understand the brilliance of the plan that he had just outlined? "I can't believe that you don't approve of the battle plan that I just negotiated," Drum stated. "I thought I had taught you better than that, daughter."

"Thank God you didn't teach her to lose her integrity as you have just done!" shouted Cdrum in Drum's ear.

"Father! Where is your integrity?" screamed Flawless. "Shut up! What do you know?" Drum retorted.

Flawless stopped short and stared at her father in horror.

"I was talking to my Conscience again," said Drum as a type of apology. Flawless was unable to comprehend the horror of what she had just heard and seen. As she finally regained her control, she wilted and put her head in her hands. "How could you have made such a terrible deal with that terrible man?" she groaned. "How could you?"

The Auras wafted over Drum. He was not going to accept the concept that he had done anything wrong. He stood up strong, puffed out his chest, and marched back and forth in front of his throne, quickly arranging an acceptable reason for his plan. His mind raced, but his manner was resolute. "I have done what needed to be done," he stated simply. "Surely you can understand that, Flawless. When we are threatened by another kingdom, we must take action to protect ourselves. This is what a strong king must do, and I, of course, am a very strong King."

Flawless looked up at her father and shook her head. "But we are not threatened by another kingdom, Father," she answered quietly. "I just negotiated a peace with Queen Luna. She has returned to her kingdom. All she asks for is a Water Rights Treaty that is fair to her and her people."

Again, the Auras swarmed Drum in a glorious cloud. He looked past his daughter. She was young. She thought she could help, but she was just a child. He shook his head. "You women think you can do things that only men can do, Flawless," he said forcefully. "Thorndike was right. You need to leave the issues of war to men like Thorndike and myself."

"Thorndike is a weasel, Daddy. I am shocked that you can't see that. And why are you calling that monster 'Defense Advisor'? Where is General Horace?"

"He retired," answered her father.

Flawless sat down in the chair next to the throne. A few minutes ago, she had been proud to sit there. She was no longer proud.

In several minutes, there was noise outside the throne room curtains. Sir Thorndike burst through the drapes with a triumphant grin. "I have routed the enemy, sire!" he crowed.

"I guess they heard that I was coming and fled back to their humble kingdom. Good riddance, I say. When I take over, Urhonordo will no longer be humble. It shall be called 'The Kingdom of Thorndike,' and it shall grow and prosper until it rivals River Kingdom! Mark my words."

The Auras had achieved a most important goal. They were now aimed for violence, and Thorndike would be their weapon of choice.

27

Consciences vs. Auras

That evening, Cflawless requested an emergency Conscience Forum. The situation in The Castle appeared to be getting out of hand. Many changes had taken place in The Castle administration since Drum had declared himself King. Cflawless was a young Conscience, and she was worried. Were all of their Conscience functions still working with humans the way they should?

Drum had replaced several old Royal Advisors with new ones. Were the new ones up to the tasks they were given? The Castle didn't seem to be running as smoothly as it did before. And now, on top of everything, there was a threat of war. All the Consciences wanted to talk to Cdrum, but he wasn't here yet. Cdrum was key.

The Consciences agreed that they missed Marvin, Sir Arnold, and General Horace. These Royal Advisors had been loyal to King Sol, and the advisors in their place were all "friends" of King Drum. What did they know about their jobs? No one could tell for sure.

The "feather man," Milton Fandango, was now the Advisor of Finance. Cmilton confessed that all Milton knew about finances was to charge The Kingdom for the daily performances of his girls and their "current events report" (gossip).

Milton had good intentions, but he wasn't really good with numbers or paperwork and paid little attention to incoming bills other than his own. Why had he been appointed to the Finance position? Cmilton didn't know, and he promised to encourage his human to try harder, but where was Cdrum?

Cdipswitch, the Conscience of the new Border Advisor, was not in attendance at the meeting. Several of the other Consciences remarked that he hadn't attended many forums in the past either and was, perhaps, embarrassed by his human's behavior. His human was a disagreeable, bossy gentleman who had no regard these days for anyone but his bossy wife.

Sir Dipswitch didn't like or even *know* any Urhonordos or Lowlanders. Why had he been given the new post of Border Advisor, anyway? He was a questionable choice for the questionable position that Drum had given him. Why? And where was Cdrum?

Rumor had it that there was some sort of deal between Dipswitch and Drum regarding construction (the Royal Guard?), building materials (the rubble from the levees?), and disgraceful treatment of Lowlanders (cages?). Did Cdrum know about these things?

The Consciences of the Forum didn't know where to start their discussion. The rules for what was right and wrong seemed to depend on what King Drum said was right and wrong. They knew that this wasn't the way things were supposed to be, but maybe Cdrum could explain.

Now the conversation turned to the new Defense Advisor. He had never been in the Royal Guard. He had never even seen a battle. But he appeared to be gearing up for a war that was more offense than defense. This was frightening and the main reason that Cflawless had called for The Forum. Drum seemed to support Thorndike's attitude and ideas, but what did Cdrum think?

"Where is Cdrum, anyway? He's usually the first one here," mumbled one of the Consciences from The Castle Kitchen. "With all the changes that have happened since Drum arrived at The Castle, he should be holding regular news conferences to help us understand what's going on."

"This new defense guy has a mean reputation too," commented Cvandyke, the Conscience for a local aristocrat. "Most of the local lords and barons think Drum has gone off the rails hiring this guy, but we didn't understand his other hires either, so what do we know?"

"I think Cdrum's confused," said Cflawless. "Drum has gone to meet with that Thorndike person again about 'gathering the troops,' as they call it, and Cdrum didn't want to go listen to war talk. I thought he was coming here, but now I don't know where he is. He may have given up. That's another reason that I called the meeting. Cdrum is upset. If

Cdrum isn't active, the rest of us may need to pick up the slack with Drum. He needs all the Conscience help he can get."

"Cdrum needs to get over it," contributed Cmorf. "Drum is not his fault. Consciences can just suggest good ideas and solutions, but they can't make a person do the right thing."

"Obviously," said Cseamstress from The Castle Staff. "Otherwise, you wouldn't have allowed Morf to force all of us to make those ugly red hats for no reason."

"That wasn't a bad thing," groused Cmorf. "It was just a loyalty thing." "Well, whatever it was, compared to now, it seems like 'the good old days' looking back on it. Today, I heard that Queen Luna brought armed troops over The Bridge *in uniform*. River Kingdom has never had trouble with Urhonordo. They are one of our allies. What was that about? Were we actually invaded?"

"No," said Cflawless. "I was there with Flawless. Queen Luna was just trying to make a forceful point. She knows that water rights are important to people who live near a river. She was just tired of King Drum blowing her off and not giving her the respect that she and The River deserve.

"Luna and Flawless worked out an agreement to meet about the whole water rights issue, but poor Flawless had to deal with her father. That man doesn't listen."

"Unless you're a farmer," snickered Cgeorge, the Conscience of a longtime farmer. "If you're a farmer, King Drum loves you. Now he is promising the farmers a pool. Did you hear that? What is a farmer going to do with a pool, I ask you? That's just crazy in my opinion, but the rest of the common folk thought that was a great idea. I don't get it, but that's just me." "I don't get it either," agreed Cflawless. "At first, Flawless and I thought the pool was a nice idea, but we don't have time for nice ideas right now. We need to talk about Thorndike before he starts a real war. Does anybody here know Thorndike's Conscience?"

"Heck, no," growled Crodney. "I'm not even sure if Cthorndike is still around. He got a real lemon when he got Lord Thorndike. He tried to make the guy kinder, more generous . . . not so mean and greedy, but I think the Eforces got to Thorndike early in his life. No matter how hard he tried, Cthorndike just couldn't get through to his human. I think he might have just given up."

"That's really sad," said Cmorf. "Morf is a disgusting suck-up, but I'll never give up on him."

"That's why Thorndike is my main issue." Cflawless sighed. "Lord Thorndike was at The Castle today talking to Drum, and that's when Drum just decided that *Thorndike* should be the new Royal Defense Advisor —a guy with no functioning Conscience, right? He and Drum are cooking up something that sounds terrible. I think they want to fight with Urhonordo and use farmers to do it. It sounds awful."

The Consciences stopped socializing and drew near to Cflawless.

"Why do they want to do something like that?"

"I never heard there was anybody that we needed to fight."

"There isn't," Cflawless retorted sharply. "Here's the problem. First, Drum got scared that Urhonordo was invading . . . which you know now they weren't, right?"

"I guess."

"Then he fired poor General Horace because he didn't have any troops to fight the invasion that wasn't happening. Then because he was scared of something that wasn't happening, he called on Thorndike to be his Royal Defense Advisor and bribed him by promising to make him King of Urhonordo when he conquers them, which nobody wants him to do. And they're going to use the farmers for troops to do it." Cflawless stopped for air.

"O-o-o-oh," gasped the other Consciences in stunned response.

An old Conscience from a retired Royal Guard was the first to regain his voice. "Farmers? He thinks he's going to use common farmers for troops? They don't know how to fight. That's crazy. And to fight who . . . and why?"

"Urhonordo." Cflawless sighed. "For no reason at all because they haven't done anything wrong." She threw up her hands.

The Consciences were silent. It was hard to take it all in, but little by little, all roads of thinking led back to Drum. Drum's plans or lack of them were the cause of everything. Plans were now being made for an unnecessary war.

"Like was said before, where's Cdrum?" grumbled Cseamstress. "Has he tried to communicate with Drum? Drum used to be a self-centered showoff, but it seemed like Cdrum had him under control. Now this king stuff has gone to his head a little—"

"Or a lot."

"Yeah, even though he used to lie all the time . . ." "But not about anything important."

"Yes, but that was before he was in such an important position," said Cflawless sadly. "Drum was kind of quirky, but he was just an odd, rich, party-prone womanizer, so nobody was worried about his quirks. He lied and made up stuff, but that was just . . . entertaining.

"Now Cdrum is really worried. Drum is scared to death about losing control of River Kingdom, and Flawless doesn't think he was thinking straight," contributed Cflawless. "River Kingdom is in danger because Drum has started something with this Thorndike person that he may not know how to finish."

"I say we should let it ride," contributed Cmorf. "There'll never be a real war. Drum is all blow and no go. He loves to bluff, and he's bluffing like usual. River Kingdom is doing pretty well. The harvests are excellent, the farmers and the commoners are happy. The only one with their nose out of joint is Queen Luna."

"You and Morf always let whatever Drum does 'ride,' snorted Cflawless. "And I resent your speaking about Queen Luna that way. She is a strong woman with a kingdom full of loyal subjects . . . *and* a Royal Guard. She is definitely no pushover. She believes in treating people and The River with respect. The River can help you *and* hurt you, and River Kingdom should honor The River and Queen Luna, not 'let it ride.'"

"How do you know so much about Queen Luna, Cflawless?" Cdrum had just entered The Forum.

All the Consciences turned at once. Cdrum was not royalty, but he was as close to it at this moment as the Consciences could get. They parted and made him a place of honor.

All but Cflawless ran to her longtime friend and hugged him hard. "How are you, Cdrum? I was worried about you. Where have you been?"

Cdrum stood back from the hug and stared at Cflawless. "Never mind where I've been. How do you know about Queen Luna?"

"Flawless went down to The Bridge and spoke with the Queen for over an hour when she invaded . . . brought her flowers too. They're friends now, you know."

"No. I didn't know that," croaked Cdrum. "They *really* talked, you say? What did they say? What did they talk about?"

"They talked about peace, of course," said Cflawless, somewhat smugly. "They agreed to put together a meeting about water rights for real this time and iron things out. Then Queen Luna and her Royal Guard went back over The Bridge."

"They didn't."

"They did, and it was beautiful. Then Thorndike showed up and messed with Drum's thinking. That's why I called this forum."

"Oh my god," said Cdrum. "If Drum heard about that, he didn't pay it enough attention and neither did I. He and Thorndike have called another rally for tonight to rile up the commoners and turn them all into Royal Guard."

"That's what I was afraid of." Cflawless sighed.

"That doesn't surprise me," said Cmorf smugly. "Thorndike has been out for what he could get from Drum since the day of Drum's inauguration. I had him sized up as a two-faced sleaze the minute I saw him."

"Takes one to know one," barked Ccook.

"Wait a minute," Cmorf retaliated. "I'm one of the good guys here."

"Your host human used to understand most stuff most of the time. Now your human is a wimp, and you know it," responded Ccook. "Even Drum knows it. Morf will get thrown under the wagon like Marvin and Arnold and Horace if Drum gets mad at him."

The dispirited Consciences looked at each other. Maybe Consciences weren't going to be as useful to humans as Flawless had always thought they would be.

Cflawless was the youngest Conscience there. She looked around at her fellow Consciences. She couldn't believe they might be giving up. She had always looked up to older Consciences for guidance. They knew so much more than she knew about the evils of the world.

Evils of the world?

Suddenly, Cflawless remembered something. The throne room was damp and cold when she and Flawless entered it this morning. The Auras must have been there in great numbers. Yes, they were, she remembered. Why had she not thought of this or recognized its significance? The Auras had obviously seen their opportunity to take over and were making use of it. Cflawless had never had to deal with real Auras before. She had heard about them. She had even heard that they loved to start wars. Why hadn't she seen this coming?

It had all happened while Cflawless watched. She was ashamed of herself. If Cflawless knew anything now, she knew that she needed to get her friends, the other Consciences, back in the game.

"Come on, people. It's not too late. Let's talk about this," Flawless coached with spirit. "What we are seeing is the work of Auras. I just figured it out. I was blind."

At first, there was silence in The Forum. Then there was uncomfortable shuffling. The Consciences had not dealt with real Auras in a long time.

Slowly, the Conscience Forum gathered back together again. This was their job. This was their calling. This was what they were made for. They took a deep breath and listened.

"I have heard that Auras are very powerful when they gather and get active. I believe, now that I think about it, they were gathered in force in the throne room and influenced the decision Drum made this afternoon," said Cflawless.

With sudden clarity, a wave of understanding swept over the tiny members of the group. This might be true. This might be what they were up against now. For some reason, the pro-war Auras had become more active. Maybe they had been taking advantage of Drum's inexperience since he took over as Royal Caretaker.

Cdrum hung his head. Why hadn't he seen this?

But the Consciences did not find fault. This wasn't something that could be handled by just one Conscience. Quickly, the Consciences regrouped and reenergized. They would all have to be in on it if they were to save The Kingdom from war.

The Consciences discussed the Auras and reviewed techniques that had worked (or hadn't) in the past. At least they now knew what they were really up against—the Auras.

28

Conscience Conflicts

Will, Ben, Guardsmen, and Lowlanders were all now working on the path that the Lowlanders had been traveling with their water jugs. The Lowlanders' way of life had been threatened. They had been lied to. Their children had been caged. They had worked all summer for no pay. But in the way typical of the Lowlanders, they saw what needed to be done, and they did it with enthusiasm. The guilt-laden Guardsmen joined in with gusto, *and* happily, they were again under orders.

First, the men dug out the big rocks and dirt that were forming the wall closest to Urhonordo land. These rocks had done the most to block The River and force it over the Urhonordo levees. Once the biggest boulders were removed and relocated at the opening of the path, they began forming their ditch, directing it south an appropriate distance from the eastern side of the new manor house.

The trapped river water above the new opening began to enter the ditch eagerly. The women and children jumped into the muddy water with joy, scooping at the sides of the new channel with their hands.

Water from the "pool" drained over the swampy edge of the ditch that was nearest, carrying drowned crops and floating farm tools with it. With removing all the debris, the progress was not fast, but the ditch began showing signs of becoming a future channel that was looking pretty good as well as functional.

The determined river lapped at the channel as though it was anxious to help dig its own way back down to The Lowland riverbed where it had flowed in the past. The Lowlanders' piece of The Great River was on its way back.

The day wore on and so did the work on the channel. Finally, with many hands digging in the mud and water, the route of The River again flowed south through a boulder-lined detour around Dipswitch Manor. They had reestablished the southern flow of The River, and the flooded farmlands were draining. There was celebration in the tents and cabins of the Lowlanders.

Will's Conscience was pleased, but not satisfied. The draining of the flood and the rerouting of The River had been successes and were important, but food for the winter was still not going to happen.

"No pool, no pay," sang Cwill in Will's ears. "You are going to have to use your creativity again. You did pretty well with the pool and The Lowland water, but you still have an obligation to pay your friends."

"Did anyone ever tell you that a Conscience was a pain in the neck?" Will griped.

"We get that all the time," Cwill admitted.

Suddenly, in the northern distance, Will saw a sight that he knew would mean even more trouble than he currently had. Coming straight toward Dipswitch Manor was the elegant caravan of Lord Dipswitch and his entourage. They were on the way to their property with great expectations of a nearly finished pool. This was not going to go well.

And that was not all. Arriving at the same time from the Urhonordo side of The River was an armed contingent of the Urhonordo Royal Guard. They were halted, standing at attention at the far eastern edge of the draining slime and mud that had been the pool.

Will's first impulse was to run. Ben had the same thought. Their Consciences struggled to say something that might encourage their humans to stand up and be brave, but the best they could come up with was, "Forget the idea of running. There is no place nearby to hide."

Will felt that this impossible situation was more his responsibility than Ben's. "Take your family and the rest of the Lowlanders back over the knoll and out of sight," he suggested. "Ask them to remain calm and quiet. We don't want them to get hurt, and there is danger coming from both sides of The River."

Ben nodded and shepherded his people past a mound of dry sagebrush and down into a small arroyo. He himself, however, crept back to keep an eye on Will.

"I was wondering if you were going to leave Will to face these confrontations on his own," commented Cben.

"Thanks for your confidence," answered Ben.

Will had decided that he would meet at least one of his two threats first face-to-face. With his head and hands up, he waded toward the Urhonordo side of The River.

"Yo ho!" he shouted to the Urhonordo Guardsmen as loudly as he could. "Yo, Urhonordos! I am William of Dale, Royal Agriculture Advisor for River Kingdom. I greet you with an apology for the ruin that your land has experienced. The Lowlander men and I were not aware of this devastation until recently. We have been trying to make amends for what was done."

Will waited. All was quiet. There was no sound but that of the floodwater draining and the fresh river water rushing into the new channel. The Urhonordo Guardsmen continued to maintain their watchful stance from the far eastern edge of the soaked fields.

How are they going to get here to talk to me? wondered Will. *They can't advance through this muck. They'll get bogged down.*

"I think someone closer wants to talk to you," answered Cwill, staring upriver from his vantage on the top of Will's head.

A stylish flat-bottomed boat suddenly nosed its way down The River toward Will from nowhere. It slid quietly up to him, large and sleek and silent. Where did it come from? Ominously, it seemed to be holding at least a half-dozen oarsmen and a small complement of men at arms.

And standing strong and steady at the stern of the boat was Her Majesty, Queen Luna.

"I heard of this invasion of water, but I had to see it for myself," she said above the burble of The River. "I must admit that I would not have believed that it was this serious if I had not seen it."

Will bowed low although knee-deep in The River. He had never met a queen before. "I am so sorry that this was allowed to happen, Your Majesty," he began.

"Hush, soulless destroyer of beauty," Queen Luna interrupted, looking down at him with contempt. "Look what you have done. Wonderful, productive farmland has been drowned by your careless greed and trampled by your troops. Does your King know no bounds to his self-indulgence? I thought I would be able to develop a treaty with his daughter, but now that is not enough. I have no choice but to take you in trade for our losses. The rest I will achieve as they did in the old days. Without an immediate apology and compensation from River Kingdom, there will be war."

Will was unprepared for such an impressive announcement. He felt as though the Queen's words were, like the water rushing past him, unrelenting forces of nature. And suddenly, he was unsteady on his feet, as without further warning, he was seized by two Urhonordo Guardsmen who had leapt into the water. In an instant, he was on the bow of the boat itself, tied and gagged and stuffed into the nose of the craft.

With deft maneuvers, the oarsmen reversed the boat's course and poled it back upriver and out of sight behind a bend and low-hanging foliage.

The River Kingdom's Royal Guard had been lounging at the manor house but had not moved from the porch. Before they could decide what to do about a boat and an armed force that had popped up from nowhere, the whole thing had disappeared. So had the armed Guardsmen that Will had spotted in the eastern distance.

"Should we go after them?" asked one of The Kingdom's Guardsmen. "It's Urhonordo land," contributed some of their Consciences. "They have a right to be there and we don't."

"But they took that guy named Will with them," said another Guardsman's Conscience. "Will is a good guy."

"We should try to help Will, but look," said the Guardsmen to each other. "We can't leave to rescue Will right now. Lord Dipswitch is coming this way. He's expecting a pool. King Drum says that he's our boss, and his pool just got drained." They were caught in another Conscience conflict. What should they do?

Ben watched in shock. It all happened so quickly that he could do nothing as well. His friend, Will, was there one minute and then he was gone. He stared after the vanished Urhonordo boat. The Urhonordos were peaceful . . . at least they always had been. Why had they taken Will? Was he in danger? Ben had no idea. But this was not good . . . maybe even a disaster. He should go after Will right away.

Now he too noticed the Dipswitch caravan. This was disaster number two. Without meeting him, Ben knew he would dislike the pushy Dipswitch in every way. The man had ordered the caging of Lowlander women and children. He had demanded a pool for his equally pushy wife. He had built his house so that it blocked The River's water without caring what it did to the Lowlanders or the Urhonordos. There was nothing about him to like.

Ben braced himself. Dipswitch's so-called pool was gone and so was Will. Will could have explained to Dipswitch about why they had drained the swamp, but he wouldn't want to hear anything from Ben. Ben was a Lowlander.

Ben's family and friends were just over the rise where they might be found if Dipswitch decided to look for them. This was potential disaster number three. Ben scooted out of sight.

Lord Dipswitch's caravan stopped in the driveway of the new manor house, and the gentleman stared at his property in shock. The beautiful water that should have been his finished pool was now rushing down a new channel and escaping toward The Lowlands. There was nothing left but an oozing mass of mud and debris. Who was to blame for this disgusting incompetence? This was not what he had paid King Drum extra for.

He growled in fury and yelled for the Royal Guard who were already rushing across the porch and up the driveway to the caravan. Tumbling in an eager but undisciplined fashion, they arrived in a jumble in front of the man whom they knew was again their boss.

Dipswitch was again their authority. They had been told to build a wall that would block The River from the manor house and The Lowlands. They had done it. They had been told to put The Lowland kids in cages. They had really hated all of that, but they had done it.

Recently, however, they had drained an illegal pool and freed children from cages. They had liked that, and their Consciences had liked that too, but now they had a major conflict. They were Royal Guardsmen, and it wasn't their duty to question authority. But which authority? The difference between right and wrong should be easier than this.

And what was worse, the Guardsmen were rushing toward the despised Dipswitch while a man they had learned to like and trust had just been abducted. They wanted to go after him, but they couldn't. They and their Consciences came to confused attention in front of the storming Dipswitch. They hung their heads and waited for Dipswitch to gather his fury and aim it at them.

Meanwhile, Ben watched from a protective corner of the manor house. He and his people had come to like the Royal Guard now that they had begun following Will's orders instead of Dipswitch's. Ben could see that Dipswitch was going to be hard on them.

Ben's Conscience wanted him to do something, but what could he do to help? Nothing. He was only a lowly Lowlander in Dipswitch's eyes.

And Will was gone! Ben loved Will like a brother. What was he doing to help Will? Also, nothing.

And then Ben's family and friends were hiding dangerously close nearby. What was he doing to make sure they were safe? Nothing.

"Are you a coward, Ben?" Cben challenged aloud. "If you're not, you could have fooled me. The Royal Guard is going to get in trouble, your best friend was just kidnapped, your family is in a vulnerable spot, and you're hiding. Really? You're not a coward?"

Ben clenched his fists. Three things needed his help. What should he do? What could he do?

I can't handle conflict. I am stupid, Ben thought to himself. I have no idea what to do.

"No. You're not stupid. You don't get off that easy," said Cben. "You just don't want to admit that what you need to do requires decision making and courage."

"What do you mean, Conscience?" whispered Ben. "I don't see anything I can do to fix this situation. I think it's unfixable."

"Let me break it down for you," said Cben. "You can't help the Royal Guard, but they can probably help themselves. Will and you could figure this whole thing out *if* you were together. That is, *you two* could create a plan together *if* you went looking for him and found him . . . that is, if you made sure that your friends and family were safe first."

That was the answer. Ben hustled from his hiding place. Maybe he couldn't figure out everything by himself, especially for the poor Guardsmen, but he *could* try to rescue Will. He needed to do that out of friendship, and he also needed Will to help him figure out a way to fix the mess that they were all still in. Dipswitch would not like their solution with The River.

But family first. Quickly, Ben made his way to where his family was hiding and guided them farther down river. Now, they were at last back in Lowland territory. They could take care of themselves and stay safe as long as *their* piece of The River was again flowing to them. Then Ben turned east, on his way to find Will.

Lord Dipswitch, on the other hand, had tired of yelling. He was accustomed to getting what he wanted when he had paid for it, and this disgusting situation was not something he would stand for. He herded his servants and a loudly protesting wife into his huge but cheerless manor.

From every eastern window, Dipswitch saw mud. Worse yet, his wife saw mud. She had expected a huge pool beside a grand estate. He had paid for it. That con man, Drum, had pocketed his own ill-gotten gain; and Dipswitch, "a deserving man of means," had nothing to show for it but an angry wife.

Cdipswitch was not involved. He had objected to Dipswitch's selfishness, dishonesty, and racism for several months now. The fact that the pool was gone and Dipswitch's wife was mad at him was poetic justice. He was pretty happy with the way things were working out.

Dipswitch had to blame someone for this mess. He turned on the Royal Guard, demanding to know how they had let this catastrophe happen.

The Royal Guard did not blame it on Will, at least not all of it. They did, however, explain that Will, the Royal Agriculture Advisor, had thought of digging the channel and ordered it. They had only followed orders.

"When I left, the Lowlanders were being contained in cages so that they could not interfere. Water was flowing out over the land and making a pool that was almost a lake. This Will person was supposed to make the pool look nice for all of us to use, not completely destroy it. Look at my beautiful pool now. It is a mud pit."

"But it's a mud pit on Urhonordo land," contributed one of the Guardsmen from the back row.

"The water was flowing onto Urhonordo land, sir, and they weren't happy about it," added another Guardsman.

"So? That was not *my* problem. It was only useless farmland. The peasants that were farming it could just farm somewhere else. Where is this ignorant Will that you speak of?"

"He was abducted by the Urhonordo Queen . . . because of the water invading her land," a Guardsman admitted sadly.

"Good riddance, then. He won't be a problem anymore. Drum doesn't care about such things as Urhonordos or their land. He's out to 'Make River Kingdom Great' and *his* pocket greater."

The Consciences of the Royal Guard squirmed. "And Lord Dipswitch is just out to make *him*self greater and richer," they whispered to their humans. "Say something."

But the Guardsmen stayed silent. *This is not our battle,* they thought sheepishly. *Dipswitch is our boss now, and Will's not here.*

Sir Dipswitch continued to fume against a king that had snookered him. As he saw it now, an upstart Ag Advisor had taken his authority too far and screwed up his real estate deal with Drum. He knew that the "pool" was on Urhonordo land, but he didn't care. The King should have chosen a more cooperative Ag Advisor.

No matter how he looked at it, neither the King nor the Ag Advisor were here where he could get at them. That was infuriating. The King had to make this bargain good for him or else.

Dipswitch made a decision. He was going to get what he paid for and then some, and the swindler that was now in The Castle was going to get it for him. The Auras that had now begun hanging around Dipswitch on a more regular basis read his mind and climbed back into his carriage.

"I am going back to The Castle," Dipswitch announced to his scowling wife, feeling the Aura incentive. "I am going to get some answers from Drum about *my* pool on *my* land. I don't care who thinks they own the land, and I don't care who thinks they have rights to my water. A deal is a deal. I am the Royal Border Advisor, and I will run this border as it should be run. Either Drum will cause it to happen or I will."

Motioning the Royal Guard to follow, he headed north. "And you, gentlemen, will enforce my wishes." The Royal Guard scrambled into line behind Sir Dipswitch. Neither they nor their Consciences liked him, but they could not do anything about it. Dipswitch was a Royal Advisor, and they were Royal Guardsmen. They followed orders, and their Consciences said nothing.

29

Rescue

As Lord Dipswitch left his manor house in anger, headed for The Castle and King Drum, Ben slipped away from his friends and family, headed for Urhonordo. The sun was still bright, but he didn't need light to find his way. He would be traveling on land that he had lived on all his life, the part of The Lowlands that was south of Urhonordo.

Easily, he crossed the shallow waters of The Lowlands' portion of The River. There was already a decent flow thanks to the work that he and Will and his people had done. The water felt good. "It truly is the lifeblood of our country," he murmured quietly.

He splashed some water on his face and drew up some in a leather pouch for his travels, but it was not a long way to Queen Luna's Castle. He just had to travel east for a way, skirting the muddy ruins of the Urhonordo farmlands and then cut up north. He had been to Urhonordo Castle many times, but under much more favorable circumstances.

Ben had grown up playing with Urhonordo children. He had even chased his friends through the Urhonordo Castle Courtyard and hidden behind its bushes and trees for hide-and-seek. He had not been to Urhonordo recently as he had spent his adult years working with Will on the other side of The River. He hadn't really chosen to do this. It had just happened.

And Ben was glad. Will had been a good friend. Even lately, when he had been given more jobs, a higher station in life, and very confusing orders from Drum, he had remained the same person.

"You really like him a lot, don't you?" commented Cben. "He's my best friend," Ben answered simply.

"It's a good thing he's worth the effort 'cause I think you might be in for some trouble up in Urhonordo."

"And what kind of trouble do you think I am going to find up there? These folks are good people. We have always gotten along."

"That was true until you started stealing their water," said Cben. "How do you figure?" Ben asked. "I never stole anybody's water."

SUNA FLORes

"Hmm," mused Cben. "Let me see. You ran your crew of Lowlanders to lower levees for almost three months so that River Kingdom farmers could get the water they needed. There was no treaty with Urhonordo that said you could do that."

"Really? I didn't know. I thought Drum was going to take care of that." "Uh-huh, but he didn't."

"That's not good."

"And you and some more Lowlanders helped dig a channel and reroute the 'pool water' around the Dipswitch house. There was no treaty that allowed that either."

"That was a good thing. We got the water off Urhonordo land." "True. But Urhonordo doesn't know that, and it looks like that was what

Will was abducted for."

"Crap!" Ben sat down on a stump. His whole plan for getting Will rescued was to talk to Queen Luna like a friend and tell her why Will was a good guy. Will had also been part of both water projects that Queen Luna objected to. He and Will had both broken the Water Rights Treaties without even knowing it. Cben was right. Luna was not going to be happy with either of them and for a good reason.

What is my tactic now? Ben thought to himself. *Will just got kidnapped and hauled away for everything that I have done too. What leverage do I have if I ask to speak to Queen Luna? Will I be trying to rescue Will or just giving myself up?*

"You're doing what you know you have to do," said Cben calmly. "I wasn't warning you to scare you off your duty. I just didn't want you to waltz in to the Queen, thinking you were something special."

"I get it, I get it."

"Good. Now get off this stump and get on with it. There's no telling what is happening to Will at the Urhonordo Castle."

And what was happening to Will?

He was lying facedown on a cold, hard dungeon floor. He was watching bugs crawl across that floor to inspect him and then hop on his face. "I'm trapped worse than these bugs," he mumbled to himself. "At least they have their freedom."

Will was strapped to the floor with wet leather that was starting to shrink as it dried. He could barely turn his head without scraping his chin on the dirt and rock. Worse than that, he was not being given a chance to talk to anyone. What had he done wrong?

The Guardsmen that had yanked him roughly onto the flat boat were not continuing to be that rough, but they were watchful as they lounged in the hall outside Will's cell.

"Seems like this is sort of harsh treatment for this guy, considering that he didn't hurt anybody," said one guard. "Maybe we should let him up."

"No, sir. Queen's orders. She said she was making a point for the King of River Kingdom. If and when she turns this guy loose, she wants him to tell the King how upset she is." The guard walked around Will and nudged at his feet. "And this guy's got good footwear. Must be in some sort of important position. Why did we have to snag him again?"

"Because he ruined our farmlands and manors by flooding 'em . . . houses, crops, everything . . . on orders from the King of River Kingdom. That's why . . . and because they've been takin' extra water out of The Great River all summer without payin' attention to the Water Rights Treaty. That's a high crime and misdemeanor, you know."

"Yeah, I heard that." The first guard lowered his voice to a whisper. "I also heard that Queen Luna doesn't believe that King Drum is really the King of River Kingdom at all. She thinks that King Sol is still alive somewhere, and this Drum guy has just taken over because he likes being king."

"Ooh, . . . that's not even legal. And *this* guy might work for that guy. That's why he has good shoes . . . Well, if this dude works for a bad guy, he must be bad too. Let's leave him here on the floor. He probably deserves it."

Suddenly, there was a commotion in the hall outside Will's cell. He strained to hear what was going on. It sounded like a fight. More guards were obviously struggling with a new and uncooperative prisoner. The heavy metal doors of the cell squeaked and clanged open, and a body was flung onto the dirt at Will's feet.

Will couldn't see a thing, but the protesting and shouting of the new prisoner sounded familiar. It was Ben.

"Ben, is that you?" Will asked through the dirt in his mouth. "What happened? Did they get you too?"

"Hey, Will. Is that you?"

"Looks like they got us both."

"How did they find you? I told you to go hide with your people."

"My people are smart. They don't need me to look after them. I came after you."

"That was dumb. You shouldn't have . . . but thanks." "Yer welcome. Now what?"

"Good question."

The guards listened in fascination. "Sounds like you guys know each other," said one.

"You sound like buddies . . . pals. Yer buddies, right?" offered the other. Ben was not lashed to the ground so he could speak freely. "Yes, we're friends. I couldn't let you guys take him off without me trying to get him back."

"That's pretty good," said the first guard. "I like that in a man. Stick up for your buddy. Go get him when he gets snatched. That's a good thing." "Yeah. That is a good thing," said the second guard. "Would you come get me if I got snatched, George?"

"Sure," said George. "You can't live without me." They both laughed at their joke.

But Will had learned something. These two guards were not bad guys either. They were just men who were doing what they were told by the Queen. They were very similar to Will and Ben.

Ben was not in a mood to care about the guards. He was mad at himself for getting caught. "I was so stupid," he whispered to Will as he moved to sit closer to his head. "I thought that I could walk right in and talk to Queen Luna and she would let you out of here."

"I'm sorry your plan didn't work out, for sure," grumbled Will into the dirt. "Why did you think you could talk to her, anyway? Why would she let you do that?"

"We Lowlanders used to play around this castle with Urhonordo kids when we were small," Ben answered casually.

"You what?" asked George.

Ben jumped. He had been overheard. "Oh nothing," he grumbled. "I heard you. You said something. What did you say?"

"Tell him," coaxed Will. "It's not a bad thing."

"I just said that I used to play with you guys when I was a kid," Ben confessed, "but that was a long time ago . . . before all these water problems." "Oh sure. You used to play with us when you were little," said Marco,

the other guard. "We're supposed to believe that. Give me a break." "Maybe it wasn't you exactly, but it's the truth," defended Ben sharply.

"We Lowlanders always played in Urhonordo as kids . . . and worked over here as grown-ups. That's no secret. We played over here. That's all."

"You say you're a Lowlander? I know lots of Lowlanders. We usually don't arrest Lowlanders. They don't do much wrong . . . at least that we know of." George pulled Ben up to a standing position and looked him over.

Ben brushed himself off and blinked. "Are you letting me go?" he asked meekly.

"Heck no. We'll let your friend up off the floor, but we don't have the authority to let you go. But we definitely need to tell the Queen about what you say, though. Wait here . . . and don't get too close to your buddy. He isn't a Lowlander, and we don't trust him a bit."

With this, the two guards loosened Will's tether and exited, the heavy metal doors clanking shut behind them. The two prisoners were left behind to wonder about their fate.

Will and Ben continued to shiver in the cold, damp dungeon. The only thing that had changed was Will's position on the floor and the tight leather straps that had held him there. The guards had closed the door but not locked it when they disappeared down the dimly lit hall.

Will could tell that night was falling even though there was no direct outside light. Their cell was getting colder.

"Should we make a break for it?" whispered Will. "We'd get caught before we reached the end of the hall."

"You're right . . . but we need to do something. We can't just sit here. Queen Luna is angry enough to start a war."

Will thought about that some more. *A war between Urhonordo and The Kingdom would be terrible, but Urhonordo had been seriously damaged and Queen Luna was very angry. In a war, people could die . . . Flawless might die . . . Flawless . . .*

Ben was thinking too. *If there is a war, I will know people on both sides, he thought. I would be friends with people on both sides.*

"Are you as dumb as you look, or did you just stop using your brain?" jeered Cben.

Ben sat still and listened. His Conscience was talking to him. Since he was in a bad spot, maybe his Conscience had an idea.

"Look at it this way," Cben explained in a kindlier fashion. "If I remember right, you actually used to play with a little girl named Luna. She might not have been *the* Luna but maybe she was. It would be something worth asking, don't you think?"

Ben thought for a minute. Cben was right.

"You know something, Will?" Ben said slowly. "I have an idea. It might not be worth anything, but it might."

Will looked at Ben through the dim light. "Speak up. I'll take anything."

Ben explained. "Okay. See, when I was a kid, I used to play up here with the Urhonordo kids. One of the kids I played with was a . . . Luna."

Will stared at Ben. "You actually used to know the Queen?"

"Uh-huh . . . at least I might. But that was a long time ago. She probably wouldn't even remember."

"Well, you remember, for Pete's sake! Why are we sitting here? Go talk to her."

"How am I going to do that? We're not exactly honored guests here." "Talk to the guards, Ben. They already know you're a Lowlander.

Maybe they'll believe you." "You think so?"

"Try it, dummy!" hissed Cben.

Ben stood up stiffly. He stood on one foot and then another. He was suddenly shy.

"Move!" said Cben.

"If you're going to do it, do it." Will nudged.

Ben was only a few feet down the hall when he stopped short. Someone was coming toward him. Quickly, he turned around. He didn't want the guards to think he was trying to escape. Then he heard his name.

"Ben! Is that you?" It was Queen Luna. Ben fell to his knees, quaking.

Suddenly, there was a hand on his shoulder. "Tag. You're it!" Then there was laughter.

Ben remembered the laugh. She had been his favorite playmate when they were young. They had played many times together. She had been a funny little girl, smarter than most and fast. He had to work hard to catch up with her, and sometimes, truth be told, he couldn't catch her at all.

He looked up. She wasn't a funny little girl anymore. She was beautiful.

Ben lowered his head with a new kind of shyness.

"Do you want us to put him back inside the dungeon again?" said George. "It looks like he was trying to escape."

"Of course not. This is my old friend, Ben," said Luna softly. "Stand up, Ben. I think you may have grown some, but I would know your face anywhere. You have a funny nose."

"You always used to say that," admitted Ben. The two grown children looked at each other. The two guards and Will stared. No one had expected this. They didn't know what to say or do.

Luna broke the spell. "What are you doing here, Ben?" she asked seriously. "Urhonordo is almost at war and then you pop up . . . and with this destroyer of our lands. Please don't tell me that you are friends with him."

"I *am* friends with him, Luna. He's probably my best friend."

Luna shook her head sadly. "I was afraid of that," she said. "I never would have thought that you would stoop to such a thing."

"Say something," said Cwill.

"He didn't do anything," said Will. "*He* didn't mess with your water. It was all me."

"That's not true," said Ben. "He's just being a friend. We both dug the levees out. We thought King Drum had worked out the treaty with you like he said he would, but I guess he didn't."

Queen Luna looked hard at Ben and Will. They were not defiant at all.

They didn't look a bit guilty.

"The levees were bad enough," she said. "That was something I was going to work out with Flawless. It was the ruin of our southern farmlands that I am most angry about. A kingdom cannot stand by and let another kingdom take over their land and ruin it without retaliation."

"Of course not," agreed Ben and Will, but Will was not finished. "You met with Flawless about the water? When did you do that? What did she say? Is she alright?"

Luna stepped back and looked at Will more closely. "You're Will, aren't you? I should have known. You look exactly the way she described you."

Will and Ben blinked. Luna knew Flawless. They had talked. Why were they here, then, standing in a dungeon? The guards were even more confused.

Luna asked the guards to untie Will and Ben and dismissed them. The guards bowed and shook their heads in confusion as, without another word, the former fugitives followed the young queen down the hall.

Upon arrival in the throne room, Queen Luna sat comfortably on her throne. Ben could not take his eyes off her. She was no longer his little friend. She was a gorgeous monarch. She had strength and beauty. She was impressive.

Will and Ben stood respectfully in front of the throne. All three had the feeling that under different circumstances, they would be friends.

Their Consciences were under the same impression and said so. "She's pretty nice," said Cwill. "She should be a friend, not an enemy." "That Will guy seems like a good person," said Cluna. "And Ben . . .

he grew up to be a much handsomer man than you dreamed he would be when he used to chase you."

"Luna's beautiful and smart. Do you think she might like you like she used to?" snarked Cben.

I am beneath Luna now, Ben thought sadly, shuffling uneasily.

Luna started the conversation. "How did you two come to be involved in that terrible mess down by the new fort? The manors on our side of The Great River are ruined. Not only their fields, but their homes were flooded. It will take them years to recover. There is nothing there now but a swamp." "I know," agreed Ben. "My people tried to tell that guy that he should build his manor house beside The River instead of blocking the water, but he wouldn't listen. His wife wanted a pool. That 'mess' on your land was supposed to be her pool. Those two even put some of my family in cages

for trying to talk them out of it."

"They put Lowlanders in cages for a pool? Really?" asked Luna incredulously. "A pool? And why did these awful people think that they could put other people in cages? Why did you let them do it, Ben? That doesn't sound like you."

"Are you kidding?" said Ben with a humph. "Of course, I wouldn't have allowed such a thing. But I wasn't there. I was up north, working on the levees. So were almost all the Lowlander men. It was the women and children that went into the cages when they protested, and it was The Kingdom's Royal Guard that put them there. Will and I let them out, though."

"The Royal Guard of River Kingdom put people in cages? Who told them to do such a thing?"

"I know it sounds crazy, but it's true. The guy who is building the house that you call a 'fort' is a business partner of King Drum, I guess," contributed Will, shaking his head. "Not only did he get the land at The Border, but Drum also gave him the title of Royal Border Advisor and sent the Royal Guard down there to do his bidding. Ben and I were sent there by the King too to finish the pool. That's why we were there . . . but we took one look at the mess and decided to dig the channel to drain your land and direct The River around the house instead."

"Oh dear." Luna sighed. "You two released the water from my land?"

"Um-hum," mumbled Ben.

"Which means that Ben and the Lowlanders that worked with me on the levees will never get paid," added Will. "That's another bad thing."

"And you two also lowered the levees?"

"Indeed, we did." Will sighed. "I am the Royal Ag Advisor that ordered it done, and I did a lot of it myself. I thought the King had fixed the treaty with you folks, but I should have checked. That was just ignorant on my part."

"And the pay?" said Luna. "Who was supposed to get paid for what?" Now she was standing.

"Again, it was my fault," said Will. "At the King's request, I made a deal with the Lowlander men to do the work of lowering the levees for the farmers and get paid with commodities for the winter, but King Drum reneged on the deal. He wouldn't pay them until they finished the pool . . . for his farmers. He counts the farmers as his main supporters."

"Since when do northern farmers walk for hours during farming season just to swim in a pool?" Queen Luna snickered.

"That's what I said," agreed Will. "But when a King says something must be done, then it must be done."

There was a long silence. Then Luna spoke.

"If a person knew that King Drum was a fake king, he wouldn't have to do his bidding at all, would he?" she asked quietly.

Ben and Will stared at Luna. "A fake king?"

Luna rose from her throne. She gathered herself with the serious dignity that her information required. "I have just received a missive by courier from Dragon Quest. King Sol and the Royal Guard were successful. The dragons have been driven back into the sea, and King Sol is on his way back to River Kingdom."

Will and Ben stared at each other in amazement.

Luna watched their confusion and disbelief. "What do you think, gentlemen?" she asked. "Could you never contemplate such a thing? King Drum was put in place as a Royal Caretaker. That is all he has ever been." The two friends didn't answer. Suddenly, all the changes that had occurred in the past months came flooding back. Treaties had been broken. Royal Advisors had been fired for no reason. Urhonordo land had been ruined. People had been caged. And the man who was now King had lied himself into the position—all for no reason.

Will was the first to find his voice. "Drum will never accept this," he said. "He considers himself a king in every way. Wait until he hears this." "I'm sure he already knows," said Luna. "The same courier that came to me was on his way to take the message to Drum when he left."

"Oh, he won't know yet." Will smiled ruefully. "He never reads his paperwork."

30

Prelude to War

Back at The Castle, Sir Thorndike, the new Royal Defense Advisor, was having a definite impact, and King Drum was thrilled with it. Finally, there was someone in that position that thought about things the way he did. Thorndike was a man of action. A man he could trust.

Flawless was the only person close to him that was not in favor of the new man.

"I don't understand you, Father. This man Thorndike is a warmonger. He's greedy. I think he's also power mad. He believes that he should be king instead of you. I'm sure of it."

"I know how to handle his type," Drum rebutted with authority. "It's a 'man thing.' You wouldn't understand, being a woman. Women are gentle and pretty. That's the way they were made. In their place, they're a perfect complement to a man."

Flawless rolled her eyes. "What happens when the woman involved is smarter than the man she is with? What happens then?"

Drum laughed. "If the man isn't too dumb to figure that out, he needs to get rid of her before she shows him up." He smirked. "Now you just run along and stop trying to mess with things you don't understand. And by the way, I liked it better when you called me 'Daddy.'"

Drum was off to The Royal Chamber to contemplate the upcoming rally. It was going to be important.

Sir Thorndike had just finished a planning session with Drum, and he was in "heaven." It had taken him months and a great deal of Aura work behind the scenes, but he was now in the right place at the right time. His position as Royal Defense Advisor was perfect.

With the look of superiority and control that had always been his style, he now entered a large drawing room. This room was not in The Castle. It was in Thorndike Manor.

And the drawing room was not empty. It was full of the wealthiest men in the kingdom. Many of them had partied with Drum in the past. Many had thought that they had the inside track for the job of Royal Caretaker when the position became available. Like Sir Thorndike, these men were envious, angry, and sure that they knew how to run a kingdom far better than Drum had ever thought of doing.

These men had also noticed Drum's ridiculous attention to commoners and peasants lately. The riffraff seemed to be taking over. Drum appeared to be more concerned by what the lowborn thought of him than the opinions of people like themselves with rank and standing. It was insulting. Something should be done about it.

These noblemen had attended several meetings together in the past few months, but their meetings had not risen much above the level of complaint sessions. Drum had claimed the position of not only Royal Caretaker, but now also king. It was galling, but he now commanded the Royal Guard and a disgusting horde of gushingly loyal farmers and peasants. What could quality men such as themselves do against a situation like this?

This was the matter that needed to be discussed today. Sir Thorndike believed he had finally found the key that would return the rule of River Kingdom and, perhaps, even Urhonordo to those who deserved it.

Lord Thorndike got straight to the point. "Yesterday, I was appointed Royal Defense Advisor of River Kingdom by King Drum."

There was a polite smattering of applause among the gentlemen. Truth be told, they were no fonder of Thorndike than they were of Drum. A gray- green fog of jealousy was a constant presence in the lovely drawing room at these meetings, but it appeared more active today as it slid across the floor, wrapping itself around available limbs and torsos.

Thorndike knew how they felt. He was one of them. If he had a plan, the noblemen would need to hear what was in it for them. He understood this. "You may not be aware of recent occurrences," he continued. "But

several days ago, Urhonordo invaded River Kingdom."

"No!"

"Yes." Thorndike let that sink in. "Repelling them in a confrontation at The Bridge was the way that I earned my position as Royal Defense Advisor. I won't bore you with the details, but needless to say, Drum was grateful."

"You know that isn't true," said Cthorndike. He had never had much impact, but as a Conscience, he thought he would give it a try. You never could tell when Conscience influence might become effective.

Ask me if I care, Thorndike thought. *I have never had a particularly good relationship with you, Conscience. Why start now?*

Thorndike's Conscience drifted away again. He could feel the Eforces.

He had been out of action too long, and the Eforces were too strong.

Thorndike's lie impressed these men. They believed that he had actually earned his position as Royal Defense Advisor. He had saved The Kingdom from invasion. That was very commendable. They chatted and rumbled and growled among themselves but, at last, turned back to Sir Thorndike with slightly increased attention.

"Drum, as we all know, is no planner of any kind. He doesn't like to think ahead so he doesn't do it," Thorndike continued.

Much head nodding ensued.

"He does, however, want to preserve River Kingdom superiority and keep it safe from all invaders, especially Urhonordos. This summer, Urhonordo tried to tell River Kingdom what to do with its own water. Some of you may have heard about this from those that farm your own estates.

"Drum, to his credit, would hear none of it and ordered the levees lowered as was necessary. This is what Urhonordo is ready to fight about. Water, as you all know, is essential to River Kingdom. After all, our kingdom was named for The River. We own it! We were here first!"

There followed a resounding chorus of "huzzah!" These gentlemen were patriots.

"This is why I have called you here today. Drum has decided to end the conflict over water rights by taking control of The Great River himself. He wants to convince Urhonordo that they have no rights to water other than what we give them. If he needs to get rid of Queen Luna in order to do that, he is willing to do so, . . . and he has put me in charge of this campaign."

The room at first was quiet. Then a rumble of opinions and counter opinions began to ebb and flow. The Auras began to swell with pride. Their influence was growing.

"He wants to take over Urhonordo?"

"I don't understand what happened to Queen Luna. She used to be so peaceful."

"But this is our land, and we were here first. We have the right to our water."

"Thorndike has always been sort of pushy, though."

"Yes, but he's intelligent. He knows how to get things done." "Urhonordo can't tell us what to do."

Suddenly, one of the younger gentlemen contributed a new and very disturbing thought.

"Sir Thorndike, if we are thinking of possibly using force to control The River, where would we get the troops to do it? More than half of our Royal Guard is out on Dragon Quest, I hear."

The crowd's interest in power and decisive action had been growing. With this question, it was stopped in its tracks. The men turned and stared at Thorndike. They hadn't thought of that. The young gentleman was right. They could not be tough and tell Urhonordo what to do if they didn't have the men to back it up.

Thorndike was ready. "This is where all of you come in," he said quietly. "The one interesting thing Drum has done is get your peasants on his side. He has given your farmers help with the levees. He has had numerous rallies for them. He has even promised them a pool."

"A pool?" the gentlemen gasped.

"Yes. A pool. I know that sounds silly, but Drum knows how to get support from the masses. The pool may be crazy, but their support for him is not. That is where you men come in."

"What have we got to do with a pool?" griped an older gentleman. "I've never taken a swim in my life."

"You mean you've never taken a bath." The man next to him laughed. The group laughed, but the discussion was serious. What did Thorndike have in mind that they were supposed to be part of?

"You men own your estates and your peasants, don't you?" asked Lord Thorndike. "So do I. All the farmers and peasants serve us, right? In actual fact, you own their allegiance, am I not right? If you think of these men in just the right way, they become troops. First, they 'troop' to work in our fields. Then they can 'troop' to defend our kingdom. It all depends on who is directing them to do what. Am I not right?"

That took a bit of thought on the part of these fine gentlemen. To be honest, they had never thought of their farmworkers as anything other than necessary labor to produce their wealth. They had not thought of them as real men such as themselves. They had not thought of their ability to do anything else but farm.

Discussion erupted into more discussion. There were pros and cons. There were ups and downs. There were ins and outs. Could their common farm workers actually be trained to be . . . an army?

The waves of ideas and counter ideas lapped in and out of the room. Thorndike sailed the waves like the captain of a sturdy vessel, dropping hints in all directions:

"They take orders from you, don't they?" "They are dependent on you, aren't they?"

"They use The River every day. Wouldn't they want to defend it?" "Don't you want to be sure that your lands get all the water they need?" "Don't you think that your workers want that too?"

"Do you want to give your water rights to Urhonordo?"

Gradually, the promise of power or the threat of losing it caused the waves to settle. As the meeting drew to a close, Thorndike was pleased with the way the gentlemen were thinking. This move would mean more power, land, and wealth than they had ever had before. They loved that.

The Aura of greed and power had started with envy but was now sharing Thorndike's power lust. It was growing and gusting through the veins of these men who felt that they had been overlooked for too long. Now they were going to be important . . . even essential.

Plus, Drum and Thorndike were ready to fight for River Kingdom. That was admirable. Now these men and their peasants would be ready to fight for it as well. The farmers and farm hands would become Thorndike's troopers, a Commoner Army.

The Consciences of the assembled barons and lords were so out of practice that they didn't question anything. They were unable to mount a counterargument in time to stop the winds of Eforce aggression that were swirling.

Before he told them all goodbye, Thorndike had only one more small request to make of them, but it was important. "This evening, Drum is going to have another rally with the peasants. He wants to introduce me as the new Royal Defense Advisor and tell them that we may be going to battle soon. I would like you all to attend with your peasants as well."

"A rally with commoners?"

"You are all generals now," Thorndike continued artfully. "You are the men that will commit your troops into battle. You are the ones that will save River Kingdom from the likes of Urhonordo. You are the Patriots of River Kingdom!"

A rousing cheer arose from the usually staid gentlemen as they envisioned themselves in their new role. They felt good. They felt strong. They were ready. They would meet tonight at The Castle.

But wait a minute. The mood was not as positive at The Castle as it was in Thorndike's drawing room. Lord Dipswitch had just arrived back from The Border with his contingent of Royal Guard, and he was angry. He had made a deal with Drum, and *nothing* he had expected was in place as it had been bought and paid for.

Lord Dipswitch rudely stormed into the throne room, followed by a slightly hesitant but still obedient Royal Guard. The King had given Dipswitch control of their duties, and as long as he demanded it, they knew they should comply.

Morf met them all at the doorway of the throne room. But he felt himself sliding backward as the anger of a furious Royal Border Advisor and his entourage overwhelmed him.

"Where is he?" Dipswitch yelled at the empty throne, swatting Morf to the floor. Morf was not accustomed to this kind of low-class behavior. That was definitely a sign of inferior breeding. He stood and dusted himself off with as much dignity as he could muster and countered, "You may be a Royal Advisor, sir, but you don't behave like one. If you would politely calm yourself and address me as one should address a fellow advisor, I would be glad to answer your questions."

Morf drew himself up to an appropriately "in charge" stance and waited.

The Royal Guardsmen behind Dipswitch grinned and held in a laugh.

Sir Dipswitch took a deep breath, squinted closely at Morf, and conceded slightly—but only slightly. He had been traveling the whole day before to get to his home on The Border. Then upon seeing the mud flats where his "pool" was supposed to be, he had returned through the night, pressing his entourage to its breaking point.

Lord Dipswitch had never been a man to be trifled with. To make matters worse, he was a man who had made a bargain with this lesser individual, Drum, whom he didn't respect before and now he regretted doing business with at all. His new wife and her formidable desires for a pool had taken him off his game in his push for his new manor house. Now, he was out for revenge.

Drum could hear the shouting from the Royal Bed Chamber. He was being entertained by the dancing girls again, a bit of relaxation before the rally that was scheduled for tonight, but he quickly decided that this was not a time to keep Sir Dipswitch waiting as he usually did. He had a very lucrative deal going with this man, and he needed to keep him happy.

Morf was just outside the chamber. "Your Highness, Lord Dipswitch would like a word," he whispered cautiously through the curtains, aware that Drum was not alone. To Morf's surprise, Drum immediately brushed by him with a determined smile. "I know," he said.

"To what do I owe the honor of this return visit so soon?" Drum began graciously, hoping to defer the man's visible anger. Something was obviously wrong at Dipswitch Manor . . . or the pool . . . or the Lowlanders. I should never have made this deal, Drum conceded to himself. This man is a pain in the neck.

"An illegal pain in the neck," reminded Cdrum.

Drum would never admit that to anyone, of course. That was not his style. On the other hand, his personal profits on this deal were already great. Everyone he had known in the old days would envy these profits—if they knew. Maybe it was worth the trouble, after all.

Drum relaxed a bit. The girls had made him feel good, so he was prepared to ask the question that he didn't want answered. "Is there a problem, Sir Dipswitch?"

Dipswitch was obviously in a dither. He couldn't get the words out fast enough. "A problem? You want to know if there is a problem?" he sputtered. "Let me tell you what is happening down at my beautiful house. The pool that was almost as big as a lake when I left to come north just days ago is now a mud pit stretching as far as the eye can see.

"In addition, there is now a ditch of some kind that siphons The River's water completely away from my pool area, which is now nothing but a muddy mess. There is no longer a pool of any kind. The whole thing is an eyesore! And I am holding you completely responsible!"

Drum couldn't believe his ears. There must be some mistake. "I don't understand how this could have happened," he began in a gentle tone.

"Surely it can't be that bad, . . . but if it is, it might have been a wayward gang of Lowlanders. You know how they are. There are a lot of them down that way, you know."

"Oh, I am sure of it. There are Lowlanders all over the place down there. I had no idea there were that many. Now that I think of it, I am sure that they are at least partially responsible for this catastrophe, but they must have had help. They're not that smart. I thought that the Royal Guard here would protect my pool and my house, but it seems they did nothing. That's why I am holding you responsible. Their help on my house and pool was part of the deal."

Drum marched in front of his Royal Guard. They looked good. Why had they not protected the pool?

"Who dug the ditch on Lord Dipswitch's property?" he demanded curtly of the Guardsmen.

"Actually, it is a channel, sire," answered the first guard in line.

"I don't care what you call it. Who dug it?"

"It was mostly Lowlanders, sire," answered the Guardsman.

"Aha! Just as I thought," growled Drum. "I should have them all locked up. They are a nuisance. There is absolutely no reason for them to be running around loose down there and ruining a man's property. Why didn't you stop them?"

"We were busy protecting the house, sir."

"Well, that was a good thing, I guess. But there is something else that I don't understand. I sent my man Will down there with some 'good Lowlanders,' ones that had worked up here and knew how to do what they were told.

"They were supposed to finish your pool, Dipswitch," Drum continued. "There was a whole bunch of them. I had it all worked out. Did you see them? Did my Ag Advisor make it down to your place?"

"I heard that he was kidnapped," said Sir Dipswitch.

"Kidnapped? By whom? I bet it was those dang Lowlanders that wrecked your pool."

"No, Drum. It's worse than that. According to the Royal Guard, it was Urhonordos."

"What? Urhonordos? That crazy woman has actually taken one of my advisors hostage? How could she have done this?" Drum turned again to the Royal Guard with a withering glare. "*You* allowed another kingdom to take one of my men hostage? Where were you when this happened? What did you see? What did you do?"

"We were in the house," said one of the guards. "And they were quick. They came by flat boat, I think. By the time we found out about it, Will was gone."

"We would have protected him if we knew," said another. "We like Will."

"So do the Lowlanders," offered another.

"Who cares who you and the Lowlanders like? The Lowlanders are not the culprits for the abduction of my Royal Advisor," growled Drum. "The Urhonordos are."

"And your Royal Guard appears to have been completely useless," snarled Dipswitch.

"The training of the previous administration was shoddy, I'm afraid." Drum nodded quickly.

"But what about my pool? What about the ditch that the Lowlanders dug? I don't care about your inept Royal Guard or your abducted advisor. Apparently, he couldn't even take care of himself, let alone my beautiful pool. You should see it. My pool is now nothing but miles of soggy Urhonordo farmland. What a waste."

Drum frowned. The mention of "soggy Urhonordo farmland" triggered a picture of Queen Luna. If it was Urhonordo farmland, she would certainly be furious about that. Thus, the kidnapping.

This was a situation Drum had not expected. Actually, he had not expected anything because hadn't thought about it much at all. He didn't know or care exactly where Dipswitch's manor house or his pool was. Will was supposed to handle this with his Lowlander friends. That was always the plan.

That plan had obviously fallen through, not that he really cared. But he had to get rid of Dipswitch and his bunch of Royal Guardsmen quickly. The rally would be starting soon. Flatter and lie. Lie and flatter. Old standard solutions were always the best.

Almost immediately, Drum had the answer. "Dipswitch, my man. I can certainly see why you are upset. Thank goodness you are such a strong man. You have taken this setback with amazing calm and intelligence. And I can see now that you are ready for revenge against those who have wronged you so terribly! Am I right?"

Sir Dipswitch looked at Drum with confusion. Was Drum taking his side on this? He reran what Drum had just said in his mind. He was a "strong man," Drum had said. He was "amazingly calm and intelligent." He was "ready for revenge." Suddenly, everything Drum said to him made sense.

The Royal Guard who still stood behind Dipswitch scratched their heads. They couldn't understand a thing that was going on, so they just watched quietly.

Drum continued with enthusiasm. "This is perfect timing," he said confidently. "I have a rally scheduled for tonight. I was only going to introduce my new Royal Defense Advisor, but now I have something even more important to announce.

"River Kingdom has been attacked and defaced. Your property has been ruined by Lowlanders, and my Royal Ag Advisor has been kidnapped by Urhonordos. This is not a time for the weak of spirit. This is a time for standing up for our rights. I will announce the solution to these outrages when I introduce my new Defense Advisor tonight! Be there, Dipswitch. You'll like what I have to say."

Morf, the Royal Guard, and Sir Dipswitch left, satisfied and ready for action. None of them understood exactly what was planned, but it sounded good. They would attend the rally.

Drum breathed a sigh of relief. Not only had he averted a dangerous run-in with Dipswitch, but he had converted a possible disaster into an even better reason for his next maneuver. The Commoner Army would be eating out of his hand.

Slowly, he settled himself onto his throne and adjusted his crown. He was good at this 'king stuff.' He had always known he would be. Tonight, he would gather his loyal supporters together to hear what he wanted them to hear.

Urhonordo and the Lowlanders no longer knew their place. They were on the warpath. They needed to be taught a lesson. They had ruined the pool and even kidnapped one of River Kingdom's Royal Advisors, someone they all knew—they had kidnapped Will. This could not stand!

Drum had not slept well since Queen Luna had come over The Bridge and threatened the security of his royal domain. *He* had built his situation. He had cultivated his position. The fear of losing it was too much.

But Dipswitch and Thorndike were here just in time. No one would dare to challenge the three of them and their demands for River Kingdom superiority. Their demands matched. They were together in this.

Drum was in the middle of this wonderful thought when Flawless slipped into the room. Quietly, she approached her father and gave him a hug. They had disagreed on some things lately. It was time to make up.

"Are you ready for your big rally tonight?" she asked. She didn't like Thorndike, but he was her father's choice for Defense Advisor. "What are you going to ask Thorndike to do, now that Queen Luna is again ready to negotiate a new Water Rights Treaty? Sir Thorndike is kind of a rough guy to like, but if you tell him what to say, I'm sure he will do alright."

Drum blinked and swallowed hard. In the hustle and bustle of Thorndike's energy and Dipswitch's fury, he had completely forgotten that Flawless said something about a negotiated peace. He loved the excitement of war talk and preparation, but here she was and now he had to admit it. She had said something about a peace talk. He had blown right by it.

"Don't pretend you didn't hear her," Cdrum whispered, thinking about what he had heard at the Conscience Forum.

Drum gave his daughter a hug as well, but now he had a real problem. Flawless was expecting a friendly negotiating meeting with Queen Luna, and Drum was preparing for possible war.

Drum stiffened and turned away from Flawless. He had to think of something quick.

"You put yourself in a box, didn't you?" sneered Cdrum. "What are you going to do? You are pretty committed to this warlike stance now, even if you did just do it to keep Thorndike happy."

"You be quiet," said Drum.

"What?" asked Flawless, a little surprised after the nice hug. "Oh, I'm sorry, Flawless. I was talking to my Conscience again." "You're always doing that, Daddy." She laughed.

"I'm telling you," continued Cdrum. "Tonight, all the men in your kingdom are going to be ready to fight unless you find a way to calm them down.

"Flawless could help you fix this. I'm pretty sure she would greatly prefer the peace she negotiated with Luna to the all-out war that Thorndike wants . . . unless she is really worried about Will."

"Will?"

"You didn't tell her yet?"

Will! Drum seized on the name. *That's it! That's how to get Flawless on my side. She doesn't know yet about Will. Will's kidnapping will trump Flawless's peace negotiation! This is perfect.*

Drum assumed a somber look and turned to Flawless with what appeared to be sadness.

"I need to tell you something, daughter," Drum said slowly, trying to pick the right words. "Dipswitch just arrived again from The Border, and he brought some very bad news with him."

Flawless was immediately interested and worried. "Isn't that where Will is right now?"

"Well, that's what I need to tell you. Dipswitch told me that Will is . . . missing."

"Missing? What does that mean? Is he okay? Is he hurt? What do you mean 'missing'?"

"According to Dipswitch, Will was kidnapped yesterday or the day before by Urhonordos. I'm sorry, Flawless. I know you liked the boy, but I am afraid he has met a bad fate. He was abducted and taken to who knows where by someone you thought was your friend—Urhonordo. I'm really sorry."

Actually, Drum was sort of sorry. He didn't care that much about Will although he had been a useful worker, apparently. But he was sorry for Flawless as she stared at him with disbelieving eyes.

"This can't be true," she cried. "Luna wouldn't do such a thing. She is kind and good. She is my friend. I even told her about Will. She would never hurt him."

"Sometimes people change," said Drum, not unkindly. "Something apparently happened down at The Border with the pool and the Dipswitch Manor House. The Lowlanders were involved. Dipswitch says it was a big mess and the Urhonordos are no longer a kingdom that can be trusted."

"You don't know that, for sure," contributed Cdrum doubtfully. "You are choosing to believe Dipswitch. You are choosing to believe what he says, but you don't know if it's true."

I know enough, thought Drum as he comforted Flawless. "I know what I need to know."

"Father, I *do* believe that you believe what Sir Dipswitch told you. And I'm sure that you are telling me the truth as you see it. But I don't believe you know the whole story. Will is smart. If he is in trouble with the Urhonordos, he will figure out how to fix the situation. Luna is a good and kind Queen. She would not take Will to hurt him. If we talk to her, I'm sure we can find out what the real story is."

Drum didn't want to know what the real story was. Flawless's forgotten peace negotiation had thrown him off, but now, that was sufficiently nullified. Drum was again committed to defending The Kingdom . . . and his position as King.

He turned to Flawless. He was through talking about Will and peace. The kind father disappeared, and in his place was a man committed to his own preservation, not the feelings of a daughter. His voice took on a determined strength. The sudden change was almost frightening.

"Enough about Will, Flawless. You know nothing about the issues of war," he stated darkly. "As I have told you before, I do not expect you to know these things. You are my favorite daughter, and you always will be. But you are not my Royal Defense Advisor. You are not a man of any kind. You have no say in these matters."

Flawless shook her head as tears welled up in her eyes. "Who are you, Father? You used to be peaceful. You were never a warmonger. Why have you changed?"

"War is business. Business is war. Rights and finances and power are all joined together in the minds of men. It is up to men to settle the conflicts between them and protect their position," Drum said forcefully. "I intend to ensure that River Kingdom will maintain its greatness. It is superior to all other kingdoms because I have made it so. Those who are loyal to me understand that. Those who are not loyal do not belong here. Are you loyal, daughter?"

"Of course, Daddy," she said meekly.

"Are you giving up, just like that?" hissed Cflawless.

Flawless didn't answer.

"Good," said Drum abruptly, content that he had made his point. "That is very good, daughter. Now that we are on the same page, I want to invite you to the rally tonight. It's going to be great. Everyone will be there."

"I will be there, Daddy," said Flawless.

"I can't believe you wimped out," said Cflawless.

River Kingdom began to bustle as night fell. Out in the manors, the wealthy gentlemen had visited their fields, their farmers, and their farmhands. They had ordered together both those loyal to them and those dependent on them *and* called them to arms.

Sir Thorndike had made it clear to the lords and barons, who made it clear to their workers as well. Their kingdom would soon be under attack by Urhonordo, and it was up to them to defend it.

The common folk were at first slow to understand this after so many years of peace, but soon, after the mention of King Drum and his need for their loyalty, they were ready to do their duty. Their King had been good to them. He had promised them their very own pool. They would do what was needed.

And there was a rally tonight. They all loved rallies. Everyone knew that they would get the details at that time.

Thorndike could feel his authority growing. It felt great. This was what he had been waiting for. King Drum meant nothing to him, but the promise of ruling Urhonordo was a prize that was worth fighting for. In his wardrobe, he carefully chose his apparel—not too flashy, but definitely regal.

King Drum would also be dressing with care tonight. He must show his commoners that he was a strong leader, someone who could lead them against any foe and win. He must make it clear that there were no alternatives against those who would dare to invade River Kingdom as Urhonordo had done.

Drum had convinced himself of the righteousness of his cause. Queen Luna had stepped over the line. She had no right to enter his territory with armed troops. That was an invasion. There was no doubt about it. And what had happened to Will? He had been abducted by Queen Luna. Surely even Flawless could see that this was an act of war.

"Will was probably helping Ben's people," countered Cdrum. "They needed the water, you know. If Luna took Will by mistake, they will give him back when they find that out. Weren't you listening when Flawless told you she had settled the dispute with the Queen?"

"My daughter is a dreamer," said Drum, checking his appearance in a large mirror.

"You are putting people's lives in danger for a war that probably doesn't need to happen. And you're not even real king!" Cdrum mourned.

"I am a king that's a lot more real than Sol ever thought of being. I am standing up for River Kingdom, which is more than he ever did. I Ie believed in treaties and giving away the rights of The Kingdom. He was weak."

Flawless entered the throne room slowly. She wore a simple gown, not in any way dressed for a rally. Her head was down. She was not happy.

Drum could not help but notice. She was his pride and joy. He loved to show her off. Tonight's rally was important. She needed to be there, and he knew how to ensure that she would be. He was getting good at this.

"When are you going to get ready?" he asked her casually, smiling. "I need you to be with me at the rally, you know."

"I'm not coming, Father," she answered simply. "I just came here to tell you."

Drum was ready for that. "I am so surprised, daughter, especially after what happened to your friend, Will."

Flawless looked at the floor. She had been thinking about Will constantly since she heard that he had been abducted. She had been trying to understand how she could have been so wrong about Luna. She understood that her father and Thorndike wanted to use force to get him back, but was that the best way to do it? Or was she just afraid to admit having misjudged Luna?

"I know you think you're right, Father, but I really don't believe that war is the best way to settle this problem with someone who has lived peacefully next to us until just recently."

"Well said," commented Cflawless.

Drum glanced at his daughter from beneath lidded eyes. "If you think you're right about this, daughter, I dare you to present your feelings tonight at the rally. If you can convince the people at the rally that peaceful negotiations are the best way to go, maybe I will change my approach."

Cdrum was astonished. "That was great, Drum. Did you really mean that? That was really brave of you."

"No one will change their mind." Drum smirked. "What?" asked Flawless.

"Just talking to my Conscience again." Drum grinned.

A smile slowly grew on his daughter's face that almost warmed Drum's heart.

"Your daughter loves you, believes in you, and is grateful. Don't you wish that you were sincere?"

"I'm as sincere as I can get, if you'll just be quiet," Drum answered.

"But, Daddy, I'll have to say something if I am going to convince people," Flawless said in surprise.

"Oh, I know, dear. You can say anything you want. You know how I argue with my Conscience."

Flawless laughed. "Your Conscience argues with you a lot," she snickered as she turned for the door. "Maybe you should just listen to him. Anyway, I will meet you on the balcony."

As the autumn sun began to set in a blaze of oranges and yellows, the farmers, farmhands, and other common folk of River Kingdom gathered in front of The Castle. Rumor had it that this rally was going to have a purpose and be more exciting than all the rest.

There was also a different tone. The lords of the kingdom had each assembled their own contingent of workers, and every manor's workers traveled under its owner's coat of arms. Determined to outshine their neighbors, many carried banners, complete with their emblems and tassels. It almost looked like a parade.

Unnoticed but definitely felt was a dark haze of greed and envy that had been developing as the lords of the manors each tried to present a grander appearance than the group next to it. There was a feeling in the air that was thrilling but also threatening. The Auras were pulling their own troops together to promote whatever came next.

Morf snuck out on the lawn to take inventory of the crowd. He thought he was prepared for tonight's turnout, but he was shocked.

"There are hundreds here tonight," whispered Cmorf. "Did you expect this?"

"No, I had no idea," answered Morf. "I knew that Drum told Thorndike to get people to the rally tonight, but I think he must have put some extra energy into it. This turnout is massive. Drum is going to be ecstatic."

"I'm just wondering if this crowd might be even more ready for war hype than Drum expected," commented Cmorf. "Thorndike may have bigger ideas than Drum."

Yeah, I know. Drum likes to talk big and threaten, but I've never seen him actually follow through on anything very violent.

Morf was rationalizing to himself, but he didn't know Thorndike that well. With a little bit of luck, the rally would make a lot of noise, but nobody would push for anything really crazy, Morf concluded hopefully.

The crowd was now in place and ready. Morf raced back into The Castle just in time to throw the curtains wide for Drum's grand entrance onto the balcony.

"Drum! Drum! Drum!" the crowd chanted. Drum obliged them as usual by strutting back and forth with a glowing face and clapping hands. Following Drum, Sir Thorndike strode onto the balcony, resplendent in robes that rivaled Drum's. Drum noticed this, but Thorndike didn't have a crown. And he never will, thought Drum. I'll make sure of that.

Morf slipped in behind the two peacocks without anyone noticing, but there was no ignoring the last entrant onto the balcony.

Flawless entered with a glorious look of strength and beauty that none of the commoners had seen before. She was impressive, and she had intended to be. She was there to make an important proposal, an alternate approach to her father's idea of superior strength and force. She would offer the idea of a peace conference with their neighbor as the best solution to their current problems. Flawless believed in this and was here to stand up for it.

Her Conscience was proud, but could also feel the presence now of a negative aura threatening the space around her. "Beware," CFlawless warned. "The Eforce energies are near and strong."

DRUM THE FARMERS

Thorndike was awed by Flawless, too, but only for a moment. *Very clever of Drum, he thought. The man is joining with this goddess for a greater impact on the crowd, but I will still win the day and this crowd will be mine.* The throng was churning with expectation. With all of today's recruitment by their lords and the hype of the obvious competition among them, the rally crowd was ready for action. Something big was coming.

Drum soaked in the energy and was about speak and take advantage of it when, surprisingly, Flawless stepped forward first and raised her hand.

The crowd quieted immediately. In fascination, they watched as "the goddess" came calmly to life and spoke to them directly.

"Thank you so much for coming to this gathering tonight," she began. "The last rally that I attended, I was not here on the balcony. I was with you and among you. I was with my friend, William of Dale. You all know him. He is a farmer like you. He is one of you. He and the Lowlanders worked with you on the levees. He helped you all to achieve the wonderful harvest that is coming this year."

The crowd responded with a respectful chant. "Will, Will, Will." "Will believes in sharing the water of The Great River. Most of you

listened when he asked you not to lower the levees too much. He believes in the treaties that allow us to share the water of The Great River with Urhonordo. If Will were here, I know he would tell you what I am going to tell you.

"Peaceful negotiation is the way to solve our problems with our neighbors. King Drum and I are here tonight to present two options to you. I am here to ask you to consider negotiation regarding water rights in exchange for peace. Will would say this if he were here. This is the time of year when we should all be enjoying and sharing our harvest. Please consider choosing a harvest of peace for the sake of your families and the whole kingdom."

Drum could not believe what Flawless had done. She had jumped in and spoken first. She had addressed the crowd truthfully, and they had actually listened. He had listened too. She had made sense.

"Did you hear that?" said Cdrum. "Your daughter is smart. If you follow her lead, everything could work out just fine."

The crowd had not expected this. It took a second or two for the whole idea to sink in. A murmuring of surprise began to sift through the banners and flags. The lords and barons looked sideways at each other. Was this what they had come here to hear tonight?

It also took Thorndike a second or two to recover, but when he did, the blood of his anger swelled. What was happening here? This undisciplined girl was about to ruin his entire plan. He had been against this woman since the moment he met her, and now he knew why. She was a threat. The Eforces confirmed it.

The Auras seemed to strengthen and began to roll through Thorndike's unprotected thinking. He was a man whose Conscience could no longer compete with his focus on evil, and the evil knew it.

Flawless has no reason to be here except that her father is weakened by his love for her, Thorndike thought. I am now immune to such things. The Auras gathered around him more tightly. He was strong and ready. He stepped forward with purpose. With a script enhanced by his personalized Auras, he could demonstrate a higher level of persuasive rhetoric than this puny female ever thought of pulling together.

"Gentlemen of River Kingdom, I do not blame you for the attention and respect you pay to the beautiful Flawless. I do the same. But we are not here tonight to hear the gentle coaxing of a girl, no matter her beauty. Do not be fooled by her misplaced gentleness. Her ideas will bring about the ruin of River Kingdom, and it will all happen because we were too blind to see the threat of another kingdom that we once thought was peaceful.

"Flawless may be beautiful, but she is flawed in her reasoning and she did not tell you the whole truth. She did not tell you the reason that your friend Will is not here."

He had the crowd's attention back, and he struck hard. "The reason that Will is not here is because he was kidnapped by the Urhonordos!

"He was down south, working on the very pool that King Drum promised you. He was kidnapped right off the work site and carried away by the Urhonordos!"

The assembled farmers and farmhands gasped in horror. "Will has been captured by the Urhonordos!"

"Those people cannot do such a thing to one of ours!" "What must we do to get him back?"

"It's a matter of honor!"

Drum stepped forward. Thorndike was stealing his thunder. If he didn't say something immediately, the authority and loyalty that he had worked so hard to develop *for himself* with these commoners might have to be shared with Thorndike. That was not going to happen.

Thorndike was on a roll, but Drum was determined to top it. The trick here was to divert momentum back to himself. The only way to do that was to bring the fervor up a notch.

Drum stretched his hands out over the rumbling, churning group. They were ready for a fight. Drum could feel it. Restlessly, they quieted somewhat, waiting for even more terrible but exciting information from *their King.*

"My fellow citizens of River Kingdom. I know that you are angry about what Thorndike told you about Will. But the Urhonordos are not our only problem. The fact is that we have been betrayed.

"Although my lovely daughter was not aware of this, her friend Will was not trying to finish the pool that I promised you. New intel that Lord Thorndike didn't have shows that Will was actually trying to ruin *your* pool! He and the Lowlanders worked together to *drain* the pool instead of finishing it. Then he left the scene *with* the Urhonordos. No one is sure that he was kidnapped. No one saw it happen. The truth is that Will and the Lowlanders were working together to destroy the pool that I promised you! "You will notice that neither Will, the Urhonordos, nor the Lowlanders have returned to River Kingdom to explain themselves. This fact alone tells us something that neither Thorndike nor my daughter knew. Will and the Lowlanders may be *v* and may now be guilty of treason! This cannot stand! It is time that I lead you forward to defend our kingdom against all this treachery!"

The crowd swelled and roared. This was closer to what they thought they were going to hear when they came. "Drum will lead us! Drum will defend our Kingdom! Save our pool. Save our pool. Drum! Drum! Drum!" Drum stepped back and let the sound of his support wash over him.

There was no more glorious sound. This was the reason he had wanted to be King in the first place. Thorndike was reluctantly joining in the chant of his name. Drum smiled with satisfaction and turned to share the glory with Flawless, but she was gone.

31

The Mission

Flawless could still hear the echoes of her father and his Royal Defense Advisor as she slipped quietly away. She had no real knowledge of what had happened to Will, but she was too worried to wait or listen to more war talk. The last she had heard was that Will might have captured himself and that Urhonordo and the Lowlanders were both involved. River Kingdom was gearing up for war for no real reason, and all they were using for rationale was senseless rumor and hype.

Dipswitch was a greedy liar. Thorndike was a power-mad warmonger, and her father . . . her father had joined them, appearing now to be a king with no Conscience. Flawless really had no idea what she was going to do, but she had to get away and do something.

Soundlessly, she tiptoed down the hall, past her room, and out a side door of The Castle. She was going to change her fancy outfit, but she suddenly realized that there wasn't time for that. River Kingdom was gearing up for war, and Will might be caught in the middle of it.

How dare her father declare Will a traitor? How dare he and Thorndike turn a simple water problem into a reason for war? Her father's speech had destroyed all hope for peace with Queen Luna. Now Flawless's plan of negotiating a peaceful solution had been scuttled by misplaced anger and panic that her father and Thorndike had purposefully ignited.

Why had they done such a thing? And what about Will? Had he really been captured by some Urhonordos? If this was true, there had to be a reason. Why had that happened? Were all the Urhonordos as reasonable as Luna? Probably not. He might be in real danger.

Hostage or traitor, Flawless understood that her father and Thorndike were now using Will as another reason to use force. She needed to find Will, wherever he was. She also needed to warn Queen Luna of a possible invasion. Her father was out of control. Thorndike was the evil creature she had thought he was, and her father's actions now were now as frightening as Thorndike's.

Flawless raced past Will's garden with no thought of stopping, but suddenly, something caught her eye. Over the top of the shrubbery rose the most amazing flowers Flawless had ever seen, but this was no time for flowers.

Still, there stood enormous flowers, tall as a queen with round flower faces surrounded by bright yellow crowns of petals. They seemed to be calling to her. They looked like gigantic royalty, rising above her head and reigning over her path like rays of sun lighting her way in the dusk.

"They should be called 'sunflowers,'" Flawless said aloud.

Without another thought, she reached up and plucked one of the huge golden blooms. She would give this royal flower to Queen Luna as a peace offering. Maybe the Queen would accept it as a positive omen. She could hope.

Sunflower in hand, Flawless scurried toward The Bridge that linked Urhonordo with River Kingdom. She had good memories of her encounter here with Luna, but tonight, it felt dark and gloomy.

The circumstances held foreboding. Might she meet enemy troops on the other side? Might she be abducted too? She hesitated fearfully as the wind off the churning river swirled around her.

"Why are you stopping?" questioned Cflawless. "Either you believe what you told people from the balcony, or you don't. Be brave."

Flawless gathered up her skirts and forged on. She was determined. "Luna is a good person. She can't have changed completely. She will talk to me, and we might still be able to prevent a war," she told herself staunchly. "And we will save my beloved Will."

But in the dark, The Bridge rose up in front of her like a monster. She had never really seen it at night before. Large jagged rocks formed its base. Huge logs like the legs of giant bodies stretched from side to side, groaning as though ready to roll over and leave their uncomfortable resting places.

Over the years, pockets had been dug under The Bridge by the rushing water, leaving gaping black holes. *Perfect for hiding anything . . . or anyone,* thought Flawless.

Cautiously, she began her crossing. The logs were slick as the water splashed up between them. She grabbed at the slippery hand rails. The wind stirred the branches of the trees on the opposite side of The River into grotesque shapes that seemed to be reaching out for her.

Suddenly, there was a commotion in one of the caves under The Bridge. A flock of geese, unaccustomed to humans being on their bridge at night, rose up in a flurry of surprise and resentment, squawking and flapping and creating its own gusts of wind. It only took a second for Flawless to lose her balance and be swept into The River. In a flash, The River had her.

Tumbling headlong over rocks, grabbing at them, careening off their sharp edges, Flawless fought her way toward the nearest riverbank. Time after time, the water teased her by flinging her close to the shore and then sweeping her away. Her elegant gown caught on the rocks and was the first thing to go, leaving only her simple shift. Flawless tried to hang on tight to the beautiful sunflower, but it too was soon swept downstream and out of sight.

Flawless was not afraid of drowning, but the water was cold and the wind whipping it against her was even colder. Her hands grew numb and devoid of feeling, but she continued to fight both the water and growing fears of losing her ability to think at all.

Finally, shivering and bruised, she clutched a strong tuft of reeds and pulled herself onto the Urhonordo bank. She was alive, but her plan for a negotiation with Queen Luna was gone completely. Covered in mud and quaking with cold, she instinctively burrowed into some grasses and pulled at the dry leaves that lay around her.

She didn't want to sleep, but she had no choice. Tortured by fears for Will and not knowing where he was or how to find him, she fought her exhaustion but finally collapsed in a fitful sleep.

Flawless was so into the depths of her sleep that she didn't move when a little hand touched her shoulder and a voice asked timidly, "Are you alive?"

The tiny boy was crouched in front of her, nose to nose. Flawless blinked in the filtered sunlight and smiled. "Hi," she said.

"Hi," said the boy. "I told my mom that I found a body by The River, but she didn't believe me. Can you go home with me so I can prove I wasn't lying?"

Flawless smiled and stood up stiffly as she brushed off the leaves. "I would love to," she said.

"But you are a grown-up girl. You should have more clothes on," scolded the little boy.

"I know," agreed Flawless. "Maybe your mommy will help me find some."

"Or my sister," added the happy fellow. "She's your size. Come on. I'll take you home."

Home turned out to be very humble but pleasant. As was the habit of many Urhonordo women, the little boy's mother was instantly friendly. She smiled and opened her arms, hugging this strange shivering woman as though she had known her forever.

"Welcome," she said, smiling. "What happened to you? Did you fall in The Great River? I've done that myself, more than once. It's tough to get out, isn't it? One time, I thought I was going to drown in the rush, but obviously I didn't. That was a good thing. By the way, would you like some dry things? I don't have anything fancy, but it'll cover you up." She laughed. Within a minute or two, Flawless was clean and dressed. As the mother had said, it was nothing fancy, but the clothes were warm and soft. "These clothes are beautiful," Flawless exclaimed with enthusiasm. The little boy giggled.

"But what were you in The River for?" the woman asked. "You're not Urhonordo. I can tell. You have quality underthings. I think you might be royalty."

"Not really." Flawless sighed. "But my father is the King of River Kingdom."

"Oh," the gentle woman said with raised eyebrows. "I hear he took over for King Sol. Pretty cheeky, I would say. But that's just me."

"Right now, my father and I don't exactly agree on things. I was on my way to talk to Queen Luna about that when I fell in The River. Maybe I should be on my way."

"Maybe you should not go *anywhere* until I find out what is happening and what Queen Luna wants me to do. Things are sort of strange with River Kingdom right now. I hear that there was a scuffle down by that new fort at The Border."

Flawless looked down and realized that her foot was securely bound to a shackle that was anchored to the floor.

"Sorry to have to do that," said the mother with true regret in her voice. "I tie my goat up to that sometimes so I think it'll hold you. I also think you are a nice person, but I don't know for sure, and I hear that your father can be a bit tricky. I'll try to turn you lose as soon as I can. I sent my daughter to Queen Luna for instructions already."

Flawless groaned. "I understand, but I'm so worried about my friend, Will. I hear he's been captured."

"He's more than a friend, isn't he?" The woman smiled. Flawless said nothing.

"I wager that the queen will know about your friend," said the woman confidently. "She knows everything."

Queen Luna didn't know about *anything* for sure at that moment. Ben and Will were sitting near her. They had all discussed the water, the mud, the new fort that was not really a fort and, of course, "King Drum."

Drum was not really a king and never had been. They all understood that now, but what should they do about it? Drum might not be a king, but he was in charge of River Kingdom until King Sol appeared. Then what?

No one here knew of the war turmoil that had taken over River Kingdom although their information was only a day old. The wife of the man who had built "the fort," now known as Dipswitch Manor, would still want her pool, Will guessed. And the Lowlanders would still be without the payment that was their food for the winter. These were many problems that still needed solving. He needed to get back to The Castle.

Luna's problems were of a different nature altogether. She had made two aggressive moves against River Kingdom that were designed to convey the depth of her displeasure with The Kingdom's lack of respect for The River and Urhonordo Kingdom. She and her troops had come across The Bridge in armor, and they had taken Will. Did Drum know about both of these things? If he did, would he understand or retaliate? Urhonordo did not want armed conflict, but Luna didn't want her rights to be trampled. It was very complex.

The Consciences got busy. The comfort of this friendly scene did not stop the Consciences from speaking their minds.

"What are you going to do to patch things up with River Kingdom and keep your water rights?" questioned Cluna. "You are sitting here with friends, but they are not the ones you need to talk to. You need to speak with Drum."

Cwill was equally blunt with Will. "You got the water directed back to The Lowlands, but Dipswitch still expects his pool, and the Lowlanders haven't been paid yet. Sitting here is not going to make that happen. You need to confront Drum."

Cben was equally insistent with Ben. "Will is your friend, and he has tried the best he can to get Lowlander pay, but without it, many may starve this winter. You need to stand up like a man and get the payment you deserve. You need to talk to Drum."

The three people in the Urhonordo throne room now sat quietly together but deep in thought that was focused on their own troubling issues. Strangely, they were all comrades but focused on completely different conflicts of Conscience. They were determined to do something positive, but their ideas ran up against too many unanswered questions. The one thing they had in common was Drum.

Suddenly, a clattering noise from outside the throne room broke into heavy thinking. A breathless member of the Urhonordo Royal Guard rushed in. "Sorry, Your Majesty," he apologized with much waving of hands and gasping for air. "I ran all the way here. Look what me and my friends just found. It got snagged on the edge of The River. We've never seen the likes of it before. My friend thought it was a head 'cause it was the right size, but I don't think so. It sure is a strange sight, though. We were afraid it was some sort of signal for a secret attack, but we've never seen a message or anything. Anyway, we thought you ought to see it right away."

The guard threw the large strange object on the floor in front of Queen Luna where it landed with a soggy thud. She peered at it. What was it? It was wet and bedraggled, but it was actually rather beautiful.

Ben stood up and gave it a bit of a nudge with his toe. "It's a really big flower, I think," he said cautiously. "What do you think, Will? You're the flower expert."

Will picked it up and then he stared. He hugged it. He looked up at the sky and hugged it tighter. "I know what it is," he moaned. "It is a message. It's one of the flowers from my garden. I planted it this spring." With fear and agony, Will turned to Luna.

"Flawless must have brought it with her," he said fearfully. "She is one of the few people that knows about my garden. She must have heard that I was taken by you and come looking for me. She would have picked it to bring to you if she was on her way here. If she dropped it in The River, it was because . . . she was in The River too. Something must have happened to her . . . She could have . . . No. I have to go find her! Maybe she is on the shore but lost! Maybe she was hurt. What if she was . . ." The thought was too much. Luna covered her face in fear. She remembered the flowers that Flawless had brought to her at The Bridge. They had talked peace then, but Luna had abducted Will since then. Will was right. This was something that Flawless would do if she were on a peace mission. But where was she now? Without hesitating, Luna jumped to her feet and spoke with authority to Ben and

Will as well as the guards.

"We all need to go find Flawless," she declared. "Who is Flawless?" said one of the baffled guards.

"She is our friend," answered the Queen and rushed from the room.

This must be a stealth operation. Speed was essential. They were to look like "a group of friends who needed to find another friend"—plus two fascinated but completely confused guards. Discarding her royal robes, Luna pulled on a common shift, determined to travel fast and without notice. They were searching for someone whose fate might be worse than they wanted to imagine. In near panic, they breathlessly set out toward The River. Were they going to be too late?

It was an uncommon sight, this unmatched cadre of Guardsmen, commoners, and a woman, all running silently down a dirt path with very grim looks on their faces. Was someone chasing them? No. they didn't seem like that. The woman looked a bit like . . . No, of course not. It couldn't be. On they ran, leaping over ruts and veering around debris, brushing aside brambles and bushes, determined to reach The River and find Flawless before it was too late.

A young girl was scrambling toward them, but they rushed past her, scarcely noticing that she was waving and yelling at them.

She halted. "Stop!" she shouted bravely.

"I'm sorry but we can't stop, young lady," said Ben as he passed her by. "We are on a very important mission to find a lady who may be in danger," he explained as he picked up the pace.

The girl grinned and cupped her hands to her mouth for an even louder shout at the quickly departing group. "My brother just found a lady in The River," she yelled. "Maybe she's your lady."

She crossed her arms and stood her ground. She knew they would stop and talk to her now.

They did stop and whirled back to the girl, but, now that she had an audience, she had something important to say. She looked each one of them over with doubt. "I know where your lady is and you don't, but I'm not going to tell just anyone where she is. I'm on my way to see the Queen."

The guards smiled at the girl and pointed at Luna. "You can tell us," they said. "This is your Queen."

"No," the girl said politely. "I mean the *real* Queen."

Luna stepped forward elegantly. "I am your Queen, child," she said. "Do you need to speak with me?"

The girl fell instantly to her knees in the soft dirt. Suddenly observing her beauty and her manner, there was no doubt who this was. "I am so sorry, Your Majesty. I didn't recognize you."

"That was a good thing." Luna smiled. "Why did you want to see me?" "We found a pretty lady in The River," the girl responded. "She's not an Urhonordo, but we don't know who she is." "Is she alive?" the hunters blurted in unison.

"Oh yes. My momma dressed her and tied her up." The happy hunters grinned.

"If you would be so kind," said Will with the respect that the girl now deserved. "I would be pleased if you would direct your Queen and the rest of us to the pretty lady you found. We are all her friends."

The girl smiled with pride and nodded. She was about to lead *the Queen* to *her* home. She turned and marched away, followed by very important people. Her mother would be proud of her.

Within minutes, they reached the little home, and the relieved mother released her "captive" along with many hugs and apologies.

"I found her, but she looked like she was dead. When I found out that she was alive, I told my momma," boasted the little boy.

"You did a very good and brave thing," said Luna as she squeezed Flawless's hand. Glancing at Will, she caught him brushing away a tear.

On the way back to Luna's castle, Flawless tried to explain the reason for her dangerous nighttime journey. As calmly as she could, she detailed what she had heard the night before. Thorndike and her father were pushing for war against Urhonordo even though she had tried to talk them out of it. "There's always somebody like that," groused Luna. "I have never been able to figure out why. What pleasure do they get out of it?"

"I think it's power," commented Will. He slipped his arm around Flawless to steady her as they walked. Luna noticed and smiled. So did Ben as he edged forward to walk next to Luna.

"It's the blasted Auras at work, Will," Cwill whispered. "Dipswitch and that Thorndike character are in thick with the Eforces."

"Thorndike was totally into his power lust last night, for sure," offered Cflawless, "and it was spreading."

Will did not know Thorndike, but he had already made up his mind about Dipswitch and his wife. They were not good.

"My father started lying about you, Will, just to sound tougher than Thorndike. He said you might even be a traitor because Sir Dipswitch said that you drained his pool."

"I did, but I'm not a traitor," Will offered.

"I believe that," said Flawless. "But Daddy and the two other warmongers have the River Kingdom farmers believing that you are somehow part of a reason for war just because they love Daddy's rallies and cheer for whatever he says."

"After all these years of living peacefully across The River from us, are they that eager to want to go to war with us?" questioned Queen Luna. "We haven't done anything to them. Don't they have any Consciences?"

"Don't blame the Consciences of the people." Will sighed. "They don't know that they have been lied to so they just believe the man they like and that's Drum." Flawless nodded sadly.

"I see your point," said Luna. "I hadn't thought of that." "And the Auras are getting stronger," offered Cflawless.

"Sounds like Auras are back after leaving us alone for a long time," added Cluna.

Flawless was ashamed of all of it. "I don't know why my father does the things he does," she concluded sadly.

"Because *he* doesn't listen to his Conscience as he should. Sometimes I think he can't, even when he knows that his Conscience knows better," said Cflawless bluntly. "It's like there's something inside him that's stronger than his Conscience and it's in the way. He has a perfectly good Conscience. I've known Cdrum all my life. Your father just doesn't listen to him."

I know you're right, thought Flawless. *I hear him talking to his Conscience all the time, but he just argues with him.* "I don't know what I'm going to do. If he doesn't start listening soon, we'll have a war."

The group trudged on in silence. The clouds of worry and almost inevitable conflict were gathering over them as they reached Urhonordo Castle. They were beginning to get depressed.

"Well, we need to figure out something fast," said Luna darkly as she slumped onto her throne. "I feel the evil flowing myself. To be honest, I have also felt the draw of meanness and retaliation. This is why I grabbed you, Will. I wanted to capture you and punish you for what I thought you had done to my people's farmland. I was willing to throw you in a dungeon. I'm so sorry for that."

"It's a good thing I am on duty." Cluna sighed. "The draw of evil is pretty strong whenever it shows up."

Ben sat down beside Luna. "Things aren't as simple as they used to be, are they, Luna?" he said.

Luna looked at Ben fondly. "I liked it back then when we were kids and we just liked each other and had a good time," she said. "I don't remember ever fighting with you."

"I had it easy back then." Cluna sighed.

"We never fought," agreed Ben. "I just chased you all day."

"And I let you catch me." Luna laughed. "Why did you stop coming over to play?"

"I grew up, I guess," said Ben. "My Conscience started talking to me about going to work and helping my family. When I finally listened, I met Will up on Drum Manor Estates in River Kingdom. That's where I've been ever since. We both work for Drum, you know."

"Sure. Blame it on your Conscience," scoffed Cben.

"So you listened to your Conscience." Luna smiled. "I guess that's a good reason. That's what I tried to do too. When my father died, I was next in line. I'm not sure I was ready to stop playing, but suddenly I was a Queen."

"And you do a good job, too," contributed Flawless. "I wish my father listened to his Conscience the way you do."

"King Drum has always thought that his thinking was smarter than any Conscience so he hears his Conscience but choses to ignore him." Ben laughed. "Now it's even worse. He's king, so he thinks that what he thinks is even more right just because of who he is."

"You know, Ben. You might be right." Flawless sighed. "No one told him 'no' all his life. Not me, not his wives, not anybody. Becoming king has made him feel even smarter, and he will do anything to keep that feeling." Suddenly, Queen Luna remembered that she had information that Flawless needed. It was going to hurt her because she loved her father, but she needed to know it. Gently, Luna invited Flawless to sit closer. "You need to hear something important, my friend."

Flawless looked up with a slight smile. "I hope it is something good," she said. "After my swim last night, I need it."

Luna didn't smile. "It is news that only arrived yesterday, Flawless. Most of us call it good news. That's a fact. But what I need to tell you is . . . that your father is not king anymore and never really was. A Royal Courier delivered the joyful news that King Sol is alive. He was successful in his Dragon Quest, and he's on his way back to River Kingdom."

THEIR THOUGHTS

Flawless didn't move. Ben and Will had heard this earlier and were not shocked. But they had not really thought about what this would mean to Flawless. They came close and sat near, but said nothing.

After several minutes, Flawless stirred, looked around at her friends, and said softly, "I'm glad for King Sol. He seemed like a good man, . . . but poor Daddy lied to become who he is. He has always known he was a fake, but I guess it didn't matter. His whole reign has been one big bluff. How sad. When people find out, he's going to be devastated."

Flawless wrestled with her feelings. Nearly everything her father had done since spring was a lie for his own pleasure. King Sol was alive and would be returning to take his place on his throne. Her father would be in disgrace. Was she mad? Yes. But she was also sad.

"He will deserve to be in disgrace," commented Cflawless smugly.

Flawless was her father's daughter and she loved him, but she had watched him during the past few months and she had grown. "Thank you for telling me, Luna," she said simply.

32

The War Is On

It was the morning after the big rally. Morf dozed on his chair by the door of the throne room. It had been an unnerving but exciting night, and an exhausted Drum was still asleep. The imagined glory of future combat had blown through the crowd like a hurricane, filling The Castle courtyard with patriotism. That patriotism had been stirred and re stirred by the dueling oratory of Thorndike and Drum until it was finally whipped to a froth of warlike frenzy. It had been amazingly fierce.

Of course, the patriotic fervor of the farmers and their lords was only based on imaginative rhetoric as no one in the throng had been damaged, threatened, or even had a cross word with "the enemy." They actually had no real reason for fighting Urhonordo or anyone else. But the horrifying visions presented by Thorndike and King Drum, each intent on topping the enthusiasm of the other, had definitely been inspiring. The men of River Kingdom were ready to fight now, even if they were not sure why.

Morf had waved a battle flag as well last night, but he had not been as enthusiastic as those around him. He was aware that the reasons for the enthusiasm were mostly hype. Morf had decided to act supportive of Drum's war talk, and Cmorf was not sure why. What was actually going to happen? Was there really going to be a war? Cmorf was still asleep now, but he was rolling about in Morf's hair in an uneasy slumber.

Cdrum was already awake but ashamed. The human that he was Conscience for appeared to be completely out of control. He was advocating war. He was championing violence for no reason. Cdrum knew that Drum's fear of Luna's invasion had started Drum's need for some sort of military protection, but now Thorndike was taking protection to a whole new level and Drum didn't seem to want to lower it.

War drums were escalating. Thorndike's lust for power was overshadowing Drum's need for protection by far, but now Cdrum had to concede that Drum's warlike stance was also his need to "out-Thorndike" Thorndike.

Second man on a Royal Balcony was not a position Drum could tolerate. Drum had risen to the challenge with outrageous predictions and exaggerated compliments of the untested prowess of his farmers. They had loved him for it. He had loved their adoration. Cdrum felt like a complete failure.

Drum was still asleep after the big rally so he hadn't even noticed that Flawless was nowhere in The Castle. Cdrum had noticed immediately, and he was sure he knew why. Flawless was furious with the things Drum had said about Will being a traitor . . . *and* she was worried for his safety. Now she was gone. Knowing why she was gone wasn't helpful now. Drum would be distraught. Cdrum needed to talk. He decided to rouse Cmorf.

"Wake up, Cmorf," whispered Cdrum. "I know that you are there in Morf's hair. I can see you. Did you know that Flawless left The Castle last night?"

"Sure. Are you surprised?" Cmorf asked with a yawn. "She is a person who actually listens to her Conscience. I wish Morf was like that, but I have pretty much given up on him."

"You woke me up," complained Morf. "What makes you think that I don't listen to you?"

"I think that because you have turned into a warmongering, flag-waving yes-man for Drum when you actually know better. You make me sick. That's why," countered Cmorf with a growl. "I have pretty much decided that you are a lost cause. I've given up."

Morf was surprised. "You mean you are not going to try to help me anymore? I didn't know you Consciences could do that. I thought being a Conscience was a lifetime commitment."

"It is, or I would have been gone a while back."

"So you're going to stay but not say anything? Is that what you're saying?"

"That's what I'm saying."

"Hmm. I didn't think I was that bad," said Morf. "I'm just trying to stay in The Castle and keep my job. Royal Advisors have been dumped at the drop of a hat around here."

"I guess you're right. All things considered, you have hung in with Drum pretty well," acknowledged Cmorf. "You haven't jumped, and you haven't been dumped. I guess I'll have to forgive you for pretending to be a warmonger. I just wonder what Drum's Conscience thinks about war since Drum seems to be all for it."

"I'm right here, people. The least you can do is talk to me instead of talking *about* me."

"Sorry," said Cmorf.

"That's okay," Cdrum answered. "And in answer to your question, I'm *not at all* for this war hype. I liked what Flawless was saying. When Drum gets up, I'm going to try to talk him down from where he ended up last night. At least I will do that until Drum finds out that Flawless is gone. That's going to really upset him."

"Maybe you ought to go wake him up and tell him. He really ought to know," Cmorf suggested.

"Okay, you're right. I guess it's my job. I'll go wake them up," said Morf reluctantly.

"Good boy," quipped Cmorf.

"See," said Morf to his Conscience as he made his way to Drum's bedchamber. "I still listen to you."

"Only when it's convenient," answered Cmorf.

Morf cautiously pulled back the curtains to find, to his surprise, that Drum was awake and sitting sleepily on his bed.

"Last night was quite a night," he mumbled. "That Thorndike was really pushing for war, wasn't he?"

"Did you know that you two were going to get everybody that excited?" asked Morf.

"Not really," snorted Drum with a laugh. "But we sure gave those farmers something to get excited about, didn't we? What a night! Everybody will remember it for a long time." Drum rolled off his bed and reached for his crown. "Of course, Flawless will be disappointed that her little idea was blown away, but she'll get over it."

"I don't think it's going to be that easy," said Morf carefully.

"Oh yes, it will," Drum responded as he shuffled into the throne room. "She always gets over things. Go get her and tell her to come in here so we can smooth things over."

Morf followed Drum into the throne room so he could say what he needed to say to Drum's back. It was easier that way.

Cmorf picked up on this. "Chicken," he whispered.

"Flawless isn't here in The Castle anymore, sire," Morf said flatly. "She's gone."

Drum stopped walking. "What?"

"Flawless is gone. I think she left last night after the rally," Morf continued quickly. "Right after you said that Will was a traitor."

Drum turned around slowly. "She's gone?" "Yes, sir."

Drum stumbled up onto his throne and pulled his robe around him like a cocoon shell. He stared at his fingers. He rubbed his nose. He looked at Morf. Morf looked at the floor.

"Where did she go?" asked Drum quietly.

"I don't know, sire, but the servants said that she left The Castle and headed south."

"She headed south?" Drum repeated.

"Yes, sir." Morf turned and left the throne room, leaving a bewildered and nonfunctioning father behind. There was nothing he could do. There was nothing more he could say.

The Castle staff, however, had everything to say to each other and anyone who would listen.

"Did you hear that Flawless left The Castle last night?" "I heard it was because of Will being called a traitor."

"Will's not a traitor. I've known his family since he was a little boy." "But where did Flawless go, then? Where is she now?"

"She's ditched King Drum. That's all I know."

As the word spread through the village, Thorndike had a very predictable response to the fact that Flawless was gone. "Thank goodness," he said with a satisfied sigh. "What a pain in the neck she was. Now Drum will be free to do what he knows needs to be done without having to run it by goody two-shoes."

Cthorndike, Thorndike's seldom used Conscience, decided to make another cameo appearance. This happened sometimes with ignored Consciences. They couldn't resist trying one more time. Maybe there was still a little bit of humanity left in him.

"I hear that Drum will be pretty broken up about his daughter leaving," he commented. "You should probably show some sympathy to the poor guy. I hear he is close to that girl."

"Too close, if you ask me," answered Thorndike. "When did you decide to wake up and get all mushy on me, Conscience?"

"I'm not getting mushy. What I'm saying is pretty normal if you had anything inside you but Eforce horse-pucky," answered Cthorndike. "This is why I don't talk to you that often. I don't think the Eforces let a kind thought register with you much anymore."

"Thank goodness again. Kindness is overrated. Now, get out of my way.

I need to inspect the troops." "They're just commoners."

"They're a Commoner Army," insisted Thorndike proudly as he buckled on a sword and marched off to where he would be drilling his men. Cthorndike knew he was no longer welcome and had not been for a long time. He drifted sadly away.

Drum watched Thorndike begin to work with his strange-looking army from his balcony. The man was really getting ready for war. He couldn't believe it. He hadn't expected it to go this far. He only wanted to scare the Urhonordos, to put them in their place, to show them who was boss.

"You're in over your head, aren't you?" said Cdrum. "What are you going to do about it?"

"What *can* I do?" asked Drum.

"I don't know," answered Morf who was walking behind him.

Drum jumped. He should have known Morf would be nearby. Now he returned to his throne and sat down dejectedly. This wasn't working the way he had hoped and believed it would. He loved being king. He loved his power. He loved the adoration of the peasants at his rallies. But the fun had gone out of all of it this morning. Flawless was gone.

"I shouldn't have said what I said about William, should I?" he mourned. "You should have listened to her or to me," snorted Cdrum. He wanted

to rub it in further, but he felt bad for Drum. He had enjoyed a good run with his kingliness, but now he was in a mess. "You might be able to fix this if you really try," said Cdrum quietly, knowing that Drum wouldn't listen. And Cdrum was right. Drum didn't listen.

"He needs to get Flawless back," said Cmorf. "What do you know?" said Morf.

"I need to get Flawless back," said Drum.

"You're right," agreed the surprised Morf. It was the first time that his Conscience and Drum had been on the same page. It had to be a sign.

Drum dressed much more quickly and much less formally than usual. Morf was ready too. But now they simply looked at each other. What were they going to do?

That was the obvious question. They went to work.

Drum forgot that Morf was an underling. Morf forgot it too. With someone they both cared about occupying their thinking, they were coming together on a mission. Together they lowered their heads and began to work on a strategy—a "get Flawless back" strategy.

First, they had to believe that Flawless was someplace safe. This had to be a given. They could not think of her being unsafe . . . or hurt . . . or killed.

No, these possibilities were not possible.

If these things were not possible, key questions followed: Where could she be? What would she do? What had been her goal?

Two possible answers that came back to both men. She went to find Will. She went to see Queen Luna.

Drum slumped on his throne again. If she went to see Luna, she might, indeed, be in danger. Drum thought. Luna had already kidnapped Will, according to Sir Dipswitch. Now she may have his daughter as well.

Morf and Drum were chewing on this difficult piece of information when they heard a noise approaching the throne room. It wasn't an unpleasant noise. They both should have recognized it, but they were too absorbed in worry to hear the familiar sound.

And of course, even on a day when Drum was at his wit's end, who should arrive but Milton Fandango and his girls on their regular morning visit. With their usual lack of invitation, they rushed up the hall, joyously dancing and giggling. Two entered first, circled Drum, and began to pet him, offering him news tidbits in their accustomed manner.

Next, without permission or hesitation, the entire noisy tangle of arms, legs, and feathers bustled through the curtains and surrounded Drum with themselves. Following close behind was the beaming Milton Fandango, now dressed more impressively like a Royal Finance Advisor.

"Great night last night, eh, sir?" he chortled. "The girls and I went out and watched the festivities. Looks like Thorndike is already out there this morning getting his men revved up for a battle. Sounds pretty exciting. When is the big battle launch day?"

Drum tried to pull himself together. If he was upset or worried about anything, he didn't want anyone to know. It was time to bluff again.

"Glad to see you, Fandango old man. Yes, you sure are right about last night. It was quite a night, alright." Milton was a strange, nervous little man, but he wasn't stupid. He had heard, of course, that Flawless had left The Castle and had warned his girls to say nothing about that. He had other things to discuss today. He was now the "money man."

"Yessir, looks like there's going to be some sort of a war, sooner or later," he commented in an offhand manner. "Sounds like it's going to be a pretty big deal. I was wondering how you thought you might finance such a war. Do you have any ideas?"

Drum looked at Fandango with a blank stare but recovered quickly. "Oh, I was going to call you up here for just that discussion," he bluffed. "I thought I might pull a little bit of something out of our storehouses if we actually do it. I was going to talk to you about that."

"That's a good idea, sire. A very good idea because we might need to think of ways to do this war on the cheap," commented Fandango with one eyebrow raised. "Supplies have been flowing out of the storehouses pretty fast in the past few months and we still have the Lowlanders to pay off for the levees. I can bring you a complete accounting tomorrow if you'd like." "Sounds good. Sounds good," Drum continued to bluff. Morf could see the little beads of sweat rolling out from under Drum's crown. "But I have some heavy-duty work to do right now, Milton. I'll have to postpone my time with the girls today. How about coming back tomorrow?"

Milton Fandango looked at Drum closely. Milton was not a nobleman. He was a vendor from the village now acting as Finance Advisor. He knew Drum's look, and he knew what was in the storehouses. Drum was not bluffing as well as usual. Very interesting. Fandango made note as he began to escort his girls back to their comfortable suite of castle rooms. Things were not going to improve tomorrow.

Drum slumped again on his throne. It was no longer a comfortable place. His daughter was missing. His Royal Defense Advisor was planning an unnecessary war, and now he knew he couldn't afford it.

Morf felt the way he had when no one had showed up at Drum's Inaugural Celebration. What Drum thought was going to happen was not happening the way he thought it would. Now Morf knew that nothing that Drum had envisioned was ever as easy as he had thought it was going to be because he never really thought past his idea of the moment.

Morf watched the dancing girls wander out through the curtains. Some stopped and gave Drum a gentle pat as they left. Even they could see that Drum was unhappy. Reality seemed to be closing in, and Morf couldn't think of a way to fix it.

"What did you expect?" challenged the grumpy Cmorf. "The man is a fraud. You knew that from the beginning. If you are surprised now, you are stupider than I thought you were."

Thanks for your support, thought Morf.

"That's what happens when you live on bluffs and lies and promises," said Cmorf. He was not going to be still now. "I can feel the Auras gathering. Thorndike is going to want to storm Urhonordo and take it over. He would like to be king here, but he will settle for Urhonordo. If Drum doesn't go along, he'll take over River Kingdom as well. The man has a power lust that won't quit."

Morf wanted to tell Cmorf that he was wrong. He wanted to make Drum feel better. He was kind of in the habit of doing that now. He struggled for something nice to say.

"I think it's sort of commendable that you feel sorry for Drum, even if he doesn't deserve it," Cmorf continued, "but there isn't really anything you can say that will help in a situation like this. You used to be creative, but I guess you lost that skill when you decided to be a kiss-up."

"Shut up," said Morf. "What?" asked Drum.

"Nothing, sire," Morf hurried to say. "I was just talking to my Conscience."

Drum looked at Morf in pain. "I used to say that all the time to Flawless," he said sadly. "I just wish she was here. She is such a good girl . . . and peaceful."

"Girls are usually better at being peaceful than we men are," agreed Morf. "Too bad we can't ask Flawless to go to Queen Luna and rescue this situation like she wanted to do. She could probably do it."

Silence reigned. Neither man had a useful thought. Both men were sad. Both knew that they had made so many mistakes by now that maybe nothing could be fixed.

"I just heard you say something interesting." It was Cmorf again. Morf wanted to say shut up again, but he didn't.

"If you don't want me to say anything, I won't, but I just heard you say that girls are more peaceful than men are and might be able to do something right now that men couldn't do as well," said Cmorf.

"So?"

"So a whole flock of lovely girls just left this room and you used to be creative. Maybe you could try your hand at creativity again and ask these girls to do something peaceful like Flawless could do if she were here. That's all I have to say."

Morf thought about that. Cmorf was right. Flawless, as a woman, had achieved a peace somehow with Queen Luna, but how had she done it? Morf thought some more, but he had no idea what her secret was. If he knew what her special skill was, maybe he could teach it to one of the girls. She must have some sort of "girl power." Power in a female was a new and novel idea to Morf, and he had no idea how to put it to work.

His first thought was to dispatch two girls to sneak across The Bridge and tie up Luna until she told them where Flawless was.

"That is sort of creative, but not very bright. These girls are really too noisy to sneak anywhere, and they would probably trip on their feathers," said Cmorf in critique.

Morf had another idea. *Two girls could go over to Urhonordo and dance in front of the Royal Guards. While the guards were distracted, two more girls could go in and untie Flawless and sneak her out,* he thought.

"That was more creative, but the problem is that we don't know where Flawless is held captive so the two who are untying wouldn't know where to find her. Try again."

I am thinking as hard as I can, but I can't honestly see how girls could rescue Flawless, and without that, I know that Thorndike will rush in, pretending to rescue her and take over Urhonordo with violence, Morf sulked wordlessly.

"You've been working with Drum too long," commented Cmorf, "but I hear what you're thinking, and I think we're missing the point. We need to think like Flawless. What did she say when she spoke to the rally?"

Morf concentrated and tried to remember and visualize. *There she was in her beautiful dress. What had she said, exactly? It was something about peaceful negotiations for water rights. It wasn't very fancy.*

"I honestly don't know, for sure," Morf groaned.

"Yes, you do," said Cmorf. "You just remembered it. 'Peaceful negotiation for water rights.' That's what Flawless wanted to do. That's all the dancing girls need to do—speak honestly and offer to negotiate peacefully for water rights."

Morf thought about it. It was too simple. It couldn't possibly work, . . . but it was creative. It might. Actually, what was their alternate plan if they didn't try it? He gave the idea more thought and went to talk to Fandango. When Morf arrived back in the throne room at noon, Thorndike was just leaving. He was in a frenetic hurry and obviously spurred by the energy of a man on an unstoppable mission.

Drum was wearing his crown and sitting on his throne as usual, but Morf was shocked to see that Drum was once more excited and responding to Thorndike's enthusiasm and war talk as he had last night. He seemed to have forgotten Flawless.

The Auras were palpable throughout the throne room, careening across the floor and swirling around the throne. Cmorf recognized them. *They must follow Thorndike everywhere,* he thought with a shiver. He brings their power with him. *We must beware.*

"What did I miss?" asked Morf. "What just happened?"

"It's going to be quick and dirty," bragged the glowing Drum. "Thorndike came swooping in here with his battle plans all drawn up and his forces ready for war. That man thinks like a battle machine. He is actually leaving with the Commoner Army tomorrow, and it should all be over by nightfall. *He* will rule Urhonordo, and I will rule River Kingdom. It's marvelous!"

"You have to get Drum to stop this now!" hissed Cmorf. "He has bought the Eforce fantasy!"

"Please, sire, nooo," groaned Morf aloud to Drum. "You can't let Thorndike wage a real war! There is no reason for it. Many people will be killed!"

"Thorndike doesn't think so," said Drum confidently. "Thorndike thinks Urhonordo is a pushover, and he plans to conquer them easily and replace Queen Luna with himself. But don't worry. If there is some bloodshed, it doesn't really bother him. It's a price he's willing to pay for what he wants." Cdrum had been listening with frustration all morning. He had argued.

He had pleaded but had, at last, given up on having any positive effect. The Auras were too strong.

But now, however, Cdrum *really* heard what Drum just said. Something clicked.

Thorndike was so determined to get his own kingdom that the idea of bloodshed didn't bother him. That was it. Cdrum had heard of this kind of Aura dominance spoken of in forums before. He had likened such a strong determination to the drive of a "Super Aura." It happened rarely, and it only happened when one overriding Aura became so strong that it ruled the mind of an individual above all reason. A Super Aura could become so much a part of such a person that it never left their side. It was part of them. It directed everything that the person in its control did. Cdrum now recognized that he was up against such a force and he had identified

Thorndike's Super Aura was power lust. He wanted to be a king and would stop at nothing to get that idea!

"Thorndike doesn't mind if 'some blood is shed' because that is the price Thorndike is willing to pay for what he wants," Cdrum informed Drum with passion. "He doesn't care if he hurts or kills other people if he gets what he wants."

Drum did not seem the least bit impressed, but Cdrum wasn't through. Another even more important truth now came to Cdrum in a flash. Drum had a Super Eforce too!

This is why the energy level was so high! This is why war talk had escalated out of control—Drum was almost as single-minded as Thorndike, but his Super Aura was different. His Super Aura was his love of himself—self-love.

Drum always knew he was right. He believed that the world should be his and conform to his wishes. He believed that his lies were truths and his wrongs were right. Drum had his own Super Aura, and Cdrum, until now, had just not recognized it.

Cdrum was amazed at his own ignorance. Drum had always put his *love for himself* before concern for anyone else. Why shouldn't *he* get what he wanted? Why shouldn't he be worried about what people thought of him? Why was he so worried about loyalty? And why did he never think of consequences for anyone but *himself?*

This was a revelation. Cdrum now realized that his thinking had been ignorant, "old-school." He had thought Drum's problems were due to overconfidence, selfishness, or thoughtlessness. These faults were usually temporary and fixable. But the powerful Super Force of self-love was something that had not occurred to him until now. This was a totally new understanding.

Now that he understood, Cdrum knew he was up against something unique. It was a force that was so ingrained as to be a mental handicap.

Undoubtedly, Drum didn't even know this Eforce existed. He wouldn't admit that it did if he was informed of it.

Cdrum knew that this was always what he had fought against and lost, but he could not quit now. He had to stop Drum from allowing this Super Eforce to rule him completely and perhaps ruin the entire Kingdom. This was a crisis.

Cdrum placed himself strategically inside Drum's ear and said, strong and loud, "Are you willing to let Thorndike pay with 'some bloodshed' if that bloodshed belongs to Flawless? Is Flawless's life a price *you're* willing to pay for *your own happiness on the throne?*"

Cdrum's voice plunged deep into Drum.

There was an almost physical reaction. A Super Aura that had secretly governed Drum since birth was being directly attacked. It was an Aura that no one had recognized or challenged until now, but it explained a lot. Drum groaned and clutched his heart. He hadn't thought about Flawless being at risk from Thorndike's exciting war. As much as he loved himself and his precious throne, this was his precious Flawless that Thorndike was threatening. Flawless might certainly be one of the people who would be hurt or even killed if Thorndike waged war on Urhonordo while she was there.

The Super Aura released its grip. How could he have overlooked this horrible possibility? For perhaps the first time ever, something had penetrated Drum's self-love—his love for Flawless. Cdrum had broken through.

Drum looked around his beautiful throne room, but now he saw it through eyes clouded with misery and confusion. It no longer looked beautiful to him. *I just approved the plan that threatens my own daughter's death, he thought. How could I have been so stupid?*

"'Thoughtless' is the word you're looking for," said Cdrum, reading his thoughts *and* trying to put his new awareness to him gently.

"Selfish and stupid," insisted Drum. "What did you say?" asked Morf in shock.

"I was talking to my Conscience," explained Drum, "but what I said was true. I just figured it out. There is no way that I can let Thorndike wage war on Urhonordo. My daughter is there, and a full-on war could kill her, not to mention hundreds of others."

The shocked smaller Auras rolled back into corners of the throne room and waited. They always waited, but they were stunned.

"Wow," said Morf. "I can't believe that you just said what you just said.

Did you say it?"

"Yes. I can't believe I didn't see it before, but now I don't know what to do about it. Thorndike will invade Urhonordo tomorrow. I am sure that Flawless is there. I have done a lot of terrible things in my life, but declaring war on Urhonordo now would be the worst. If anything happens to Flawless, all is lost."

"Your Majesty," Morf began timidly.

"Speak up, Morf," hissed Cmorf. "This is not a time to be your usual weak-kneed self."

"Right, right. I'm on it. Your Majesty, you might not remember this now," offered Morf, "but this morning, I had an idea of using 'girl power' to resolve our problems with Urhonordo rather than giving in to Thorndike's war effort."

Drum said nothing.

Morf shuffled his feet but continued. "I kind of took it upon myself then to ask Fandango's girls to come here. I hear them coming down the hall now. I asked them to come back because I might have a plan to avoid war." "If it'll avoid war, I'll listen to anything right now." Drum sighed, his head in his hands.

As the girls filed in, they began their usual dances and gathered around Drum as was their custom. With their soft hands and gentle smiles, they surrounded him and patted him. He smiled slightly at them, but they did notice that something about him had changed. So did Fandango.

"What's the problem, King Drum?" he said, looking at Drum from the corner of his eye. "You do not look happy. Thorndike is marching his men up and down through the village, barking out orders and getting ready for war. That man is a force."

"I know." Drum sighed. "He is more of a force than I ever should have wanted." Drum took off his crown and laid it to the side. It was now getting in the way of his thinking. The girls and Fandango stepped back and stared, but Drum did not explain.

Morf looked from side to side timidly, but Cmorf poked him. Morf wasn't sure how to do it, but now he needed to test his idea.

"Ladies," Morf began. "Have any of you ever been to Urhonordo?"

Great giggling began to ripple through the dancing girls. It was apparent that many of them had traveled over The Bridge more than once.

Drum raised his eyebrows. This thought had never occurred to him.

Morf continued. "Since some of you have been there before and possibly have friends there, would it be possible for you to do your King and your kingdom a big favor?"

The girls stood blankly staring at Fandango. He was their boss. What was this all about?

Fandango snickered. He knew more than Drum imagined. In addition, he had already been talking to Morf in the hall. Come to find out, Fandango was even ready to become a patriot. "The girls are free to do as they wish, no charge" he declared. "Especially if it will help The Kingdom."

Morf now felt he was on stronger ground with his plan than he had expected to be. Drum was not throwing a fit. He actually seemed to be listening. Fandango was being generous. Morf cleared his throat. He had to say this right.

"You dancing ladies that work for Sir Fandango are loyal citizens of River Kingdom, but now I hear that you have many friends that are Urhonordos as well. My idea is that we ask you ladies to form a Peace Corps and send it across The Bridge to . . . talk to Urhonordo about peace." There was a long silence. The dancing girls looked at each other timidly.

This was a strange request. They had never thought of doing such a thing. They were dancers.

Drum frowned. Fandango appeared deep in thought. Morf stood on one foot and then the other. The Eforces waited to move back into position.

Finally, a small girl from the back of the group stepped forward. "I'll go," she declared simply. "I'm in favor of peace."

That was all it took. Suddenly there was a chorus of "Me too" and "I can do that" and "Count me in." Much chattering ensued as the girls giggled some more and tried to think up catchy things to say to the Urhonordos. It was then, however, that Drum raised his hand for quiet.

The girls stopped talking immediately, seeing the look in Drum's eye. Without any further communication, they pulled together in a protective circle.

Drum began to pace, stopping to look at the girls for a moment and then returning to his pacing.

Morf was worried. He began to stammer. "We can do this differently if you wish, sire. If you think it is a bad idea, I can send the girls away."

"Hold your ground. You're acting like a weenie again," counseled Cmorf.

"For Pete's sake, stop pacing," hissed Cdrum. "You're scaring everybody to death."

Drum stopped pacing and faced the dancing girls. "Do you understand what we are asking you to do? Urhonordo is now enemy territory. Do you understand the danger that you will be in?" he growled.

The girls shrank into a tighter circle as their eyes widened.

THE WARRIN

Drum's voice became deeper and more menacing. "My daughter was captured by the Urhonordos. William of Dale has either been captured or has joined the other side against us. Neither the Urhonordos nor Will may be the people you think you know. They may now be ruthless enemies."

"Come on, Drum," whined Morf. "If you didn't like my idea, you could just say so. I'll send the girls away, and we can let Thorndike go to war tomorrow."

"Are you trying to scare the girls to death?" asked Cdrum.

"No," said Drum forcefully.

"What?" asked Morf. "Are you talking to your Conscience again?"

"Yes," Drum said, continuing. "Ladies, I need you to understand that the Urhonordos are against us because of water rights and they have taken up arms. If you go across The Bridge, you will be on your own. The River Kingdom cannot protect you."

Cdrum suddenly realized with shock what Drum was doing. He wasn't trying to scare the young women. He was trying to warn them. Drum was actually thinking of someone else instead of himself. Cdrum couldn't believe it, . . . and he was thrilled. This was a Super-Force breakthrough.

Morf blinked at Drum.

"Don't back off," warned Cmorf. "Keep pressing your idea before the girls get too scared to do anything."

Morf said his piece. "When Flawless spoke to the rally, she said that she wanted one simple thing. She wanted to go to the Urhonordos and negotiate a peaceful Water Rights Treaty. That was all she was asking for. That may be where she went last night."

The dancing girls listened to Morf and then looked at Drum and looked back at Morf. They relaxed slightly.

"King Drum is right to warn you," said Morf, "but this is what I think. Flawless is an intelligent woman, and I believe that her beauty and intelligence have kept her safe. I believe that you young women are beautiful too. Your beauty and intelligence will keep you safe as well.

Urhonordo is not as safe a place as you may have known it to be, but if you go there to negotiate peace, you will be safe. This is what I believe."

"Wow," said Cmorf. "I didn't know you had it in you. Good job."

The dancing girls began to talk things over. Their fear shifted from panic to realistic discussion. Milton stepped forward and spoke to them a bit and listened to them a bit. At last, he turned to Drum and said quietly, "The girls are ready to serve The Kingdom, Your Majesty."

Drum and Morf combined to give the girls simple instructions. "Tell the Urhonordos that we don't want to fight with them. Tell them that we are ready to negotiate water rights."

Then surprisingly, Drum added another idea of his own. "And tell Queen Luna that I didn't know water rights were such a big thing, and I am sorry if water did them any harm."

"Do you really mean that?" Morf asked.

"Most of it," answered Drum. "If it will get Flawless home safely, I'll say anything."

Cdrum frowned. Drum was doing better, but he still needed his Conscience with him at all times. The Super Aura was not as in control as it had been, but it was not completely gone.

33

Wages of War

An hour later, the dancing girls left The Castle, crossed over The Bridge, and disappeared. They were dressed in their finest feathery best, their hair shining and confident smiles on their faces. This was a mission they were proud of. They were going to save their friend, Flawless, and maybe even *all* of River Kingdom. They were important, and they knew it.

Fandango nervously watched his girls until they were out of sight. He was worried about them. He had never been a brave man, so his role of shepherding girls and arranging for their performances had always been a lucky position for him. He hoped that their mission would be successful.

But what if it wasn't? What would King Drum do then?

Milton's recent appointment to Royal Finance Advisor had not been a welcome advancement for the timid man. Surprisingly, he was very good with numbers, but only with his numbers, not someone else's.

He had accepted the position, only because he didn't know how to say no. He knew Drum was a spender, and as a "non-nobleman," he could not tell someone like Drum what to do. His first reaction had been to ignore the job and hope that Drum would change his mind.

When he finally took the time to look in the Royal Storehouses, however, Milton understood what Marvin, the Finance Advisor before him, had been trying to tell Drum. The storehouses were no longer full.

Now, the nervous Fandango had just dispatched his girls on a mission for peace. He hoped they would be successful, but he knew that if the girls came back empty handed, Thorndike would be getting The Kingdom ready for war. A war that The Kingdom couldn't afford. River Kingdom was nearly broke.

The trembling gentleman returned to the throne room where Drum was pacing and waiting. Milton bowed low and began to say what he knew he needed to say. "Pardon me, King Drum. I know that you have many things on your mind today, but I feel that I should inform you as to the condition of The Castle finances."

Drum had never worried about finances, his own or The Kingdom's. Such a concern was not interesting to him. "Not today, Fandango," he murmured.

The man gulped, but continued. The bravery that his girls had shown was contagious. "But I believe The Kingdom has a problem you should be aware of, under the circumstances, sire." No response.

"I have been counting the commodities and coin in the storehouses of The Kingdom. I am very careful with money so I even asked the girls to help me count, and I wrote it all down." He pulled some notes out from under his robes.

"Good for you," Drum answered nonchalantly.

"I know I should have spoken with you about such matters before," croaked Sir Fandango, twisting the paperwork. "But now, with Lord Thorndike preparing the farmers for battle, I feel that I should make you aware that many of our storehouses are almost empty."

"We should have plenty in our storehouse." Drum sighed dismissively. "If we don't, what have you been doing with it?"

The timid little man was ready. "Well," he began, "I *do* have a list." He smoothed out his papers. "First, there was the cost of the remodeling and enlargement of the Royal Party Hall, which we are still paying off. Then there was the food, drink, entertainment and red hats for the Inauguration Celebration. Then there has been the coin necessary for the constant purchase of oil for lamps and heat for The Castle. In addition, there is the excess payment for the Royal Guard, which has been deployed down south as well as a recent additional payment for pool finishing. Last, there has been the care and feeding . . . and dressing . . . and housing of my girls. They have been working for you daily and almost exclusively."

"The girls have been worth every penny of it." Drum smiled.

"Of course," agreed Fandango. "On the positive side, we do have a storehouse which is beginning to fill with the results of our current harvest, but we owe much of that to the Lowlanders for their work on the levees."

"Don't worry about the Lowlanders. I told them that I wouldn't pay them until they had completed the pool for the farmers. Dipswitch told me yesterday that they actually emptied the pool instead of completing it, so I'm not really worried about it," smirked Drum.

Milton shook his head. "I continue to worry about the cost of war if we have one." He sighed.

Drum reached over and retrieved his crown. Money problems never bothered him. He had figured out a solution before, and he would do it again. "Don't worry. We might not even go to war at all if the girls are successful. Even if they're not, I might change my mind and just tell Thorndike to forget the whole thing. I'll just go over to Urhonordo and get my daughter myself." The self-love Eforce might already be making a comeback, Cdrum observed.

"By the way, what did Thorndike say when you told him to wait for the results of the girls' 'peace talks'? I bet he hated that."

"What?" asked Fandango.

"What do you mean 'what'? Don't tell me that you didn't say anything to Thorndike yet? Flawless and the girls are negotiating in enemy territory, and you didn't tell Thorndike?"

"Me? *I* was supposed to tell Thorndike?"

"Yes, you, Fandango. I can't do everything. I am the King, not a messenger boy. You should have told him immediately that we were trying Flawless's peace idea and we might not even need him. That would have been fun to watch. He will be furious when he hears. Maybe I should tell him myself, just for sport."

Fandango stopped his financial discussion in midair and looked at Drum with concern. The timid little man wanted to explain to Drum that it wasn't really his place to tell a man like Thorndike what to do, but his girls were on their way to Urhonordo and could be in danger with Flawless if any fighting started. He knew that Thorndike would be frustrated with his message, but the safety of his ladies was important. He rushed from the throne room.

It was only a few minutes later that Fandango returned with frightening news. Thorndike and his enthusiastic Commoner Army were already on the march for Urhonordo!

34

Dance Diplomacy

At Urhonordo Castle, Will and Ben were huddled with Luna and Flawless and in deep discussion. The four were in a sticky situation, and they knew it. From what Flawless had heard, the recruited farmers of River Kingdom could be launching an assault on Urhonordo in the near future. Flawless was sure that the eager Thorndike would want to move soon.

"I took my frustration too far when I captured you, Will," Luna said regretfully. "Kidnapping an important person from River Kingdom took things to a whole new level, but I really felt I had to do something to get the King's attention."

"First of all, Will isn't an important person." Ben laughed. "He's just Will."

"He's important to me," said Flawless, taking Will's hand. Quietly, they found a corner where they could talk. Technically, they were in an enemy camp. Flawless and Will were in unchartered territory for both of them. What should they do?

Flawless had been at River Kingdom Castle just the night before. She had heard Thorndike. She had heard her father. She had come here to warn Luna and negotiate for a peaceful solution, but such a solution seemed out of reach now.

"I thought I could help us all iron out our problems and work together.

How naïve can I get?" Flawless said glumly.

Will was sympathetic to Flawless's desire for a negotiated peace, but this situation was more complicated than she knew. He had seen the flood on Urhonordo land that had been taken over as "the pool." Flawless hadn't. That flood was massive. If Will thought about it from Luna's point of view, a wealthy citizen from River Kingdom had stolen water from The Lowlands and used it to flood Urhonordo. They had done so with the on-site help of the Royal Guard of River Kingdom. This actually was an invasion of Urhonordo. Did the people of River Kingdom even know what had been done in their name to either The Lowlands or Urhonordo?

This "invasion" had left the Queen in a rough spot. The Urhonordos blamed River Kingdom for their ruined lands and homes, but wouldn't they also blame Queen Luna if she didn't retaliate?

Will began to share what he knew with Flawless. "By not even thinking about it, your father made things more complicated than you know," he began. He explained the new manor house that blocked The Great River, the massive flood that had ruined Urhonordo farmland, and the channel that he and the Lowlanders had dug. Flawless listened, a pained look on her face. "We don't have time for those two to get mushy." Ben smiled as he watched them in serious discussion.

"Maybe they needed to take time," countered Luna, looking at Ben fondly, "but *I* may not have much time. I must ready my forces. It sounds like River Kingdom may decide to invade us tomorrow and come after Will."

"They are more likely to come after Flawless," said Ben. "I'm sure they know she's here. I want to help you, Luna, but that will mean that I prepare to fight people I have worked with for years. That doesn't sound right, somehow . . . even though my River Kingdom friends will be in the wrong." "This is very confusing for me," confessed Cben. "I'm not sure what side we're on."

"I have never fought against anyone," said Ben, "so I have no idea what to do, but they say that the best offense is a strong *defense*, so I'll work on your *defense*, Luna. Does that sound like an okay plan?"

"Sure, but how are you going to do that?" Luna laughed as they began to walk off together.

They didn't get very far. One of the Royal Guards burst through the door. There was a confused look on his face as he announced, "Queen Luna! We are being invaded, but you won't believe who the invaders are." The guard was holding a spear in his hand, but he bowed low and motioned "the invaders" into the throne room. This was an invasion that his training had not prepared him for.

The dancing girls walked in shyly, occasionally smiling at the cohort of guards that had followed them from The Bridge. Most of them seemed to know each other.

Queen Luna cocked her head to one side and smiled quizzically. "Hello, ladies," she said. "Is this a social call?"

One of the girls stepped forward. She was the tiny woman who had been the first to volunteer earlier. "We are a Peace Corps from River

Kingdom," she announced bravely. "We have come to negotiate with Queen Luna because we don't want to fight with her . . . or any of her men." The rest of the girls smiled and nodded.

Queen Luna was charmed. "I am Queen Luna," she said to the girls. "What would you like to negotiate?"

The girls looked at each other. This was not their usual line of work. How should they do this? What should they say? Again, the little woman spoke for the group. "We are worried that there might be a war," she began carefully. "We have heard that Urhonordo has kidnapped some of our people and there are many among the people of River Kingdom who are ready to fight to get them back."

Suddenly, she got a burst of courage. "I may just be a dancing girl, but I am here to speak up for my friend, Flawless. Flawless is a nice person, and she didn't deserve to be kidnapped!" The young woman stood strong, her fists clenched at her side. She looked determined.

Flawless was watching from the corner where she had been sitting with Will. Quickly she raced to the little dancing girl and hugged her fiercely.

"Emma! Is that you?" Flawless was friends with all the dancing girls. They had become close when the girls had moved into The Castle. "What are you girls doing here? Aren't you afraid? Did my father send you?"

"We came because we wanted to save you, Flawless," Emma offered truthfully.

The closely bunched ranks of the dancing girls broke apart to hug Flawless as the Urhonordo Royal Guard joined them in what looked more like a happy reunion than a formal negotiation.

Will and Ben and Luna watched in amazement. This was even nicer than a negotiation, but no one was exactly sure what should happen next.

At last, Queen Luna felt the need for some decorum. She was on a war footing. "Royal Guard," she said sternly. "Return to your stations . . . now." Obediently, the Guardsmen dispersed, leaving the dancing girls smiling but a bit confused. Now, what should they do?

Seeing their discomfort, Flawless found them some chairs and assured them that they had done a good job of negotiating. She was not sure at all that this was true, but neither she nor Cflawless saw any harm in her saying so.

Cflawless was less kind in her observation of Flawless herself. "You thought that you could fix everything with negotiation, just like these dancing girls, didn't you?" she chided.

"It was better than going to war," Flawless said with a pout. "What?" asked Will.

"I was just talking to my Conscience," said Flawless. "My Conscience thinks that the girls' and my attempts at peaceful negotiation were useless. I hate to think that this is true, but maybe it is. We don't seem to have solved anything. The problems are much more severe than the girls and I knew." "Attempts at peace are never wrong," said Cflawless, "but maybe the side that needs negotiations now is more River Kingdom than here. Luna wants peace, but she wants your father to respect her kingdom and the rights of everyone who lives near The River. What about your father? Who is negotiating with *him* for peace?"

This question was an unexpected blow. Flawless was stunned by what it revealed. Why had she not understood this before? Who had broken the Water Right Treaties? Who had hurt both the Urhonordos and the Lowlanders? Who was threatening war? It wasn't the Urhonordos that needed to be asked for peace. It was River Kingdom. It was her father and Thorndike.

Flawless was amazed at her own naïve ignorance. How had she become so stupid? Was it her love for her father? Was it her lack of thinking things through? Or was it just her pride at believing that she could solve problems by herself? Probably all three.

She looked sadly at Will and Ben and Luna. They already knew what she now knew. It had just taken her longer to understand it. "I need to talk to my father," she told them bluntly.

Her friends understood and agreed.

"I will take the girls with me," she continued. "We all thought that we could make things better by talking to you, Luna, but now I see the problem more clearly. River Kingdom is the place where peace talks need to happen and behaviors need to change before it's too late."

The dancing girls were listening and now began talking to each other in an almost frantic way. They were looking at the Queen and then at Flawless and then back to the Urhonordo Royal Guard. They were worried about something. They were upset. Now they went to Flawless. She was their friend.

Again, the littlest dancing girl spoke for the group. "It may be too late already, Flawless," the girl whispered fearfully. "A huge armed invasion force already left River Kingdom at the same time that we came over here. They passed us on the road. There were over a hundred of them!"

"What? Who was leading them? Where were they going?" asked Will, standing nearby.

This was a bloodcurdling announcement. A River Kingdom Army was already on the march!

"Oh no," cried Flawless in despair. "Daddy has already gone to war? Why would he have done such a thing so fast? You say that he sent you girls here? Why wouldn't he have given your peace negotiation a chance to work?"

Now all the dancing girls began speaking at once.

"I don't think King Drum was with them," contributed one of the girls.

"I don't think he knew the army was going until after we were gone."

"He was worried about *you*, Flawless. He wouldn't have sent the army until you were safe. He loves you."

"It was that mean rich guy, Thorndike, that was leading the farmers down the road right past us . . . *and* right past The Bridge."

"They passed The Bridge?" Will questioned in amazement. "Where were they going?"

"I don't know, but that bossy Dipswitch was with them," the dancing girls contributed all at once.

"That's right. And Lord Dipswitch took the River Kingdom Royal Guard with him."

"I don't think the King knew about that either."

"Looks like they all just took off before anybody could tell them not to do it."

The chatter finally slowed. The Queen and those around her stood silent, taking in the sudden news.

The dancing girls looked at each other. They suddenly realized that they may have given away some information that they shouldn't. Maybe they were traitors now. They circled tight together and covered their heads, awaiting punishment.

Flawless recovered from her shock and fell to her knees in front of Luna. "Oh, Luna. I am so sorry. I had no idea this was happening. It sounds like we are truly at war. I can't believe it."

"You came here with a good heart," said Luna. "Your father sent the girls here to negotiate as well. Maybe his heart was changing. It's impossible to tell what the man that is leading the River Kingdom Army is thinking now, however."

Flawless bowed with respect for her friend. Her position as the negotiator was no longer valid if it ever had been. Now, news of a mobilized River Kingdom Army had turned her and the dancing girls into hostages.

Ben and Will looked at each other. River Kingdom had armed troops on the move, and they were headed for *v*The Lowlands. What in the world were they going to do in The Lowlands? Were the Lowlanders considered enemies too?

Ben's mind raced back to his homeland. Thoughts of caged children and blocked river water jumped into his mind. And Lord Dipswitch was part of an invasion force that was already on the road, headed south.

Will and Ben were thinking the same thing. "My people are in danger," Ben said quietly. "I don't know why, but they are about to be invaded."

Queen Luna went to her throne and sat upon it stoically. She said nothing, but all could see in her manner that she was carefully considering everything she had just heard.

She spoke first to Ben. "You must go home, Ben. I see that your mind and heart are already there. Your people may be in danger, and you are one of their leaders. They will need you."

"You read my mind, Luna," said Ben sadly. "I have no choice. I don't want to leave you, but I can't imagine the terror my people will feel when they look north and see armed farmers, not to mention the Royal Guard marching toward them. They will not know what to do or where to turn. They have never fought with anyone before."

"I will go with you," said Will, but then he glanced at Queen Luna. "That is, I will go if I have your permission, Luna," he added.

"Of course," said Luna with a nod. "I expected that you two would want to go and help the Lowlanders together. You cannot leave them at the mercy of these forces and the evil men that lead them. It is men like this that are the reason for the terrible situation we are in now. Of course, you both must go immediately."

Tears ran down Flawless's cheeks. Her world seemed to be falling apart. Her own River Kingdom was going to war, and now Will and Ben were possibly heading toward violence as well. And then there was her father. He had slid from king to liar while she tried to talk peace like a child. Nothing was wonderful anymore. Nothing was hopeful anymore. She felt lost.

"Pull yourself together, Flawless," hissed Cflawless. "You are not your daddy's little girl anymore. You are a grown woman. You have a mind. Get busy and figure out what you should do with this situation you're in."

Flawless took a deep breath and looked around her. The beautiful dancing girls were now huddled nearby. They were away from home. They were possibly in an enemy kingdom with no protection and no leader. They remained circled together as they always did when they were afraid. Flawless tried to smile reassuringly.

"You didn't expect this kind of situation when you came here, did you?" she said kindly. "You were very brave, though. And you said nothing wrong. You did what you thought you should do to help me and The Kingdom, right?"

The girls nodded fearfully.

"Well, you did a wonderful thing," said Flawless with new energy. "You brought us the information that we needed. Without knowing about our troops heading south, we wouldn't be able to help anyone or do the things we need to do. You girls are heroes."

The girls looked at Flawless closely. They could tell that she was telling the truth. They relaxed a bit.

Queen Luna helped by smiling at the girls. "Don't worry, ladies," she said gently. "You came here as a Peace Corps and all of us here are for peace, so we are actually all on the same side." Flawless was grateful. The girls felt much better.

Will and Ben began to get ready for their immediate race for The Lowlands. Slowly, Flawless reviewed her current situation. She was in Urhonordo, which might be attacked by her own kingdom's troops. But her father had not assembled or dispatched them. According to the girls, he hadn't even known about it. What was going on? She knew she should go home and find out.

As though reading her mind, Luna spoke up solemnly. "You shouldn't go home now, Flawless. You must stay here. You will be safer."

"But my father . . ."

"I know. Your father still believes that you may have been kidnapped by me. I'm sure that he's worried about you. We need to make sure that he knows that you are alright."

"You're right," agreed Flawless. "So . . ."

"So we will send these brave ladies back to The Castle to let him know that you have not been harmed. They will be our messengers."

The girls nodded up and down vigorously. "We can do that," they all offered vigorously.

"And you must also give him a very important message just from me." Luna pulled a scroll out of her pocket. "Please give this to the King and tell him that I send it. But you must not read it. Can you do that?"

The girls nodded.

"But I need to—" offered Flawless.

"You need to stay here, Flawless," Luna interrupted firmly.

Flawless blinked. "Am I a hostage?" she gasped.

"Yes," answered Queen Luna. "We are at war."

35

The March

Thorndike was marching south, and he had never felt better. *His* Super Aura was in control. He had the power he wanted. *He* was the leader of a massive Commoner Army, and he was completely in charge.

Stretching out behind him was row after row of armed men. They may have been armed with picks and shovels and hoes from their work in the fields, but they were armed. They marched in rhythm to Thorndike's command, lustily calling out fighting cadences that spoke of bravery and a righteous cause. The Eforces surged with them now as well.

Thorndike and his Commoner Army had left earlier than expected. He knew that Drum would be surprised when he found out, but what did he care? Drum was not a man of action such as he was, and Thorndike had a plan that was so masterful and unexpected that he was guaranteed a win over the hapless Urhonordo forces. He would then take over as their king. He had worked it all out with Lord Dipswitch.

Dipswitch was marching alongside Thorndike, but he had his own agenda. He also had a partnership with the Eforces. He was not returning to his angry wife and his mud flat "pool" alone. Oh no. Thorndike's Commoner Army was now *his* army too, and the size of the Commoner Army would get him what he wanted more efficiently than the Royal Guard alone—through more force.

Dipswitch had gone after his land deal and the results he wanted by using Drum's greed to buy the location, materials for building, and rapid construction of his manor. Now, however, he could see that he had exhausted this strictly backroom strategy. At this point, he needed something stronger if he expected to rebuild his pool . . . and plant some fruit trees . . . and capture workers to maintain them . . . and create a kingdom of his own. The Aura power lust was contagious.

Dipswitch had the Lowlanders on his mind. The Urhonordos had rid him of the troublesome Will, but not before Will had obviously directed the Lowlanders to dig the channel that had drained his pool. Dipswitch now realized that controlling the troublesome Lowlanders as Will had done could be the key to his future labor needs and a lucrative manor in a lovely warm climate.

Fruit trees! A kingdom covered with fruit trees planted and cultivated by local labor under his command—this is what he was after. Lowlanders appeared to be hardworking and able to follow orders, just what Dipswitch needed—slaves.

And how would Dipswitch accomplish this? By conquering the Lowlanders in the same way that Thorndike planned on conquering the Urhonordos and with the same army. Dipswitch had discovered at the rally what he and Thorndike could and *should* accomplish together.

Dipswitch had something to offer to Thorndike as his part of the bargain. The Royal Guard was still working for him on Drum's orders. If Thorndike was going to war with Urhonordo, Dipswitch and his Royal Guard could overpower the Lowlanders, but then his Royal Guard could move on and help Thorndike and the Commoner Army invade the Urhonordos. Sweet.

Thorndike welcomed the addition of the Royal Guard. Both of these greedy men could get their own personal kingdom. There was something wonderful to be won for each of them. Their mutual Aura were ecstatic. With Dipswitch joining the movement, Thorndike had rewritten his original frontal attack on Urhonordo from The Bridge. Now he was going to attack Urhonordo from the rear where they least expected it.

He and his troops would first arrive at Dipswitch's property. They would conquer and cage the Lowlanders. That would be easy. Next, they would circle behind Dipswitch Manor, cross The River where it was shallow, and proceed north to Urhonordo.

This would allow them a nighttime invasion on Urhonordo Castle from the south, just as Urhonordos were expecting a bridge assault from the west. The plan was brilliant.

Back at The Castle, neither the battle plans nor the reasons for them were understood by anyone including King Drum. Thorndike had left with many of the farmers in the area, his farmers, but Drum had no idea where they were going.

*What are they planning to do? They are **my farmers**. I was the one that earned their loyalty. They were willing to fight **because of me.** But where are they now?* he asked himself miserably.

Drum realized that he had lost control. He had to admit it. He had lit the match of war, but he had no idea where the fire was going to be lit or who would be burned. It had all seemed so glorious at the rally. What had gone wrong?

For the first time, Drum felt the impact of all he had done—all he had always done. Also, for the first time, he had no idea what trick he could pull out of a hat to fix it. There were no deals to make. There were no rubes to con. The gullibles that had been at his bidding for months were marching to war. He slouched on his throne in the beautiful throne room, but there was no pleasure in it. A war was starting somewhere, and his daughter was missing. His Conscience was strangely silent.

Morf sat on his chair by the door. He was depressed and unmoving as well, but his Conscience was not going to let him dodge responsibility for the part he had played in this current fiasco.

"Well, this is sure a mess," Cmorf said to Morf. "You thought you could just hang with this self-serving, corrupt wannabe King and approve of everything he did and your life would be easy, right? Flawless is nowhere to be found, the Royal Ag Advisor has been kidnapped, and the Royal Defense Advisor is off somewhere starting a war with a bunch of farmers. How is this 'go along to get along' policy of yours working for you?"

I tried, Morf thought sullenly. I thought that asking the girls to go for a peace talk with Luna was a good idea.

"That was a good idea, but it was too little too late. You should have stood up for doing what's right a long time ago, instead of just smiling and bowing," grumbled Cmorf. "You thought you were so smart to kiss up to Drum. You thought you could just ride the wave of always hanging with the main guy, getting to feel like a big cheese, and not worrying about the right and wrong of things. Am I right?"

I guess so, thought Morf. *But you could have told me I was wrong stronger like a good Conscience should, so it's your fault too.*

"Oh, that's good. Go ahead and blame your Conscience. See if that helps you out much," countered Cmorf. "I don't think you really get the gist of Consciences, Morf. Let me spell it out for you. We Consciences can't *make* you do anything you don't want to do. We can only give you an idea of what might be better or more honest or—"

"Okay," said Morf aloud. "I get it, I get it. But now what? And where in the heck is Thorndike?"

Morf had hoped that the girls could open the door to negotiations and keep Thorndike from actually marching on Urhonordo at all, but obviously, those hopes were no good now.

Morf thought he understood Queen Luna. She would have been willing to talk to the girls and perhaps arrange a meeting to discuss treaties, but she was not stupid or weak. Her Royal Guard was well trained and disciplined. Thorndike's Commoner Army was not going to be able to rout the Urhonordo Royal Guard like they might think they could. Flawless and the girls could definitely be caught in the middle. Morf sank deeper in his chair.

Drum stood up suddenly. He could not admit that he was wrong. The Super Aura of his belief in his own infallibility had been with him too long. The dancing girls had not yet returned with his daughter, but they would. He was sure of it. Thorndike's army had left without final instructions from him, but he and Thorndike had discussed Drum's grand objectives and were both excited by them. He was undoubtedly implementing them at this moment.

As King, I am, after all, the commander and chief, Drum thought. He began to pace. He got an idea.

"Go tell Thorndike to get back here immediately," Drum barked to Morf. "He works for me. I am the King, and I am not ready yet to give him my final orders."

Morf stared at Drum. "He left quite a long time ago," Morf hedged lamely. "He's probably way past The Bridge by now."

"Oh . . . you might be right," said Drum, but he stopped pacing. Drum's Aura was down, but not out. It reloaded and tried again.

"Maybe Thorndike met the girls and my daughter and they will all soon return with news of Urhonordo's surrender to me," Drum said with a new more favorable read on the whole thing. He grinned at Morf confidently. "That could be true, don't you think? I hadn't thought of that. My dancing girls are very persuasive. I've seen them in action. Sending them out to negotiate for me was an outstanding strategy on my part. Maybe one of my best ideas of all time."

Cdrum was listening, but said nothing.

Morf winced. *Drum's losing it,* he thought. "Your Majesty," he began, "it might be a good idea now to discuss the information that you may be getting from the girls when . . . and if they return.

"I hope that Flawless will be with them, but the message that they bring may not be the queen's surrender. Queen Luna feels that her water rights are important enough to fight for. Urhonordo may even be fighting with Thorndike's army right now. We have no way of knowing."

Drum shook his head in pity at Morf's ignorance. His Super Aura was completely back. "I've been negotiating with rich people like the Queen all my life," he said. "I know how they think. They are all out for the best deal they can get, but I am the best negotiator there ever was."

"I understand that," said Morf, "but we are the ones that are in the wrong here, sire. We need an opportunity to tell Queen Luna that we understand that and won't trample on her kingdom's rights anymore."

"Good job . . . finally," said Cmorf.

"I thought you understood me better than that by now, Morf," lectured Drum, walking back and forth aimlessly. "River Kingdom is the big dog here, and the big dog gets what he wants. When 'Queenie Luna' opens up her front door to find a huge band of my Commoner Army in front of her, she will roll over and beg for the bone of whatever water we give her. Just let me get my daughter home, and then we'll talk deals."

Morf smiled.

Cmorf groaned. "Get that sappy look off your face, Morf. Drum hasn't learned a thing, and neither have you. Drum doesn't think about anyone but himself, and you're smiling like a nitwit. Don't let him think that he knows what he's doing, Morf. He listened to you about the girls. Maybe he will listen again. Say something."

"He can't listen right now," said Cdrum. "He's in the grip of a Super Aura." Cdrum sighed. "I didn't want to admit it, but I am sure that it's true."

Cmorf groaned. "A real Super Aura? I've heard of them, but I wasn't sure they were real." He didn't know how to explain that to Morf.

I don't think Drum can think this through rationally anymore. He may be past that, Morf thought sadly without knowing he was feeling the strength of the Eforce.

Cdrum was exhausted, but he tried again to speak to his human. "You might not have all the facts you need here," said Cdrum calmly. "You might want to knock off all that 'big dog' talk until you have Flawless. You have no idea what's going on with Thorndike. You don't know what Queen Luna is thinking. When Flawless is safe, and she can give you some understanding of Queen Luna, you might have better ideas."

Drum's Super Aura was ready to lock down its position. "I'm tired of small thinkers," said Drum confidently. "Shut up and watch me operate. I'll show you how the big dogs do things."

"What?" said Morf.

Drum just shrugged. "I was just talking to my Conscience again," said Drum, "and just in time too. I think I hear the girls and Flawless in the hall. Now you'll see how the real battle is going to be won, Drum-style."

Drum marched to the curtains himself and held them open. As he predicted, it was the dancing girls. All were smiling and began hugging Drum while he grinned like a schoolboy, receiving their familiar affection. It was a joyful moment. Morf stood back and watched closely.

"I knew you girls would be successful," Drum chortled. "Come over here and tell me all about it. What did you say? What did the 'little Queenie' say? Where is Flawless? Why is she taking so long?" Drum scampered to his throne and plopped himself down on it like a young boy waiting for a present.

The dancing girls followed him and surrounded the throne as had always been their custom. Emma had now become the spokesperson for the girls. She stepped forward but suddenly became hesitant. She knew that what she needed to say was not what King Drum wanted to hear.

She began slowly. "The Queen was very nice to us," she said, starting on a positive note. "And we saw Flawless. Flawless was nice too." The rest of the girls nodded vigorously and agreed.

"Then where is she?" Drum grinned. "Is she waiting to make a grand entrance? Did she need to change into something fancy just to give me my news? She didn't need to do that. I am her father." He giggled happily.

Emma looked at the floor. "Flawless did not return with us," she said simply. The dancing girls withdrew silently into their usual circle. No one said a thing.

Drum stared at the girls. First, he smiled. Then he looked at each one.

Then he smiled again. "You're joking with me, right?" he asked.

Emma swallowed hard. "No, sire. The Queen said that Flawless needed to stay with her because she said, 'We are at war.' She also said to give you this." Emma held the small scroll out in front of her. "She wouldn't let me read it, but she said I should tell you that it was a message from—"

Drum rose up in a rage. Slapping the scroll from the frightened girl's hand, he glowered down at the trembling group. "You girls are failures! You were sent to that stupid castle to bring home my daughter and you failed! Why do you even dare to show your faces? Get out! Get out of my throne room and never come back. You're fired!"

The girls scattered and ran for the doorway in panic. Morf gathered himself quickly and began to shepherd the frantic girls into the hall, speaking gently and trying to console them. "You didn't fail. You did a good job. You did the right thing. The King is just angry. He'll get over it. Go find Fandango."

Morf stood in the doorway, listening to the scurrying footsteps of the girls as they retreated down the hall. *Poor things,* he thought. *And what was Drum doing?*

Drum was standing motionless in front of the throne, staring at it. Behind him was the scroll that Emma had brought for him. Morf picked it up and silently read it.

"A message from Dragon Quest: King Sol and the River Kingdom Royal Guard have successfully concluded their combat with the dragons of the east. The dragons have been driven permanently out to sea, never to return to dry land. King Sol and his troops will return to River Kingdom soon to celebrate this great victory."

36

Path to Leadership

Will and Ben had already left Urhonordo Castle and were on their way to The Lowlands. They had no time to wait. According to the dancing girls, the Commoner Army had a head start, and it was massive. There were farmers and peasants of all kinds, not to mention the Royal Guard. There were a lot of them.

"We probably know almost everybody in that so-called army," said Will.

"That will be a good thing," Ben called back from up ahead. "We'll need to talk them out of this war." Ben was leading the pair. This was familiar territory, even in the dark. He was again on the southern end of Urhonordo where he had played as a child.

"My feet know every inch of this ground," he said nostalgically. "I had a lot of fun here. This was like a playground."

"We should probably get closer to The River," called Will from behind. "Swinging wide like we are now will take longer, don't you think?"

"Nope. That's not what I think." Ben laughed, coming back to his friend. "Back in the day, you would have been right." He was not laughing anymore. "Remember the lake? Remember the mud flats? That's what is close to the River's banks now."

"You are so right." Will shook his head. "I forgot about the swamp. It's a mess, and it will be for a long time. Lead on, Ben."

They hurried on through the early evening. It may have been Ben's playground as a youth, but the fall chill was lowering onto the land. Ben and Will pulled their hoods up over their heads, one foot after another, heads forward, plunging through the lessening light.

After what seemed like hours, Will broke their silence. "Are we there yet?" he whispered. "It seems like we should be there already."

"We are," whispered Ben, putting his finger to his lips. "Right over that rise is Dipswitch Manor, and then of course, beyond and south, The Lowlands. The question now is, where is Thorndike's army?"

The two men crawled silently to the top of the rise and peered over it. Just below was the sight they feared. Beneath them lay the remains of the swamped Urhonordo farmland with The Great River beyond. Stretched out in a mass of humanity on the other side of The River was the Commoner Army. It was a motley-looking crew of farmers mixed with Royal Guard, pitchforks mixed with swords, rough shawls mixed with shields.

Dipswitch Manor rose up in The River between the two sides, blocking the water except for the channel that now let it slide by to the east of the manor.

And standing between Dipswitch Manor and "the army" was Sir Dipswitch himself.

"I didn't expect that," said Will. "What do you think Dipswitch is doing with the troops? And where is Thorndike? I thought Dipswitch would just be inside, trying to make his wife happy without a pool. I wonder why the troops are stopped here, and what is Dipswitch doing?"

"Hard telling," whispered Ben, "but I don't think he is part of a welcoming committee. I think he's talking to the army. He is standing up there in front of everybody like a General. Look. He's waving his arms and pointing to The Lowlands. He's up to something. Come on. We've got to get closer."

Will and Ben snuck down the rise and out behind the manor, avoiding the swamp below them and The River. Slogging through their new channel, they crawled up on the bank and slunk across the backyard of the manor to get a better look. There at the edge of The Lowlands was where they got another surprise. Cages.

Will and Ben stared. In front of them were rows of cage like structures, roughly cobbled together out of the scrub trees and thorny brush that grew in The Lowlands. And who was building the cages? The Lowlanders. Obediently, the Lowlanders were doing what they were famous for. They were working.

Ben and Will snuck up to the Lowlander workforce and mingled in without notice. No one was guarding them. They seemed to be working voluntarily.

"What are you doing?" Ben whispered. "Who are these cages being built for?"

The nearest Lowlander stood up straight with pride. "Lord Dipswitch says that these cages are for conquered bad guys, Ben," he announced with pride.

Will looked at the cages closely and then back to the Lowlanders. "These cages are pretty sturdy," he complimented. "You folks do good work."

"Thanks, Will." The Lowlander grinned, recognizing Will from working with him on the levees. "And it looks like we're finally going to get paid for the levees and these cages and everything all at once, just as soon as we finish. We're helping the war effort."

"The war effort? Really?" questioned Will. "Who are we fighting? I don't understand who you're building cages for."

"That's the best part." The man proudly smiled. "These cages are for bad guys when they get caught. These will save their lives," he explained. "We call it 'catch and release.' When our enemies get caught, the Commoner Army will put them all in these cages. They will just be locked up where they can't hurt anybody until they learn to be good guys. Then we will let them go. Cool, right? Isn't that a good idea?"

Ben and Will looked at the cages and the proud Lowlanders building them. They nodded and smiled but backed away slowly. These were cages for "enemies and bad guys"? *What* enemies and bad guys?

"I'm going to talk to Dipswitch about this," Will said and started forward.

"You don't need to go up front to where Dipswitch is," said a strong, deep voice behind him. "I'm building them for him." It was Lord Thorndike. Ben backed slowly into the crowd of working Lowlanders and blended away out of sight. Quickly, Cwill climbed close to Will's ear. "Be careful," he warned. "This guy has no Conscience right now. If he had one, I would know. He's pure Eforce. I can feel Eforce all around us. Say little and learn." Will stuck out his hand. "Hello, sir. I'm just taking a closer look at your operation here. As a farmer, I know that these Lowlanders are good workers. It was pretty smart of you to ask them to build these cages." Thorndike accepted the compliment with pride. "I recognize you now,"

he said. "You are William of Dale. I am glad to see you, but . . . I thought you had been abducted by Urhonordos," he added suspiciously.

Will gulped. Busted.

"Stay loose," instructed Cwill. "You can handle this."

"I just got away," Will offered quickly. "I was abducted by Urhonordos. I thought I would never get loose, but I finally did. I got lucky. I came down here to see if I could help Lord Dipswitch before heading back to The Castle. But why does Dipswitch want cages?"

Thorndike relaxed. *This guy has escaped from the Urhonordos. He must be pretty smart*, he concluded.

"Let me tell you," Thorndike boasted. "These cages are an important part of our total operation. Pretty impressive, wouldn't you say?"

"Indeed," said Will, nodding wisely. "Impressive, to say the least. And there are quite a lot of cages here. How many Urhonordos do you think they will hold when you win the war?"

Thorndike laughed, a rough soulless laugh, and looked with sympathy at Will. "That's right. You've been a captive so you are not in the loop about our plan."

Thorndike put his arm around Will's shoulder and led him away from the busy workers. "These cages are not for the Urhonordos. The Urhonordos will be *my subjects* as soon as they are conquered by the Commoner Army out there. They will be under *my* control, so there will be no need for cages. These cages are for Lowlanders."

Fortunately, Will was not facing Thorndike. The shock on his face would have given him away immediately. "Easy . . . easy," counseled Cwill. "I should have known that," Will managed to say. "And the Lowlanders will belong to Dipswitch, right?"

"You're thinking like a General," said Thorndike. "I like that. Of course, they'll belong to Dipswitch. He'll have his own little Kingdom down here. No more fighting over water . . . no more hassle . . . lots of low-cost workers. If the Lowlanders want to get out of their cages, they will have to do what Dipswitch and his Royal Guard tell them to do.

"We may not need the Guard for the Urhonordo takeover. We'll see. I predict that the Queen's forces will be pushovers for a robust

Commoner Army like ours. By the way, there may be a place for you in Thorndike Kingdom when I get settled.

"Meanwhile, having just escaped from the Urhonordos, do you have the energy to help us finish our operation here? I could use a man I could trust." "Don't do this," exclaimed Cwill in Will's ear. "This man is pure Eforce. He will turn you into an evil person too. He's smooth." "I would love to," said Will with a smile.

"That's great," responded Thorndike. "Dipswitch doesn't like to get his hands dirty. Come with me." With that, Thorndike turned confidently and strode past the manor house to where Dipswitch stood lecturing the assembled troops.

"So in conclusion, let me summarize what we are going to do here: We will line up the low-IQ Lowlanders in front of the cages. We will march them into the cages and only hit them if they resist. Those who resist will be beaten and thrown into a special cage full of cacti, a very painful result. They won't resist long."

Some of the farmers groaned and protested. The farmers knew many of these Lowlanders. They had worked together. Why did they need to put Lowlanders in cages?

The Auras had been becoming more active with the farmers as they had marched toward their forecasted battle. Thorndike had made the patriotic need for war obvious. But here, in the dusk, on the edge of their expected war with the Urhonordos, the need for caging their friends, the Lowlanders, was *not* obvious. Their Consciences became active. The Auras flattened into the ground and waited to reemerge.

"Are you sure we have to do this?" a farmer asked. "The Lowlanders are good people. We've all worked with a lot of them for years."

Dipswitch nodded. "I know," he agreed. He was prepared for this. "That's why we won't leave them in the cages for very long . . . maybe only a day."

"Why do it at all?" grumbled one of the Guardsmen. Will recognized him from before. He had helped dig the channel that had released the water from the Urhonordo farmlands. He had liked the Lowlanders and helped them.

Will listened intently. How would Dipswitch get around this question? Thorndike joined the Dipswitch lecture now. "It's for their safety, of course," Thorndike contributed with a smile. "The Lowlanders have been friends with the Urhonordos in the past. They may want to warn the Urhonordos of our coming. The only way we can invade the Urhonordos without the Lowlanders warning them or being caught in the middle of the fight is to lock them up until our battle is won."

The farmers and Guardsmen mumbled among themselves. They had never been in a war, and this move was confusing. They didn't like it.

"We won't hurt them," assured Sir Dipswitch. "As soon as we win our battle with Urhonordo, we will take the Lowlanders out of the cages and let them go back to work. They will build your pool for you!"

The farmers cheered. That is what Drum had promised, and that promise hit the right note. It was brilliant.

"Now, I have a surprise for you," announced Thorndike. "Right here with us tonight is the very person that we thought had been abducted by the Urhonordos. But he escaped! Look behind me. Here is the one and only William of Dale!"

Will stepped forward with humility. The crowd of farmers rose to their feet and cheered. They knew Will. They liked him. He had always been on their side. "Will, Will, Will," began the familiar chant.

"You are acting like 'Mr. Popularity.' Is this the place for that?" sneered Cwill.

Will ignored Cwill and walked among the farmers and Guardsmen, shaking hands, receiving hugs and pats on the back. He was among friends. He was in his element.

Cwill was furious. "I thought you were a good person," he chided. "I've been proud of you most of the time. What are you doing? You're joining the bad guys."

Keep the faith. I'm not a bad guy yet, thought Will. Although I feel like one right now.

Thorndike had an idea. He watched Will walk among his friends and knew his idea was a good one. He was watching leadership.

Thorndike called Will back to him with a suggestion. "Now that you know our plan, why don't you pick out some men to help you round up the Lowlanders? The Lowlanders seem to know you. They'll never suspect you," he whispered confidently. "Pick out men that you know you can work with."

Will nodded. He knew who to pick. One by one, he chose the Guardsmen that he had worked with on the channel. The farmers were relieved. They had not wanted to put the Lowlanders in cages even if it was only for a short time. The Guardsmen felt honored that Will had chosen them and came forward eagerly. They had trusted Will before. They would trust him again now.

"Just follow my lead," he said quietly. "I think I have a plan."

"What are you going to do?" challenged Cwill. "Just because you have other people to do an evil deed for you, that doesn't mean that you're not responsible for doing it. I think I'm going to be ashamed of you."

Will heard his Conscience and felt bad. He didn't like what he was doing either, but it had to be done.

"The cages are ready," announced Thorndike.

Will winced and motioned to the Guardsmen to follow him. He could see that they were not keen to do this job either. Quickly, he gathered them together and tried his best to quickly explain a plan he had just invented. It could backfire. He wasn't sure.

Cwill closed his ears in shame.

With solemn acceptance, the Guardsmen followed Will toward the collection of hastily constructed cages behind the manor. The Lowlanders were resting wearily in front of the cages. They had been working hard for hours and were proud of their work.

"Lowlanders. May I have your attention," Will called out loudly.

The Lowland men were surprised at the call, but came forward without hesitation. They knew Will. They knew these Guardsmen. They trusted them. Soon, nearly all the Lowlanders were lined up smiling in front of Will and the Guardsmen. And in front of them all stood Ben.

Ben . . . Ben. Oh my god. For some reason, Will had not thought about Ben in this. How could he lock Ben up with the rest of the Lowlanders without explaining?

Ben grinned. "What do you want us to do now, sir?" he joshed. Will gulped.

"Tell them all to run!" yelled Cwill.

"Get into the cages and close them behind you," Will instructed loudly. "Do what I say or the Royal Guard here will force you to do so."

The Lowlanders stared. What did he say?

Will and the Guardsmen took a step forward. "This is an order," said Will. "Lord Dipswitch is requiring all of you to place yourselves in the cages that you just built and stay there until further notice. This is for your safety."

"What are you talking about, Will? Are you crazy?" said Ben. "You are talking to us Lowlanders. We are your friends. These cages were built for our enemies, not for us."

"Tell your people to get in these cages now, or I will put you in them myself. Do it now!" Will ordered and walked forward, grabbing Ben by the shoulders and shoving him backward.

Ben stumbled back in shock. The Guardsmen, moving forward in a line and on cue, began pushing and nudging the Lowlanders, pulling and shoving the befuddled, disbelieving workers who had until a moment ago been part of a team that seemed to have turned on them. They were so off guard that they offered no resistance.

It took less than five minutes to herd over one hundred confused Lowlanders into their primitive but sturdy cages. Sirs Dipswitch and Thorndike stood back a way and observed the procedure with admiration. "That was amazing," glowed Thorndike to Dipswitch. "I heard that William of Dale was a good farm manager for Drum, but I never suspected that he had this kind of command expertise. He and a few Royal Guard moved a hundred men into custody without hesitation. This young man is a blooming General."

"I hear what you are saying and I agree," said Dipswitch with a superior air. "His ability to subdue the lower classes is impressive. He has a way with them and even with the Guardsmen. And tonight, he had the fortitude to escape from Urhonordo. That means that he is brighter and more daring than the average farmhand."

"Hmmm . . .," mused Thorndike. "And he is one of them, isn't he?" He glanced over Dipswitch's shoulder at his makeshift Commoner Army, now sprawled in disarray on the west lawn of Dipswitch Manor.

"His escape also means that he knows the quickest and best route back to Urhonordo in the dark," added Dipswitch. "And who better to lead a Commoner Army than another commoner? Hmm . . ."

Immediately, the two called Will to them. They patted him on the back and shook his hand. The Royal Guard stayed back with the cages full of Lowlanders.

"You were magnificent!" gushed Dipswitch. "I can't believe how efficiently you moved those unsuspecting lowlifes into their cages. As you did it, I had marvelous visions of my future, putting them all to work to rebuild my pool as soon as this messy war business is concluded."

Will looked at the ground in a humble fashion.

"Keep looking at the ground, you two-faced jerk!" shouted Cwill in his ear. "You just put your best friend in a cage! Dipswitch is going to turn them into slaves. You should be ashamed of yourself! You are no better than these guys!"

"Thank you," Will responded to Dipswitch.

I know. I feel terrible, he thought grimly. *But I had to do it.*

"We were extremely impressed," continued Thorndike. "You have shown yourself to be a man who can get things done. I never saw anything like it. The Lowlanders just jumped and obeyed your every command."

Will continued to look at the ground. *They are my friends, he thought. They trusted me. What are the Guardsmen doing right now? I hope I haven't done the wrong thing.*

"How could this not have been 'the wrong thing'? You have given yourself to the Eforce!" growled Cwill.

I have not joined the Eforce. I have a plan, Will thought. *Or at least I think I do. A Conscience should trust a person.* Cwill said nothing.

The two "generals" looked at each other, looked at the humble Will, and nodded. They had made another decision. They were going to ask Will to lead the forces of their Commoner Army to Urhonordo. Who else among them could do it better?

Will followed the two older men to the porch of Dipswitch Manor where they spread out the drawings of their complex battle plan. In the torchlight by the doorway, Will studied their map and listened as the two discussed the attack that would win Urhonordo for Thorndike.

It was a perfect plan. Will would lead the invasion force of farmers up to Urhonordo. If there was any fighting, Will and the farmers would be the first to be in the fight. "A brave position," they assured him.

"The cowards will lead from behind," commented Cwill.

"The Royal Guard and I will provide the final blows of the war and take over Urhonordo as the prize of victory," Thorndike added. "And you, William, will be my new Defense Advisor, of course."

Will smiled in a shy fashion.

"Dipswitch will stay here with his Lowlander workforce. One kingdom won. One more to go! Upon my victory, I will take over Urhonordo, and Dipswitch will carve up The Lowlands here as he wishes and rule The Lowlands as his own, complete with a built-in permanent workforce."

The glow of Thorndike's Super Eforces was clearly visible. How could they fail now? Selfishness, greed, and power were in place. Total disregard of anyone else was secure. All Auras were finally going to win in a big way.

Will had to admit that it was an imaginative plan. First, the Commoner Army would edge quietly around behind Dipswitch Manor, pass the cages, and cross the channel. Then they would charge north through the night toward Urhonordo Castle and take Urhonordo's protective troops completely by surprise.

The Urhonordos would put up some sort of a fight, most likely, but they would be easily overcome and forced to become prisoners until they agreed to accept Thorndike as their king. The plan was foolproof—from Thorndike's point of view.

Will listened while Dipswitch and Thorndike congratulated themselves on their inventiveness. He nodded sagely and appeared to agree about everything. But at last, Will offered one question. He had been waiting for this.

"What portion of Urhonordo territory do you plan to pass through when you head north?" he asked in a concerned fashion. "Lower Urhonordo is wild and hard to cross in some places. There are dense forests. Where there are no forests, there are farms. Where there are farms, there will be Urhonordo farmers. You will probably meet with resistance. The going could be slow, and there could be a lot of bloodshed. Your surprise attack before dawn could be impossible."

Thorndike smiled broadly at Will. "This is where you come in," he said happily. "Thorndike and I watched you handle the Lowlanders tonight. You are a true leader. And you just escaped from the very place where we are going. We figure that you are the best person to lead us back up there by the quickest route."

Will blinked. He wanted this. This was part of his still-forming plan. They wanted him to lead the invasion. He would be the one to lead a mass of patriotic farmers who were his friends against the Urhonordo people who were now also his friends. That sounded terrible.

"And now you're going to be a traitor," Cwill said with contempt.

"I would be glad to do this duty for my kingdom," Will answered Thorndike with enthusiasm.

How wonderful, thought Thorndike and Dipswitch. This young man is eager. It was almost as though he had anticipated this role. Dipswitch and Thorndike smiled at each other. They had chosen well.

Will tried to look calm. "First, I need to make 'arrangements' with the Royal Guard," he said simply.

Cwill was unusually quiet as Will walked deliberately back to the cages where he noticed that the Guardsmen were paying extremely close attention to their captive Lowlanders. They almost looked friendly.

"They're all squashed into these cages tight and quiet like you asked," said one of the Guardsmen with a strange, hidden grin. "But the doors ain't locked and they understand. They're all okay with it."

"What?" whispered Cwill. "Did I miss something?" Cwill peered into the cages more closely. The Lowlanders were smiling back at him.

"You have to look more upset if Dipswitch or Thorndike come by," whispered Will to the Lowlanders, glancing behind him to make sure neither was near. The Lowlanders grinned and tried to look sad. Will shook his head and almost laughed. They weren't very good actors. "Where's Ben?"

Now Cwill was really confused. "What's going on here? You just locked up all of your friends and they don't care? What's going on?"

Ben moved to the front of one of the cages and looked seriously at Will.

Cben heard Cwill's confusion and answered him. "We Lowlanders and the Guardsmen are Will's new partners, Cwill. The Guardsmen let us in on it. Will and Ben will be in charge. It's cool. Don't worry. Will hasn't gone over to the Eforces. This is plan A."

Will spoke directly to Ben now. "Ben, my friend, I have put you through so much."

"It's a matter of trust," answered Ben.

"Thanks," said Will simply. "Before this is over, you'll have to do more crazy stuff. Are you still willing to work with me?"

"Just tell me what to do," said Ben.

"When it's time, you'll be using your own ideas, not mine."

"You know I can," said Ben, opening his already unlocked cage to shake Will's hand.

Cwill was flabbergasted . . . but grateful. He had not heard or understood any of this. "I'll have to pay closer attention," he admitted aloud. Will understood Cwill's confusion. He had cringed at what he was doing too. He was still worried. Was plan A going to work?

Will leaned in to the caged Lowlanders. "I am so ashamed that you have been put here. You are my friends," he whispered. "I had no right to do this. Your lands are your lands, and Dipswitch has no right to them . . . *and* he has no right to The Great River. He will learn this soon. Ben and I will be leaving. Listen for our army and Thorndike to move up the rise.

"With all of us gone, Dipswitch won't be paying attention to you until morning. He will come here to treat you as the slaves that he expects you to become, but you will not be here. You will have ditched these cages and be free again.

"You have been treated like slaves by Dipswitch . . . but also by me. You have never been paid. This is my fault and I know it, but if this battle that I am going to ends well, I will not forget you."

The Lowlanders understood and nodded. They trusted Will too.

Will turned away from the cages and raised his hand to the Royal Guard waiting nearby. His manner changed. For the benefit of Thorndike and Dipswitch, he was now the leader of an invasion force. Cwill hung on, still in confusion, but more ready to hear what would happen next.

"Follow me, men!" Will yelled and ran toward the back of Dipswitch Manor. The Guardsmen followed with a roar. "Wait here," he called next. The Guardsmen halted behind the manor. They knew the plan.

Now Will returned to Dipswitch and Thorndike who were watching Will's control of the Guard with admiration. Will stood up straight and pulled together all the outward appearance of gravitas and importance that he had seen other gentlemen of importance exhibit. He stepped up to his bosses with a demeanor that he hoped resembled the confidence that he didn't actually feel.

"The Lowlanders are secure. The Royal Guard will constitute the rear guard of our fighting force, gentlemen," he said in the deepest voice he could produce. "They are now in position. Sir Thorndike, if you please, gather your Commoner Army now and tell them that the moment is at hand. Let them know that this will be their moment of glory and assemble them in front of the Guardsmen. Then I will lead them across the shallows of the channel as your plan so cleverly indicates and position them for the grand assault northward . . . along the bank. You, sir, can then follow a safe distance behind with the Royal Guard."

Dipswitch and Thorndike thought they understood the implementation of Thorndike's grand plan. Having never led an army themselves, it sounded good to them, and they were thrilled. This young man understood everything. He had the courage and the leadership ability to see that their evil plans actually happened, something neither of them really wanted to do.

Thorndike patted Will on the back and smiled like an expectant father. His vision was going to happen. "How far will we march east before we cut north to storm Urhonordo?" he asked excitedly. This scenario was just as Will had envisioned it.

"That part of the invasion is my contribution," offered Will, joining his bosses in their excitement. "I know this area. I just traveled it tonight. I know the pitfalls of clustered farms and dense forests inland that will present the greatest obstacles to the progress of our march.

Drum Manor Estat
Drum Manor Estate
THE CASTLE
WINS GARDEN
UNHONORDO
The Brown Cloud
Dragon Quest
RIVER
KINGDOM
THE BRIDGE
THE FLOOD
DIPSWITCH MANOR
The Lowlands

"That's why I believe that the shortest and least obstructed distance between here and Urhonordo Castle is along the bank of The Great River. The recent flooding for 'the pool' wiped out all the farms along the bank. Our march will meet no resistance there," Will concluded his description with grand hand gestures and a grim face.

Thorndike and Dipswitch were even more impressed with their new discovery than they had been earlier. And due to their complete ignorance and disregard of the deep destruction that had been caused by "the pool" on the Urhonordo shore, the plan sounded excellent.

The night was at its darkest. The timing was perfect. Thorndike marched with a show of great solemnity to where his gaggle of farmers and farm hands were stretched along the west side of The River.

Seeing his demeanor, the Commoner Army began to gather itself together. They had marched down here with spirit and determination. They could now see that their real reason for coming was about to be tested.

Their excitement began to grow. They were going to show these Royal Advisors of their hero, King Drum, that they were ready to defend him and their Kingdom. It was to be a preemptive strike. They would be attacking Urhonordo and its "stupid Queen" before she could attack them. It would be a win for King Drum, and they were patriotic. The chant began. "Drum, Drum, Drum." They were doing this for Drum.

The popularity of Drum was somewhat galling to Thorndike and Dipswitch, but they decided to overlook it. The man was a dishonest, selfish imbecile who never should have been in his position, but his popularity now served their purpose. They joined in the chant. Thorndike tried to explain what they were going to do over the din of the army's cheering. Will understood that they couldn't hear a thing and began waving hand signals, which boiled down to "Follow me."

Like a huge animal with many feet and legs, the Commoner Army began to move as one with Thorndike and Will in the lead. The mass of men rumbled past the cages full of Lowlanders and the waiting Royal Guard.

Strangely, the Lowlanders and Guard were silent, staring boldly at the farmers as they passed by. On any other day, they might have acknowledged the farmers that they knew, but not today. They all had their orders, and old friendships did not match the current mission—for any of them.

Dipswitch and Thorndike did not notice this anomaly. They were intent on their own goals. Their upcoming power was their motivation.

Small inconsistencies along the way were of no concern. Their Eforces had provided their focus.

Now the army turned left and crossed behind the manor and crowded over Will's channel. How strange. Even though it was still pitifully shallow at this point, neither Dipswitch nor Thorndike really wanted to get wet. Amazing, thought Will who was already knee-deep in the water. With a silent snicker, he decided that their hesitancy might be a good thing.

"Gentlemen," Will said with respect. "I see no reason for you to get yourselves wet this early in the game. If you wish, you may want to go back to the porch of the manor while I get our troops past the channel and on to our staging area for the march northward. When the Royal Guard is in place, you can join us, Lord Thorndike. You will be able to see our progress from the porch until then."

Dipswitch and Thorndike gratefully scooted around to the front of the manor as Will picked up the progress of the men behind it, through the water, and out the other side.

Slowly, the farmers and other assorted commoners reassembled on the launching site leading to the eastern bank of The River. The group knelt down tensely, staring ahead and full of enthusiasm. Their energy was high. They had never gone to war, but this was exciting. They were more than ready to "get on with it."

To their left was Dipswitch Manor and the channel that had liberated the River flow again although that history was not part of what they knew or cared about. Ahead was what was important: a dark vista of smooth dirt, glistening in the moonlight and looking as though it had just been cleared and made ready for their marching. They couldn't wait to begin.

Will checked his troops. The first phase of his plan was about to begin. He stood tall in front of them. "Who among you are the strongest runners?" he hollered.

"Make way! Make way!" men called from within the ranks, and soon a cadre of the burliest farmers and farmhands had taken over the front row of the assembled army. These men were the Kingdom's finest and strongest. They all cheered.

Will spoke directly to them. "You will lead the way," he announced. "You will show the rest of the army how it's done. You are the fastest. You are the strongest. If you do well, all of them will follow and do well. It's up to you."

The front row stood proud and flexed its collective muscles.

Will turned to Dipswitch Manor and the two gentlemen on its porch who were straining through the dark to see the staging of the upcoming battle. They couldn't see it well, but they were nearly as excited as the troops. They heard Will call the strongest and fittest to the front of the group. They sensed that he was ready to go.

Will called across the channel. "Sir Thorndike, are you ready to lead your troops to victory?"

Thorndike blanched. His plans had been great. The setup for battle was now in position for forging ahead. He had always dreamed of what it would be like to lead his men into the throne room of Queen Luna to claim her throne.

The part that he had left out of his dream, however, was the hard march northward and the battle that would follow. Now, hearing Will's call of readiness from across the dark, it suddenly occurred to him—he didn't need to lead it.

Dipswitch had been listening to Will's preparations too. He moved closer to Sir Thorndike and asked a most logical question. "You're not going to go first, are you?" Then he added a personal fact, "There's no way that I would do it."

Lord Thorndike assembled his dignity and authority and moved to the edge of the manor's porch. He stood tall. "Your preparations have been excellent, Will, but I now realize that I would only slow you down if I was in the lead. I now believe that you would be the best man to lead the charge while the Royal Guard and I will follow behind as planned."

Will nodded in agreement, and his heart leapt. This is what he had hoped this coward would say. It was perfect.

"Thank you for your confidence in me, sir. I am up to the challenge. These men and I will take pride in doing what needs to be done!" he yelled back.

A great cheer went up from the Commoner Army. They were ready to march.

37

Revelation

Drum crouched warily on the throne. He had just been informed that his daughter was still a captive of the Urhonordos. He had also chased his beloved dancing girls from the throne room. A group of loyal farmers were somewhere headed for a battle that he had encouraged, but he had no idea where they were or what they were going to do. Everything was out of control. His situation could not be worse. At least that is what Drum thought.

Morf stood in the doorway with the small scroll in his hand. Half of him wanted to read it to Drum. Half of him wanted to throw it away and pretend he had never seen it.

"If you ignore it, you will be acting like the same coward you have been since Drum got to the Castle," said Cmorf flatly. "If you are ever going to return to the man of integrity that you used to be, this would be a good time to start."

Morf walked slowly toward the throne. "You need to read this," he said quietly. "It's for you from Queen Luna."

"I don't need to read anything that that woman sends me," Drum snarled.

"Queen Luna didn't write it. She just passed it on. It's a note from Dragon Quest."

Drum stopped breathing for a moment. Then he sat up straight. "Read it to me," he commanded.

Morf read the note aloud. For a long time, there was silence in the room.

Cdrum broke the silence. "You knew that was what it would say," he murmured.

I did know, thought Drum. He reached up and took the crown from his head.

He didn't bother to look at it, but handed it directly to Morf. "Put this over there where it used to be," he said flatly. Then he stood and walked toward the doorway of the throne room. "Come on," he said to Morf. "Show me where the Royal Caretaker's room is. I've forgotten."

Morf froze. He stared after the departing figure of Drum as he ambled toward the doorway. "Go get him," Cmorf ordered. "He's lost it. He doesn't know what's going on."

Quickly, Morf put the crown on its pedestal and ran to meet Drum. He jumped ahead and started toward the bedroom that Drum had occupied for only one day before he moved into the royal bedchamber. As usual, the room was empty though the lights were lit as they always were throughout the Castle.

Drum looked around the room. He scarcely remembered it, but it looked comfortable enough. He found a chair and sat down. Morf was not sure what was coming next, but he followed and also found a chair. No one spoke.

Drum seemed to be deep in thought. Every once in a while, he would look up and smile at Morf and then return to his thoughts.

Finally, Morf couldn't stand it anymore. He had no idea what Drum was thinking. He had to find out. "What are we going to do now, sire? What are your thoughts about all this?"

"All of what?" Drum asked matter-of-factly. "Try to be more precise, Morf." Drum smiled, but a low heat was burning behind his eyes. He wasn't thinking. Drum was calculating.

Morf sputtered. He stood up. He sat down again. At last he managed to squeak out what he was thinking. "What are you going to do about the fact that King Sol is alive and coming back to the Castle?" Morf looked at Drum with sympathy. This was hard. Morf actually felt sorry for the poor guy.

"Don't waste your sympathy on Drum," groused Cmorf. "He deserves anything that comes to him."

But Drum just smiled. "Where else would he come? He lives here."

"But he's King. You're not King anymore."

"I was king when I wanted to be king and now, I'm not. Don't worry about me. Nothing has changed. It was an act. That's all it ever was. You know that."

"What?" wheezed Morf.

"What?" repeated Cmorf. "This is a trick," he whispered next. "Watch him. He's up to something. Drum is not going to go down without a fight. Stand back. You don't want to be part of wherever he's going with this. Keep your mouth closed. He's crazy."

But Morf couldn't keep his mouth closed. "What do you mean you were never really king? You have been king for months. You have been wearing the crown. You've been holding rallies. You've been ordering people around. You've even started a war. And you say it was all an act? *You were the King!*"

"Come on, Morf," Drum said sternly. "You've been around the Castle a long time. Many people thought I was king. But you just read that King Sol is alive. The note didn't say anything about me. A lot of people say I am good at being king. A lot of people still think I would be a good king. Maybe yes, maybe no. Who knows? Time will tell. But River Kingdom has always had a king. How could I be a real king when it already has one?"

"But you said—"

"*I* never *said* I was king," said Drum. "A lot of people said it, but I never said it."

"Yes, you did. I heard you."

"*I* never said I was king. Other people may have said that, but not me. I know what I say. That's fake news. You shouldn't repeat it."

Morf stumbled back to a chair and sat down, trying to figure out the whole thing. Finally, he had one more question. He squinted narrowly at Drum. Drum had to acknowledge this question with the truth. "If you were not the King, then who sent the farmers off to war with Urhonordo? If you didn't do that as king, who did?"

Drum stared intently at Morf. "I am so surprised that you, of all people, would ask such a question, Morf. You and I both know that we found that out only this afternoon. It was Sir Thorndike. For some reason, he fancies himself a Royal Defense Advisor. He just marched off to war with a bunch of farmers without telling anyone. King Sol is going to be pretty upset about that. Thorndike took matters into his own hands."

Morf didn't get up from his chair. "*You* made him Royal Defense Advisor, sire," he stated flatly.

"Get it straight, Morf. Thorndike was only 'acting Royal Defense Advisor.' The man is a warmonger. He's power mad . . . always has been. I have never been in favor of war. That was an illegal operation."

Cdrum was confused. He had to admit that Drum was partly right. Drum had talked a good game against Urhonordo, but Thorndike had gone off to war without permission. That much was true, but Cdrum was sure that Drum had appointed him to his Defense Advisor position . . . hadn't he? Morf sat still in his chair. The room seemed to be spinning. In was out.

Up was down. Wrong was right. Nothing made any sense.

Drum, on the other hand, was completely calm.

Cdrum had not said a thing yet. He studied Drum from one side and then the other. He still could say nothing. He, too, was shocked. Drum had just lost the best position he could ever have asked for, and he didn't seem upset. Why?

He slid down Drum's arm and stared back up at his face. It was only then that he saw what Morf had seen. Behind the calm exterior that Drum was demonstrating, Drum was calculating. He was reconfiguring what needed to be done. He seemed to have no feeling for his loss. That was the key. He had no feeling.

Cdrum suppressed a shiver. That could only mean one thing. Drum's Super Aura was in the building and helping Drum construct his next move.

I should have known, thought Cdrum.

Drum looked over at Morf and shook his head. *Morf seems upset and sad, Drum thought. I guess he's not very bright, so he doesn't get the way I operate. But he will.*

"Hey, Morf," Drum said with a smile. "You're good at arranging parties, I hear. Let's get The Castle staff together to welcome the King!"

38

Plan A, Plan B

Meanwhile, down at Dipswitch Manor, at the edge of the yawning mud pit, the most athletic men of the Commoner Army were stamping their feet like impatient horses. These men were nearly all of Will's fellow farmers. He knew them. He could feel that they were tense and ready to go.

Although the night was dark, they could all see the sheen that the flooding river water had left behind when it receded a day ago. The land was free of debris and litter. To the inexperienced fighting force, it looked like they could make good time on its smooth surface.

Will grinned at the remnants of "the pool" that lay in front of him. He held up his fist and pointed north. "Let's do it, friends!" he yelled. With a roar of enthusiasm, the men were on their way, leaping from the boulders and dry land of their staging area and into . . . the muck.

With a groan of realization, their impossible journey began. The first line of hefty farmers sank immediately up to their knees and stopped. Will could hear the men cursing.

This was what Will had expected. He had toiled with this mess just yesterday. He had slogged in it. He had dug out the channel where its water now flowed. Tonight, however, if he had figured right, this sodden farmland was going to be his friend. If the unsuspecting farmers had enough trouble plowing through the mire toward Urhonordo Castle, maybe he could get them to change their minds and avoid going to war altogether. The muck would act as a time delay to leave room for thinking. On short notice, this was all he could come up with for plan A.

"How are you doing out there?" he called to the first mucking farmers. The strongest farmers had only struggled a few yards. Every foot they picked up dragged wet mud with it, but they were not stopping. They had been chosen to lead the entire group of fighting men, and they were not about to say that they couldn't handle it. "It's gonna be slow, but we're doin' it," one of them yelled proudly.

The men on the shore began to laugh and encourage their friends with taunts.

"Pick up your big feet," they yelled from dry land. "Quit griping. It can't be that bad."

"You guys said you were warriors." "You look more like mud hens." "It's only mud, for Pete's sake."

"Come join us, Will," the leaders yelled back from the goo.

Will had to do it. He had ordered it and now he had to be part of it. He jumped into the mud and slogged his way to the front of the line. The rest of the farmers cheered their support and followed. After several exhausting minutes, most of the Commoner Army was completely clogged in the morass.

From the dark of the porch, Thorndike had no idea how his mired army was struggling. The entire Commoner Army, however, was now knee-deep in the mud. The last ones to jump into the mud instantly recognized what the early sloggers up ahead of them had been complaining about.

"This stuff ain't mud. It's glue." "I'm up to my knees."

"I'm up to my waist." "I'm stuck."

"I'm in it up to my eyeballs," yelled one of the men angrily. "There's got to be a better way."

They aren't thinking about why they're going to war like I hoped. They're just getting mad. Is my plan A going to work? Will asked himself. Cwill finally caught on. "Slowing them down so they could think was your plan A, right, Will? I see that now. That was a good idea, and they *are* slowed down . . . and mad. But they're only mad at the mud right now. They need to learn the truth about this mud and what it has to do with the war." "I know," Will answered, "but how are they going to find out? They believe in their cause. They won't believe me if I tell them their cause is a lie."

Cwill waited. Will was going to have to admit that he had led them into mud on purpose and their reason for going to war was not valid. Will was not in a good position.

"I don't know, but I think these guys are going to keep going to war if somebody doesn't tell them they got snookered," Cwill said quietly.

Will cared about his friends. He couldn't let good people fight good people for all the wrong reasons. And the men were persistent. They might even finish their muddy march and go straight on to Urhonordo if he didn't think of the right thing to do. Too bad, Morf wasn't here. Somebody needed to get creative. Will stood in the mud and felt hopeless. He needed a plan B.

A tired friend stopped and leaned toward Will. "This trail looks like it's muck as far as the eye can see, Will. Maybe we should try another route that's drier. How do you suppose this trail got flooded like this?"

Will came to a halt in the wretched goo. He finally understood what his Conscience wanted him to do. Someone needed to tell them about this mud and what it had to do with their war. This was plan B.

"You're a little slow, but you've got it," snarked Cwill.

Will climbed up on a fallen tree and looked back over the wet, dirty mass of humanity he had been leading and shouted as loud as he could. "Hey, you guys! I wasn't with you when you were all recruited. This muck is awful. Before I go any farther in it, I just want to understand the main reason for our great mission. Maybe it'll give me more incentive to slog through this mud. Do you all know why we're going to war with Urhonordo?"

"Sure, we know," puffed a regular rally-goer, as he pushed through the mire. "We're not stupid."

"I'm not sure *I* know as much as you know," said Will. "This is a lot of work so I really need some incentive. Who told you that we needed to go to war in the first place?" Will wiped some mud from his nose.

"King Drum and Thorndike told us," one of the early runners shouted fiercely. "They laid it all out for us at the rally. Urhonordo plans to invade us so we've got to invade them first. That's what it's all about."

"Oh, I see," said Will. "That's a very good reason, I guess. But why is Urhonordo going to invade us? They've always seemed like such peaceful people."

"It's all about some stupid water rights," said the farmer closest to Will. "I heard that the queen didn't like our levees."

"Okay," said Will. "Now I get it. But is that all? It seems like lowering a few levees is not enough to start a war."

"Yer right," said another farmer. "That's no reason for them to invade us at all. That's why we need to invade them before they can invade us. Understand?"

"I guess so," said Will. "I just thought that the biggest reason they were threatening us might be because we flooded their farmland and ruined their homes, but I guess I got it wrong."

"What do you mean by that?" an angry slogger asked. "When did we ever do that?"

"Just a few days ago," Will answered, "River Kingdom flooded miles and miles of their farmland. We ruined a lot of houses and crops and tools. We really made a mess."

"You're crazy. Nobody from River Kingdom would ever do something like that."

"Yes, somebody would . . . and did. If Urhonordo is mad at us, I thought that us flooding their land might be the reason."

The muddy farmer shook his head. "I don't believe River Kingdom ever flooded Urhonordo land. We don't do things like that." The farmer plowed ahead silently.

Then he stopped and turned around. He knew Will. He had farmed with him. He knew him to be honest before. He plowed his way back.

"Okay, Will. If you say that somebody from River Kingdom flooded Urhonordo land, I think you believe it, but I have trouble believing it. I never saw it. So if anybody ever did that, tell me where that happened," he concluded with a challenging look.

"I don't have to tell you. I can show you. You're standing in it," said Will simply.

The farmer looked down. "You mean somebody from River Kingdom flooded this mud flat? Really? Who?"

"Lord Dipswitch."

"No . . . no way . . . Really?"

"Yes. Really."

"On purpose?"

"Uh-huh."

"Why would he do such a thing? What was his reason? This is disgusting. He had no right to do that. Why would he have done that? You don't just flood another kingdom on purpose. It's against the rules."

Will shrugged. "You saw Dipswitch Manor, right? Sir Dipswitch had it built so that it would block The Great River. When he did that, he knocked down the levees over here, and this land flooded. When it got nice and deep, he decided this would be his pool. None of you knew that?"

"Of course, we didn't know that."

"But if it was deep at one time, where did the deep water go?" challenged a doubter. "If it was deep before, this here is just mud. Where is all that water now?"

"The Lowlanders and I drained it into that channel we just crossed over so that the Lowlanders could get their water back. Dipswitch Manor had cut all The Lowlands' water off."

The first farmer's eyes grew rounder with everything that Will said. Now that he thought about it and looked carefully, even in the dark, he saw the evidence. With effort, he struggled around in the mud and began to talk to the men near him. The men around him began to talk to the men around them and so on and so forth. Soon, all the mud-stuck men were aware of the reason for the mess. They had the proof. They were in it.

The Commoner Army was stunned. They had never heard this before. They had been lied to. None of them thought that this was right, and there, in the mud and goo, in the middle of the night, they got mad.

They began to grumble and plot. They had been tricked by Thorndike and Dipswitch. It was all a scam. They were furious. The Auras that had been following this group toward war changed focus. They now swarmed from group to group throughout the angry farmers. Maybe they could get some violence going out of this anger.

"You did good," chortled Cwill. "Well done! Everybody gets it!" "Why weren't we told this?" yelled one of the nearby farmers, stomping heavily in the slime.

"Dipswitch was wrong to ruin Urhonordo land just to make his stupid manor house," said another, shaking his fist.

"Then he wanted to leave Urhonordo land ruined and use it for a pool?" "A pool that the King said he was making for us?"

"Was King Drum in on the flooding too?"

"And we were going to war with Urhonordo for a pool on *Urhonordo land?*"

"We should tell the King's rich friends that they had no right to do this to us."

"Let's go back to Dipswitch and Thorndike and string 'em up."

"Uh-oh," said Cwill. "I think you did too good a job. I smell Eforces." Will looked back over the angrily waving fists of the Commoner Army. The roar that came from the crowd had now changed from enthusiasm for a righteous war to enthusiasm for revenge. They had been betrayed and sent into combat for no reason. Fury was mounting.

Suddenly, as though the entire body of men were one, they turned and began grappling back through the mud toward their staging area. They were on their way back to confront Dipswitch and Thorndike. They had almost gone to war to defend Dipswitch's own evil behavior, the invasion of someone else's land . . . with water. They hadn't thought much about treaties before, but they knew River Kingdom was in the wrong.

The crowd of wet, mud-covered humanity was oozing back now, preparing to climb back onto dry ground and charge the selfish men that had not told them the truth. Those men were still sitting safe, dry and comfortable in Dipswitch Manor. They deserved to be rousted out and beaten for their lies.

Suddenly, a barrier rose up in front of them. And the barrier was strangely familiar. It was the Royal Guard of River Kingdom—and part of plan B.

From the front of the line, trapped by the mud with the rest of the army, Will watched nervously. He had asked for help from his friends among the Guardsmen, but the help he had asked for was difficult to achieve. These men were fighters, not negotiators.

"What's going on with you, guys? Didn't you hear about your sleazy boss, Dipswitch?" The questioning farmer was standing next to the Guardsmen bellowing to them for blocking his exit from "the pool." "Drag your worthless bodies out of the way so that the rest of us can get at that guy in the manor!" he yelled.

Now, the word came back through the ranks. "The Royal Guard won't let us out of this blasted slime pit. Whose side is the Royal Guard on? Don't they understand what happened here?"

Will had slid down from his fallen tree, but now climbed back onto a closer one and waved his arms. "Wait!" he yelled. "Wait! Listen to the Guard. They do understand. They have something to tell you. Just listen for a minute. Just listen to the Guard."

Grudgingly, the men decided to follow Will's advice. Very slowly, the gaggle of famers quieted each other down. When the din was low enough, the Royal Guard pushed one of their number forward. They had chosen him to speak, but this was not something he was used to.

"We in the Guard were here to dig out the levees and block Lowlander water for Dipswitch. We were told to help build the manor. When we followed orders, we didn't say anything, even when our Consciences said it was wrong. That was a bad thing. But we also helped Will and the Lowlanders dig the channel to release the water. That was a good thing. Now we want to help get some peace going, if we can."

"What happened to you guys now? Did you suddenly get an attack of Conscience?" some of the farmers jeered. But strangely, the Guardsmen remained quite serious.

"Actually, yes. Now we might have a chance to fix a problem we helped cause. We're ready to go with you to Urhonordo, but this time, for a peace conference."

The army of wet, disheartened farmers slumped where they stood. The enthusiasm they had had for their patriotic mission had driven them initially, and then their anger had fueled them in the opposite direction. Now they had neither.

And to top it all, the Royal Guard wouldn't let them out of the mud. What were they supposed to do now? They looked at Will. They looked at the Guardsmen. Somebody needed to say something.

"It's your turn," whispered Cwill. "They understand the problem now, but they are still stuck in the mud. You can't just leave them here."

"I know, I know," whispered Will, "but I'm waiting to start the rest of plan B."

The men again became very quiet, but they were wet and cold. They now knew what kind of a fix they were in. They had been used. They were embarrassed. Their own Consciences were beginning to nag at them for being gullible and accepting lies as a reason to fight with the Urhonordos. Now, however, a quiet rustle occurred at the edge of the mud pit.

Someone was pushing and nudging the Royal Guard from behind. Very few dared to do such a thing. The Guardsmen were fighting men. In this case, the Guardsmen just stepped aside. It was a few Lowlanders—Ben and several of his men.

"Hi, guys," said Ben sympathetically. "I know you're all ticked off. We don't blame you. So are we Lowlanders. We were all lied to by the two warmongers back there on the porch. We even got thrown into cages. But Will is on our side. Let him speak for us so that we can all get home safely without fighting. I trust Will. He's been straight with me so far."

The commoners looked at each other. They were cold and miserable and sort of mad at Will, but they had to admit that Will had told them the truth, a truth they probably wouldn't have believed if they weren't seeing it for themselves. Grudgingly, they nodded.

"I am just here to show you a quick way to get to Urhonordo Castle if you decide to go there. If and when you're ready, I know a shortcut, one with no mud. It won't take us long to get there."

"Where were you when we needed you before we got into this gunk?" grumbled one of the farmers. He reached up a hand, and Ben pulled him up onto dry land.

"In cages," Ben reminded them. "This was a hard way to learn about what has caused this so-called war, but sometimes, only seeing is believing." Now the other Lowlanders passed the word. They had just spotted

Thorndike coming their way.

Ben looked over his shoulder and spoke quietly to those closest to him. "Pass the word, men. Thorndike still thinks you all want to go to war, and he will be here in a minute. If we are going to give peace a chance, we need to convince him that we still want what he wants. The idea is to get him up to Urhonordo Castle where he has no other choice but to talk peace. Let Will do the talking. Follow his lead."

With that, Ben stepped back through the Royal Guard and out of sight while the other Lowlanders snuck behind the manor house and returned silently to their unlocked cages.

Will crawled out of the mud and stomped the mud off before it dried and crusted.

"When Thorndike gets over here, I'm going to have a lot of explaining to do," he warned those around him, shaking his head.

Will took a deep breath. "Lord Thorndike," he called through the darkness. "I think we have a problem."

39

Preparing for War

Up at Urhonordo Castle, Queen Luna expected an attack from Thorndike and his Commoner Army with dread, but she was ready for it. Her lookouts had reported back on a regular basis. Runners were posted from The Lowlands up to her castle, running with great speed in relay formation.

The runner closest to Urhonordo Castle had just reported in. The invading River Kingdom Army was an army of mostly farmers. They had blundered into the mud pit that had been "the pool" only a day before. Now they were stuck.

"Why would they do such a stupid thing?" Luna asked, laughing. "Didn't they know they would get stuck if they tried to travel through mud?" Flawless didn't feel like answering. She was stuck too, but not in mud. "It's dark," she commented gloomily. "They probably didn't see the mud." Luna had sympathy for Flawless. She knew that Flawless was trapped away from her family and her people at a difficult time. She also knew that Flawless did not want a war, but Luna felt she had to keep her here. The actual fact was that Urhonordo would be under attack by River Kingdom shortly.

Queen Luna's troops were at their guard posts. They were ready to fight off any challenger, but they still couldn't believe that this was happening. A couple of weeks ago, the dancing girls had traveled back and forth with no problem. A healthy trade exchange between the two kingdoms had been humming. Why were they suddenly in danger of being invaded? They had done nothing wrong. The people who had broken the rules regarding water rights were River Kingdom people.

"You know," said Luna as she sat down next to Flawless. "Looking back on this whole situation, I wish that I didn't force your father's attention to water rights by showing up with troops the other day. That might have caused him to think that we were invading."

"He didn't really think that." Flawless sighed. "I told him that you and I had talked."

Flawless wasn't tied down. She was free to move around, and she was comfortable with Luna. "But he didn't bother to tell the real warmonger. Thorndike was really looking for a war, and my father didn't know enough to talk him out of it. He even encouraged him. He does that a lot. He says things and does things that he likes at the time without thinking them through."

"Not a good thing for a king."

"I know. And he's not even a king, but it may be too late for the real King to show up and keep us from killing each other," responded Flawless. "I wish there was something I could do."

"You tried," said Cflawless.

"I messed up." said Flawless. She stood up and walked around. "I wish I was older and wiser," she said quietly, "or maybe a man. Maybe I could have steered my father and Thorndike away from war if I was a man."

"Never wish for that." Luna grinned. She gazed out over the lawn of her castle. The sky was clear and dark. It was a beautiful night. Without notice, her thoughts strayed from war preparation to peaceful times that she had spent with her childhood playmate, Ben. He had been such a good friend—kind, smart, funny. It was too bad that they had not kept up with each other as grown-ups.

"What do you think of Ben, Flawless? He seems like a nice man. He was a great kid, but that was a long time ago. Is he really as nice as he seems now?"

"Yes," said Flawless without hesitation. "I like him a lot. He's Will's best friend. They've worked together for years." Flawless glanced sideways at Luna. "You like him, don't you?"

Luna grinned. "You could see that?" she asked sheepishly.

"Anybody could see that," answered Flawless. "It wasn't hard to see. You two picked up right where you left off when you were kids." She smiled at Luna but suddenly became serious again. "I wonder where Ben is now. I'm sure he's with Will. I'm glad they're together, but where are they? They were headed down south to try to stop Thorndike's army from invading you, but who knows?"

"My runner said The River Kingdom Army was stuck in the mud. Obviously, whoever is leading them is not too bright," Luna snickered. "I wish I could see that."

Flawless grinned.

Silence set in. The women were in an odd situation. They were friends, but their kingdoms were at war with each other. Neither one of them wanted to cheer for a winner, but peace seemed too far away from their ability to influence it.

In actual fact, Luna had already done a great deal to influence the outcome of any war waged against Urhonordo. Troops were deployed in defensive positions around the villages, and a stout perimeter was in place to protect her castle. Her forces were well trained even though they had never been used in combat.

Luna had always known that River Kingdom was not the only other kingdom that might someday attack Urhonordo. Back in the day, the history of Urhonordo had not been peaceful at all.

To the east lay broad expanses of territory where fighting was a much more common occurrence. Urhonordo had benefitted from their location across The River from River Kingdom. Their potential enemies had known that they could not attack Urhonordo without involving the friendly forces of River Kingdom. That is, they had known that until now.

Luna sighed. An existing Mutual Protection Treaty with River Kingdom was now as useless as the Water Rights Treaty. Why had Drum been so difficult? Couldn't he see that there was no reason for this ridiculous war? Luna was lost in contradictions and questions.

Flawless was also deep in thought, but she was having a very curious one. *What if, she thought. What if Will had lured the River Kingdom forces into the mud to slow them down and keep them from fighting?*

"That would be a good idea, if he had a chance to do it," mused Cflawless. "Maybe they slowed Thorndike down with mud. Stranger things have happened, and they're pretty smart."

"And Thorndike is pretty stupid," added Flawless.

"What?" asked Luna, looking up from the map she was studying. "Oh nothing." Flawless smiled. "I was just talking to my Conscience." "You feel bad about this, don't you?" asked Luna. "Me too. Seems like there should be some way to shut this war down before it actually hurts people."

Flawless sighed and nodded and walked to the window. The castle's yard stretched out into the night. It was becoming dark green, almost as black as the early evening sky. The eastern prairie beyond looked like a velvet carpet rolled out as far as the eye could see, but suddenly, there was something else, way out beyond the reach of that carpet. It wasn't evening sky. It was a brown dirty smudge forming a narrow unmistakable cloud above the ground.

Flawless wasn't sure that she was seeing anything but night. Maybe the sun was rising. No. It had just gone down on the other side of the castle. Cautiously, she walked to the front door of the castle and squinted toward the east.

There it was. Whatever it was, it was definitely something. It might be a fire. It might be the dust of a herd of animals. She had heard that there were wild herds in the Urhonordo flatlands, but she couldn't see anything but a brownish cloud. Some nearby trees were silhouetted against it, catching wisps of moonlight. Was it a good thing or a bad thing? It didn't look good. It was eerie and frightening. What should she do about it?

"Are you going to tell Luna about this?" Cflawless asked directly. "Do you think she should know about it?"

I don't know, Flawless thought with sudden conflict. *What if it's River Kingdom invading from a surprise direction? What if Will is with them? What if I alert Luna and she alerts her troops?*

"Do you think that could be Will . . . coming from way over there?" asked Cflawless. "If it is, how did he get troops over there without any lookouts seeing them?"

"I don't know. I don't know," Flawless moaned.

"What?" Luna asked again. "Are you alright, or is your Conscience still giving you a bad time?" She smiled and put her head back into her work.

With that, Flawless saw what she needed to do. Luna was her friend, and the brown cloud was not Will or The River Kingdom army. It was something else, and it wasn't good.

Flawless made up her mind. "Luna, come here. I'm looking at something that you should see."

"What's that?" Luna asked absently.

"I don't know, but I think you need to see it."

Luna got up from her map and stretched. It was late, and it had been a long and eventful day. "What do I need to see, my friend?" she asked, peering over Flawless's shoulder.

Flawless pointed.

"Oh my god," Luna whispered. "Not now. Please don't let this happen now."

Flawless watched in awe as her friend, the gentle Luna, suddenly evolved into an army General. Grabbing a heavy robe from a chair, she rushed from the throne room and up the stairs to the lookout tower. "Stay here," she called over her shoulder.

Flawless was alone. It was the first time she had been alone since Will and Ben left. Obviously, Luna trusted her to stay where she was and not try to escape.

Escape? She thought. Why would I escape? Where would I go? Will and Ben are down south, trying to stop a war. My father is back at River Kingdom, pretending to be a King. Luna is now my friend, and it looks like she's in trouble of some kind. Why would I leave my friend when she is in trouble?

Flawless walked back to the doorway and stared at the mysterious brown haze on the eastern horizon. She squinted and tried to make it out. From Luna's reaction, she now understood that the "something" that she was looking at was most likely "someone," and whoever it was, it was probably not going to be welcome.

Who was this new threat? She had heard of marauders that roamed the plains at night, attacking unsuspecting travelers or ransacking unprotected castles and manor houses. This must be what she was seeing.

Or could it be the troops of a rogue kingdom, out to conquer an unsuspecting kingdom whose focus was now to the south? If that were so, Urhonordo could be challenged from two directions at the same time.

Flawless shuddered. Her mind flew from one possible catastrophe to another. And what was even worse was the thought of Will being caught up in either scenario.

"And here you are, alone in a room, doing nothing," observed Cflawless. "Everyone you love is on a mission, working on the problem, being useful, while you sit here doing nothing."

"What can I do?" Flawless questioned sadly. "I don't know who is out there that Luna is so afraid of. I don't know who is waiting to attack her or even Will. I don't even know where Will is. Maybe he has already been captured. I don't know anything."

"There is only one way to find out." Cflawless nudged.

Flawless thought about it. Her Conscience was right. If she could get a closer look at whoever it was that was causing the dust or smoke to rise in the east, she would know. If she discovered who it was, she could come back and warn Luna so that she could prepare. It was probably the only useful thing she could do.

Without further deliberation, Flawless made up her mind. She would scout the oncoming force and find out who they were and what they were doing out there on the plains in the night.

Quickly, she looked around for something that would disguise her female attire. She was still wearing the simple peasant garb that the farm woman had given her, but it was light in color and would be clearly visible. She needed to do her scouting without being noticed. In a nearby hall, she found the worn tunic of a Guardsman hanging on a hook. It was brown and dark and would easily blend in with the night. Slipping it over her head, she was pleased to see that it dropped to her ankles. It was perfect.

Flawless was now ready. She had her own mission. Silently, she slipped out into the dark.

40

Onward

Down south, Thorndike stormed out of Dipswitch Manor, shaking his fist and shouting. He and Dipswitch had congratulated themselves on a successful launch of the troops toward Urhonordo a few minutes ago. Their new protégé was in charge, and Thorndike definitely did not expect to see him still standing on the bank, covered in mud and surrounded by equally muddy commoners.

And meandering around, talking to all of these bedraggled souls were members of the Royal Guard, looking like they were ready for something but they didn't know what.

"What happened here?" Thorndike screeched. "Are you commoners too stupid to find your way north? You all look like pigs from a pig trough! And you act exactly like stupid pigs! What are you doing here? Where is your leader? Where is that Will kid?"

The Commoner Army was tired and wet. They were not in the mood to be called pigs. They glared at Thorndike. They now knew the true back story of the war they had been encouraged to fight. They were more interested in attacking Dipswitch than anything else. It was time for Will to intercede and change their focus. But what was he going to say?

Cwill got pushy. "The farmers are mad, Will. You made them that way. Are you going to sit here and let your farmer friends get insulted because of what *you* told them, or are you going to say something intelligent? Stand up. Say something smart. If you don't, things are going to go from bad to worse here."

Will slowly stood and faced the furious Thorndike, his mind scrambling for an acceptable lie. "It's all my fault," he sputtered slowly. "I misjudged the depth of mud left behind when the water flooded the land. I thought that going along the shore was a quicker way to Urhonordo Castle, but I had no idea that the mud was this thick."

"That was a good start. Try groveling too," counseled Cwill. "It's disgusting, but this is worth the effort."

Will got down on one knee. "I apologize, but the men and I are ready to try a higher, drier rout. *Also*, we have all decided that we will do much better with *your expert leadership* instead of mine."

"Good job," whispered Cwill. "Disgusting, but effective."

Thorndike looked at Will with rage. His men were a mess. Their march toward *Thorndike Greatness* in Urhonordo had lost time *and* focus. And it was all this kid's fault.

On the other hand, if he didn't get to Urhonordo Castle before dawn, his grand scheme of a surprise nighttime attack from the rear would be foiled, and the truth was, Thorndike didn't know exactly how to get there. In addition, there might be some fighting along the way. That was not something that a man of his breeding and quality wanted to do.

He looked again at Will. Without any noise or hint of its presence, Thorndike's Super Eforce began to contribute to Thorndike's thinking. *This kid is a commoner. He's expendable. No one will miss him if something happens to him,* Thorndike quickly rationalized. *Throw him back into leadership. At least you won't have to fight when you take over the castle.* Now the kid was on his knees. He was humble, and he also knew the way to the castle even though he had chosen the wrong way first. This commoner could get him and his stupid Commoner Army to Queen Luna in time to take her out and replace her before the sun came up.

This revised Eforce-energized way of thinking took hold and provided a new surge of power to Thorndike that was even stronger than he had felt before. He knew now what he was going to do. His way to his glorious destiny was again clear.

"Rise, William of Dale. I forgive you for your stupid mistake. To show you that there are no hard feelings, I will allow you to lead the troops again, being assured that you now know a better way this time, of course."

"Indeed, sir," said Will with an inward sigh of relief. Cwill said nothing, but smiled.

"You will lead us forward, young man," Thorndike continued forcefully, "followed by the army, the Royal Guard, and myself. I have decided that we must continue to assign the honor of first strike to the brave Commoner Army to ensure victory before daybreak."

"And to take all the possible casualties while leaving Thorndike without a scratch," Cwill observed loudly.

Will and the Commoner Army heard and understood both the instructions and the reason for them, but lined up as requested. It was actually the lineup they wanted to have as they arrived at Urhonordo Castle, but they now had a much different mission in mind—peace.

"Thorndike is in the complete control of his Eforce," signaled Cwill. "Watch him closely. He will sacrifice anyone or anything to get what he wants."

"I know," whispered Will.

Now the farmers and Royal Guard began to move eastward.

"Sir!" Will shouted to Thorndike as he passed by. "Can I enlist just one of the Lowlanders to help me navigate the lower part of Urhonordo? Lowlanders are the most familiar with this land as it is close to theirs and they have spent much time here. They will get us where we want to go fastest."

"Do what you wish," Thorndike acknowledged flippantly. "Take the one you want as a prisoner. We have dozens to choose from behind the house in cages." No one said anything, but within moments, Ben joined Will at the front of the forces.

Now the lineup was complete, and the fighting force quietly undertook their new, more peaceful mission. Will and Ben began to lead through the nighttime mist with purpose. It would take hours, and arriving before dawn was going to be a challenge.

And what would be waiting for them? Will really had no idea. His first thought was of Flawless. Was she still with Queen Luna? He had no way of knowing. This was not a good position for her to be in, but he and his forces wanted peace and would try immediately to speak to Queen Luna about peace before Thorndike knew what they were doing. Ben could definitely help with that.

But Luna didn't live by herself. She had advisors and Royal Guards of her own. Would they try to protect her when they saw another army approaching on their soil? Huge battles had been started for less. He would have to move quickly to speak of peace as soon as they got near.

Will and Ben chatted about all this quietly. "I had no idea what you were doing when you headed off into the mud flats tonight," Ben commented. "At first, I thought you were crazy."

"Me too." Will laughed. "I got lucky with the guys that were around me when I tried to explain the whole thing. I knew a bunch of them."

"And they knew you. That was what was key," Ben answered. "I told my people that I trusted you. I guess the farmers and Royal Guard trust you too."

"But Will still hasn't paid you guys," reminded Cben. "You can't eat 'trust,' and if we don't get paid soon, Lowlanders will starve this winter." Cwill heard Cben even though Will didn't. "I won't let him forget," offered Cwill.

On they trudged. They had finally passed the flooded farmlands, and now, under Ben's navigation expertise, they turned due north, directly toward Urhonordo Castle. By Ben's calculations, they would get there while it was still dark. They were traveling at a good pace and had not been stopped by anyone or anything along the way. So far, so good.

After another half hour, however, one of the farmers tugged on Will's tunic. "Looks like the sun's coming up already," he warned.

"It won't be up for another hour or so," Ben said confidently, plowing forward.

"Then what's that?" asked the farmer, pointing eastward.

There, on the far distant edge between earth and sky, was a light-brown haze.

Will stopped and squinted east. So did the rest of the marching force. Thorndike dropped his secure position at the rear of the line and rushed forward, again beside himself with fury.

"I told you we were going to be late. I told you that we wouldn't be able to attack under the cover of night. The sun is coming up, idiot! Our surprise is ruined. The Urhonordos will be able to see us a mile away. There will be massive bloodshed, and it will be your fault."

Thorndike began pacing back and forth, waving his arms at the distant view and cursing.

"That isn't sunrise," said Ben quietly.

"Then what is it, Lowlander?" Thorndike sneered. "You think you know more than the rest of us? I doubt that. Shut your mouth. You need to know your place."

Will squirmed. He couldn't stay quiet. "Be careful," warned Cwill.

Will swallowed hard. "Ben played in this area when he was a child, sir," Will offered with as much control as he could find. "This is his stomping ground. This is something that he knows about and I don't. We need his expertise."

Thorndike scowled at Ben. "You say that he knows something about that brown haze over there, Will? What do you know about it, boy?" Thorndike growled.

"You've got this," whispered Cben. "Keep your mind on the mission. Say what you need to say, but say as little as possible to this jerk."

"It's not sunrise. I think that somebody is out there, sir," answered Ben. Will squinted eastward. "I think he's right," said Will.

"Somebody else . . . another army . . . another fighting force? Somebody else that wants to take over Urhonordo? How can that be? Urhonordo is mine. It is meant to be *mine*. This can't be happening."

Will shook his head. Thorndike was obsessed. He was possessed by his battle mania to such an extent that he couldn't think. But the brown cloud on the horizon was real. If it was another kingdom on the march toward war, it could be a threat to Urhonordo and to The River Kingdom forces. They needed to know who it was and what their intentions were.

"I think we should wait here," said Will calmly. "If this is a fighting force, we need to know it before we get to Urhonordo. Stay here and I will sneak up on them and find out what they are doing out there. It could be a peaceful group. We don't want to provoke them unnecessarily. Wait for me here, and I will be back shortly."

"No!" shouted Thorndike belligerently. "There will be no waiting. We are moving forward. If that is another fighting force, it is even more important that we get to Urhonordo and conquer them before someone else does."

"But—" Will began.

"And you are not going nowhere, Will," Thorndike continued. "We'll send this Lowlander. He says he knows everything. *He* can go out there, find out what we need to know, and come back. If he doesn't make it back, no one will miss him. Go on out there, boy, and see what you can find out without getting killed."

Ben nodded. "I'm ready to go, sir," he announced. "I know this area well. I can go and come back to find you wherever you are if you keep going. I'll go."

"Ben," said Will. "Let me do it. You take over leadership. You know the best way to the castle so much better than I."

"This cadre will not be led by a Lowlander!" thundered Thorndike. "I have my limits. I allowed him to come along because he knows the territory, but that is all. Now he can be useful in another way."

Thorndike turned to Ben and glared. "Go out there and find out who that is, Lowlander. If you don't come back soon, you can consider yourself a deserter, and you will be killed when you are caught. Do you understand me?"

"Yessir," said Ben obediently.

"Then go. What are you waiting for? Get out of here," Thorndike shouted.

But Ben didn't answer. Will was already gone.

41

Drum Beat

Back at River Kingdom Castle, all was quiet. Drum appeared to be asleep in his bed while Morf was nodding fitfully in a chair nearby. He had decided that Drum was not "right in the head" since he had found out that King Sol was alive. He did not seem at all concerned about an impending confrontation. That was not normal.

Now Morf had completely reestablished Drum in the quarters that had been assigned to the Royal Caretaker. There was no longer any sign that Drum had ever been in the throne room or its adjacent bedchamber.

The Royal Caretaker's room was actually just down the hall from Morf's own room, but tonight, Morf had remained camped out in Drum's space.

In spite of Drum's dishonesty, extravagance, and warmongering, Morf had developed his own type of defensive loyalty to Drum. Morf would never admit that, not even to himself, but it was true. Morf knew that Drum had no right to declare himself King and never had, but life with King Drum had been entertaining for Morf, and he had stayed on in The Castle. That had been his goal.

Flits and bits of these thoughts skittered through Morf's dreams as he slumped in his hard uncomfortable chair. He squirmed and changed position, trying to find a more accepting piece of the smooth wooden surface.

"Sit still or find a different place to sit," ordered Drum from his bed. "That chair squeaks."

Morf woke up with a start. "Are you awake, sir?" he asked groggily. "I guess so, thanks to you," yawned Drum. He sat up and swung his

legs out from under the covers. "Some people make too much noise to let other people sleep. That would be you, Morf. What are you doing here in my room, anyway?"

"I'm just keeping an eye on things," Morf said honestly. "A lot has changed since yesterday afternoon."

"Not that much," said Drum. "We're in the same castle. We've got the same staff around us. I've got a good bed. I don't know what yours is like, but mine is just fine."

Morf stared at the ceiling. How was he going to deal with this? Surely Drum realized by now that his life was changing drastically. He had appeared to blow it off yesterday, but the reality had to have sunk in by now. Morf approached the subject delicately.

"You *do* understand that you're not the King anymore, don't you?" he asked gently. "That's why you're sleeping down here."

Drum slipped his feet into his cold slippers and stood up. Slowly, he ambled over to Morf and looked him in the eye. "Do you think that I lost my mind when I lost my crown, Morf? Is that what you think?"

"That's what *I* think," commented Cmorf. "The guy has lost it. He doesn't know up from down. He can't handle it."

"Of course, I don't think that," Morf lied. "It's just that this is such a big change for you, that I was worried about how you would feel."

"This is only a temporary setback, Morf. I've had a lot of reversals in my life and moved on to better things. And I feel that we have a lot of work to do now," said Drum. "Have you begun to line things up for the King's celebration?"

Morf shrugged.

"I told you," said Cmorf. "The guy is balmy."

"You think I'm crazy, don't you?" Drum laughed. "Maybe you're right. Maybe 'crazy' is the way I've always been, but this is me. My life is all about *me*. And now . . . *I* want to throw a party. *You're* the Royal Community Relations Advisor. Parties are your job, right?"

"Um . . . hum . . ." mumbled Morf. "But I don't understand, sir. A party? You are stepping down from your position as King. In essence, you are giving up all your power. Aren't you upset?"

"Yes," said Drum. "I'm upset because you haven't started preparations for our welcoming celebration for King Sol. When are you going to get busy? Do you want the King to think that I don't know how to throw a party? You don't have any time to waste. *And* I have *not* given up all my power. I am still the Royal Caretaker. Do what I ask you to do, or I will have you replaced."

Morf stood up in shock. His emotions no longer teetered between sadness and sympathy as they had a few minutes before. He had been put in his place.

"By the way, Morf. Fetch me my dancing girls. There's no reason for me to stop enjoying their presence. They are the best part of living here in The Castle. And tell my Financial Advisor to come with them. I need to make some adjustments in my finances."

Morf sidled toward the door. He stared back at Drum. He had thought, if Drum wasn't sad about not being king, maybe he would at least be humble.

Drum *had* called himself king. He *had* lived like a king. He had done a lot of things that were just plain wrong. He should show some guilt, at least. But it didn't look like humility or guilt was going to happen with Drum. How did he manage to do that?

Cdrum was beginning to understand Drum at last. Like a ship heading for its North Star, Drum was heading for his next port of self-love with his Super Auras. His Auras didn't allow him time for guilt or regret. Like a magnet, they pulled him toward appreciation or success without taking time out to acknowledge failure. Drum had not failed. He was just moving on.

Morf turned and shuffled down the hall. *What should I do now?* he thought. *Should I really be putting together a celebration . . . and why?*

"You should be rehearsing some guilt and humility to offer your King for your own behavior," answered Cmorf.

"Me? Why should I feel guilty? I didn't do anything wrong. I have no reason to be worried about King Sol coming home."

"I guess not." Cmorf smirked. "Unless you consider it wrong to assure everyone that King Sol was probably gone for good and they should go along with every stupid thing 'King Drum' wanted. And how about toadying up to Drum's every royal whim . . . bowing and scraping and not doing anything to keep Drum from overspending The Kingdom's money while taking bribes for himself?

"And here's a good one: How about cheering him and watching him encourage a war for no reason? If you are really proud of the role you have been playing while King Sol was gone, then you have no reason to feel guilty."

"Oh," said Morf to himself. "I think I had better start planning a party." Morf headed quickly down the hall to the kitchen. The Cooks would need to get busy.

"I rest my case," snarked Cmorf.

Back in the room of the Royal Caretaker, Drum was having a rough time with his Conscience as well. It had started out quite nicely, however. Cdrum had not given up entirely.

MORAHDRUM

"I'm really proud of the way you're taking this demotion, Drum," said Cdrum. "I thought that you would be upset when it happened, but you have been quite the gentleman. I hope you can keep it up."

"Keep what up?" asked Drum calmly. "I am doing what I always do. I'm moving on. I'm not worried about a thing."

"Come on, Drum. Show some remorse. You know you made yourself King when you shouldn't have. Now you're not King anymore. Aren't you sorry, sad . . . mad . . . worried about King Sol . . . what he'll say, what he'll do . . . anything? Pay attention! You're not King anymore! Don't you get it?"

"No. You're the one that doesn't get it, Conscience," answered Drum.

"I do what I want to do when I want to do it because I want to do it. Some people like that. Inferior people don't. I am a man of business. I do whatever works while it works. When it stops working, I do something else. I'm just resetting my future goals. And as you know, I'm the best negotiator in the world. I will land on my feet . . . no harm, no foul."

"But you hurt people. You lied. You spent money on your lifestyle that wasn't yours to spend. You took bribes. You made bribes. You even started a war. All of that was against my advice as your Conscience. Can't you see that?"

"Sure. I can see that," agreed Drum, "but that's not my problem. You're the Conscience. That's your problem. Now, stand back and watch my dancing girls. Where's Fandango? I have some affairs to settle."

Soon the dancing girls arrived. They seemed a bit shy now. They had just heard that King Drum was back to being Sir Drum. They weren't sure how they should act. The nervous Milton Fandango was not the least bit shy (or nervous) anymore, however.

"Got knocked back down to nothing, eh, Drum? Thought you were a big-shot King for a while, right? Too bad, so sad. Now you're nobody again like the rest of us. How does it feel?" Fandango strutted across the room, looking around with disdain.

"You're not in the King's quarters anymore, are you?" he continued sarcastically. "Thought you were pretty important while you were King, didn't you? I guess you're not important anymore, right?"

"I'm important to you," Drum said flatly.

"How so?" Fandango fired back.

"First, I am still the Royal Caretaker. That means that I am still your boss . . . and I can still fire you."

Fandango said nothing.

"Second, I am the 'King' that appointed you to your current position, so your position is definitely linked to my reign. Have you thought of that?"

Fandango glared at Drum. "You've spent the Royal Storehouses of The Kingdom into a hole, Drum. How are you going to explain that to King Sol

when he gets here?"

"I'm not going to explain anything," Drum said calmly. "You are. I have nothing to do with it. You are the one that has been handling the money. If we were running low, I know nothing about it. And it is probably notable that much of it has been going to you and the dancing girls."

"But you have been throwing rally after expensive rally and keeping the lights burning in The Castle every night. Those things have cost The Kingdom money," Fandango sputtered.

"And you have allowed it. And observe . . . the commoners now love the rallies and me. That's called popularity, Milton. Do you have any of that?"

Drum sat down on his bed. He fluffed his pillows and lay back. He waited. Milton Fandango felt his nervous quiver begin again. He said nothing, but he nodded at the girls. Several climbed up on the bed while the others began to sing and dance in front of it. Drum had made his point.

42

The Brown Cloud

Flawless slipped into the dark side yard of Urhonordo Castle and darted to the nearest shrub. Peeking up to the ramparts above, she realized that she would have to time her mission just right to avoid the castle lookout's detection.

The beautiful front yard would be the hardest part. Run, hide, and watch. Run some more, hide, and watch. Carefully, she made her way from bush to bush and into the tall grass beyond the landscaping. Crouching low beneath the tops of the grasses, she headed for her target, the large brown cloud that hovered over the distant horizon line.

She was a good runner. Now that she was out of sight of the castle, she ran as fast as she could. She was making good time. She could barely see the castle anymore. That was a good thing. She continued running through the tall grasses. She was determined.

Flawless had no idea what was causing this cloud in the distance, but she felt it was her duty to find out. Her Conscience had two opinions on the subject.

"This is a pretty courageous thing you are doing," Cflawless commented. "You are trying to get information that will help Luna and maybe even Will. Your heart is in the right place. You may be risking your life, but you're doing it for a good reason. I'm proud of you." This was Cflawless's first thought on Flawless's daring journey to discover the possible threat.

"You are a complete idiot for doing this!" This was the second and equally strong thought of her Conscience. "You have no idea what you're doing. You have no idea who or what is causing this cloud. If it's bandits or a rogue kingdom and you are captured, you will become a bargaining chip to be used to get concessions from Queen Luna. That won't help her at all. Even worse, you may become a plaything for evil men who consider you to have no value above that. Either way, this is a stupid move."

Flawless sat down on a rock to rest for a moment. She thought about what she was doing. *Am I doing the right thing? Might I be causing more harm than good?* She was out of breath and tired. She was frightened, but as she stared ahead, she could see that she was much closer to her goal than she thought.

It was time to hide. She lay down in the grasses and parted them carefully with her fingers. Now she could actually make out the forms of some figures—men huddled around smoky campfires. And there were horses, many horses, some grazing, some pawing the ground impatiently. Above them rose a combination of smoke and dust and firelight—the brown cloud.

She had come far, but not far enough. Were these men good or bad? Why were they stopped here in the middle of nowhere? She turned back toward Urhonordo Castle. It was so far away that she couldn't see it above the grass. The castle was nowhere in sight. It had disappeared. She was disoriented.

For a minute, Flawless panicked. If she had an important message to deliver, which way would she go to deliver it? The tall grasses had covered her trail.

"I told you this was a dumb idea," mused Cflawless. "Now what are you going to do?"

"I'm going to get the information I came for," Flawless said out loud. "What information did you come for?" said a deep voice from above her.

Flawless froze. She was lying on her stomach. She could see feet. Two men were standing over her. It was humiliating . . . stupid . . . frightening. She said nothing.

Large hands swooped down and grabbed her by her armpits. Roughly, they stood her up and shook her.

"Look what we've got here," said the owner of one set of hands. "It's a little page boy of some kind. Looks like he snuck out in his father's tunic. Wonder how he got way out here."

"Looks like an Urhonordo tunic by the markings," said the second man. "This kid's a long way out, unless we're closer than we think we are. At any rate, he's ours now. Let's haul him in and see what he looks like by firelight."

The men shoved Flawless forward in front of them.

Good, she thought. *At least they think I'm a boy. I'm safer if I'm a boy. But who are these men? They know where the Urhonordos are, and they're heading me in the opposite direction. It must be an invasion force! I'll have to find a way to escape.*

Flawless kept her head down. Her long hair covered her face. Dirt from her travels and the huge tunic that hung to her feet completed her disguise. Several times she fell into the grass, and the men hauled her upright by a rope that they had thrown over her head. She was a captive.

Flawless had not achieved her goal. Resolutely, she made no noise. If she was going to do anything to help the people she loved, she would have to . . . be a boy and escape.

Finally, the trio reached the firelight. Flawless glanced from side to side. The encampment was huge. Separate fires were strung out in a long line, and smoke curled into the sky, causing a greasy haze over wonderful- smelling shards of game roasting over the flames.

Now Flawless realized that she was hungry, of all things. She was supposed to be a spy on a mission, but she was starving. And why not? In the confusion of her captivity with Luna, she had forgotten to eat. Now she was someone else's captive. Her stomach began to growl.

Her captors threw her to the ground, but laughed. "I hear the little beggar's stomach growling," hooted one. "Should we feed him or let him starve?"

"Better throw him something," answered the other. "He ain't too big. He might blow away."

One of the rough men reached into the nearest fire and pulled out a shred of meat, tossing it to the ground at Flawless's feet.

A boy would eat this and not worry about the dirt, Flawless thought. How would a boy do it? I am a boy now. Quickly, she crouched to the ground and grabbed the stringy morsel, stuffing it into her mouth.

"Whoa!" one of the men shouted as he jumped back. "Don't stand too close. This little guy will eat your foot off if he gets too close to it."

Huddling close to the ground with her meat, she took the opportunity to look more closely at her surroundings. It was then that she realized with a shock who she was looking at. She was surrounded by the Royal Guard of River Kingdom!

This was amazing. These men were King Sol's men. Her mind began to race. Luna had said that the King was returning from Dragon Quest, but she had no idea when. Obviously, it was now.

Cflawless was fascinated. "Think about it," she said. "Your mission has completely changed. You came here to gather information about enemy soldiers and warn Luna. Now you need to warn your own Royal Guard *about* Luna. She won't know that this isn't an attacking force."

Yes, she will. She'll figure that out right away. I don't need to warn these men about Luna. I need to warn them about Thorndike, Flawless realized next. Dropping the piece of meat to the ground, Flawless stood suddenly and wiped her long hair from her face. "I am Flawless Drum," she announced to her startled captors. "I must speak to King Sol immediately." The first Guardsman stepped back and looked at Flawless more closely.

Then he grunted in disgust. "Yeah. And I am the Queen of Sheba," he snarled. "Look here, Wallace. This here boy turns out to be a girl. What she's doin' out here, dressed up like a boy, I don't know, but she don't look right to me. We need to tie her tight, up 'til we can find out." Immediately, the two Guardsmen began to tie Flawless's hands.

"Stop! You have to let me speak to King Sol," Flawless insisted, struggling away. "There's a war party that may be attacking Urhonordo from the south at any minute. If you proceed any further, you might become part of that war."

"She's a feisty one with a crazy story. You'll have to give her credit for that," said one of the Guardsmen. A crowd had begun to gather around their new captive. They looked at her more closely.

"She might be sort of pretty if you get the dirt off her," said another, brushing her hair back again. "But she wouldn't have come out here alone. Somebody must've come with her." "We should go back out in the field and check for others. She may be some kind of a trick."

Now, a great shout arose from somewhere out in the darkness. "Look what we found! We found a spy out in the tall grass. He's a dirty one, but he's young and brawny. He's up to no good, that's for sure."

Two more Guardsmen struggled in with a man who was in no way a willing prisoner, but this man had already found his voice. "Put me down, you guys! I'm not the enemy. I'm a friend. I'm William of Dale."

The Guardsmen flung Will to the ground, keeping tight hold of the rope they had tied around his neck. He tried to come back to his feet again, but these men were not about to let that happen. They paced around him, scratching their chins and comparing notes with each other.

"He's got good shoes. He looks like he might have a position of some kind."

"But he's covered in mud from the waist down."

"But the mud is all dried up. It didn't come from around here."

"Look at his hands. His hands are rough like a farmer. He ain't no gentleman."

Will tried again. "Look, men. You're partly right. I'm a farmer, but I'm also the Royal Ag Advisor. I need to find King Sol so I can tell him what's going on in River Kingdom before he gets there. He could be in danger."

The Guardsmen didn't know what to make of Will. They continued to discuss it among themselves.

"He speaks like a pretty smart guy."

"He lies, though. Everybody knows he's not the Ag Advisor."

"Yeah, that would be Arnold. But he seems to be all worked up about King Sol. Is he dangerous?"

"Maybe we should take him to King Sol and let him decide."

Flawless's captors had lost some of their crowd of admirers when Will was brought in. That took some of the fun out of it. The first Guardsmen decided to move their prize and join with the crowd that was now surrounding Will. With little concern or deference, now that they knew she was female, they dragged their prize by her leash-like rope into the space around Will and threw her down near him.

"Look," said one of them. "We got a female to go with your guy. That makes a pair of 'em. We should check again out there in the grass. Maybe there's more."

"Will! Will! What are you doing here?" Flawless cried, crawling closer through the dirt. "Are you hurt? Have they hurt you? Do they know who you are?"

Will looked up in shock. "Flawless?"

It was Flawless, here in the middle of a war camp. Where had she come from? How did she get here, of all places? He tried to move closer, but a Guardsman stepped on his leash.

"Look," he said as he bent over to see them more closely. "Look, they know each other." Now he tried to understand what he was seeing. "They know each other, but they didn't come together. They both say they're from River Kingdom, but they can't prove it. They don't have any papers or passage. Who are they?"

The Guardsmen were now even more intrigued . . . and interested. But they were members of the Royal Guard. They were well trained.

The King needed to know about these two and make a decision about what to do with them.

Yanking them roughly to their feet, the Royal Guardsmen who had captured the prisoners in question marched the pair to the tent of King Sol and called inside.

"Who calls?" said a sleepy voice from inside the tent.

"We have prisoners, Your Majesty," responded the self-nominated spokesman proudly. "We thought you might like to see them. They say they they're from River Kingdom, but they can't prove it."

"Prisoners?"

There was the sound of rustling clothing and scraping shoes coming from inside the tent. After a few minutes, the crownless head of a tired monarch shoved itself through the flap in the tent and squinted.

First, he looked Will up and down with little interest. "You're a muddy mess," he observed as the guard turned him around for inspection. "Did somebody throw you in The River?"

"I tried wading in a mudflat down south," Will answered truthfully. "It's hard to make mud in a dry area down south, boy," Sol offered skeptically.

"Not if you dam up The River with a manor house," Will responded. "That would be a stupid thing to do," said Sol.

"Yes, sire. It was," agreed Will.

King Sol raised his eyebrows. This was interesting. Now he focused on the girl.

"Are you trying to look like a boy?" he asked.

"Not really," answered Flawless. "It was all I could find to travel in, and I was in a hurry. Luna might be in danger, and I didn't know who was out here."

King Sol backed away from Flawless and squinted at her more closely. "You call the Queen by her first name, young lady. Do you know her?"

"Yes, sire. We're friends."

King Sol brushed Flawless's hair away from her face. "I believe I have seen you before," he said slowly. "Have I?"

"Yes, sire. I met you with my father. I am Flawless Drum."

King Sol folded his dangling robe over his nightshirt and stood up straight. He was not dressed appropriately for this. Neither was she, but that didn't matter. She was a lady and, from what he could remember, a beautiful one.

"These circumstances are very strange for a lady of your family's station, Mistress Drum," he said politely. "Please allow my men to show you to private quarters where you can freshen up. Is your companion here a servant?"

"A servant of The Kingdom," Flawless responded stoutly. "He is the Royal Agricultural Advisor . . . the new Royal Agriculture Advisor. And I believe that I speak for both of us when I say that we both need to speak with you, immediately. Your forces and the kingdoms of both Urhonordo and River Kingdom may be in great danger."

King Sol stood up tall. He was no longer tired or sleepy. He scowled at Will. "What danger do the two of you believe that my kingdom and Urhonordo are in? Who would attack two such fortified kingdoms?"

"They may attack each other," said Will simply.

43

Plan A and Plan B No. 2

Leading the Commoner Army on the trail north toward Urhonordo, Ben was struggling. It was not due to the fact that he was tired although that was true. He had been marching steadily, dodging around farms and forests, trying to keep the Commoner Army and the Royal Guard behind them from meeting up with Urhonordo people that would question them or, even worse, feel that they needed to defend themselves.

None of the Commoner Army had anything against the people of Urhonordo, but emotions were mixed about the encounter that Thorndike was leading them to. This was part of the reason for Ben's struggle. The farmers had been to too many rallies. They believed what King Drum had told them:

"The Urhonordos, led by their heartless Queen, are trying to take away River Kingdom's entitled water rights!"

According to Drum, the Urhonordos were trying to enforce a treaty that would rob the farmers of the precious water that they knew they needed for their crops. That was what the levees were all about. King Drum understood the need for lowering levees. King Drum understood them, and King Drum didn't like Queen Luna. They didn't think that they should like her either. It wasn't that the Commoner Army didn't believe Will, but what he had shown them and told them about was mostly about that scoundrel, Dipswitch, and what he had done. He was definitely a bad guy. That had been easy to see . . . and feel. They would show him no mercy when they caught up with him.

But the levees and an ignorant queen were something else. Their upcoming peace talks might involve some serious "levee talk" as well.

Ben listened to the grumbling behind him and hoped that Will would be back soon to calm the negative chatter and get the peace talks started.

Thorndike was wrapped tight in the power lust of the Super Eforce that was now part of him. Other Eforces knew that he was in position to become a new champion of evil. They continued to feed him with the thoughts of his coming control of Urhonordo, and if those thoughts flagged, they added the racism that he had always used to enhance his feelings of superiority and entitlement over Lowlanders.

This was another reason that Ben was struggling.

"How much farther do we need to go, boy? How far away from Urhonordo Castle are we now?" Thorndike asked impatiently. "Do you still think that we'll be there before dawn? Do you even know?"

"We're getting close," answered Ben without emotion. "If you don't hit him, I will," groused Cben.

No, you won't. Neither one of us will, but maybe we'll get lucky and he'll get captured by Luna, Ben thought with an inward snicker. *Can I wish for him to get killed?*

"No." Cben sighed. "That is beneath you, no matter how much he deserves it."

"Too bad," Ben concluded aloud. "What?" asked Thorndike.

"Uh, nothing," answered Ben. "I was just talking to my Conscience." "I didn't know that you Lowlanders had Consciences," responded Thorndike.

Ben swallowed his response. This was a time to concentrate on his mission, not the man *who* was beside him. This man was a menace. The closer they got to Urhonordo, the more menacing his presence became. He had no respect for Luna. He might easily try to hurt her or, at the very least, enslave her. They were now very close to Urhonordo Castle, but where was Will?

Will always talked about plan A and plan B. Plan A at Urhonordo Castle was for Will to talk to Queen Luna and Thorndike and try to talk both sides out of a battle and into a peaceful solution, an eventual peace treaty. Will was a good talker. Luna was intelligent and reasonable . . . and beautiful and nice and . . . Ben shook his head and grinned.

If Will was not back in time, Ben would have to figure something out himself. Ben knew very well that *he* was plan B.

Ben was sure that Luna would listen to what he had to say about peace and treaties, but he also knew that Thorndike would never do the same— particularly since he was a Lowlander. Plan B was obviously a little iffy.

Thorndike had no respect for Ben, and Ben knew it. The Commoner Army was a bit defensive about the issue of water rights and their levees. Things could go wrong easily.

"If plan B is going to work, you better start on it now," counseled Cben. "I advise strategic groveling."

"I am very proud that you have allowed me to walk beside you all this way," Ben said smoothly.

"Oh my god. Don't overdo it." Cben whispered. "You shouldn't even have to *talk* to a man like this, let alone grovel."

"I have a plan," said Ben to both his Conscience *and* Thorndike.

"Oh, is that so?" responded Thorndike. "*I'm* the General of this army. *I* am the only one who needs to have any kind of plan for Urhonordo. My plan is simple. March on the little Queen and knock out her flimsy defenses with my superior numbers and conquer Urhonordo. That's my plan—a simple plan, but effective."

"It sounds amazing," crowed Ben enthusiastically. "It sounds as though you have it all completely thought out. You have quite a military mind, sir. Congratulations."

"Oh, brother," growled Cben.

"I don't know why you think you know about these things, but you're right," said Thorndike with a shrug.

"I am just guessing that *your* wonderful plan is the reason that you want me to go on ahead and scout out the location of the 'little queen's' defenses, right? That way you can find exactly where they are and conquer them quickly. Am I right?"

Thorndike looked long and hard at Ben. "Did I say that?" he asked. "Of course," said Ben admiringly. "How else would I know that your

plan will work? You've thought it out so well that it can't fail."

Thorndike puffed with the praise. *That sounds like a pretty good idea. Maybe I did say that,* he thought. "When do you think I should dispatch you to scout Urhonordo Castle?" he asked, staring northward.

"I could go now," Ben answered in a shy voice, "if you think it's best.

I will go at your command."

Thorndike struck a pose. He lifted his chin and straightened his back. He was already posing for an inaugural portrait. "I will look forward to your feedback on the enemy," he said in impressive tones. The Commoner Army that was lined up behind him had heard the whole conversation and chuckled to themselves.

44

An Impossible Plan

Queen Luna peered eastward as the brown cloud she had been watching was joined by a slowly rising sun. She knew who was causing the cloud. She had no doubt now although she was still very concerned. This was King Sol and his troops. Two pieces of The River Kingdom army were approaching her from two different directions. She had no idea what either one of them was going to do. As a queen, she felt that she had done all she could do to get ready.

She had sent out a runner to King Sol's troops to inform them of her current situation. How would King Sol interpret this? They had always been friends, but this was very different. Would he feel that he needed to take the side of his southern troops? Perhaps they had already contacted him.

Luna paced the ramparts at the highest point of her castle, straining east at the approaching army. "Stand ready," she commanded her men. She couldn't afford to take chances. "Do not fire until my signal."

A commotion now could be heard at the front door. Who could that be? There was shouting and scuffling and the sounds of dragging and scraping.

Luna yelled, "Stay calm. Do not initiate violence!" She ran down the stairs, expecting Flawless.

"Luna!" screamed a voice from a squashed face against the castle floor and under a boot. "Tell them I'm me."

This was not a time to laugh, but Luna had to suppress a smile. "Let him up," she said quickly. "It's Ben." The men backed off and looked at him closely.

Ben scrambled to his feet. "Wow," he puffed. "Your men are prepared for invaders. That's a good thing. River Kingdom's Commoner Army is just down the road and ready to attack."

Luna was dressed for war, both physically and mentally. She was not ready for small talk. "Why are you here, Ben?" she asked bluntly.

Ben noticed her tone. She was all business.

"It depends on who you ask," he replied. "Thorndike thinks I am here on a scouting mission. I think I am here trying to arrange for some sort of peace conference, . . . and I need to do it fast because Thorndike is all excited and ready to invade."

Luna raised her head and glared. "I dare him to try it," she announced. "No, you don't! No, you don't!" said Ben loudly. "You can't let him do

that. Many good people will be killed for no reason."

"Why do you say that, Ben? Are you afraid we can't defend ourselves?" Luna asked boldly.

"No. Just the opposite. I know that you can defend yourselves. I can see that. That's what I'm afraid of."

Luna stomped forward and placed her face squarely in front of Ben's. Her men stepped forward protectively. "Whose side are you on?" Luna challenged.

Ben was impressed but taken aback. She wasn't his childhood friend anymore. She was a queen.

"Both, Luna," he answered honestly.

It was Luna's turn to step back. She was also impressed. Ben had come here to an armed castle, which was now more like a fortress. He had come on his own to try for some kind of peace talks. This took bravery.

"I can understand that, Ben," said Luna, relaxing a bit. "I believe that you want to avoid war. That's what I thought you and Will went down south to do. But I have to say that I don't understand why you came up here with an invasion force. Did Will join with Thorndike too?"

"Neither one of us 'joined' Thorndike, but we did come up here with him. That's true. We decided that we should march up here with him and try to think of some way to negotiate peace on the way or when we got here." "Did that work? Did you figure something out that would end this mess?" Luna asked.

"No," Ben admitted sadly.

"Too bad," said Luna. "I know that I have been trying to think of something like that too. I don't want to fight. My men don't want to fight. But soon there will be somebody here that does want to fight, and we can't stop them unless we fight back." Dejectedly, Luna walked toward the window.

"Look, Ben. Do you see that huge troop of men in the distance? They are marching this way. I'm pretty sure that's King Sol and his men."

"I figured that might be who that was. Will and I spotted them hours ago, and Will went to check it out. But he never came back."

"I sent a runner as well. Not only that, Flawless ran off last night. She may be out there with them or captured by them or heaven knows what." Luna looked at Ben. "I wish you could have come up with a solution. I am worried. When Thorndike's invasion force and King Sol and my men all meet together on one battleground, it might become a bloodbath."

Both friends stood and looked out the window. What had happened to their peaceful lives?

Suddenly, Ben turned from the window. "Luna, I have an idea," he announced. He stared at her fondly. "But you're not going to like it."

"Tell me," Luna answered. "Any idea is better than no idea. Tell me." "Surrender," Ben said without hesitation. "Get ready to surrender

right now."

Luna blinked. She stared at Ben in disbelief. "What? Surrender? Are you crazy?"

Luna whirled around and confronted Ben in fury. "I thought you believed in me, Ben. I thought you could see that Urhonordo is prepared to defend our territory. You said that Thorndike was a warmonger. How could you even *suggest* that I surrender to him?"

"Luna, wait. Listen. I have an idea that might work. Just listen." "Why should I listen? I see now that you have chosen a side, and that

side isn't Urhonordo. You just want us to give up." A tear welled up in her eye. "I thought you had more faith in me than that."

"I do have faith in you," protested Ben. "That's why I'm saying this to you. You and your men are the one force that could actually stop this war without bloodshed. Please . . . just listen."

Ben stood his ground and looked Luna in the eye. She was furious. She was insulted, but she knew that violence was just around the corner. Instinctively, Ben reached for her hand. The old trust of a little girl playmate crept unbidden to the surface of her mind.

"What have you got to lose?" contributed her Conscience. "Listening to someone is better than fighting them or locking them up."

"You're right," said Luna to both her Conscience and Ben. "Tell me your idea, Ben."

Ben took a big breath and began. "I know Thorndike's army. They are not real soldiers, but they have been goaded into thinking that you want to take their water. They would not be dangerous at all if they knew the truth. The Royal Guard of River Kingdom is with them, but they already know the truth and don't want to fight at all. If Will tells them to stand down, they will."

Luna listened carefully. Was this true? She was skeptical. "What about that man, Thorndike? He wants war right now, doesn't he?"

"Yes and no," Ben offered with a grin. "He wants somebody to go to war, but not him. He wants to wait in a safe place until any fighting is over and then claim Urhonordo as his spoils. He's not exactly brave."

Luna studied Ben. He seemed the same as he had always been— honest, brave, and funny. But she had to admit now that she cared for him. Was this clouding her judgment?

Luna's Conscience weighed in. "Let Ben complete his idea, Luna. Don't jump until you hear it all."

"Okay, Ben," said Luna in a more accepting tone. "What miracle do you think will happen if I give up?"

"If you surrender and you tell your men to step back, the men on the other side will see that you're not fighting, so they won't need to fight either. Then there will be no fighting, right? People can start talking. No one will get hurt."

"But, Ben, Thorndike will think that I am weak and take over my kingdom. Isn't that what he wants?"

"Yes, of course. You're right. That's definitely true."

Ben's face took on a more serious appearance, and he looked closely at Luna. "I would have to convince him that he's wrong, Luna. But I am more than willing to do that. I will fight for you . . . and win. He is only one guy, not a whole invasion force. I can do that."

Luna sat down on a common chair to think. There was little time to truly consider Ben's plan, and she knew it. But her anger had fallen apart. Ben wasn't challenging her ability to protect herself. She knew that too.

Ben was presenting a difficult challenge. Would she be willing to step back and appear vulnerable in order to stop a battle?

"Ben's plan is smart strategy, but risky," offered Cluna. "And it will take more courage for you to look weak than to meet this Thorndike with force. Do you think Ben's plan will work?"

Luna's queenly mind tried to answer all the angles of that question. *How would her Royal Guard react to this? Would the farmers of The Kingdom be willing to lay down their arms? And what about King Sol? What would he think? Whose side would he be on? Would he understand the difference between strategy and cowardice?*

Ben seemed to read her mind. "Will went to scout King Sol last night.

I believe that the King may understand a white flag." "Oh no, Ben. Not a white flag . . ."

A rumbling now became clearly audible. The sounds were coming from the prairie and the advancing troops of King Sol. "I have to go now," Ben said quickly. "I need to get back to Thorndike with my scouting report, and the King is nearly here. This is a terrible plan for you to consider, but I know you will do what you think is right." Ben looked one last time at Luna and ducked out the door.

Through the brambles and untamed foliage, he ran, his mind now clouded with fear and doubt. *Have I said the right thing? Was my idea a good one? If Luna surrenders, will Thorndike and the Commoner Army simply take over Urhonordo?*

"You have done your best," Cben assured him.

What good is that if the woman I love is made captive by a tyrant? Ben thought desperately.

"Now you're admitting that you love Luna?" questioned Cben.

"Be quiet," ordered Ben, diving through the heavy brush that was surrounding Thorndike's seat on a ridiculously padded forest stump.

"Don't ever say such a thing to your betters, boy," growled Thorndike, rising stiffly from the stump.

"Just talking to myself, sir. We are very close to the Urhonordo Castle, sir. I took careful measure of all their battle positions and fortifications, sir." "Are there a lot of 'em?" questioned one of the closest farmers, hoisting

his shovel to his shoulder in readiness for his upcoming assault.

"Do they have fire-loaded oil on the ramparts?"

"Are we going to have to storm the castle?"

"Do they have a mote?"

"I can't swim."

"How about bows and arrows? I'm pretty good with my bow, and my quiver is ready."

"You and your quiver are both quivering, Jake."

"I'm gonna take on whoever I meet with my bare fists. Urhonordos won't know what hit 'em."

"I like your enthusiasm, men," growled Thorndike. "You are all strong men of action, and your moment of destiny is almost at hand. Some of you may not make it through this war, but I will remember your bravery toward our goal."

"What, exactly, is our goal?" asked a familiar voice from the other side of a clump of brush. Will stepped out into the clearing and stared at Thorndike.

Cben spoke up in Ben's ear. "Don't move. Don't say anything. This is a delicate moment."

Thorndike backed up in shock. He had almost forgotten Will. There was a moment of silence, but then the Commoner Army recognized who they were seeing and erupted in cheers.

"Hooray for Will!"

"He scouted the unknown and survived!" "He is a man among men!"

"What did you see out there on the prairie?"

Thorndike strutted forward and stood in front of Will with a dominating glare meant to put him in his place. "What took you so long? Where have you been? My men are about to attack Urhonordo without you."

"I was captured, but I got away," said Will. "The camp that I visited was very large, and they are headed this way."

Ben stared at Will, but heeding his Conscience's warning, he said nothing.

Thorndike bristled. "Then we need to storm Urhonordo quickly before this new army can get there and take over the castle before we do!" sputtered Thorndike. "Go for it, men! You can do it! I'll be right behind you!"

"Wait!" shouted Will. "What's the hurry, Sir Thorndike? The men and I really need to know what we're going to do. I would rather talk than fight, wouldn't you?"

"Yeah, but we came all this way for a reason. Maybe just talking won't do it," said a young farmer.

"We need to win something for our trouble," contributed another. "So we can get River Kingdom water like we should."

"So Urhonordo won't have anything to say about it."

"And Drum says that Urhonordo wants to attack us so we have to attack them first," shouted an eager farmhand in the front row.

"Drum ought to know. They've got Flawless! What about that?" The farmers looked at each other. Yeah, what about that?

Will was losing his plan for peace talks. The rallies with Drum had taken their toll, and they had marched a long way. Their anger had rekindled, and they were ready to fight.

Ben stepped up. "I need to warn you, men," he said gravely, "and Lord Thorndike too. I have just returned from scouting Urhonordo. I must tell you that they are well fortified. The queen's warriors are positioned at every possible location. They are on the ramparts. They are at every opening in the castle. When you approach, unless you are welcomed, you will be met by a cadre of well-trained swordsmen."

Will looked at Ben with admiration. This was the Ben that he knew and admired. He could see that Ben was pushing for peace talks in his own way. "Woah," Will responded. "That sounds serious. I would like to avoid full-on bloodshed if I could, Lord Thorndike. Since you are our leader, what do you say? Wouldn't this be a good time to discuss things rather than fight?" The Commoner Army shuffled within its ranks. The farmers weren't used to fighting. Trained swordsmen didn't sound very good to them.

Talking was suddenly sounding better.

Thorndike blanched noticeably. What should he do? His idea was to march in without a scratch and take over. Being part of a charge toward an armed castle was not what he had in mind. He hesitated.

"Stand pat," warned Cben. "Thorndike is thinking it over, but his Conscience has completely checked out. He is in control of an Eforce. Stay calm."

Suddenly, Thorndike remembered his previous revelation. If there was bloodshed, he didn't want it to be his, but all around him were expendable humans. As he had noted earlier, he could forfeit the lives of these men, and nobody would care. Between him and any violence would be a hundred useless farmers and his Royal Guard. The Guard could come in and mop up after the farmers had taken the hits and worn out the Urhonordos. Then he could just walk in. This was an excellent plan.

"I say forge ahead with weapons drawn!" Thorndike shouted. "Will and Ben know this area. I say that they lead our invasion force onto Urhonordo grounds so they can show you men how to take out any fortifications. I will follow, of course, behind the Royal Guard. Together, you men will put that queen and her flimsy fighting force in their place, and I will win! What do you say, men?"

The farmers looked at each other. Thorndike said that Will and Ben would lead. They knew what they were doing. That sounded pretty good. They could do that. A roar went up. Everyone gathered up whatever they had for weapons—shovels, axes poles, hoes. Energy circulated from one excited patriotic man to another. They felt powerful. They knew they could do this.

Will and Ben had no choice. They were trapped and started forward at the lead, down a grassy trail toward Urhonordo Castle.

"Do you have any idea what we're going to do when we get to the castle?" whispered Will fearfully.

"Actually, I think I do . . . or at least, I hope I do," said Ben. "I spoke to Luna, but she never said she agreed with my plan so I don't know for sure."

"You spoke to Luna?"

"Yeah. On my 'scouting mission.'" "What did you say? What did she say?"

"I asked her to surrender," answered Ben. "She listened and considered it, but we could hear King Sol's troops approaching so I had to leave before I got caught in the wrong place."

"In this situation, what is the 'right place'?" asked Will. "Wait a minute. You asked her to surrender? Luna? Luna would never surrender. She's too strong, and she has too much pride."

"Not if surrender was strategic," said Ben quietly. "Strategic?"

"Yeah. It was just the idea. We'll have to see if it works. If it doesn't, we'll probably be dead."

They had arrived at the edge of the beautiful grounds of Urhonordo Castle. The grass sparkled in the dew of the early morning light. There was no sign of anyone in the yard. All was quiet. Will and Ben could hear the heavy shuffling of the Commoner Army behind them.

"I am going to step out and ask for the surrender, Will," Ben announced. "Do you want to come with me or wait for a sign?"

"I'm ready to be 'strategic' *with* you," Will answered with a small sideways grin.

Slowly, aware that it could be their last living move, they stepped together out onto the castle lawn. They walked slowly forward. The men behind them watched tensely. Were they supposed to follow? They weren't sure, and nobody wanted to make the first move.

Now a door in the castle opened a crack, then a bit wider. What happened next was completely unexpected . . . by most. An elderly female servant opened the door the rest of the way and stood aside. Queen Luna, no longer dressed in warrior garb, appeared in the doorway.

The early rays of the rising sun caught the tips of her hair and glistened off the folds of a royal purple robe and the silver gown beneath it. Ben, Will, and the first row of the Commoner Army inhaled as one. She was a beautiful . . . and shocking sight.

Next, the elderly woman reached beneath her apron and handed what she retrieved to the queen. The queen, with deliberate and stately grace, proceeded alone to the center of the lawn and revealed what she was holding—a small delicate scepter and, attached carefully at the top, a white flag.

Ben walked forward and joined her. Luna looked at him closely, but handed him the scepter. Will, who had not come forward with Ben, stared at the pair in astonishment. She had done it. She had followed Ben's suggestion to be strategic, but now what?

Almost automatically, Will turned to the men behind him, issuing an order. "Stand down, men. The queen has delivered a notice of surrender, but her Royal Guard is still well armed and out of sight behind her. I am sure of this. Lower your arms, but stay ready. Await my signal."

Will joined Ben and Luna. "What do we do now?" whispered Will anxiously.

Luna spoke quietly, but strongly. The situation was still dangerous. "Will, please keep your people from invasion, or my men will need to defend me. Ben, what you said would happen has happened so far. There is no bloodshed. Please go east and bring the troops you find there to the yard."

Will and Ben didn't understand, but for only a moment. They knew Luna was strong, but they were not sure what was going to happen next. Then without further hesitation, they both initiated their assignments. These were actions of trust. No one's Conscience advised against them. Ben gave Will the flag and rushed off in the direction that Luna had indicated. Will held the white flag high in the air as the Commoner Army slowly lowered their makeshift weapons.

But immediately, the fragile quiet was shattered. With arms flailing, Thorndike crashed loudly through the Commoner Army, his anger bursting out loudly in an uncontrolled frenzy. On his face was the unmistakable fear that he was losing control. Will was holding a surrender flag and looked strong. Will was threatening his claim on the Urhonordo victory. The kid is trying to take over, he thought, suddenly realizing that perhaps he had never really had control at all.

"What are you doing, standing there in my place?" Thorndike shouted accusingly. "What's going on? Do you think you're in charge now just because of that ridiculous flag?

"This stupid woman should have given me the white flag! She should never have surrendered to you. Give me that flag. I'm taking over. I order you to put this woman in chains."

"Her army is still under arms, Sir. They are waiting to defend her if they need to," responded Will quietly. "If anyone touches Luna, they will be killed." "You and Ben were right up here next to her and nothing happened to you. Why was that so?" the overwrought aristocrat barked.

Then Thorndike's eyes narrowed. Logical thinking submerged to nothing as his Super Eforce mania took complete control. "Or do the two of you have a special deal on the side?" he sneered. "Do the two of you plan to take over Urhonordo for yourselves? Is that your hidden game?"

Thorndike's power was being threatened. He was losing it! He stumbled toward the Commoner Army. They were ready. *He* would lead them. They would fight for *his* power!

Thorndike was crazed with suspicion and jealousy. His reasoning was gone. Now the Commoner Army was getting excited again and looking for their tools. To keep the peace, Will would need to fight a different kind of battle and fight it right now.

"Grovel for peace," advised Cwill.

Will nodded. "You are gravely mistaken, Lord Thorndike," said Will submissively, lowering himself to a knee in front of Thorndike as he had done earlier. "The queen simply awaits the attention of the man in charge of this invading force, sir. She doesn't want to talk to a nobody like me."

Thorndike grabbed the white flag and studied Will closely. Luna stood like a statue with no expression. He squinted at Will with suspicion and turned the flag over and over in his hands, but he was, as usual, susceptible to groveling. Predictably, his fear began to lessen.

He walked around the immovable queen several times and began to see things as Will had described them. Now he understood the queen's reasoning. She wanted to surrender to *him*. She was being appropriate. Everything was under control. The situation just needed to be taken over by himself, the new royalty. This was exactly the way he had envisioned it.

Without further discussion, he brushed the kneeling Will aside and planted himself in front of Luna. Will, in turn, stood and came closer to the Commoner Army. "You have responded perfectly," he whispered to the troops. "The Queen is surrendering without a shot. Your presence has made a definite impression on Queen Luna. Continue to stand down and wait for my signal if things go wrong."

Thorndike was now in his glory. Visions of Luna's future submissiveness danced in his brain. She was a beautiful woman. He had never seen her before so he had never really known that. Maybe he would keep her around for . . . entertainment. He straightened his attire and slicked back his hair. Conquering this woman was even more enjoyable than he had dreamed.

He strutted before her. "Hello, woman," he greeted Luna rudely. "Are you ready to get down on your knees and pay homage to your new King?"

"No," Luna replied flatly.

Thorndike stopped in his tracks. How dare she speak to him that way? Who did she think she was? She had surrendered. She was now his prisoner. She obviously didn't know how to behave like a prisoner.

But Thorndike had become used to being rebuffed by women in the past. He could handle this. "Get down on your knees, woman," he ordered again, with a threatening stare as he pointed to the ground at his feet.

"No," Luna answered and raised her head high in a queenly pose.

Thorndike was appalled by her behavior and pulled back a hand, ready to slap his uncooperative prisoner to the ground. But then, he heard a strange, but very recognizable noise—the clanking and stomping of troop movement.

But this noise did not come from the direction of the Commoner Army. Rounding the corner of the castle yard to the east was Ben, followed by over one hundred Royal Guards. But these were not

Urhonordo Royal Guard. These men were dressed in River Kingdom armor. They were not smiling. They marched like the well-trained force that they were, slowly and calmly onto the yard of Urhonordo Castle, stopping only a few feet from Queen Luna and Thorndike, whose raised hand seemed to be frozen in midair. Slowly, in complete shock, two reactions took place.

The first one was Thorndike, of course, who had allowed himself to be lured into an exposed and vulnerable position. His Auras had carried him so far into his fantasies that he was now unable to comprehend what was happening. What was happening? Who were these new and intimidating people, and why were they here? His hand dropped uselessly to his side.

The second reaction was astonishment in the Commoner Army who recognized the newcomers immediately. This was their Royal Guard. They had some of the Royal Guard behind them, but these men in front of them were the ones that had followed King Sol into Dragon Quest. The only question now was what were they doing here?

The answer was wonderful but baffling. Without fanfare, from behind the ranks of the rough and grizzled Royal Guard stepped two more surprises—the beautiful Flawless Drum accompanied by their king, not King Drum, but King Sol.

Will grinned at Ben. "Strategy," he mouthed silently. Ben nodded.

For a moment, the Commoner Army just stared, then dropped to their knees. The King that they had admired and thought of as dead was alive and standing before them. It was a miracle. There was silence.

The Royal Guard that had been bringing up the rear of Thorndike's force surged forward and peered over the heads of the kneeling farmers. Bumping into them clumsily, they finally saw what was causing the notable quiet on the very edge of a war. Their brothers in arms had returned successfully from Dragon Quest, and the King was with them . . . King Sol! At first, they hesitated. Then the Commoner Army stood aside, and the combination of Royal Guardsmen rushed together in Queen Luna's yard like the military fraternity they were. There was no holding them back as a beaming King and Flawless quietly moved to Queen Luna's side. Ben and Will joined them. Standing together in peace, they all looked on while the

Commoner Army gathered about them and cheered.

Now content that they were not going to be fighting, the farmers sighed in relief and patriotic joy. Rather than the aggression they had been encouraged to anticipate, they slapped each other on the back and appreciated the peaceful moment.

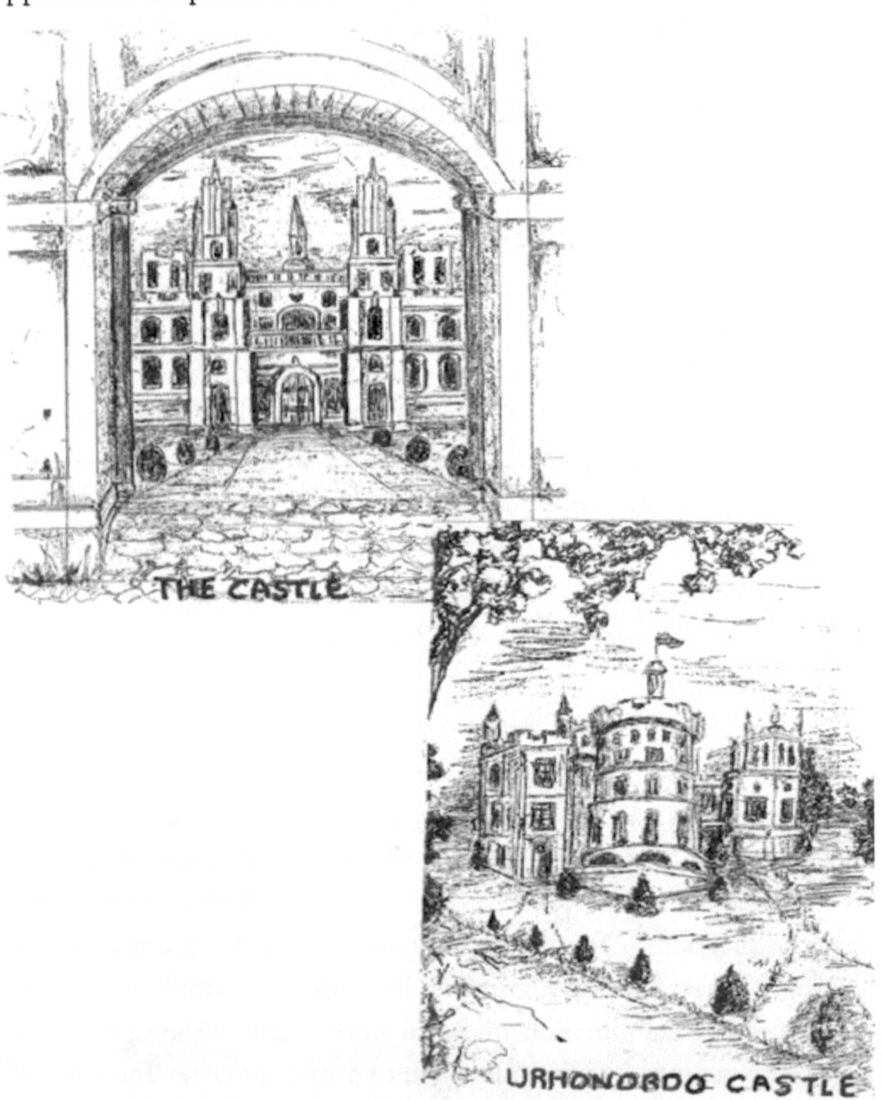

45

The Road Home

What happened next was a happy scramble. The Commoner Army had decided immediately that an assault on Urhonordo was not going to happen. There was so much joy in all of them at the King's return that they could not remember why they had thought they should fight Urhonordo in the first place. Thorndike had disappeared, but no one went looking for him.

Queen Luna toured her castle and sent out runners to inform all of her Guardsmen to stand down and return to their usual stations. Peace was at hand.

King Sol had returned from Dragon Quest triumphant and healthy. Everyone wanted to know the details of his triumph, but he modestly held back as was his style and referred the inquisitive to his Royal Guard who were more than ready to share the details of their fine exploits.

But Sol and his men were anxious to get home. King Sol took the lead and headed out on foot as everyone gathered themselves together and followed, their livestock and equipment straggling behind them.

Ben chose to stay behind in Urhonordo with Luna, telling Will with a smile that he would catch up with him later.

The morning was young as the now reunified Royal Guardsmen fell in line behind their King and slowly headed for The Bridge and home. All were exhausted. They had marched toward different and uncertain fates the night before but were feeling much better now. They were all on the same side—River Kingdom.

The Commoner Army followed the Guard, still equipped with their shovels and hoes . . . and with many questions. Did they have two kings now? What was going to happen? The farmers had thought their King was dead and had adopted a new one. They had given their hearts to King Drum. He had treated them to rallies and parties and promises.

Last night, Drum was their man, but today, King Sol was their king. How was that going to work in the future?

With more questions than answers, a motley crew of farmers and Guardsmen, royalty and peasants began to wind their way toward the Castle, this time taking a shortcut over The Bridge. Flawless and Will traveled at the head of the procession with King Sol.

They were keenly aware of everything that had brought them to this point and also equally aware of what King Sol did not yet know.

Neither of them had been clear or completely honest with him when they had met with him in his tent the night before.

"You should have told King Sol about Drum last night," chided Cwill as he rode along on the shoulder of Will's still muddy tunic. "That would have been the smartest thing to do."

I didn't have time. I had to stop an invasion. Explaining Drum would have taken more time than I had, Will thought. *But I wish I did. I have no idea what I'm going to say about Drum now.*

Cflawless was equally critical of Flawless. "Why didn't you tell King Sol about your dad yet and all the trouble he caused?" she snarked. "You know the whole invasion and all the water rights problems were your dad's fault . . . not to mention the fact that he has been calling himself 'King' and telling everyone that King Sol was dead. What happened to you when you had a chance to say something about all that to King Sol yesterday?"

He's my father, Flawless thought gloomily. *He's been awful, but it didn't seem right to turn on him in the middle of a possible war.*

"I guess I sort of understand that," Cflawless responded. "He's terrible, but he is family."

The dreary travelers trudged along the worn trail that led to The Bridge. All were deep in their own thoughts. They were weary but anxious to be back in River Kingdom. As they neared The Bridge, their spirits lifted and their pace quickened, but the first of the many surprises was awaiting them.

On The River Kingdom side of The Bridge was a stout cage, and in that cage were the very angry and highly verbal Lord Dipswitch and Lord Thorndike. Guarding the cage was a solemn contingent of Lowlanders.

King Sol led the procession over The Bridge but came to a halt. "What's this, my friends?" he asked the Lowlanders. He walked around the caged men who had suddenly become very quiet.

Thorndike and Dipswitch were dumbstruck. They were caged and furious, but they were staring at the face of King Sol. Their recent interactions with Drum began to bubble up through their memories. But King Sol was alive. Now what?

They decided to bluff.

"King Sol," began Sir Thorndike, standing tall in the cage as though still in charge of something. "I have no idea why these ridiculous persons have caged me. I did nothing to them. They don't even belong in this kingdom.

They are only Lowlanders. Are you going to allow these foreigners to trespass in River Kingdom and jail an upstanding citizen such as myself?"

King Sol smiled at Lord Thorndike. "Hello, Thorndike. I remember that I saw you just recently, didn't I? Yes, I did. This morning, to be exact. "Perhaps these Lowlander men heard that you tried to start a war with Urhonordo and take over the kingdom of Queen Luna. Do you suppose that might be the reason that they have caged you?" Thorndike hung his head. His bluff had failed.

"And you, Dipswitch . . . what is your story?" King Sol continued. "These ignorant foreigners have no right to do what they are doing,"

Dipswitch fumed. "They are only Lowlanders, as you can see. They have no value. I did nothing that I did not have a perfect right to do. "

Now he looked up and smiled. "Ah-h-h . . . I see that the Royal Guard is here. Come here, men, and release me immediately." Lord Dipswitch stood forward boldly. He was in a cage for no reason,

for goodness' sake. These no-count Lowlanders had no rights. He smiled confidently and motioned to the Royal Guard that had recently been under his control.

A nearby Guardsman stepped forward. He had been down at The Border all summer, and he knew the story. "If I may speak, Your Majesty." King Sol nodded.

"The last time I put someone in a cage like this was yesterday, and it was a whole bunch of Lowlanders. I did that at your command, Sir Dipswitch. You ordered me to block their water and lock 'em up like slaves. Me and some others did that. We're pretty ashamed of it now." He hung his head as a rumble of agreement and apologies rose from among the ranks of the Royal Guard.

King Sol shook his head. "I'm ashamed to hear that," he said, "but it's good to hear that you understand now." The Guardsmen nodded, and their Consciences were quiet. They didn't need to say anything.

King Sol turned to the Lowlanders. "Thank you for not harming these two men, my friends. I appreciate your restraint, and I will take care of their punishment from here."

The Lowlanders smiled and nodded as several Royal Guardsmen took Thorndike and Dipswitch into custody and began rolling their cage toward The Castle. The Lowlanders were satisfied. They nodded at Will with respect and headed south.

"You know these Lowlanders well, don't you?" observed King Sol as he and Will and Flawless resumed their trek toward home. "Did you work with them this summer while I was gone?"

"Indeed," answered Will. "Many Lowlanders joined Ben and me to lower the levees. It was a dry summer."

"Oh," mused King Sol. "You lowered a lot of levees, did you? How did Queen Luna feel about that?" He looked at Will from the corner of his eye.

"Not very good," Will answered honestly. "We never even looked at the Water Rights Treaty. In fact, water problems were at the start of what ended up being Thorndike's invasion of Urhonordo. And worse, water problems got out of hand with Dipswitch down south. That is still a mess."

King Sol Kept walking. "I am surprised that Arnold didn't take care of things like that. He's always been right on top of issues with The River. And Queen Luna is usually very reasonable."

"She would have been reasonable about the levees this spring too if we had just consulted her about them first," added Flawless.

Will cringed. "It was my fault, sire," he confessed. "I am the Ag Advisor now, and I didn't take care of things as I should have."

"I know," said Sol.

Will and Flawless blinked but looked straight ahead. How much more did King Sol already know?

They were nearing The Castle. "How's your flower garden doing?" asked Sol with a smile as they passed by.

"It probably needs weeding," offered Flawless. *Here is another thing that King Sol already knows,* she thought.

Now, The Castle came into view. It looked magnificent. The King stopped and stared as did everyone. The Castle was bedecked with flags and banners. Servants were standing at all the doorways. They were leaning out the windows, shouting greetings and dressed in their finest.

And strutting toward them now, dressed in an elegant but simple robe, was Lord Doran Drum. "Welcome back, King Sol! It is so good to see you!" He took a knee and bowed his head.

Flawless and Will watched as King Sol smiled, asked Drum to rise, and shook his hand. "The Castle looks wonderful. It looks like you have arranged a welcome for me. I am impressed. Let's go inside and enjoy it."

RIVER KINGDOM CASTLE

46

Homecoming

The Castle was sparkling clean, and the celebration had been arranged perfectly. Morf and The Castle Staff had worked all through the day to make it that way. All Morf had needed to motivate The Castle Staff was to tell them the amazing truth: King Sol, the real King, was coming home. Everyone was excited . . . and grateful. The past few months had been stressful.

In the halls of The Castle, the kitchen, the bedrooms, the royal quarters, and every corner, all the servants had responded with joy to the knowledge that King Sol was alive, and their preparations were for him. Did they have questions? Oh yes.

"Did the King kill any dragons?"

"How many?"

"Was he wounded?"

"When did Drum know?"

"Does King Sol know about King Drum?"

But the questions were reduced to little or no importance as King Sol entered The Castle smiling, with Drum at his side, also smiling . . . and with no crown.

King Sol retired to his room to freshen and change into fresh kingly garb . . . and his beloved crown. But when he emerged to partake of the dinner that had been prepared for him, strangely, he still had no crown. No one could find it. (?)

The maids were in a dither, but Sol assured them that he was not worried. "I don't need a crown to prove that I am King," he said calmly.

The celebration was held in the Royal Party Room. It was the first time it had actually been used. At the table of honor, Flawless and her father were seated next to King Sol. Will sat next to Flawless at the same table. Local wags noticed Flawless and Will with smiles. They had suspected they would be a permanent couple and were pleased to see that they both enjoyed the King's favor.

The complete Royal Guard was also honored at their own special tables throughout the hall. They were shocked to have been invited to sit *inside* the Royal Party Hall *and* in the presence of the King. This had never happened before. In truth, Morf had had to scramble for enough food to serve this great throng of hungry men. But King Sol was pleased.

A picnic of sorts had been arranged by Drum in the courtyard for the Commoner Army as well. Music played. The dancing girls danced for them. Everything was festive and joyful. Drum oversaw the whole operation, thanked them for their service and its peaceful conclusion, and assured them that this was the way he had known it would work out. All cheered as he hinted that he had plans for the future and promised he would see them again soon.

After dinner, King Sol rose as if ready to retire. The Guardsmen were still chatting and drinking and sharing war stories. Suddenly, with a gracious but ominous look at Drum, King Sol turned to Drum and asked him, Flawless, and Will to join him in the throne room.

Conversation in the Royal Party Room suddenly ceased. The truth would now come out. The sins of the past months would be laid bare. Everything had been aimed at the King's joyful return until now, but this would be the time for grim reality at last.

Lord Drum was the object of universal focus as he waved confidently to the throng and followed the King to the throne room. What was King Sol going to do? What was Drum going to do? The King's closest personal guards rose expectantly, but the King waved them away.

Flawless and Will followed Drum into the familiar throne room with dread. They were sure that this was going to be a confrontation. It was not going to be pretty.

Drum smiled confidently, but he couldn't help looking around. This had been his room, but it was definitely not his room anymore. For a moment, he *did miss* that. He could still feel the remnants of the Auras that had occupied the room with him. They were telling him that it should still be his room, but they were greatly subdued now in the presence of the real King. Cdrum stood tall on Drum's shoulder.

Drum looked around slowly. He used to have control here, but he no longer had any control and the beauty and power of this place sank into his being. He had *owned this Castle.* He had *worn the crown.* For a brief moment, he was experiencing a real feeling of loss, something he rarely allowed himself to feel.

Cdrum began to work on him. "You thought you were going to get away with it forever, didn't you?" challenged Cdrum as he moved into Drum's ear. "Now is the time to stand up like a man and admit your mistakes."

But Drum's Super Auras rose from the floor and occupied the very space where Cdrum had been standing only a moment before.

Drum heard his Conscience and responded without hesitation. *Get away with what? I didn't do anything wrong,* he thought without hesitation. *The Castle is in good condition. River Kingdom is prosperous, and the harvests are great, thanks to me and my farmers. I was great at this job. The King can see that. He should be grateful.*

Drum glanced at King Sol to read his demeanor, but his face was turned away. King Sol had not taken to his throne. Instead, he stood at the doorway to the balcony, looking down at the courtyard where the rally crowds had gathered for Drum.

The King would be jealous if he knew the size of the crowds that gathered down there just for me, Drum thought proudly. *I should tell him about that.*

"I don't believe you" hissed Cdrum from his place in Drum's ear. "You declared King Sol dead and took over his throne. Do you really think that he wants to hear about how wonderful you were as King?"

He should. He could benefit from what I did if he knew about it, Drum thought. The Super Aura relaxed. Drum's self-confidence was intact. No worries.

King Sol turned and faced Drum squarely. "You drew a lot of common folk to your rallies down there when you were King, didn't you?" he asked bluntly.

Flawless held her breath. This is what she had been dreading. Poor Daddy.

Drum looked at King Sol without flinching. "Are you talking to me?" he asked calmly.

"Who else would I be asking?" asked Sol.

"I guess you are asking me," Drum responded. "If that is so, I just need to assure that I have never been King. Any rumor to that effect is a hoax. That's a shame, of course, as many people see it, but I'm not of royal lineage, you know."

King Sol stared for a moment, but went on. "So you never wore my crown and told people you were king. Is that what you're saying, Drum?"

Drum smiled. "I admit that I tried your crown on a couple of times just for fun, but I never said I was King. That's what I'm saying."

Will and Flawless listened and watched with fascination. What was Drum trying to do?

King Sol scratched his beard and thought about what Drum had said. Drum was not admitting that he had acted as king. He would try another approach. "If you have never thought of yourself as King, how did you think you had the authority to start a war with Urhonordo?"

"I never started a war," answered Drum. "That is strictly the responsibility of the King, and of course, I was never the King so I couldn't authorize a war. If someone told you such a thing, that was fake news."

King Sol became notably frustrated. "That scoundrel, Thorndike, was definitely engaged in a full-fledged war, complete with Royal Guard and even common folk. That was your war, Drum!" King Sol said fiercely.

Drum's face was almost forgiving. "There is no proof of that. No, sire. I fear that you have been given incorrect information. Those who are jealous of me say things like that sometimes. That was Thorndike's war. I never told him to do that . . . and I never would have. That story is a hoax."

King Sol looked at Drum quizzically. Drum smiled confidently back and stood tall.

"So . . . you maintain that you have been doing only what I asked you to do," stated Sol.

"Indeed," answered Drum confidently. "And extremely well according to the town folk."

"And under your supervision as Royal Caretaker, I shouldn't worry that you have emptied nearly all of its Royal Storehouses, built levees on The River without reviewing or consulting Urhonordo, used Lowlanders as slave labor and allowed them to be caged, built a manor house blocking The Great River with the Royal Guard as laborers, cut off Lowland water, and encouraged a war with Urhonordo. Is that what you're saying?" Flawless covered her face.

"Not exactly," corrected Drum. "You are saying that. My opinion is quite different. Since I have been in charge, The Castle has gained in size and beauty due to my instruction. River Kingdom has become 'Great,' and this year's harvest is going to be the greatest ever. I have utilized the efforts of our neighbors, the Lowlanders, and I just sent runners to them with a more than generous payment for their work on the levees in response to a promissory note that I had signed." Drum nodded in Will's direction.

"Trade was brisk with Urhonordo before Thorndike, and will be again now that Thorndike has been put in his place. What more could you want? I ask you, Sire, what more could you want?"

Will winced but smiled. Morf's promissory note had worked. Finally, the Lowlanders will get paid, he thought with relief.

"Everyone is glad that you are home safely from Dragon Quest, as am I," added Drum, "and although I have labored to do the best job for The Kingdom that could have possibly been done, considering what you left me to work with, I regret that I am not available to continue helping you, Sire. I have more creative plans for my future." Drum stared directly at King Sol with a smirk.

Cdrum grabbed Drum's ear. "You have perfected lying without getting caught. I must recognize talent, even though it is misused. But you have screwed up and taken advantage of an entire kingdom! How can you calmly refuse to take responsibility?"

That's the point of view of an unimaginative Conscience, thought Drum calmly. And I don't agree. If you can't see the truth of what I am saying, catch up or find another job. I don't take responsibility for anything that you think was bad when I know better than you what is good. On second thought, you're fired.

"I Made River Kingdom Great," Drum concluded aloud, "without any help from you. The farmers of The Kingdom believe in me. I know what they like, and I know how to provide it. For that reason, I will return to private life and spend my time where my skills will be more appreciated, if you don't mind."

"What?" asked King Sol.

"Never mind," answered Drum with a smile and a wink. "I was just talking to my Conscience."

Will and Flawless had heard enough. They slipped out of the throne room undetected, leaving the two men to themselves.

"Your father is smooth," Will observed to Flawless. "He has a cover for everything." Flawless nodded sadly.

"Look again, Will," countered Cwill. "Drum's not covering. He loves who he is and what he has done. He actually believes what he is saying."

"I guess I see that now too." Cflawless sighed. "He doesn't believe that he has done anything wrong."

Drum now exited the throne room, and after smiling and waving at his daughter, he strode proudly down the hall with no backward looks of regret. Cdrum hopped off Drum's shoulder and joined Cflawless.

"I heard you, Flawless," grumbled Cdrum. "I hate to admit it, but you're right. And truth be told, a man who does 'nothing wrong' doesn't need a Conscience. I've been fired."

"What? Fired? Can a human just fire their Conscience?" Cflawless cried aloud.

"My dad fired his Conscience?" cried Flawless. "He can't do that. Daddy really needs his Conscience. What's wrong with him? Is he crazy?" "In a way, yes," Cdrum responded. "He has been completely captured

by the Auras of self-love now."

Flawless couldn't hear Cdrum's answer, but Will answered her. "There have been times when I was sure that your dad was . . . off,"

Will said gently, "but he is your dad."

Flawless sighed. "Actually, I was just talking to my Conscience, but she agrees with you. Daddy can't help what he does because he is . . . handicapped. After all that has happened, I love my dad, but I hope he'll never be in charge of anything important again. He can't tell right from wrong anymore."

Will scratched his chin and thought about what Flawless said. The fact that Drum was handicapped explained a lot of what had happened. "The King can obviously see now that your father 'isn't right.' What do you think he's going to do?" whispered Will.

"Not much," predicted Flawless. "The King is a good man and he may not ever know the whole truth, but I think he understands."

"Understands what?" asked Will.

"He understands who my dad really is and that he will never change, but as long as he can't make decisions for The Kingdom anymore, he's not a problem. My dad's not really a bad man, but he loves himself too much to be a good man. I think what will happen to my dad is what has always happened. He'll just keep on keeping on."

47

Conclusion

A year after the return of King Sol, the Conscience Forum held a massive meeting on The Bridge. It was a fitting place to meet since this forum included Consciences from The Kingdom, Urhonordo, and The Lowlands. After all they had been through the year before, they decided to take stock, appreciate what they had learned, and ready themselves for the future. Written reports were presented regarding the major incidents of the past year.

The Report:

Ben and Queen Luna were married and became King and Queen of the Urhonordo Kingdom. The couple currently live at Urhonordo Castle but frequently vacation at Dipswitch Manor.

The Lowlands again have enough water and continue to be completely independent without royalty to mess things up.

Lord Dipswitch was released from the dungeons early due to an executive pardon requested by Ben after Dipswitch attended civil rights training. Lord Dipswitch reformed (according to his Conscience) and opened a bed-and-breakfast at his manor house, graciously hosting royalty, Lowlanders, and commoners alike.

His wife learned to make tortillas, a favorite dish of the neighboring Lowlanders with whom she became friends.

*Lord Thorndike's Conscience, Cthorndike, requested and received a formal release from his obligations as a Conscience to the Super Aura–controlled Thorndike and became a freelance anti-Aura Consultant.

*Cdrum received the same release and went into partnership with Cthorndike. Cdrum still visits Lord Drum every now and then, but it is more of a social call.

*Upon release from the dungeons, Thorndike himself left the area in search of dragons whom he desired to recruit for his own purposes, but returned to start up a Jr. Militia Training Camp.

*King Sol happily maintained his position as king, having dismissed Lord Drum as Royal Caretaker without punishment. Csol had requested this as he had confirmed the common knowledge regarding Drum's handicap. King Sol did adopt Drum's idea of rallies, however, which he intended to hold yearly on Dragon Quest Triumph Day.

*Will and Flawless continued to live and work at The Castle with Will continuing as Royal Ag Advisor and Flawless acting as Castle Hostess and Urhonordo Ambassador. They were married the following spring and the current rumor was that King Sol was seriously considering appointing Will as King when he retired.

*Morf stayed on at The Castle but took law classes in his spare time. He became Drum's personal lawyer and was kept on retainer because Drum continued to do as he pleased and constantly required defending.

*Drum returned to his manor houses, but soon built a bigger one by taking over Dipswitch Manor in a shady real estate deal with Dipswitch. He and Fandango combined to turn the new manor house into "Drum Commoner Castle" with the dancing girls in charge of entertainment and hospitality and Fandango in charge of finances.

*Drum Commoner Castle became a big success and was frequented often by the peasants and farmers who still loved Drum and always would. He could be seen there regularly, striding the red carpets, talking politics with visiting dignitaries, and wearing head gear that was amazingly regal.

End of Report

The Consciences were frankly amazed by the positive outcomes that had resulted from the months that Lord Doran Drum had been in possession of both Castle and Crown. They gave Cdrum a medal for his "Discovery of Super Auras" and put him in charge of a commission to study the issue of Aura Deep State investigation and better ways to improve the Royal Government.

In general, the Consciences were proud of their influence, all things considered, but they were humble. They knew what they had always known, of course. Consciences could try to advise their host humans, but they could never really force humans to do what was right if they didn't want to do so.